Thy Father's Shadow

The Sanctuary Series
Volume 4.5

Robert J. Crane

THY FATHER'S SHADOW
THE SANCTUARY SERIES
VOLUME 4.5

Copyright © 2013 Midian Press
All Rights Reserved.

1st Edition

This book is a work of fiction. Names, characters, places and incidents are products of the author's imagination or are used fictitiously. Any resemblance to actual events or locales or persons, living or dead, is entirely coincidental.

The scanning, uploading and distribution of this book via the internet or any other means without the permission of the publisher is illegal and punishable by law. Please purchase only authorized electronic editions, and do not participate in or encourage electronic piracy of copyrighted materials. Your support of the author's rights is appreciated.

No part of this publication may be reproduced in whole or in part without the written permission of the publisher. For information regarding permission, please email cyrusdavidon@gmail.com

Author's Note

With the exception of the Prologue and the Epilogue, this book takes place during chapters 22-33 of Defender: The Sanctuary Series, Volume One. The Prologue and Epilogue take place during Chapter 116 of Crusader: The Sanctuary Series, Volume Four.

Maps of Arkaria and Saekaj Sovar can be found for your convenience at http://www.robertjcrane.com/p/arkaria-maps.html

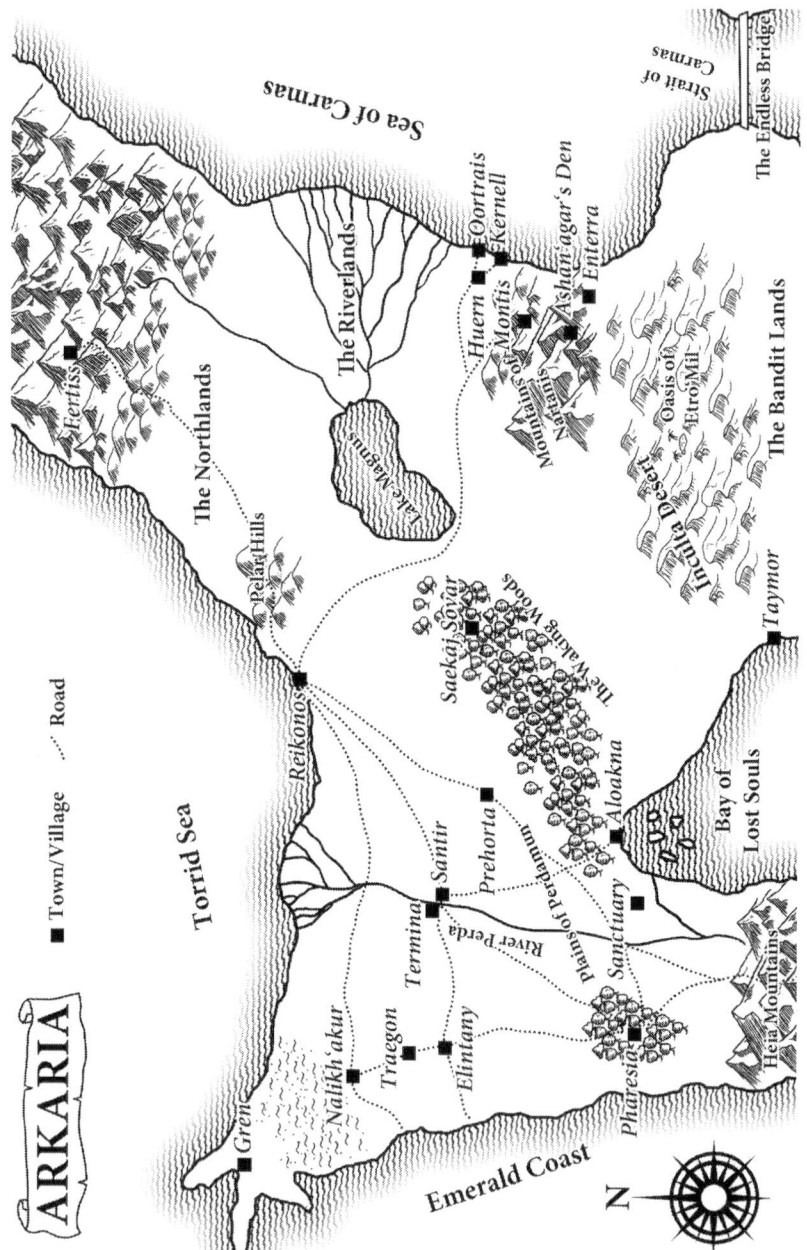

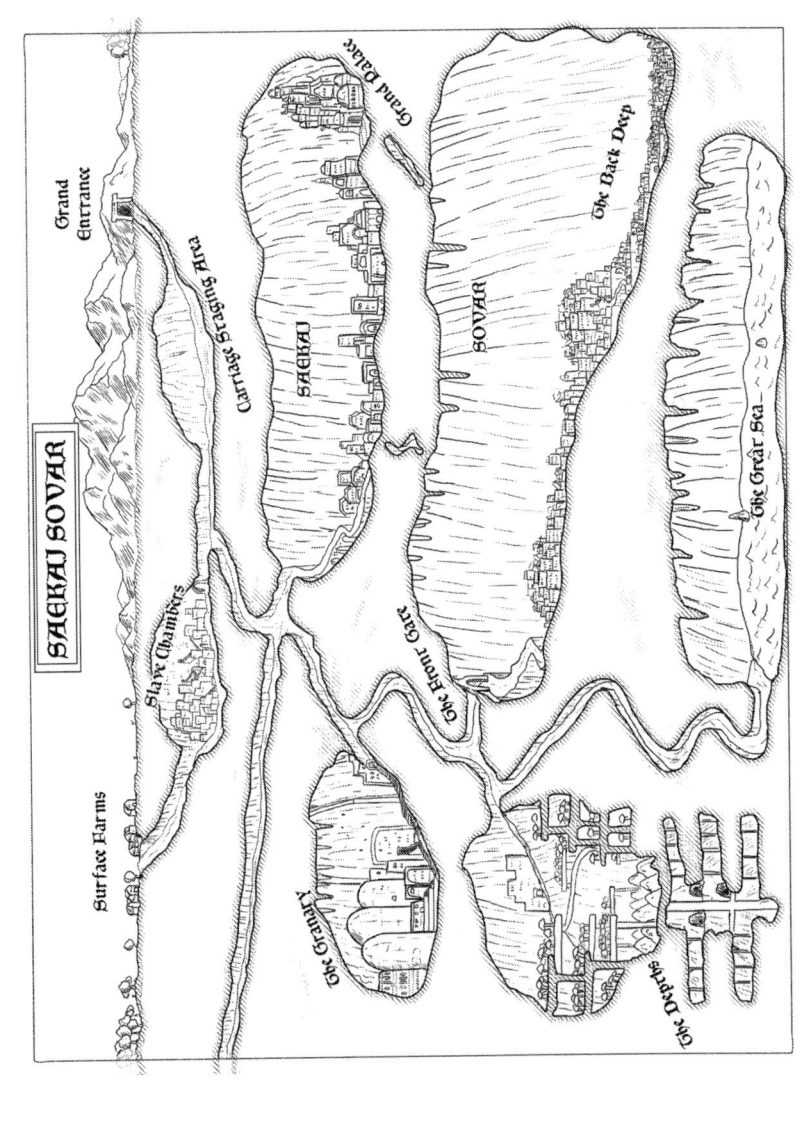

Prologue

"Alaric is dead," Terian said. The sound of his boots echoing against the stone surface of what remained of the Endless Bridge was the least of the noises clamoring for his attention, but he noticed it nonetheless. The gentle wash of the sea against the supporting pillars of the bridge below and the buzz of muted conversation from the nameless, faceless grunts in the Army of Sanctuary that still gathered in clumps atop the bridge vied for Terian's attention as he strode toward the shores of Arkaria.

"He was the Ghost of Sanctuary," Samwen Longwell said, carrying that barbaric pig-sticking lance of his over his shoulder. "I find it hard to believe that a man who can go incorporeal on cue somehow drowned in the wash of the strait below."

"He was not invincible," Curatio said stiffly. Terian turned to see him sweep his white robes behind him as he walked. "And while he was certainly a proficient swimmer, I do not think he would be able to swim out from under the multiple tons of stone he brought down upon himself just now. Nor if he had, would he deceive us by hiding his survival." Curatio's normally quick smile had been absent of late—*for most of our journey across Luukessia*, Terian reflected. *Well, our retreat. Which may be the reason it's gone missing.* "I think it is safe to say—"

"That he's dead," Terian said, the heavy thump of his boots coming back to his ears. "Much as I said just a moment ago." *Much as I've been thinking since he cast that damned spell and ruptured the bridge.* He nearly swore aloud but curbed it. *Damn you, Alaric, for saying what you did, for being what you were and then—*

And then—

Terian glanced off the edge of the bridge and stopped, placing a palm on one of the grey stone pillars that stretched like towers above them. He took a long, slow breath of the sea air, felt the salt breeze wash through the holes in his helm to chill the sweat gathered beneath in his hair, on his face. *Gods, what a fight.*

He felt his chest deflate, felt his stomach drop. *What a year.*

It's all been a fight. From beginning to end.

"So what do we do now?" The voice came from Odellan, a blond-haired elven soldier who looked entirely too pretty to Terian's eyes. Terian looked sidelong at Odellan, who stood earnestly waiting for an answer as the others—the whole damned army—stood knotted on the bridge, waiting.

"Cyrus is swimming along the bottom of the bridge," Curatio said, and Terian turned his head to look at the healer. Every word he spoke was like venom squirted into a wound. "We need to go to him; he is the General, after all. We will go to him, and then we will ... determine our next move."

Terian felt his arm shake where it stretched out against the bridge support. *General Cyrus Davidon. The favorite son. Of course we have to go find out what he has to say.* Terian felt his face twist in anger—in anguish—some combination of the two, like a knife thrust into his heart.

"What do we do without Alaric?" This voice was smaller—near quiet. It was J'anda Aimant, the dark elven enchanter who asked, in a voice that was barely audible.

"We go on," Terian said, surprised his voice did not crack. He pushed off the bridge support and stared at the beach far ahead, barely visible in the falling darkness that heralded the arrival of night.

Like he would want us to.

1.

Three Years Earlier

"Do you want me to leave?" Terian stared at Alaric, the Ghost's only eye looking back at him with a strangely impassive expression. Alaric was many things to many people; unreadable was not one of the things he was to Terian. *They just don't know him well enough*, Terian thought.

"No, I do not wish you to leave," Alaric said, standing by his chair. The Council chambers felt mildly cold, in spite of the Plains of Perdamun's utter rejection of typical winter in favor of warmth nearly year-round. The sun was below the horizon now, and Terian looked past the Ghost to the windows to see the darkness fallen over the plains. The fires were crackling in the hearths on either side of them, and Terian heard them acutely; there wasn't any smoke to speak of, but he could smell the faint aroma. "I wish you to do your duty as an officer."

"He's scum, Alaric!" Terian let loose this time, unrestrained, his voice hitting a defiant tempo. "Orion is a piece of self-absorbed trash, whose only reason for being here was to trade up. He's been waiting for an excuse to leave, to move up in the world, and we're better off without him."

Alaric stared at Terian with an even eye. Only minutes earlier they'd seen members of the guild walk out the doors, almost countless. *Half the guild, for all I know.* "That is certainly your opinion," Alaric said quietly, "which you have every right to. However, you are the Elder of Sanctuary, and there are things expected of you, duties—"

"Don't lecture me on duty," Terian said. "I just did what was best for Sanctuary, letting that poison be excised. Orion and the gnome have been destined for this collision for months, circling each other while the wound grew more and more infected. I just got it all out in one burst."

Alaric moved quickly, sweeping his hand across the table and knocking his own helm to the ground. Terian took a step back, flinching at the motion. "And lost us half the guild in the process!" the Ghost snapped, his face drawn in a look of quiet fury. "Your duty is not simply to your internal feelings about what is best for Sanctuary; it extends to our bylaws as well, to enforcing our system of justice and law, so that our members are not left rudderless, guided by whatever presiding whims come upon our officers on any given day!"

"What is right," Terian said, trying to regain his mental footing after the Ghost's outburst, "goes beyond law, goes beyond whim … it goes to the very heart of the direction you've chosen for Sanctuary, Alaric." *How can he not see the truth of this?* He pointed a finger at the paladin. "You told me when I came here that this was to be a place where we would fill ourselves with a purpose— defending the people who can't defend themselves. Fighting the fights nobody else will." He let his eyes fall as that unreasonable darkness settled itself around his heart once more, the one that had plagued him for so long. "Making amends for … sins past." His eyes came up again and found Alaric's lone eye watching his. "You sold me on the idea that we wouldn't be bound by the politics and strictures, the petty stupidities that keep the Kingdoms and Sovereignties and Confederations from doing right. Now you're telling me it's not so?"

"Our ability to do right rests in our bylaws," Alaric said, a calm quiet settling upon him. "It is grounded in the idea that there is process and law to hold back our baser natures. To 'do right' without any restriction is the slow path to tyranny. Many a despot has thought himself 'right' as he inflicted untold horrors upon his people. Many a tyrant has thought he was treading the path of righteousness when he had lost his way years earlier. Our bylaws guide us. They are our North Star to keep our intentions and our lying hearts from leading us astray in the heat of emotion. They bind us from hasty, foolish action."

Terian let out a low snort of disbelief. "They bind us from righteous action." *They keep us from our duty,* he thought but did not say. "They stack the deck of Sanctuary against those of us who care for her and put more power in the hands of those who would use her for their own ends. They keep us from expelling low trash such as Orion, even when it becomes obvious he is not the sort that will give us any aid beyond that which will profit himself."

Alaric's lone eye narrowed, and the room seemed to grow hot to Terian. "You do not know how it would have played out. You do not know what further consequences will rise from what you have let happen this day. Orion had done no real wrong, had not crossed any lines beyond simple selfishness. Had he done anything of the sort, anything provable, there would have been action from us, you know this—"

"I don't know anything, anymore," Terian said with deep disgust. *How can he be so blind to what that worm was? What his deceitful little trollop was doing?* "He was using us. He was biding his time, waiting to make a move—"

"And now his move is made," Alaric said with unsubtle calm, "and along with him, we have lost half the guild in an unsettled dispute gone amok."

"We're better off without them," Terian said, waving his hand dismissively. He wanted to sit in his chair, felt the vague pull of it, but resisted.

"So say you," Alaric replied. "But it was not your decision."

"It was," Terian said, "it was my decision in the moment that they started going at it in front of me, bringing their grievance to the fore and having it out. It was my decision, and I let it be, let it play the way it did." He took a deep breath. "And I would do it again, for the good of Sanctuary."

Alaric stared back at him. "So this is what I can expect from you? A man unfettered by rules, by restraints?"

Terian didn't glare, but it was close. "You helped elevate me to officer, then to Elder. You know who I am, what I have done—what my aims are. If you don't trust that I'm doing what is right for the guild—"

"I don't trust intentions," Alaric said, his head bowed. "Not yours, not mine, not those of anyone, truly. Not to operate without oversight, without restriction, with absolute power. Decency goes adrift in small moments first then larger ones when someone believes they are unfettered by any rules. You may set out to do good by this guild, but without rules, you would play favorites. Those who were annoyances to you would not be treated the same as those who have ingratiated themselves to you. There is no equality of members in such a case, and soon enough someone who is outspoken would become your target, and you would land upon them with all your grievous fury. Your guildmates can become your enemies without the rule of law to help guide you, without it to equalize your reaction."

Terian felt the pull of hot anger in his blood. "Do you truly think me so petty? So low? Do you think me without scruples or decency?"

Alaric turned away, letting his steps echo through the room as he made his way to the windows that lay to either side of the balcony doors. "Perhaps it was not you of whom I spoke." He gave a faint look, over his shoulder. "Power is a corrupting influence, Terian. You might use it from a desire to bring about the best results for Sanctuary, but your moral compass is not some indefatigable thing, unswayed by emotion or your judgment. It is not a fixed constant that will hold you on the same course for all your days. We all need a true north, something to help guide us so we do not lose our way on the darkest of nights."

Sanctimonious bastard. "That's you, I suppose?" Terian let the bitterness run out in his words. "Are you the all-knowing guide? Are you our compass, Alaric? The one who will light our steps and tell us the right way to go when all is shadow and blackness? Will you set our course, always? Tell us when we err, gently take us by the hand and lead us back onto the path, like children who've lost their way?" He drew in a deep breath, and it seared his nostrils as if he were inhaling brimstone. "Is that what we are to you? Do you call us brothers but really mean 'children'?"

Alaric's steady gaze wore on him. The look was jaded, calm, placid, but Terian could see a little of the fury buried deep. *Because I know him.* "You are no child, and you should not look to me as your example. Our bylaws are our guide, etched in place to restrain the darker voices in all our souls, to light the path to good conduct for all of us."

"You say of all of us," Terian said with a little more hostility, "but I kind of get this feeling you wouldn't be having this conversation with Vara." *As though he doesn't play favorites already.* "I don't need a father, Alaric. I've already got one more of those than I care for. I don't need a compass, because I know my way around the world."

"And what about a purpose?" Alaric said quietly and let his head turn to look back out the window to the darkened plains.

"Look at me!" Terian said and watched the old knight's head make a slow turn to see him. "Don't ignore me; don't look away when I'm talking to you, like I'm some matter of unconcern to you! I have seen darkness, I have seen death, I have seen horror and evil, all on a scale so massive and inordinate as to be immeasurable. You think I don't know which path is right and which is wrong? I've known since long before I darkened the doors of Sanctuary what the right damned path was, what the right intention is, because I've seen the application of it in the wrong ways." He let his voice settle. "I don't need a guide. I don't need your path, or your purpose, or your laws." Terian looked down at Alaric's helm on the floor and gave it a gentle nudge with his foot. "I know what's right."

He felt the weight of the one eye on him, even as his mouth felt dry. "Do you?" Alaric asked.

"Damned right I do." Hot fury boiled in Terian. *I can't believe I'm saying this.* It was as though he had crossed a forbidden line, airing all this, and yet the reckless fury and pride would not allow him to turn back, not now. There was one more thing yet to be said. "And I don't need you to tell me any of it, to show me any of it." The last of the fury slipped out. "In fact, I don't need you. Or Sanctuary." He gave one last encompassing wave of his hand, waited for a reaction, and when none was forthcoming, he turned and went for the door, not pausing as he opened it.

"Then I wish you the best of luck in your path … brother."

"Don't call me that," Terian said, holding the door, feeling the weight of it in his hand, like it was a hundred tons of regret. "I'm not your brother, not your son, not your anything anymore. And I damned sure don't need your luck." He let the door slam shut behind him.

2.

One Month Later

It was a rowdy crowd in the Brutal Hole, a longshoreman's bar in Reikonos, the capital of the Human Confederation. *Rowdy is good,* Terian thought. *I like being surrounded by troublemakers, laborers, men who think they're strong.* The low winter daylight barely shone down through the front windows, reflecting off the darkened mirror that lay behind the bar. Rosalla was behind the bar, as usual, and she was a good one. He liked her, which was rare. *I don't like much of anyone. But she's okay. More than okay.* He didn't want to think it, but outside of some of the girls down at the Silken Robe, the local brothel that catered to dark elves, he hadn't spoken to anyone but Rosalla in more than a week.

The crowd crashed around the bar like waves breaking on docks. There was laughter, cursing, angry shoving—sometimes from the same person all in the span of seconds. Terian watched it all with a careful eye. It wouldn't do to have the place degenerate into a melee, after all, not with him still nursing his drink. He'd feel obligated to get involved, and that would most likely end with him walking down the snowy streets of Reikonos rather than warming his arse by the hearth. He took another long pull of his ale and pondered that thought. He didn't care for it.

It took a few minutes, but he finished another. He had barely set it upon his table before Rosalla appeared, another already filled for him, green ale not even sloshing over the sides as she put it down in front of him. She didn't bother with a tray, just brought it right to him, careful as anything, her yellow eyes looking down at him from beneath her frizzed white hair. "Is this going to be another night where I have a cart man wheel you home?"

Terian studied the green ale as though it held the great mysteries of Lake Magnus's depths somewhere within it while he fished into the coin purse at his belt and came back with three bronze pieces only slightly smaller than his littlest finger's first knuckle. "It is beginning to turn that way, isn't it?"

She looked at him, bereft of any amusement as he laid the bronze on the table. She waited, expectantly, and after a moment he put two more down. She scooped them up then finally graced him with another look. "Shall I have him standing by, then? I know a good one, wheels a corpse cart around the slums most days, but at night he's quite discreet about delivering drunken souls to their beds. And quite cheap, too—"

"The last ride," Terian said, letting his fingers play over the smooth surface of the glass, "didn't cost me a thing."

She gave him a look that was all fire and attitude. It filtered past him and came to rest on his helm, which was hiding in shadow on the bench next to him. "Can't imagine why someone would hesitate to run afoul of you by haggling over price of service when you're drunk."

"Especially when I'm so sweet and pleasant of disposition, right?" Terian took another sip, long and measured. The ale was room temperature at best. Other establishments might have taken advantage of Reikonos's snowfalls to cool their beverages. The Brutal Hole never even bothered. Terian suspected that was a management decision, though he didn't rule out Rosalla simply not caring.

"You're not a mean drunk, that's certain," Rosalla said with a cool indifference. "Many's here that are. So … will I be having the cart man pick you up later?"

"Sure," Terian said, watching the bubbles drift up to the top of the glass. "Why not?"

"Why not?" Rosalla asked. "Are you looking for a legitimate reason?" Her voice carried a rough, guttural accent. She was plainly used to speaking dark elvish, but she spoke the human tongue here. He looked behind the bar at the jars filled with pickled meats and wondered idly if they served human tongues, real ones.

"Can you give me a reason not to?" Terian wondered if he'd care if she could.

"Perhaps you have work tomorrow?" She cast an impatient gaze at him. He didn't care. She turned a nervous eye to the bar, as though she could sense a riot impending, the longer she was away from pouring drinks. "An early morning? Or plans for later tonight?" She gave him a mirthless, though wicked, smile. "A visit to the Silken Robe, mayhaps? Need to keep your sword rigid for the work that might entail?"

"Sword rigidity is not a problem for me," Terian said with only a little irony, "since I carry an axe."

"Is there some semblance of meaning to be found in that?" Rosalla asked, and he could see the genuine amusement in her face. "That you carry an axe, inflict bloody wounds with it, and spend your nights chasing—"

"I wouldn't delve too deep into that thought," Terian said and drank again. The brew was foul, fouler than anything Larana would dare to put out back at Sanctuary. *I only miss the beer,* he told himself. *And possibly the companionship.*

"Hrm." With a last sound of amusement, Rosalla turned away from him, heading back to the bar.

He wasn't too shameless to watch her as she walked away, either. *More genuinely interesting than anything I'd find at the Silken Robe, I'd wager.* His view was suddenly blocked by a dark cloak and he felt a flash of annoyance. He looked up to see who might be approaching him and had to suppress the desire to grasp the axe hanging behind his back. He let his hand relax after a moment's thought, and it found the familiar ale in front of him again as he tossed it back in one good drink. "My first temptation was to split your godsdamned head from your body. Then I realized that it probably wouldn't do a bit of good."

"Forbearance never was one of your top qualities, dear boy," came the slick, oily voice of the figure that stood before him. He wore a deep blue cloak with a cowl up, and in the dim light it looked almost black. His mouth was just visible, an underwhelming, bony chin peeking out from under the cowl.

"Malpravus," Terian said, setting his empty glass back on the small table, "what the hell do you want?"

"I want what anyone wants," Malpravus said, drawing a skeletal hand to his chest, letting it run over the exterior of his cloak. "Power, and all the trappings that come with it."

Terian let himself chortle, but it was a dry noise, free of any amusement. "Well, at least you're honest about that much."

The necromancer's eyes weren't visible under the darkness of his cowl. "The way you say that would imply that I am dishonest about other things."

Terian didn't flinch, even as the darkness under the cowl seemed to deepen as if by magic. "As you said, you want power.

Might just be that power doesn't come as easily to those who always speak the truth."

Malpravus's skeletal grin widened. "You are such a rarity among your former brood. I do so enjoy my time among your brethren of Sanctuary, but their naïve honesty and virtuousness leaves me a bit tired. It is as though the realities of life have never settled hard upon their bones, and they remain comfortably cocooned in that guildhall of yours, ensconced from the harshness of outside forces." He gestured toward the chair opposite Terian. "Do you have a few moments to parlay? To discuss possibilities?"

Terian paused before answering, but only briefly. "Well, I'm supposed to be catching a ride with a guy who runs a corpse cart here in another hour or so." He picked up the glass and stared forlornly at the last hints of foam at the bottom of it. "It won't kill me to listen to you until then, though I warn you—if you begin to annoy me, I'm going to drink faster, so I can get to passing out more quickly."

Malpravus seemed to ponder this for a moment while Terian stared at him. "Quite a state you've worked yourself into. If the voices I hear are to be believed, you've taken work with a mercenary company, watching warehouses during the day to keep marauders, the impoverished and street urchins at bay? And at night you rotate between this ... place," Malpravus gestured to the dingy interior of the Brutal Hole with a skeletal hand, "and another establishment not far from here, rather less prestigious—if such a thing is possible."

Terian let his tongue run over his front teeth and felt the glaze over them from the meals of the day. The aftertaste of the ale was still strong on his palate. "I do what I have to for money so I can do what I want to in my off hours. It's called working for a living." He sat forward. "You're probably not familiar with the concept."

"It's ... sliding by on the minimums," Malpravus said, with an air of distaste. "Shooing orphans away in the cold because they're in front of a warehouse you're guarding is hardly work befitting a dark knight of your station and power, dear boy." He stiffened and smiled slightly. "Perhaps I might offer you ... a path."

Terian's eyes fell to his empty glass, regarding it with a thought as Malpravus's words echoed in his head. *It doesn't usually stay empty this long ...*

As if in response to his thought, there was a grunt followed by a cry from the bar, and Terian's head wheeled to see Rosalla trapped, a wide longshoreman gripping her tightly from behind and lifting her off the ground. Her feet dangled just beneath her.

"The Silken Robe ..." Rosalla said, struggling for breath from inside the muscled arms that had hers pinned to her sides, "... is just down the road!"

"Don't want no whore," the beast of a dark elf who was gripping her said. He was bigger than any of the others in the establishment, Terian realized as the big longshoreman dragged Rosalla from behind the bar. Most of the faces in the place were down, focused intently on their drinks, and an air of discomfort was palpable from the regular patrons. There was suddenly a wide, open space in front of the bar as the crowd dispersed to give them wide berth.

"Excuse me," Terian said, cutting across the near silence, and punctuating it by smacking the bottom of his glass on his table, drawing the startled attention of everyone at the bar. "I need another ale."

The beast who had Rosalla in his grasp wore an expression even uglier than his actual face. "She'll be with you in a few minutes." His smile grew wide and malicious; Terian noticed there were teeth missing from beneath the navy lips. "Maybe. If she can walk afterward."

"It'd take more than you've got to put me bowlegged," Rosalla said and brought her head back with a smash into the big dark elf's nose that caused him to cry out and drop her. She dropped and spun, kicking him solidly in the groin before disappearing behind the bar.

"I like her attitude," Terian said, watching the big dark elf hit his knees. Terian waved his hand at him once in a leisurely fashion, as if he were simply fluttering his fingers. The big dark elf was too busy clutching at his groin and took no notice of it.

Malpravus, on the other hand, saw it and broke into a broad grin. "Dear boy, if one didn't know better, one might mistake your actions for a virtue of some sort."

"That would be unwise," Terian said shortly, staring at the empty glass again, almost forlornly. "I just take delight in the misery of others, that's all."

"Is that it?" Malpravus's smooth voice belied his amusement, and he cast a little look over his shoulder as Rosalla popped up from behind the bar with a crossbow in hand. She froze, though, as she saw her attacker on his knees, groaning and gasping quietly for air. The subtle, sucking noise the big longshoreman was making had an almost tragic, desperate quality to Terian's ears.

"Hmm. The Lockjaw plague spell?" Malpravus asked, regarding the scene with a raised eyebrow. "Swells the tongue? Makes it difficult to breathe, yes?"

"It's one of my favorites," Terian said, watching the longshoreman, a dark elf big enough to stand favorably against Cyrus Davidon—that giant human—clutching at his throat, unable to move from the floor. "The only downside is that it won't kill him. He won't realize that for a few more minutes yet, though." *A seasoned fighter would know to just keep going; but a dumb longshoreman will flop about like a gutted fish until it wears off.* He clinked the glass idly against the table again, and it sat at a terrible tilt on the uneven planks. "Still, I do so love the misery, especially for this sort." He glanced down at the flailing man once more and felt a thin, unsatisfied smile break across his lips.

Rosalla stormed out from behind the bar, her white, frizzed hair flaring as she wheeled her head around until it settled on him. The rest of the Brutal Hole's patrons were clearing now, standing and leaving, shuffling toward the door. It was no stampede, but close, the thudding of leather boots against the wood planks filling the entire bar. "You!" she called as she closed the distance between them. "You did that?" She gestured to the blue-skinned man on the floorboards, clutching at his knees as if he could curl up like a baby.

"I did that," Terian admitted lightly, as though he were confessing to swatting a fly and with all the concern one might have for doing such a thing. "I could use another ale, by the way, if you're looking for a way to thank me."

"Thank you?" Rosalla was flushed, her cheeks dark blue. "You drove away every patron in the place!"

"Nonsense," Terian said lightly, "I'm still here. And waiting on that ale, by the way."

Malpravus made a gentle coughing noise. "I would not decline a refreshment either."

"You don't count as a patron," Terian said darkly. "Maybe a patronizer."

"Who's going to clean this up?" Rosalla said with a darkness of her own, waving to gesture at her attacker, who was now pounding the floor as though it would clear his throat.

Terian shrugged. "You sent for the man with the corpse cart already, didn't you?" He held up the empty glass almost like he was saluting. "Problem solved." He glanced at Malpravus, who nodded sagely. "Don't you love it when all the pieces sort of intersect together in convenient ways?" Terian paused and frowned. "Never mind."

"I do love it when that happens," Malpravus agreed.

"Yeah, but the rest of us don't, because when your plans come together it almost always involves us getting screwed in an unenjoyable way." Terian looked up at Rosalla. "I thought you'd be happy. He was planning to—"

"These types always plan to," Rosalla said, leveling a finger at him. "They always plan to, at least once a week. And every time I disabuse them of the idea, every time I put the pain into them, make them suffer and they change their minds, I don't lose all my patrons in the process! Now what am I supposed to do?"

Terian surveyed the empty bar, the overturned chairs and tables, the still-struggling lout lying on the floor, and he lifted his glass toward her. "Get me an ale?"

With a noise of sheerest frustration Rosalla left, and Terian watched her step over the longshoreman to return to her place behind the bar. "I'm guessing that ale isn't going to be just ale," Terian mused idly while he watched her go. *She has a wonderful walk.*

"Indeed not," Malpravus said, drawing Terian's attention back to the Goliath Guildmaster. "May we come back to addressing my proposal?"

"The one where you give me a path?" Terian eyed the empty glass forlornly and sat forward, favoring Malpravus with his full attention. "The problem is that I presume any path you're likely to give me is going to be one that leads to the edge of a cliff, where a helpful shove will be waiting to aid me in going over."

"Such unkind thoughts do you no credit, dear boy," Malpravus said, steepling his long, thin fingers.

"They keep me alive, though," Terian said, watching for any movement beneath the darkened cowl. The fact that the necromancer's eyes were not visible was only a little disquieting.

"You could be a great dark knight," Malpravus said, leaning back as though to hide his eyes further. "I have seen the seeds of the true darkness within you, waiting to take root. You did the pact, your soul sacrifice; I have heard the tale, and it was truly a great one. But you pulled away afterward, threw away all your dark works and left, seeking a ... less harried way, perhaps." The smile became a grin, teeth bared. "Something that required less personal sacrifice?"

Terian blinked only slightly. "I made about the biggest personal sacrifice I was willing to."

Malpravus took a deep breath in through his nose. "The path I would offer you is one much easier than that which you trod before. It would lead to officership in Goliath, one of the foremost guilds in the land. With your experience, you could step right into our council, help guide our armies in our ever-expanding role in the world. Help lead us to prominence."

"Easier?" Terian said, and let the doubt creep into his tone. "If your version of easier is anything like—"

"It isn't," Malpravus said smoothly. "You've done your sacrifice, your bit to cement your knighthood. I can show you ways to grow your power. To bring you money, status, women if you seek them. You need not pace cobbled streets watching for burglars, or drink green ale from kegs that were sealed only yesterday." Malpravus dismissed the empty glass with a wave.

"There are finer things out there. You need not coast along on the margins any longer if you don't desire to."

There was an almost smoky feeling around Terian's eyes, the barest hint of a sting in them. "All I have to do is join Goliath, right? Follow your orders? Help recruit and guide the next generation of your brood as you take another step toward surpassing the big three?"

Malpravus's grin was unfettered delight now. "Yes. You have it exactly."

Terian leaned back in his chair. "Why me, Malpravus? There are countless dark knights out there."

"Yet so few available," Malpravus said. "And fewer still with your particular set of experiences—"

"We come to it at last," Terian said, not sadly, but almost. "You mean my officer experience. In Sanctuary."

"As I recall," Malpravus said, almost innocently, "you were not just a mere officer, but Elder of the guild. Such a post is undoubtedly one of trust, of leadership. Someone inhabiting such a post in a guild as august as Sanctuary might know things that could be a valuable commodity—"

You bastard. Terian didn't say it out loud, but he knew it was writ across his face. "You want me to betray Sanctuary by telling you all about everything I might have learned in the Council Chambers."

If Malpravus was shocked, he hid it well. "I can't imagine anything that would be discussed in the Sanctuary Council that I would need to be privy to." He still wore the wide grin. "Still, I would expect your new loyalties would win out over the old, should the day ever come when it might be necessary to choose between one and the other—"

"Malpravus," Terian said and felt the light whistle between his front teeth as he said it, "I'm a son of a bitch. I might even be a damned son of a bitch. But I'll kill myself before I become a damned, traitorous son of a bitch."

"I couldn't imagine your mother being all that pleased about your assessment," Malpravus said, his slitted eyes just barely visible now, a gleam of light shining off of them.

"The 'son of a bitch' thing? I was actually talking about my father," Terian said and rapped the edge of the table with his knuckles. "I've left Sanctuary. Parted ways with them. But that doesn't mean I've abrogated all loyalty with their membership." He let his jaw settle tightly. "My issue is with Alaric; with his sanctimoniousness, with his steadfast refusal to do what's right when it's necessary. I will never …" He leaned forward, letting the heat of his emotion seep out, searing the table between the two of them, "… never betray my friends. Count on that."

The necromancer did not stir. "Dealing in absolutes is infantile."

"Well," Terian said, letting the chair legs squawk against the floor as he stood, "compared to you, you old bastard, I'm probably an infant." He held up three fingers and saluted in rough style. "Go molest a corpse, okay?"

"Such unkindnesses—"

"Are part and parcel of who I am," Terian said, watching the cloaked necromancer as he backed toward the bar, toward the exit. "I thought you wanted me to join you?" He gave off his best, most infuriating smile and stopped by the bar. Rosalla waited just behind it, her arms folded and her lips puckered as though she'd had the Lockjaw spell cast upon her. Terian pulled his entire coin purse out and dumped the contents on the bar. "Here. My attempt to make amends."

Rosalla's jaded eyes were still narrowed, but they flitted back and forth from the pieces of bronze, silver and the one of gold that rested, gleaming, on the old, pitted wood that made the surface of the bar. "That will almost cover it."

Terian shrugged. "It's what I've got. It's not like I have a house on the bluffs; I guard warehouses for a mercenary company. You want it or not? Because I'm pretty sure they'll take it at the Silken Robe if you don't—"

Rosalla lunged and put a hand over it, but not before Terian's darted out and snagged one of the knuckle-length pieces of silver. She glared at him as she scraped the rest off the bar's surface and into the pocket of her apron. "What the hell was that for?"

"I still have to eat and drink between now and my next week's pay," Terian said, pocketing it. With a last look at the sullen figure of Malpravus, still sitting at the table, watching him go, Terian made a gesture at the necromancer. "You might want to clean that up."

"The cart will be along shortly," Rosalla said, head down, counting the pieces of metal.

"Not the big guy," Terian said as the handle of the door slid into his grasp, clinking against the metal of his gauntlet. "Well, him too."

"I thought *you* were waiting for the cart," Rosalla said, looking up at him warily.

"I guess I'll be walking," Terian said with a smile, and lifted up his last silver piece. "Besides," he gave a last look at the big longshoreman on the floor, coughing and hacking as though her were dying, "I think the cart is going to be full up."

3.

A snowfall a few days earlier had blanketed the streets of Reikonos, and the usually dark avenues of the slums were even darker now. The sun shone directly on the filthy streets for only about an hour a day anyway, less in the winter, and Terian had doubts that the snow would be going away anytime before spring. He had seen the freshly scraped and shoveled streets in the commercial district, down by the docks where the warehouses lay. Even the markets were given some attention, snow pushed aside by merchants wielding shovels, trying to draw passersby to their carts by giving them clear lanes. The slums, however, remained a wasteland, with tracks cutting through the stained white blanket of the snow, and dark spots to mark where chamberpots had been emptied and animals had left deposits of their own.

The whole city carried a filthy smell, and Terian wrinkled his nose as the door to the Brutal Hole was shut behind him. *Don't know how Cyrus lived here for so many years.* He gave it a moment's reflection. *I suppose Saekaj is no picnic, either, though it's Sovar that carries the real stench.* Drawing his cloak tighter against a sudden wind, he set himself to walking against the shin-high snow that hindered his way.

He felt the bite of the cold seeping through his armor as he walked, the familiar clank of his boots dampened by the snow covering the cobblestones. He looked over the darkened streets and saw only vague hints of any life. A few scattered souls: some beggars, a merchant cleaning up his cart. There were lamps everywhere, but only every third or fourth one was lit. It was the way of the slums, he knew, that not all of them got oil. That thought caused him to recall the magical fires of Sanctuary, and he suddenly felt a longing to be far from Reikonos, far from the home of the humans, and surrounded by a very different group of humans.

Never going to happen.

His breath frosted in front of him when he let a sigh of despair cross his lips. The thought of what Malpravus had offered him was fresh in his mind. *I'm not nearly drunk. Not nearly. And giving away almost the last of my money?* He wanted to curse himself for it, but couldn't find the strength to do so, not huddled as he was against the cold. *There'll be more along next week. Enough to get by.* He felt his teeth chatter just slightly. *And that's about all.*

Still better than going with Malpravus. He inadvertently looked right, toward the Guildhall quarter. The faint sounds of the city echoed—dogs barking in the distance, a rattling down an alley, and voices raised in conversation. The Guildhall quarter was far off, but on a clear night one could hear the revelries within, the sound of an army marching through or to it, or one of the largest guilds returning from the Trials of Purgatory. It was quiet tonight, though, or the noises of the slums were blotting it out.

There is no way he would let me simply be an officer in his guild. There would have to be a price. His eyes flicked left and right, as though trouble was bound to dart out at him from behind the dilapidated stall that he turned past on the way back to his boarding house. A cat screeched at him and raced away into the darkness. He shrugged at the sight of its retreating hindquarters; better than rats, he supposed.

The boarding house was in sight just now; a wooden structure mostly, sandwiched between a burned-out husk of a house and a butcher's shop that dealt in lower quality meats of dubious origin. Terian had bought from them on several occasions; they had finer things than one would find even in Saekaj, though he knew most humans would turn their noses up at the offerings. A mad city, he'd decided, one where even the poor got a better chance than the mids of Sovar did.

The boarding house had a worn look about it, with warped boards that let the wind in every chance they got. Lying in bed on the nights when he hadn't enough coin for firewood was a challenge and had required him to spend precious silver on a heavier blanket, an old quilt that might have been hand-stitched during the last Elven/Dark Elven war, for all he knew. It was worn but heavy, and it kept out the chill enough for him. Still and all, he preferred to buy firewood, or if that wasn't available, coal, though it left a film of dark ash on everything.

He opened the door to the boarding house with a squeak, peeking inside to see if anyone was still in the entry hall. There was no one in sight, though a fire burned in the hearth in the meal room. It was low, though, and Terian knew instinctively that the proprietress—one Madame Hawthess—would have gone to bed hours earlier. She never pronounced judgment on him for the hours he kept, at least not audibly, though she did let him know by sigh and snort what she thought of his presumed activities. That he could handle, though. He had been dealing with thwarting the expectations of others for all his life, hadn't he?

"You are earlier than I expected," came a vaguely familiar voice from one of the chairs turned to face the hearth. If there was someone sitting on it, Terian could not see him. He let his hand fall to his axe handle, slung as it was across his back, and prepared to pull it. His cloak would come off with it, true, but it would be clear and ready to swing in just seconds. "Don't bother with the axe, I'm quite unarmed." The voice was low, smooth—not like Malpravus's—it held a dry air as though the speaker was perpetually starved for amusement, as though he had never had any in their entire life.

"I don't care for visitors," Terian said. "Which is why I never have them."

"I had assumed it was because you had no friends left with whom to visit." A head poked its way around the steep back of the chair. It was clearly a dark elf, that much was visible to Terian's eyes immediately. Grey-white hair backed by the firelight shone, almost platinum in color. The rest of the face rested in shadow, however, but the shape of the head in general was elongated.

"A foolish assumption," Terian said, chewing his lower lip, his fingers still holding tight to the axe handle. "I have friends. Countless friends."

"Yes, a veritable wealth of them, I'm sure." The man stood, drawing himself up to his full height. He was taller than Terian, taller than almost anyone the dark elf had ever met, save for perhaps Cyrus Davidon or Vaste. "In fact, I suspect every one of them that you possess surrounds you at this very moment, ready to launch themselves to your assistance, to your service at the slightest command."

Terian squinted his eyes to see through the light of the fire, blotting out the face of the man. A crackle of recognition caused him to shake. "It is you. Guturan. Guturan Enlas."

"I hoped that you would still know me by sight," Guturan said, drawing carefully at the lines of the jacket he wore over fine clothes. He took another step toward Terian and his face became visible through the backlight of the fire. It was lined, an old face, one he had known since childhood. "But it was only a faint hope, as you never were the sharpest child."

"You were always such a kind soul, Guturan." Terian let his hand leave the axe handle and ran it across his cloak to smooth it back to position to protect him from the cold. "I have so missed you these long years since I've been gone." He didn't bother to say it with anything less than a lethal dose of sarcasm, fit to kill any good intention that might have been brought into the conversation.

"Yes, well," Guturan said, now stepping closer, almost within arm's reach of Terian, "I come bearing a message."

Terian felt a seething distaste, one only a step up from what he had experienced at the sight of Malpravus only minutes earlier. "Gods, I hope it's a good one. Something cheerful, like a summons to my father's funeral."

Guturan barely raised an eyebrow at that. "Would you rejoice at that news?"

"Honestly," Terian said, "who wouldn't?"

Guturan Enlas regarded him carefully for a moment then turned and shuffled back to the chair he had been sitting in, retrieved a cloak from where it lay over the back, and wrapped himself in it. Terian watched him do so; it was a fine cloak, made of the threads of vek'tag hair, smoother than the silk that the elves of the Emerald Coast cultivated for their finery. Wordlessly, Guturan straightened his clothing and covered himself in the cloak.

Terian waited while he did so, and it was not until Guturan began to step past him to leave that Terian finally spoke. "What the hell does my father want, Enlas?"

"Nothing that would appeal to an ungrateful whelp," Guturan said with a sneer that wasn't remotely feigned. He leaned closer to him, lowering his voice as though he had just recalled that they were in a boarding house with very thin walls. "He told me that you would be intractable about this, that I would be wasting my time, but I argued for you. I argued with Lord Amenon that times had changed, that perhaps you had grown up, you foolish, naïve boy. He told me you had certainly not, and I argued for you." Guturan let a slight smile drift across his long face. "Once more, your father's wisdom proves why he is the master and I am but a humble steward in his house."

"Stick it in the darkest reaches," Terian said, unimpressed. "If you have some offer to make, be on with it. If all you've come to do is chide me in my father's name, then I invite you to enjoy your walk back to Saekaj."

"Your father—!" Guturan stepped close to Terian, and there was an air of menace about him. He regained control of himself, and his expression smoothed out. "Your father ... has heard about your recent ... difficulties."

"He's heard I'm sleeping in a boarding house at night, frightening away children for gold by day, and drinking and whoring my way through the evenings?" Terian said, amused. Guturan's eye twitched with loathing. "I don't know what's so difficult about any of those things, but I suppose that my father's view of the world is somewhat darker than my own."

"He heard," Guturan said, voice crackling and scratchy, as though it were steel scraping on steel, "that you had been cast out of your former guild and were adrift on a sea of meaningless actions. Magnanimous man that he is, he consented to allow me to come here and make you a most generous offer."

"'A most generous offer'?" Terian said, scoffing slightly. "This ought to be good. So what is it? I can become a member of his household guard? Stand at a post for ten hours per day staring at the empty street in front of his house? Or keep an eye on his interests down in the Back Deep of Sovar? At least that would put me near to the best whorehouses and bars; Saekaj has never been much to my taste—"

"He has consented," Guturan said, cutting Terian off without amusement, "to allow you something that no other member of the Sovereign's Army would surely give." Terian listened, quiet for once, waiting for the next verbal volley to land. "He wants you to return to Saekaj." Guturan pulled himself up straight once more, as though to become as august as a messenger should be for this sort of news. "He wants you to take up that which you once scorned and threw back at him. He wants you to rejoin him as his Lieutenant, his adjutant. To become his right hand and serve the Sovereign once more.

"He wants you to come home."

4.

Twenty Years Earlier

The glow of the lamp light was all Terian had to go by as he stared into the mirror. He did not consider his face youthful, not compared to his peers, but he knew how the other adults saw him. His hands shook as he fiddled with the fine cloth tunic, adjusting it over and over to find the perfect resting point on his thin frame. *Today, I am fourteen years old*, he thought.

Today I am a man in the eyes of my people.

A soft knock came at his door, preceding its opening by only seconds. He turned sharply, heart beating full in his chest. The door did not finish opening before a thin little slip of a girl snuck in through the crack, closing it behind her. She put her back against it, near breathless.

"Ameli," Terian said, turning back to the mirror, "I'm getting ready to go to the Legion of Darkness."

"For a day," Ameli said, almost squeaking. Terian regarded her in the mirror—her black, frilly dress, her thin face. She was only eight.

"It's important I make the right impression," Terian said, adjusting his collar once more. The neck was not quite right; it hung loose around his throat like a bowl with too little food in it. *I'm too skinny for this tunic.*

"You know all the instructors already," Ameli said with a scoff worthy of her age. "You know the head of the League. Father has already introduced you to everyone of consequence, and showing up in a suit that your neck rattles around in like a scabbard with too little sword is not going to impress them. They're already impressed enough because of Father."

Terian froze, the truth of her words eating into him. He tugged at the collar once more. "We have … a family image to maintain. Father expects us not to shame him in front of these people. They will be my instructors for the next four years. I have to take this seriously."

"Puhahahah," she said, pushing off the door and making her way toward him. Her laugh was distinctive, like nothing he'd ever heard before. She was shorter than he was, reaching only to mid-chest. "You take everything seriously."

"And you take nothing seriously." He squinted into the mirror, shooting her a thin, impatient smile.

"Because I'm eight," she said with a guffaw. "I have at least a couple more years before I have my sense of humor magically removed."

"They have not invented a spell that could pull that off, or Father would have had them cast it on you long ago," Terian said, finally reaching a rough truce with his collar. *It's not going to get any better than this.* He straightened, and it tilted to the left, provoking a sigh from him. "Son of a—" He stopped himself, catching sight of Ameli in the mirror before he completed his sentence, "… Shrawn."

"Puahahah," Ameli said, breaking into a grin that made her skinny face look like it was stretching at the bounds. "Nice catch. But the way you finished it gave it the same meaning."

"But I didn't curse," Terian said, staring forlornly at the collar, "and that's what counts in Father's eyes."

"Father, Father, Father," she said mockingly, rolling her eyes. "Maybe while you're in training at the Legion of Darkness, you can pick up some new people to talk about all the time? It'd be a nice change."

Terian stared at her in the mirror. "He's our father. He's the General of the Armies for the entire Sovereignty. You should show him the respect he deserves."

He could see Ameli look slightly chastened at that. "I know he is, but ... he's not you, Terian. He's not like you."

Terian felt his brow furrow. "What do you mean?" *I have done everything in my power to be like him! And who wouldn't want to be?*

"He's kind of ... mean sometimes," Ameli said, now mousy, like she didn't want to show him her eyes. "He yells a lot, Terian. He's always mad about something."

"But not at you," Terian said softly.

"No," Ameli said, still not looking up. "Not at me. Not at us."

"Running the Sovereign's Army is difficult work," Terian said. "He's under a lot of pressure."

"Now you're just repeating what Mother says."

"You asked me to talk about someone else," Terian said, letting a half-smirk out.

"Doesn't count, you were still talking about him."

"Ameli, Father is the most respected man in Saekaj and Sovar save for Dagonath Shrawn," Terian said. "We owe him our respect as well. If that means I'm talking about him all the time, good." He turned and gave his collar one last tug, but it did no good.

"He's done things no one else ever has. Carried us to the top of Saekaj. We would be living in dirt and filth in Sovar right now if not for him."

"Maybe that wouldn't be so bad?" she asked. "Maybe then he wouldn't be so angry all the time ..."

Terian stared at his collar in the mirror, and let out a sigh. "No price is too high for what we've got. Anger is a small thing to put up with to be in the second largest manor in Saekaj."

Ameli started to say something but lowered her voice. "You're talking like him again."

"Ameli," he said, letting a hint of impatience inflect his tone. *She just doesn't understand.*

"Sorry," she said, and now she truly was chastened, he could see. She took a couple steps toward him, her dress swaying as she walked. She reached up to his face and ran a cold hand down his cheek. She paused, just for a second, at his collar, and gave it a sharp tug. Then she wrapped her arms around him and gave him a strong, short hug before she ran from the room without another word.

Terian turned and looked at himself in the mirror. "Huh." The collar was smooth and perfectly in place. *How did she do that?* he wondered.

"Terian!" His father's voice echoed outside, and Terian straightened involuntarily, giving himself one last look over in the mirror. *Flawless.* He hesitated, looking around the room one last time before he walked out. It would hardly be his last time here; he would continue to live in his parents' house as he trained at the Legion during the days, but still ... it was a change, and worthy of reflection. *Once I walk out of here, everything will be different.*

"Coming, Father," Terian shouted back over his shoulder, and he gave one last look around the room before he walked out the door.

5.

Dawn found Terian riding into the whispering entry of the Waking Woods; a forest so massive that it girded the heart of Arkaria. They had hired a wizard in Reikonos Square, an elf with a shock of white hair, and after Guturan had tipped a few pieces of silver into his palm, the fury of energy that accompanied a wizard teleportation spell had risen to a crescendo and enveloped them.

When the light faded from his eyes, the snows had receded and they had stood on a flat plain turned brown by the rising tide of winter. "This is as close as I can safely get you," the elf had said, already disappearing into the bright light of his return spell. Terian had ridden south with Guturan at his side, the sun beginning to rise over the eastern horizon. He wondered at his decision. It hadn't even been a question, really. His father called, and he came. *Curious, that—especially given how we left things after ...* He felt a black despair crawl through him.

As they crested a hill, Terian looked east and saw the reflection of waters, a massive glow upon them as far as his eye could take in. "Lake Magnus," he whispered, keeping his gaze upon it a few minutes longer than he normally would have.

"It does have a certain majesty, doesn't it?" Guturan sniffed. "Though I still prefer the dark, quiet beauty of our own Great Sea."

"Phosphor-lit cave waters don't exactly do it for me anymore, Guturan," Terian said as their horses crossed the outermost tree and Lake Magnus disappeared from sight behind a moss-covered oak.

"You have the constitution for the outdoors, then," Guturan said with another sniff, reaching into the breast pocket of his cloak and coming out with a vek'tag-spun silken cloth, smooth and silvery in the gleaming morning light. "So many of our people do not. I collapsed upon my first sojourn out of Saekaj, you know."

"A common tale," Terian said as he passed under the boundary. It was a simple enough marker that only knowing eyes would catch: the oaks of the outer perimeter had cave cress flowers hanging from the boughs. Deep brown, dried out, they lay suspended from the branches at a height where they might escape notice if one were not being particularly observant.

"We now return to the glorious lands of the Sovereign," Guturan said with a whisper, solemn, but loud enough for Terian to hear him clearly.

"If it was so damned glorious, he'd still be here," Terian muttered.

"Be careful how you speak in this realm," Guturan said, a dark expression covering his face. "You have grown unaccustomed to the ways of our people. Loose tongues and disrespect go hand in hand, and they are a quick path to the Depths and all the tortures within for the careless."

"Yeah, yeah," Terian said. *I'd almost forgotten that the liberty of speaking one's mind is not a privilege granted to my own people.* He'd seen more than one person lose their head, their tongue or their freedom for an ill-chosen rebuke of the Sovereign. *Which is ironic since he hasn't even been here in the last century. Heavy is the shadow he casts, to still shroud us in such darkness.*

Visible behind the trees were shadows, and Terian knew they were small, hidden huts of the dark elven guards. Many a wandering foreigner had been unfortunate enough to miss the signs of the cave cress warning them off. *Trespassing in the Sovereignty carries a steep penalty all its own.* He shuddered. *And one I would not care to pay, were I a traveler who accidentally wandered astray.*

They carried on, their horses cantering along and bringing them deeper into the forest. The boughs of the trees grew closer together for a spell; thick and knotty branches denoting the old growth of the forest. The underbrush became nearly nonexistent, having long ago been taken for fuel to burn, and signs of the trees having been harvested for firewood became apparent. The larger trees had stumpy limbs where they had been cut and taken for burning.

There was sound ahead, and now the first guards of the Sovereignty were obvious. Before they had been mere shadows, hidden, but now they were apparent, and designed to crush the will of any who had bothered to penetrate the defenses of the Sovereignty this deeply. They held another purpose, though, a darker one, and Terian tried to hide the chill of it within him as he attempted not to ponder it. *It won't be long before I can't ignore it, though, as the evidence of it is coming upon us rapidly.*

Troops of the Sovereign were on parade march, their angular armor clearly visible, their swords out and on display. The road had widened sometime in the last hours of travel and Terian had not even noticed. It was now large enough for ten men to walk abreast between the trees. The armor of the foot soldiers was clanking in time, and they paid no attention to Terian or Guturan, who maneuvered their horses off the road to yield the right of way to the army. "As it should be," Guturan said, though whether he was referring to their giving primacy to the army's passage or the idea that there were a thousand dark elves presently on the march, Terian did not know. *Nor care, truly.*

The sound of clanking armor receded behind them and the trees grew thinner ahead. Terian could see the sun shining down on a massive clearing, and all around the perimeter sprang fortifications. Tree stands, interconnected by bridges and walkways, marked their entry into the wide-open space. Archers stood upon the platforms, facing inward. Their passage was acknowledged by a soldier on the ground with a simple nod and nothing more; his task was not to keep them out, after all. No one unintended ever made it this far anyhow. *Not freely, at least.*

The clank of metal ahead drew Terian's attention. The clearing was more than a simple forest meadow. It was hectares of open space, tilled land, farms that stretched to the regrowth of the trees in the far off distance beyond the reach of his eyes. "It's gotten bigger," he said under his breath, not really intending to speak the words aloud.

"Saekaj Sovar has gotten bigger," Guturan returned, the steady clopping of the feet of their horses drumming along as they kept on down the dirt road. "The farms have to grow correspondingly, though they have discovered some strange mechanism of switching the crops grown in each field every season, and apparently it has slowed the need to clear more land."

Terian looked across the wide expanse of open fields. *Couldn't prove it by me.* His eyes fell upon figures in rags off the path a short distance. A tree trunk stood clear in the middle of the farmland, a platform built atop it. It was a funny thing, bough-less, turned into a watchtower in the middle of a field. There were others he could see, every several hundred feet. Archers stood atop them, watching the fields with a dispassionate eye. They kept watch on the figures in rags, who had implements in their hands to break the earth.

Terian looked at the ragged souls and felt a little pity. At least a quarter of them were small, no higher than to mid-thigh on him. *Gnomes.* Others reached his belly or perhaps a little higher. *Dwarves.* The tallest of them were the most stooped, bent as they were to do their labor. *Humans and elves, I suppose.* He felt a shudder run through him. He'd spent time in Reikonos freely, and even been on a sojourn or two to Pharesia, the elven capital, and Termina, their foremost city. There were no dark elves in chains there, breaking the ground ahead of winter settling in.

He looked away abruptly, ignoring the sick feeling in his stomach and keeping his eyes to the path in front of him. *Slaves. How many of them are there now, I wonder?*

They passed the next hours seeing spectacle after spectacle of the slaves working the land. Taskmasters stood with whips at the ready, and it was not an uncommon sight to see them being applied with zeal. Some of the overseers even seemed to delight in it. The crack of the lash made Terian uneasy, and he kept his eyes on the road ahead. Hills were rising in the distance, and there was a deep relief that accompanied them in his mind.

"I shall be glad indeed when we have crossed into the gates," Guturan said quietly over the screams of a gnome being whipped without mercy just across the field. It was a pitiable noise, and Terian felt a sickly unease.

"Indeed," Terian said, his voice tight. "I know exactly what you mean."

"Do you?" Guturan asked. "I had thought you thrived in the out of doors?"

Terian felt his face go slack, letting the tension bleed out as the shock filtered in. "I thought you were talking about the …" He stopped himself. His mouth was dry, and he felt a pallor settle over him. *Slavery is as natural to the residents of Saekaj as indoor plumbing is to those of Sanctuary.* "Never mind." The screams across the field died off at last, and he did not turn to see if it was because of the death of the owner of said voice. The sick feeling, however, stayed with him as they rode closer and closer to the approaching hills.

6.

A series of buildings was visible just to the east of the hills. A bevy of young dark elves stood nearby, squinting under the weak early winter sun. Clouds lined the sky and Terian's breath still frosted the air, even as the hour ground closer to noon. He hadn't eaten an official breakfast, just some stale bread that had accompanied Guturan in his saddlebags. Terian could sense his destrier's pull toward the long grass that filled the ditches on either side of the road, but he kept the steed moving onward, until they reached the cluster of dark elven youths, two of whom ran up to them as they began to dismount.

"These two belong to the House of Lepos," Guturan said stiffly to the older of the boys. Terian watched to see if any coin was passed to the stableboys; none was. *Not tremendously surprising; it is their duty, after all.*

"Yes, sir," the older stableboy said, bowing his head and taking the reins of Guturan's horse. The younger took Terian's in hand and started to lead the destrier away. He was a speckled lad, the black freckles on his cheeks a match for his dark, wavy hair. They continued on past their fellows, who stood stiffly at attention while Terian and Guturan were in sight. He suspected that once they had passed on, the boys would be back to playing hardscrabble games of some sort or another; the dirt on the knees and elbows of their ragged clothes seemed to bear out his assessment.

"Not far now," Guturan said, turning from the stableboys waiting for their next arrivals and walking toward the hills. There were two steep ones just ahead, almost a sheer cliff face on the side of one of them, and Terian could see the grand entrance tunneled into the hillside. It had stone towers built to flank it, with countless guards standing all around the base, monitoring the traffic coming in and out. It was a little ebb and flow, only a few people passing here and there, all of them dark elves. *How unlike Reikonos.*

They came upon the gates, and Terian felt a great discomfort settle over him. *How long has it been? Twenty years?* He felt a little twinge in his muscles, a mixture of discomfort and anticipation. *Not long enough.* He glanced at the wary guards looking him over from behind their dark plated armor, and the archers on platforms above, and he drew a breath of cool air piping out of the caves. *Not nearly long enough.*

"State your business," one of the guards said as Guturan approached, holding a simple piece of parchment before him. The guard took it, never removing his gaze from Guturan.

"I am Guturan Enlas, steward of the House of Lepos." Guturan made a small bow of respect. "I bring with me Terian Lepos, heir to my master's house."

There was a rough whisper that passed between the guards. There was an opposite lane, too, one checking the papers of those leaving the tunnel, and activity within it stopped as heads swiveled to take in Terian. He wanted to dip his head further beneath his spiked pauldrons, to recede within his helm, to disappear beneath the cresting spires of it, but he couldn't. *The heir of House Lepos is a dark knight of great renown,* he told himself. *There is no retreat for such a man.*

Guturan's parchment was thrust back to him and Terian received a sharp, deep bow from the head guard. "M'lord, you are expected." He gestured with a long arm toward the entry tunnel. "Your vek'tag carriage waits in the courtyard."

"Thank you," Guturan said, taking back the parchment delicately and then beginning his walk again toward the darkened mouth of the cave. He gave Terian a smile as he looked back. "No point in walking all the way down, after all."

There was indeed a carriage waiting about a hundred feet down the passage where the chamber widened. The cave floor was a well-worn path, and Terian could see the faint outlines of ancient steps once cut on either side of the passage. They had long ago been smoothed out to allow for passage of wheeled carriages and wagons, but at the edges of the tunnel the remnants of them could still be seen.

The cave opened up into a terraced courtyard, with ramps leading down on either side into a wide chamber. Carriages and wagons were lined up end to end, and storehouses were carved into the rock at either side of the room. It was a grand courtyard built into the underground, a staging area for all the cargo shipped into and out of Saekaj Sovar, the city in the deep.

The dirt under their feet gave way to stone bricks laid out to smooth the passage of wheeled vehicles. It was the dark clay of the beaches near the Great Sea, harvested and mixed with straw, hauled up and shaped underneath the blue skies of the out of doors by the slaves, then dried in the sun and fired in a kiln. It clanked with every step of his boots, and the humid air flooded his nostrils with the smell of the beasts that filled the courtyard—there were horses, oxen, donkeys and vek'tag as far as the eye could see—the vek'tag being swapped out on the outbound wagons and swapped in for the ones descending into Saekaj and Sovar.

It was a bustle of activity, hundreds of carriages and wagons, and yet the courtyard was hardly full. Terian's eyes took some time adjusting to the dark, to the glow of the occasional lamp. The tunnel behind them admitted only the most fractional amount of light from the surface, and it faded the deeper they got into the courtyard.

Guturan Enlas approached a carriage that bore a familiar sigil. Two vek'tag were harnessed to the front of it. Enormous spiders, large as oxen and nearly as docile, clicked their broken mandibles while waiting, chattering to each other. The carriage hitched to their backs was draped in red cloth, though it was hard to see in the fading light. It was built of fine wood which showed from underneath the velvet coverings. Wood was a luxury in Saekaj, necessary for so many things that it was carefully rationed. Terian knew the display of even this much rich wood was a statement about the owner of the carriage. Most wagons or sleds were simple things, with no more material than necessary to get the job done—and sometimes less.

The sigil on the velvet coverings was a darkened eye, stylized with lightning bolt-shaped protrusions from the top and bottom. It gave the whole thing an angry appearance, to Terian's mind. *Which seems appropriate.*

The carriage driver gave them a nod as they approached, and Guturan opened the door for Terian with a short bow. Terian climbed in and seated himself on the hard bench in the back. Guturan sat across from Terian and slapped the wall behind him. The carriage drew to motion with the crack of a whip.

Terian endured the bumps and turns silently for a few minutes as they left the great courtyard and the tunnel took an easy slope. After only ten minutes, however, he knew his face was showing discomfort.

"It is a fine carriage, is it not?" Guturan asked, apparently unaware of Terian's expression. *Or ignoring it. That wouldn't be surprising.*

"I could do with a little less Saekaj opulence." Terian adjusted himself on the hard bench. "I know wood is a sign of wealth that should make the lessers heed their betters, but they have this thing called padding now. Sure, it gets in the way of showing off, but it certainly eases the passage."

Guturan snorted. "Human and elven comforts," he said, making it sound like a curse of the lowest sort. "Let them have them, their pampered ways, their soft luxuries. Our people are of the earth, hardened. We are one with the darkness, and enshroud ourselves in the righteousness of Yartraak. When the day of our reckoning comes, the humans and elves shall be ill-prepared, having grown cumbersome and fat on their comforts."

"Right." The carriage bumped along down the tunnel, slowing and speeding up as pedestrians moved to the side to allow their passage. Terian heard the driver's shout more than once followed by the crack of a whip and a cry of some poor soul who hadn't moved out of the way fast enough for the driver of the noble carriage. "Well, there certainly isn't much comfortable about life down here."

"As it should be," Guturan pronounced haughtily. They lapsed into silence for a moment before he spoke again. "I presume by your earlier jibe you have not heard the glorious news of the Sovereign's return?"

Terian's ears perked up and he looked away from the window, where he had been studying the narrow line of foot traffic that was heading up to the surface, broken by the occasional open-topped wagon. He had seen no noble carriages heading in that direction. "What?"

"He has returned, our Sovereign." Guturan said it with the satisfaction he might have expressed over a bountiful meal being served. "Returned, and has taken up his rightful place at our head once more."

"That's ..." Terian remembered Guturan's earlier chiding and suppressed his first response. "Marvelous. Simply wonderful."

"I can tell when you're feigning." Guturan's reaction was one of measured annoyance. "You have not lived under the glory of the Sovereign. All you have known is the weakness of the tribunal that has led us since before your birth. This last century has been dark days indeed for our kind, with the withdrawal to lick our wounds, sulking about here in our own dark territories and not reaching forth our hand to take rightfully what has been ours—"

"Because it worked out so well for us last time we tried that," Terian said without enthusiasm.

"You know nothing of our last war," Guturan said with a scoff. "You are not yet a half century of age, yet you think you know all about things that came before your time. We were a power on the rise, destined to engulf the whole of Arkaria."

"Until the wretched humans and hated elves banded together in the lightest alliance," he gave the word 'lightest' all the vitriol due it in Saekaj, being the curse it was within the city, "and sent us running from lands that we had, blah blah blah—"

"Curb your wicked tongue," Guturan hissed. "Lest you land yourself in the Depths for sedition."

Terian blinked. *This may be more difficult than I thought.*

Guturan's slitted eyes receded as he seemed to faded into the seat of the carriage. "There have been many sent down to the Depths of late for saying less than you already have. Whatever leniency of expression might have crept into Saekaj and Sovar with the century of tribunal rule has been swept away in recent weeks."

He raised his voice. "And I think it a good thing. Traitorous thoughts should not be countenanced, and the Depths require the labor of our ill-behaved and wayward brethren to keep us marching forward."

Terian let the silence hang after that. He had been down to the Depths once to visit while in training at the Legion of Darkness to become a knight. It was a prison by any name. It was broken into segments depending on the severity of the crime: the uppermost chambers were manure composting sites; below that were mushroom gardens and root farms—where the natural crops that fed Sovar, bereft of the luxuries of the surface foods that were so enjoyed in Saekaj—produced the bulk of their daily sustenance. Below that were the mines, dank and forbidding, where the most heinous perpetrators were sentenced to be worked to death. Terian let himself shudder only slightly at that thought. While thieving could get one sentenced to the root farms, seditious sentiments were the quickest ticket to the mines and labor unto death.

Shouts rang ahead from the carriage driver, and Terian put his head close to the left side window, though he thought he knew what was coming next. Traffic stopped in the opposite lane, a wagon halting with a stream of pedestrians behind it, cowed by the shouts of the Lepos carriage's driver. When the last of the slow-moving walkers was nearly clear of the lane, the driver sent the carriage into a turn to the left, crossing the opposite lane of traffic. Terian turned to look out the right window, caught the gazes of a crowd of haggard people walking behind and around the wagon, trying to get a glimpse of the carriage and the sigil it bore. When they saw Terian looking out, whispers echoed quietly in the tunnel as the carriage made a slow, careful turn into a side passage.

A gate lay ahead, and Terian could see it just beyond the walls of the tunnel they had crossed the lane to get into. It obstructed the view of the chamber beyond. Luminescence from the phosphors and fungi on the chamber's ceiling lit the cave with a cool blue color. It was a cavernous place, beyond the gate, one of the great cities of the dark elves. They pulled up close to the gate, the wheels of the carriage clacking against the cobblestones beneath. They didn't even grind to a halt, merely slowed for a moment as the shout went up to open the gates. Terian could hear the heavy wood pulled open with the effort of laboring workmen who were kept in place solely for the purpose of opening the doors. The hinges squealed the tiniest amount and a guard swore then appeared at the window of the carriage. "Apologies, m'lord. We'll be having that oiled immediately."

"Excellent," Guturan answered for Terian. *Mustn't have the gentry speaking to the lowborn soldiers himself.* "I expect no less from the Saekaj guard."

The guard bowed and retreated as the carriage started to move once more. Terian did stick his head out the window this time as they passed through the gates.

Saekaj.

The upper city was spread out before him, the road dipping down into the main street that ran through the heart of the noble city. There were other avenues, to be certain, but the main road led through the primary square, where stood the markets, where stood the great fountain from which the servants and slaves drew water for the least of the noble houses.

The chamber was a roughly ovoid shape, and in the far distance against the opposite wall stood the Grand Palace of Saekaj, the seat of government for the entire Sovereignty. It was a blocky and boxy structure built into the far wall of the chamber, but with an unmistakable majesty of its own. Twin waterfalls flanked either side of the main tower, washing down into a moat inside the palace grounds. There was a wall surrounding the grounds, with great gates of metal and wood, fully displaying the opulence of the Sovereignty. Terian had been inside before, for formal events. *I doubt the Sovereign will throw nearly as many parties in his house as Dagonath Shrawn and the godsdamned tribunal did in his absence.*

The incline of the road leveled off as they reached the ground level of the chamber. The carriage's smooth movement through the streets was unbroken. The avenue was teeming mostly with servants, though the occasional carriage was passing in the opposite direction, pulled by vek'tag as large as the ones which guided his own conveyance. The smaller houses in the center of Saekaj were those of lesser nobles. Greater nobles had their estates against the walls, with plenty of room to expand their houses by burrowing deeper into the chamber walls. Lesser nobles had to content themselves with the space they had.

The noble houses grew more opulent and the chamber grew wider as they approached the market. At the square, the carriage turned to follow the circular road. The chamber reached the full extent of its width and height and began to taper again toward the back of the chamber and the Sovereign's palace.

The smell of food and dirt was prevalent around them. Terian could see faces blurring into the crowds. A great many of them belonged to servants, obvious by the garb they wore. A few nobles were interspersed, always obvious by their black, white and greyscale garb. *Bright colors are still for the poor, I suppose.* The servants wore colors, but even their clothes were muted and fit within acceptable ranges for their station. *Enough to allow you to discern them for what they are, but not so much as to be an embarrassment to their masters.*

The carriage moved slowly, the noble traffic thick through the streets. The markets rang with the quiet voices of costermongers.

So different than Reikonos, Terian thought, *where they raise their voices as loud as possible to advertise their low prices.* Here, the merchants kept almost silent, and the bargaining for low prices was done only in whispers. *Appearances are everything here. Better to have the watching eyes and listening ears believe you to pay too much rather than too little.* Terian smiled but knew it was more of a sneer. *The foolish preening of Saekaj is a constant.*

His eyes traveled over the crowd with dull disinterest. *Servants, merchants and nobles as far as the eye can discern.* The modest garb of the females in the crowd captured his attention. High noble girls were too prim for his taste. *Besides, every one of them has a parent over her shoulder telling them to wait until marriage.* He smiled. *They don't all listen, thankfully, but still ...*

His eye fell on a servant, her hair dyed a faint blue. *It's the servant women that pay the price for the nobles' prurience.* He felt his lips curl in disgust at the thought. *I'd rather pay a whore than take advantage of the servants the way these chamber pot scrapings do.* He swept his gaze over the crowd, looking for a nobleman to fixate on, to direct his hateful gaze to. He found one and gave him a daggered look that was doubtless invisible to the recipient. *I may be here, but I'll never be like you and your ilk, whoever you are.* He turned his eyes back to the blue-haired servant, finding her once again in the crowd. *I'd rather be like—*

He paused as the servant girl turned her head toward the carriage. It took Terian a moment to realize she was unaccompanied, a strange thing for a servant in the Saekaj markets. He saw her face in profile as the carriage inched along. A slight bump on the cobblestones rattled Terian's armor as he leaned toward the open window, mouth slightly open as he stared out. *It can't be ...*

It is.

He opened the door to the carriage and jumped out onto the street as Guturan shouted, "Halt!" behind him to the driver. Terian ignored it; he would walk the rest of the way from here if need be.

His boots hit the cobblestones and a servant exclaimed quietly under her breath as he brushed her out of the way. His eyes were fixed on the blue-haired girl, only a half-dozen paces away now and caught in a throng as she moved slowly along.

Terian pushed people aside without shame or grace. He checked the nobleman he'd caught sight of from the carriage particularly hard and without remorse, drawing a sharp rebuke from the man that faded once he caught sight of Terian's armor. Terian gave little thought as to whether it was simply the armor heralding him as a dark knight or whether the appearance of it gave hint to who Terian was that silenced the man. *Probably the former*, he decided.

He reached the blue-haired girl with a few more steps. She was in the midst of a throng of servants but headed in a different direction, crossing diagonally against the crowd. It was that which gave her away, he realized. Servants would not dare to come to the marketplace alone. It would make them prey for noblemen seeking easy conquest.

He came up behind her and grasped her upper arm as carefully as he could. She turned to give him a fiery look, speaking before she had even fully turned her head to take him in. "Release me, fool. I'll have you know I am—"

"Kahlee Ehrest," Terian said with a smirk, "in the market unattended, with blue-dyed hair and servant's clothing. Tell me, are you looking for a nobleman to take advantage of you? Because there are easier ways; you could just show up at the gates of the House of Redrigh Thornn without a stitch of clothing on."

"Terian Lepos, you cad," Kahlee said with a slight rolling of her eyes. "The streets of Saekaj have not missed you in your lengthy absence."

"Indeed not?" Terian asked. "Unfortunately, my father apparently did miss me, and so the streets of Saekaj will have to suffer in order for the great Amenon Lepos to be happy."

"Happy seems a strong word for Lord Amenon," Kahlee said, still looking entirely unimpressed. "I'd ask you to release my arm, but I know how little you listen to the commands of your social lessers."

"Oh, Kahlee," Terian said, still smiling, "I've never once thought of you as my lesser at anything, especially being social."

"I'd like to think I'm lesser than you in the realm of rudeness," Kahlee said. Terian stared at her face, which was still pinched with irritation. *Cute, though. And hardly aged since last I saw her*, though she had gained a certain thinness of face that he didn't remember. "Presently, you are proving my theory on that." She flexed her arm slightly under her faintly-dyed clothes as if to illustrate the point.

"Oh, I'm sorry," Terian said, still not relinquishing his grip. "I'm just trying to save you from falling prey to that utter arse over there." He jerked his thumb back in the direction from which he had come.

Kahlee craned her thin neck to look past him, and he wondered again if she'd been this thin when last he'd seen her. No, she hadn't. Thinness was not a prized attribute among the nobles of Saekaj; the plumper the noblewoman, the more prosperous the house, it was said. *A young and unattached woman such as this would practically be force-fed by her parents, yet she's looking surprisingly waif-like.* He smiled wider. *And blue hair?* "I doubt Guturan Enlas could be described as an 'utter arse,' even by you, Terian Lepos," Kahlee said.

Terian turned, not letting loose of her arm. "What? Not Enlas. Well, Enlas too, if you knew him." He pointed at the nobleman he'd knocked down, who was speaking to Guturan in hushed tones. "Him. He's plainly circling the market looking for servant girls to make his conquests."

Kahlee laughed, causing heads to turn in the hushed market square. "Yaren Machin?" She kept her voice low so that Terian could hear it without letting it drift as his words had. "He's a fool, but he's not fool enough to accost me twice. I've warned him off before and he knows who I am." She gave him an unamused look. "Now that we've established that I am perfectly safe from the predations of others, will you drop this pretense—and my arm?"

"I'll drop one," Terian said, frowning, "you decide which."

Kahlee sighed. "My arm, then."

Terian let his mouth snake slightly upward as he let her arm fall. "Now, about that supposed pretense—" Kahlee Ehrest turned away without comment. "Hey, wait!"

"No," she said, moving through the crowd of faintly colored garb. She paused to let an older noblewoman clad in a black dress cross in front of her.

Terian stepped forward to follow, and three servant girls in their teens nearly fell over themselves to move out of his way. "I really didn't have a pretense when I grabbed hold of you. I was just trying to catch you so I could say hello—"

"Which you've yet to say," Kahlee said, whirling around to face him. "So get it out of your system and we can both be on our way."

He stared at her, the angular lines of her high cheekbones and dark blue skin flush and faint against the blue hair and pale red dress. "Hello, Kahlee."

"Hello, Terian," she said, almost tonelessly. "And good day. Now that we've got that out of the way, I hope we can avoid speaking for another twenty or so years." She drew herself up. "Which will not be nearly long enough for me to forget what you did—and who you are." She gave him a look of faintest reproach then turned about on her heel and faded into the crowd.

7.

Terian felt the sting of her contempt coloring his cheeks as he made his way back to the carriage. Guturan waited silently but with furious eyes. "Are you quite finished accosting the serving girls? You need not be as flagrant as that fool Yaren, you know? Arrangements can be made without resorting to public displays of—"

"That was Kahlee of the House of Ehrest," Terian said, the smells of fresh yeast bread from the market filling his nose. His flesh felt surprisingly warm given the coolness of the caves.

"Sovereign's grace," Guturan said in shock. "I'd heard she'd defied her parents, but to see a girl of one of the noblest houses dyed and garbed in such a manner—" He halted in the middle of his sentence. "This is hardly a matter to be discussed in polite company."

Terian stopped before the door of the carriage as the driver waited for him, holding it open. The man was stooped low in a bow. "I could stand to discuss it a little more," Terian said. "She looked …" He turned his head, trying to catch a glimpse of her through the crowd. "… good."

Guturan made a hacking noise deep in his throat. "You have been away for far too long, Master Terian. She was rangy as a street orphan of Sovar, and those clothes—"

"You don't have to agree with me, Guturan," Terian said. "You can shut up any time, though."

They fell into silence as Terian climbed back into the carriage. Guturan latched the door behind him, and the faint noise of the market square faded as Guturan started to pull the cord of rope to shut the curtains. "Don't," Terian told him, and Guturan let it be.

The carriage began to move again, the light thumping of the wheels against the road allowing Terian to drift into thought. *Kahlee Ehrest ... oh, how you've changed ...*

They passed back onto the main road at the far end of the square, and walls cropped up to separate the street from the noble manors on either side of the avenue. The sides of the chamber quickly gave way to the largest and most prominent noble estates. Each manor they passed was grander than the last in the line.

Here sit the most favored. Terian's eyes swept to the left, to the next-to-last house. *The House of Ehrest. Third in the line for the most favored in Saekaj. Though I'm certain Kahlee's behavior isn't helping them at present.*

Terian's eyes were drawn to a familiar house, and the carriage made a turn through the gates of the estate nearest to the Sovereign's palace on the right-hand side of the road. *My right, not the Sovereign's. And that is important.* He glanced out the window and caught sight of the manor house directly opposite. *The House of Dagonath Shrawn.* Terian's eyes narrowed. *The most feared and hated man in Saekaj Sovar. The Right Hand of the Sovereign.*

The House of Shrawn passed out of sight behind the gates, and there came a smell of familiar gardens as they crossed through the wall. Guards were present, clad in the livery of the sigil of the eye that hung over the carriage. A small waterfall flowed out of a rocky streambed against the wall of the cavern. A large, blocky estate house waited at the end of the drive, built into the rock. The lines of it were sheerest elegance, aping the palace of the Sovereign wherever possible. The carriage squeaked to a stop in the roundabout in front of the front door, and Terian drew a deep breath of cool air.

"Don't forget your cloak," Guturan told him, not even looking at him.

"I never took it off," Terian said.

Guturan looked back at him, frowning. "Why not? It is abundantly warmer here in Saekaj than it is outside in that awful wind, out in the frigid elements of that city you were living in."

Terian shrugged. "I suppose I've become accustomed to the warmer temperatures humans and elves prefer."

Guturan made a disgusted noise. "Comforts."

"I'm sure we don't have any of those here," Terian said, "in our palatial estate." He brushed past Guturan and stepped out of the carriage first, taking care not to miss the hinged step that had been kicked down for him by a well-dressed doorman who had come out to greet them. Terian let the clank of his boots against the stone carry him up the steps to the entrance where a second doorman opened the front door with a deep bow.

Terian strode into the house, where wooden floors varnished and dark awaited him. There were lamps burning in the entry, concessions to the fact that the bright luminescence from the ceiling of the cave was not present here, and that even a dark elf could not see in total blackness. He eyed the nearest lamp, saw the slosh of the fuel oil that he knew had been dredged out of the Depths by prisoners, and pondered idly whether it was the slaves on the surface or the dark elven criminals who truly had it the worst in the Sovereignty.

"My son," came a quiet voice from the corner. He turned and saw her, rising up from an unpadded hardwood chair, . Olia Lepos wore a dress of cotton grown on the surface by slaves. She was thinner and frailer than he remembered, much more so than the other noblewomen he'd known, though she was less than a century old. Her face was lined in the manner of humans who had spent days in the sun, but he knew that daylight had never touched her skin, even now. She stopped only a pace away, her reserve clouding whatever emotion she might be feeling. The room was smallish; a foyer with a staircase leading upward, the majority of it carved stone, built in the style of the noble houses of Saekaj to conserve space. Terian could have reached up and touched the ceiling were he of a mind to but even so, she appeared miniscule within it.

"Mother," Terian said and felt the tug of a worried smile. She looked so faint and worn, as if a thousand years had passed since last he had seen her, when in truth it hadn't even been two decades. *An eyeblink for a dark elf, really.*

"I am pleased that Guturan was able to find you," she said, her hand reaching up and running across the pitted surface of his breastplate below the pauldrons. There were only small spikes here, twice as wide as his thumb, near each armpit where he could ram them into a foe with a sharp shoulder check and cause bruising, at least. She kept her small hand well clear of them, however, as though fearing he might employ them on her. *She needn't worry about that.* "It has been so long," she said in a voice tinged with regret.

"Not so long for our people," Terian said as cavalierly as he dared.

"But for the humans whom you have been living among," Olia said, her eyes still not meeting his, "half a lifetime, almost."

"I've also lived among elves," he said, as gently as he could. "And for them it would be considered nothing more than a season."

She finally raised her face to stare at him, and though he could see the clouds of unease beneath them, not a word of condemnation came out. "Still, it pleases me to look upon you once more, especially here in this place, returned to us safe and whole."

"The blessings of Yartraak have surely been with him," Guturan said from behind him. "Is Lord Amenon in his office?"

"Of course," Olia said. "One of the servants brought him that atrocious mushroom, suet and beansprout gruel only moments ago." She had seemed almost indifferent until the food was mentioned. When she spoke of it, a hardening of the lines around her eyes became evident. "Cooked for only seconds, the way he likes it."

Terian let that hang in the air for a moment before he spoke. "The way the poor eat it, you mean."

If Olia was affronted by her son's comment, she hid it behind the facade of her purple eyes, as indigo as the dyes he had seen in the Reikonos markets. "No matter how far above his beginning station your father has risen, he continues to shun the luxuries afforded him by his Lordship, his fortunes and the continuing favor of the Sovereign." She shook her head ever so subtly, so subtly that Terian could not discern whether she was mentally chiding her husband or merely dismissing his faults. "To think that the son of a vek'tag herder and a seamstress could rise so far. Truly the Sovereign is gracious."

Terian bit back his immediate response. *Truly gracious, to allow only those who have sacrificed what you have sacrificed to rise up from the pits of Sovar. Never mind those languishing there who have been given no such opportunity.* "Truly," was all he said.

"We must take you to your father," Guturan said without further ado, striding up from behind to lead him on.

"You don't think he saw our arrival out his window?" Terian asked with returning amusement.

"You will go to the lord of the house; he need not come to you," Guturan snapped, his long, lanky legs now resting on the first step of the staircase, giving him an even more pronounced height advantage as he looked down at Terian. "Or have you forgotten your manners and your place, having lived so long out in the cold daylight of the filth above?"

Terian let that one pass, feeling more pleased at riling the steward than stung by his ineffectual reply. "I don't recall ever knowing any manners, actually. Who was in charge of teaching me those? I can't remember."

Guturan let out a low exhalation of frustration. "My apologies, my lady, for failing you so in the instruction of this one—"

"My son has always found his amusement in defying the expectations of others," Olia said dismissively. "Do not trouble yourself over it, Guturan, you did your best. After all, if he confounded the responsibilities handed him by his father, his mother and his Sovereign, it cannot be expected he would take the education you gave him with any seriousness—"

Terian sighed. "Do you hear that?"

Olia and Guturan both stopped, caught by surprise, and listened. "What?" Olia asked.

"You might not be able to see it, here in the dark," Terian said, striding forward to the stairs and dodging past Guturan as he began to ascend, "but it was the sound of my eyes rolling."

He climbed the stairs, the long, pacing steps of Guturan Enlas following behind him. When he reached the landing after the third floor, he slowed and Guturan overtook him. There was only one room here, at the top of the house, and the stairs cut straight up toward it. Double doors marked the entry. They were not wood but stone, and heavy, as Terian knew from experience. He recalled many a time as a child trying to push them open, just a crack to glimpse a sight of his father at his desk, poring over parchment that seemed to come from messengers arriving at all times of day and night.

Guturan stopped and used a solid metal knocker built into the door to sound a heavy, thunking call that echoed down the stairwell through the rest of the house. Terian remembered that noise as well, all the way back to boyhood, awakening him at times in sleep. The smell of something deep and earthy was in the air: the gruel his father had eaten every day for as long as he could recall.

He never made any of us eat it, though, Terian thought. *Not even once.*

"Come," came the voice from within the study, and Guturan shot a look at Terian, something between disapproval and a warning to behave, something that had roots in Terian's childhood. He felt himself subconsciously straighten as Guturan pushed open the door, and Terian stiffly went up the last steps into the study.

8.

"Your son," Guturan announced as Terian strode through into the study. The aroma of the gruel was even stronger in here, in spite of the weak nature of the stuff. It was hardly fit to feed the poor, yet his father consumed at least a bowl of it per day along with all the other meals that were served in the house. *Doesn't affect the old man's waistline, though,* Terian noted.

"So it is," Terian's father spoke. His hair was a dark, lustrous black, like the oil that came from the Depths, and his skin showed nary a wrinkle in spite of his several centuries of life. It was all combed back in smooth lines and slicked down, as though it had been wet with water from the well. Not a strand was out of place and Amenon Lepos stared at Terian down a nose that was as pointed as his son's.

There was little enough noise in the study, an almost ominous silence in the book-lined room. A few lamps hung in the corners and a small hearth blazed with heat and light to Terian's right, the only sign of comfort in the room. A picture of a dark elven girl was hung above the hearth, but Terian averted his gaze from it as quickly as he saw it.

Ameli.

The chair behind his father's desk was a simple thing, functional wood and not nearly enough to be considered extravagant. His desk was a table, well crafted but spare, and with parchment carefully organized in stacks on top. A quick look toward the hearth showed Terian his memory was not in error; the remains of parchment turned to ash lined the front of the hearth. The fire was as much for the destruction of the countless secret missives his father received as it was for any sort of warmth. The smoky aroma filled the room, reminding him of more than one uncomfortable memory of this place.

Terian's eyes fell upon a single red gemstone centered in the middle of the desk on a small pillow. He pursed his lips when his gaze fell upon it; it was the lone decoration on the otherwise Spartan surface, the only item not made of paper. "You still keep that?"

Amenon Lepos did not even raise an eyebrow. "I prefer to surround myself with reminders of the blessings of the Sovereign, to always keep my remembrance centered on thoughts of gratitude for what has been given unto me."

Terian stifled the bitter reply he wanted to make. He shuffled from foot to foot for a moment before he spoke again. "You summoned me, Father? Called me home?"

Amenon looked past Terian. "Leave us, Guturan."

Guturan nodded. "If I may, m'lord, do you require—?"

"I need nothing further right now," Amenon said curtly and turned once more to look out the large window behind him. Terian stole a glance and saw that it was as he remembered, a full view of the approach to the house. And directly across from it, clear and proud against the far cavern wall, was the manor of Dagonath Shrawn. "My son and I have things to discuss."

"As you wish," Guturan said, making his retreat with a last bow. He shut the door behind him, the sound of the stone's heavy weight on the hinges as they closed almost palpable to Terian.

They stood in silence, Terian's skin prickling at his last memory of this place, of the last conversation he'd had within the walls of this study. Echoes of that conversation had played in his head for years, but not a word was spoken now.

"I heard you fell on hard times," Amenon said, turning at last to face Terian. "That you had taken to selling yourself in menial guard duty, drinking and whoring in your off time." His countenance was dark and serious; grave.

"Well," Terian said with lightness, "I was all about the drinking and whoring in better times, too, but I had more money to pay for it then."

Amenon studied him without amusement. "I've told you this before, but it bears repeating. The wit that comes so naturally to you is familiar to me. Your grandfather made a constant jest of everything in his life, and it took him no farther than the vek'tag pens of Sovar. You would do well to remember that when next you interrupt a serious topic with your pointless levity."

"In fairness to him," Terian said, without much levity at all, "anyone who worked the vek'tag pens for very long would need to have a sense of humor about them. After all, shoveling spider dung? When does that get fun?"

Amenon did not even blink, keeping his gravely serious aura. "I suppose it would be too much to ask for you to listen to the words I speak to you."

"I'm listening," Terian said. "I'm taking it all in. I'm here, ready to serve as your adjutant, if that's what you want." He didn't have to force his face to turn serious. "But if you think I'm going to do it without making light of amusing situations, then I'm not sure what you expected when you summoned me here."

Amenon wore a wary look. "I expected you to have matured, perhaps. To be ready to assume your duties as my heir."

Terian gave a moment's pause. "I'm as ready as ever I'm going to be for that."

Amenon studied him shrewdly—*looking for a smile or laugh to mark the joke, probably.* "I expect you to fulfill your unquestioned duty to the Sovereign and to the Noble House of Lepos. Do you think you can do that without exposing us to too much embarrassment and scorn from your … eccentricities?"

"I'll keep the drinking and whoring at levels acceptable for the nobility," Terian deadpanned. "It'll require me to step up my efforts in both of those areas to keep up with that old sot Mangrein or to bed as many whores as Lady Irinset does serving boys, but I'm willing to apply myself in order to properly represent our house." He snapped to formal attention, just as he had learned in the Legion of Darkness. "I shan't fail you in this endeavor, Father."

Amenon Lepos did not so much as narrow his eyes, but his hand rose faster than Terian could react. A vise grip found its way across Terian's neck in spite of Amenon being a good ten steps away from his son and having a desk separating them. Terian dropped to his knees immediately, prying at his throat, trying to rip off the gorget that was there to protect him from attacks to his neck.

Terian gagged as he felt the pain of his fall on both knees, the shock of the drop not nearly as heavy as the pressure on his throat. *Can't breathe …!* He tried to mouth the words for the countercurse to Lockjaw, but his sublingual casting skills were mediocre at best, and he knew it even as he tried and failed the first time. *It's not fatal*, he told himself. *Not fatal.* The crushing pressure around his windpipe was only in his mind, the logical part of him knew, and yet it felt as though a pearl as large as a troll belly had been forced down his gullet and he choked again, making the same gagging noise that he'd heard the night before in the Brutal Hole.

"Perhaps you labor under the illusion that your wit impresses me," Amenon said calmly. Terian had a dim vision of his father standing behind his desk, unmoved, not even watching the spectacle of his only son crawling on the floor, fighting for breath, trying to reverse the spell that had been cast upon him. *It will pass.* Terian tried to force the thought to calm him, but failed. *It will pass it will pass it will pass—*

"It does not," his father went on, still calm. "Skill in battle impresses me. Dutiful service impresses me." He looked back at last, now, and Terian met the cold, disinterested gaze of his father as his own surely screamed *Help me!* to the man who could spare him. "A good jest is fine for a working man of Sovar, whiling away his nights drinking the mulled brews that allow him to dull his senses. Not for a man of purpose. Not for a scion of one of the most noble and exalted houses of Saekaj." He flicked his wrist toward Terian and the pressure in Terian's throat released in one gasping outrush. Terian collapsed to his face on the stone floor. "Not for a Lepos. Not for you."

Terian saw boots appear in his vision, the clouds of red in his eyes finally starting to dissipate. "I summoned you here to take your place at my side." Terian looked up and saw his father looking down, examining him dispassionately, as though he were something accidentally scraped onto the floor by an ill-cleaned boot. "I expect you to perform your duty as part of my unit, to give me your all in battle, and to keep your indiscretions well and truly under our feet." Amenon did not deign to lean down. "If you find yourself compelled to drink and whore, do it the way the other nobles do—in Sovar, in quiet, deniable secrecy. Shame me, fail me, fail in your duties, and you won't need to look to the Sovereign for punishment." His expression remained level, as though he were talking about nothing more vexing than the weather. "For I keep my house in order in his name, and I shall not suffer weakness or foolishness within it that does not aid in our ascent."

9.

Terian scraped himself up off the study floor after lying there only another minute. There was nothing further to be said in his father's eyes, apparently; Amenon had seated himself in the chair and begun examining parchments.

Son of a bitch. Terian's glare went unnoticed. *I don't have to take this shit.* He wheeled and started to leave, but his father's voice held him at the door before he opened it.

"Terian," Amenon said. "See Guturan before you storm out. And be back tomorrow morning, early. We have an assignment from the Sovereign and shall be leaving after surface sunrise. Matters to attend to."

Terian ran a hand across his throat. The pain was fading but still noticeable, so he said nothing, merely forced the stone door open and slid out.

"I have this for you," Guturan said, waiting just outside. His hand was extended and a coin purse dangled from it, filled to the brim, a sight Terian's eyes hadn't beheld very often in the last few years. *Especially of late*, he realized with some chagrin. "You will of course have all the privileges of a noble heir, all the access, receive all the invitations to the balls and events while you remain with us."

"That last one is not exactly a selling point," Terian said hoarsely, his fingers massaging his throat.

"Nonetheless," Guturan said without expression, "you will be expected to conduct yourself in the manner of House Lepos's heir, including in the social arena."

Terian eyed the money pouch and knew instinctively that it was gold, all gold. No bronze or silver needed, not for a true nobleman's purse. He eyed it, gave it thought, considered passing, just brushing it aside and leaving. He wavered, stared at it, and Guturan moved it closer.

Terian thought about the boarding house again, of the communal kitchen, of his hour per day to prepare his meals. The memory of clutching his blanket tightly around him when he slept. Of the time that a street urchin hit him in the head with a snowball while he stood outside a warehouse. The thoughts ate at him and he tasted something sour on his tongue.

He took the extended coin purse.

"Your father told you to be back before surface dawn, yes?" Guturan called to him as he started down the stairs.

Terian thought about firing back a sharp look as he clacked down the wooden steps but he refrained. "I'll be back by then."

He didn't see his mother when he reached the foyer, so he simply stepped out of the front door as the doorman opened it for him. One of the servants ran up to him and started to ask him about his need for a carriage, but he waved the man off. *Walking will do me good. Besides, there is no shortage of carts and wagons willing to haul me back from Sovar, if I so need it. And very few of them haul corpses.*

He passed the gate guards and they saluted him. He ignored it as his heavy footfalls clattered along the main avenue. He looked to his right at the Sovereign's palace; at the enormous, smokeless fires that burned on the top of its guard towers, and he felt a seething anger at the mere sight of them. From there he turned his head to look at Shrawn's manor, and felt his fury grow stronger. *You bastard, Shrawn. How different would my life be if my father didn't constantly feel your dagger at his back?* His anger flashed, then settled. *Possibly not any different at all.*

He stormed off to his left, trying to control his steps lest they become a fitful stomp, petulant in his anger.

The walk to the square took only ten minutes, and it was bustling with all manner of servant activity. Terian felt the weariness in his legs from the morning's long ride, and the thought began to settle in about the walk to Sovar. *Why am I even going there?* It was an idle question, one he didn't really need an answer to. He already knew the answer, anyway.

Because it's where I always end up. Every time. It's the only place in this dank hellhole where I can be ... me.

By the time he'd come to the far end of the square, the novelty of walking had worn off. He was weary from the journey, and he ached from the Lockjaw curse his father had cast on him. A man with a small cart waited at the far end of the market, a wide bench pushed against the high back of the open cart. It was a vehicle with one purpose, and that was to convey passengers around the city.

He signaled the man as he approached and was met with a wide grin. The blue face of the cart man was made even more accentuated by the phosphorescence glowing above them like a milder version of an azure sky. It was not a blinding light by any means, but Terian could see well enough by it. The cart clacked through Sovar as the cart man hustled along, using his own legs to convey the vehicle and his passenger.

They were stopped momentarily at the gate as the guards made note of his name on a roll of parchment. He knew the same roll would be checked again, later, when the time came to readmit him. Terian was unworried about that, though; he knew more than one secret path into Saekaj if it came to it. Sometimes it had.

The traffic stopped in the lane of the tunnel immediately outside the gates, and he watched the cart driver make the turn across the traffic as they began a slow descent into the tunnel that led to Sovar. Within a hundred feet, the smooth brick gave way to rutted clay and the passage became rough and bumpy, and Terian felt the shock of the journey in his bones. A thin pad lay between his backside and the bench, and he was thankful for this concession to comfort.

The journey down to Sovar took almost a half hour as the foot traffic increased around the Granary, the enormous chamber between Saekaj and Sovar dedicated to the storage and sale of foodstuffs grown in the Depths, as well as to fish brought up from the Great Sea. The crowds were heavy around the tunnel that led there and continued to be heavy as they slowly made their way down into Sovar.

There was no gate at the entrance to the lower chamber, no guards to keep anyone out as the tunnel split off from the main road that led down further into the earth, toward the Depths and the Great Sea. The air became danker and dirtier down here. The air was choked with coal dust; that awful-smelling stuff mined from the Depths and often burned for fuel in Sovar. There was no chance of wood down here; what little made it underground became furniture, not fuel.

There was a thick layer of soot over everything, in spite of a dozen natural chimneys that allowed the worst of the coal smoke to gradually filter out and be replaced, in time, with cleaner air from outside the caverns. Terian had seen Sovar on those occasions, and there was no cooking of anything on those nights. Cold, yeasty, unbaked dough or rough, unsoftened roots with raw mushrooms were a welcome feast on those days. He suspected many of the occupants of Sovar simply didn't eat on those occasions.

The noise of the place was a low roar, countless voices talking over one another, barking commands, shouting transactions from the thousand stalls that lined every single step of the thoroughfare. Barkers promoted their goods in voices so loud it would put the cart merchants of Reikonos to shame. The things being sold were of little interest to him, however. There were other bars, better ones, in Saekaj. Ones that served real liquor, distilled whiskey, things made from the good grains and barley and oats that came from the surface. But there were limits in those places, and everyone was always listening, always watching. *Shrawn is always listening in those places.* As his father had said, nothing in Saekaj went ignored. Nothing within its proper circles could be ignored; it was too tightly knit.

Sovar, on the other hand, offered the veneer of anonymity. That was all it was, in practice, he knew, but it was enough. *Shrawn is probably still watching down here, but even his eyes might miss something, and even his ears are necessarily deaf to what goes on in Sovar.* Everyone in Saekaj might indeed know what a noble did in the pit that they called Sovar, but although it was whispered about, it would never be brought up in polite circles. *And that is its strength,* Terian reflected as the cart pulled through a street and barkers surrounded him on either side, trying desperately to catch the noble visitor's attention.

He ignored them all, though, and the wild colors that surrounded him. While the majority of the structures were simple mud dwellings carved into the rock, there was vek'tag hair cloth everywhere, some of it shaded by wild dyes of a sort that would have been unusual even in Reikonos. He had been gone so long he had nearly forgotten the strong pigment of the wildroots that grew in the Depths, the flowers of which were an inedible byproduct of the growing process. It was cheap, being a principal castoff of a vital part of the food production that allowed the entirety of Sovar to subsist. It gave Terian's eyes something to look at in any case, garish distractions from the dull and dark structures that had been built in nearly every available square foot of Sovar.

The smells were a distraction of their own. They ranged from the sooty, permeating odor of the coal that was burning in the communal ovens to the scent of thin stews that were fragrant with the mushrooms, wildroot, and vek'tag meat that seasoned them. *And season them is about all those things do, in the amounts the poor of Sovar have.* Terian blanched, recalling the time he'd traveled into the Back Deep of Sovar with his father to visit one of Amenon's childhood friends. It had been an awkward experience, one that brought the hot flush of shame to Terian's cheeks even now. He could recall asking when the real food would arrive after being served a thin stew with a piece of wildroot floating in it. A look from Amenon had been enough to quell any further comments. Only later had his father told him that as honored guests, they had received the wildroot as a reflection of their status. The rest of the family had gotten only the stew, with perhaps a few fragments of the root to gnaw on.

A bump in the road brought Terian's attention back to the increasingly crowded lane. They'd turned onto a narrow alley, barely wide enough for the cart, and Terian smiled. *At least some things don't change.* The cart stopped in front of steps carved down into the basement of a building that reached three stories in height. Terian stretched as he got out of the cart and handed the quiet driver a piece of gold, earning a grateful—and enthusiastic— thanks. He realized that the cart driver didn't make that much in a day of labor under normal conditions and immediately handed the man a second piece of gold from the full purse that he'd tied to his belt.

He walked down the steps and opened the door, pausing to look inside before he stepped in. The place was dim, a lone lamp burning over the bar. The man standing behind the bar—which was made of stone quarried in the Depths—was unfamiliar, as gaunt as most of the residents of Sovar, and he glared at the intruder for almost a second before he registered surprise and then bowed his head rapidly at the sight of his noble guest.

Terian didn't strut as he walked in, but he knew many a time in his youth he surely had upon entering this establishment. It was called the Unnamed, or at least so called by anyone who knew it. Most of the establishments in Sovar had names painted outside to draw attention, banners of vek'tag cloth with names dyed on them. Not the Unnamed. It remained hidden in a darkened alley, and catered to a very specific brand of clientele. In a sea of establishments fighting for attention, it went nearly unnoticed.

Nearly.

Terian's eyes roved around the room, picking out a few day laborers with their skin darkened by exposure to the light of the surface, a few layabouts with the tell-tale shiftiness of con men who would sing any song they could for another piece of silver, and even someone dressed like a noble, in the corner. He did a double take when he saw who it was, and a broad grin crept over his face as he made eye contact, altering his course to carry him to the corner table where the man waited with a smile of his own.

"Xemlinan Eres," Terian said, matching the man's smile. It felt good to smile. Unusual but good, like he hadn't done it in quite a long while.

"Terian Lepos, my own personal hero," Xemlinan said, with a deferential nod of the head. His smile never wavered.

"Me, your hero?" Terian said with a laugh. "You were always my hero. Living in Sovar but richer than most nobles. Buying this place," he indicated the Unnamed with a wave of his hand, "I mean really, who doesn't dream of owning a bar where they can drink for free?"

"It's not free," Xemlinan said, taking hold of a bottle that rested on the table next to him. There was already a glass across from him, as though he'd been waiting for someone to show up. "But this … is on the house."

Terian sat down, looking at the glass as Xemlinan poured it full of amber liquid. "You already had a glass out, and a bottle of Pharesian brandy on the table." He looked across at his friend, who poured with a steady hand. "You knew I was coming?"

"I got a message from your father," Xemlinan said, picking up his glass, "saying that you were on your way down from the surface. That he would be meeting with you and to expect you shortly thereafter."

Terian stared across at Xem, then down at the brandy, before picking up the glass. "It's like he knows me or something." There was an unintended mournful quality in the way he said it.

"That would be fair to say." Xem picked up the glass lightly in dexterous fingers, and slugged it back in one. The faint red of his fine wool coat, made from the small number of sheep that were grazed on the surface, was almost distracting in its lack of bright color. "I consider it also possible that he knew the message he would have to deliver would be unpleasant, and suspected your natural desire to retreat to more comfortable surroundings afterward."

Terian stared at him, glass still in hand. "That would be fair to say as well. He certainly delivered an unpleasant message." Terian's fingers went to his throat, massaging it almost unconsciously.

"Did he lay down the law upon you?" Xem asked with a faint smile that wasn't remotely genuine.

"Martial law," Terian said, finally drinking the brandy. It was good, burning all the way down to his belly. "'Keep your drinking, whoring, shameful tongue to yourself and do your duty.'" Terian felt his face go taut from the memory of the Lockjaw spell. "Or something of that sort." He took another long, burning drink.

Xem filled his own glass once more and topped Terian's off. "Your father is not a man for mincing words."

"Indeed not," Terian said, and removed his hand from his throat. "It didn't take many words at all to get his point across."

Xem raised a thin white eyebrow at him. "Did the point sink in?"

"Does it matter?"

"It does," Xem said, looking at him seriously as he put the bottle back down and picked up his glass, cradling it close to his fine wool coat. "I have joined your father's ... team, as it were—"

"His 'team'?" Terian said mockingly. "It's not an army unit?"

"The army is idle," Xem said, head cocked to the side in amusement. "We are not at war, so they maneuver, they drill, they do the things an army at peace would do. Tend to homeland issues, when asked. Your father's armies await, at his command at all times, but the balance of his time is spent on something more ... subtle."

"And here I thought I was going to be the adjutant to a regiment at peace," Terian said, raising his glass in a mock toast. "The old bastard fooled me again."

"If you had any desirable options left," Xem said with a slight wince, "you would not have let yourself be 'fooled.' My sources placed you in a ramshackle boarding house in Reikonos, spending what little gold you had in a tavern so foul that only the longshoremen drank there."

Terian shrugged. "What's wrong with longshoremen?"

"By and large, nothing," Xem said with a shrug. "I'm certain most of them are fine people. But in Reikonos? The human capital? It is hardly a high paying job, attracting the finest of candidates."

Terian rolled his eyes as he shook his head. "That's your problem, Xem. You think such work is beneath you."

Xemlinan gave that a moment to simmer, and then spoke quietly without any accusation. "And your problem seemed to be that you didn't think any type of work was beneath you."

Terian felt his cheeks blush. "Maybe nothing is. Someone has to guard warehouses against thievery."

Xem took a long drink of his brandy before delicately setting his glass back on the table so quietly it didn't make a sound. "Someone indeed has to. It's a vital job, as is being a longshoreman in Reikonos." He leaned forward and caught Terian's gaze with his own. "But someone who has the gifts of the dark knight, who has spent years of their life training to follow in the footsteps of the single greatest knight of the shadows to ever step out of the darkness of Sovar—"

"Don't call him that," Terian said, looking away.

"*Everyone* calls him that," Xem said. "Everyone knows him. He's a legend. Have you ever even heard of someone rising to the station he has? It doesn't happen. Ever. Nobility is nobility. The Sovereign does not raise a family up through mercantile activity or civil service. Our little corner of Arkaria is not Reikonos, where even one of our kind might have a house on the bluffs. The ladder in Sovar has no rungs, and there is only one direction one goes on it—down."

"It would seem at least one man figured out how to shimmy up the damned thing," Terian said with mild amusement.

"And you should pay careful attention to him," Xem said, finishing his drink.

"I find it hard to take him too seriously," Terian said, "for whatever reasons. My own, mainly."

"You were his truest disciple," Xem said with a hint of sadness, "before you left. Before—"

"My reasons," Terian said, firmly enough to close the topic of conversation. "My own."

There was a near-amiable quiet for the next few minutes as they drank in peace, Xem refilling the glasses wordlessly every time they got low. "Tell me about this ... team," Terian said finally.

Xem gave him a wan smile. "There are six of us. Seven, counting you."

"A real baker's half-dozen," Terian said without amusement.

"We're sent to deal with problems that the Sovereign needs taken care of," Xem said, tilting his head a little and straightening his coat. "Quietly."

"Assassinations," Terian said with a nod. "Not really my forte."

"We haven't done any assassinations yet," Xem said, watching Terian with jaded eyes, "but I'm certain if one was needed—"

"My father would assassinate anyone, anywhere, at any time in the Sovereign's name," Terian said.

"Perhaps not your mother," Xem said with a laugh.

Terian did not laugh. After a moment he allowed, "*Perhaps* not."

Xem grew serious. "We have traveled the world a bit. Dealt with things in faraway places. A bit of thievery," he bowed in his seat, a most elegant maneuver. "My specialty, of course. We've slain a rare monster or two, brought back trophies for the Sovereign." His face grew more serious. "Killed a few heretics. Weeded out some dissidents and undesirables here at home."

Terian gave a subtle laugh. "There's some irony in you killing undesirables, since it wasn't that terribly long ago that you might have been counted as one yourself."

Xem's dark blue lips became a thin line. "You well know I am entirely focused on my own survival. When the choice was presented to spend the rest of my life in the Depths or to turn about and give my full service to the Sovereign, it was easily made."

Terian looked around the Unnamed. "You even got to keep all your stuff. The Sovereign is not usually so forgiving of the sort of transgressions that would leave your survival in question."

Xem's face puckered slightly. "There were others much less fortunate than myself, I will say that much. Your father's assistance was vital. There was no one else whom the Sovereign would have listened to who would have interceded on my behalf. He sold the Sovereign on what an asset I could be, how much I could help him by being in his service." Xem looked down. "I have not seen your father so persuasive ever before."

Terian's hand went back to his neck. "He has a way of getting his point across, however he needs to do it."

Xem looked up. "I owe him much." He poured another round. "Therefore, drink as much as you like, and I shall have you taken home at the end of the night, or to a brothel whose owner I have an arrangement with. All this I do in service of what I owe him, which is more than I can possibly repay."

"I find myself strangely not in the mood for female company tonight," Terian said, letting his fingers drift from his neck back to his glass. "But I'll keep in mind in the future that you're the one to go to for all my baser needs."

"It is what your father has instructed me to do," Xem said. "To keep things quiet. To keep your indiscretions out of Shrawn's sight."

"It's touching how much he cares," Terian said then paused. "About not allowing his house's reputation to get sullied. Not about me, obviously."

"I do not think he would have sent for you if he did not earnestly desire to have you with him—"

"You don't know him all that well, then," Terian said, hot blood running through him. "This is all about appearances. He has no heir without me." He was just beginning to feel the drift of the alcohol in his veins even though he'd had three times more already than he'd have had on an ordinary night in Reikonos. "I'm his greatest failure, the fact that I so greatly deviated from the path and shamed him."

"He was so proud of you up until Ameli died," Xem said. "You were his most devoted follower. Then you leave? Without notice, without a word—"

"Oh, there were many words," Terian said dully. "Loud ones. Unforgivable ones. Ones he'll never call me to account for, thankfully. This is how I know it's all for the sake of appearances." Terian leaned closer to the table, almost conspiratorially. "Because if he truly cared about this gaping rift between us, he'd actually address the night that rift happened." He leaned back. "But he won't, because he doesn't care about my respect for him as a father, and he doesn't respect me as a son. He only wants to ensure that the House of Lepos survives his death without pitching back into the abyss of Sovar." He smiled at Xem's expression of near-disbelief. "I take it now that the Sovereign has returned, the Shuffle has resumed?" He waited for Xemlinan to nod once. "Then you know as well as I do that if my father died without a loyal heir on hand to take up the reins, within a year House Lepos would be housed toward the gates of Saekaj. Within five they would be back in Sovar, without a piece of bronze to bite on." He shook his head. "No, my father feels the clutching fingers of mortality, and he wants to make sure his name and his retinue continues past his death."

Xem said nothing at first. "Is he so low in your estimation that your mother does not even rate a mention in that concern?"

"I'm sure he cares for her somewhere in there," Terian agreed, "but I'm not sure it matters to him as much as knowing his name will live on after he dies."

"A grave assessment," Xem pronounced and took a hard drink.

"I'd forgotten how much more it takes to get drunk down here," Terian said, staring at the glass in his hand. "I barely feel it yet."

"You'll feel it more acutely as you rise back to Saekaj," Xem said grimly, "so go easily on it. We have an early morning tomorrow, after all."

"And what is this about?" Terian asked, studying Xem as he drank.

"I have no idea," Xem replied. "Your father will talk about our assignment on the morrow."

Terian nodded slowly, taking it all in. "That feels like a very long time off."

"It will be here before you know it."

"Perhaps," Terian said and took a large enough swig to finish what was in his glass, then gestured for more. "But I have expectations to live up to," he said with a twisted grin, "and I'm not nearly as drunk as I need to be in order to still be feeling it at his morning meeting."

Xem gave a slow nod of his own. "I suppose you expect me to join you in this bit of madness?"

Terian grinned. "Why, Xem … how can I think of you as my only friend in Saekaj Sovar if you won't get utterly, stinking drunk with me?"

10.

Dawn was irrelevant in Saekaj and Sovar. There was no sky to look to, just the steady, dull glow of the phosphors on the ceiling and high cave walls of the chambers. Still, even that faint blue glow, a pittance of light compared to what had shone down on Terian just yesterday, was almost too bright for his eyes this morning. The fire and lamps that lit his father's study were oppressive. *Take a man out of the light for a day, he forgets what a proper hangover feels like. It's all perspective, I suppose.*

There was a small gathering crowded in the room, and no one was speaking. Guturan had fetched Terian early, far earlier than he had wanted after drinking the night away with Xem. He'd been carted back to his father's house in a litter with dark shades. Frankly, he hadn't even remembered getting there, nor being settled in his own bed, though the force with which Guturan shook him awake suggested to him that the steward likely had something to do with getting him to his bed.

He stood near the hearth, in spite of the heat, so as to avoid looking up at the painting mounted above it. He kept his eyes fixed around the room. Two unlikely compatriots were seated at a small table in the corner opposite him, nearest the door and away from the desk. One of them was Grinnd Urnocht, the single largest dark elf whom Terian had ever laid eyes on. The man was enormous, not in terms of height but width: bulky as a troll, wide as a dwarf. He wore a perpetual smile, but not a stupid one. He was friendly and was even now whistling while studying the game board that lay between him and his companion. His black hair was short and carefully groomed, and he wore heavy mail across every part of his body. A large, visored helm sat precariously close to the edge of the table.

"I'd ask you to stop that infernal whistling," the slender man across from him said, "but I've known you long enough to know you'd never do it." Verret Horras's deeply contemplative look was hidden from Terian, although he'd known Verret long enough to know it was there. Deep thoughts were brewing; Verret kept his quiet, though, a long, white hank of hair was tied in a careful queue down his back. He wore gray clothing, a subtle shade that was dark enough to blend with the night itself. A cowl and mask lay around his neck like a scarf, ready to be pulled up when needed, and a long, curved sword was draped across his back.

"Sorry," Grinnd said with contrition, and the whistling stopped. He smiled, almost embarrassed, around the room at each of the other occupants of the office then turned his attention back to the board in front of him. After a moment, he began to whistle again, and Terian almost laughed when he saw Verret's teeth appear in a grimace. The slender man said nothing, though. *Those two haven't changed. Never have I seen a greater contrast than them—large, friendly Grinnd paired up with quiet, slim, angry Verret.*

Xemlinan leaned against Terian's father's desk, which was now clear of any parchment at all. Xem wore a suit again today, but this one was much less flashy, without any shiny buttons to catch attention. It was a duller shade of grey, and he wore a cloak around his body that suited what Terian suspected was his role in this team; the quiet, stealthy member, prone to be in charge of slyer occupations.

"You know, Grinnd," came the voice of a man who stood across from Xem, wearing white robes and a sash that marked him as a healer, "if I didn't know you better, I'd swear you were trying to provoke Verret into killing you."

"Hm?" Grinnd looked up from the board again, blinking his eyes in surprise. "I'm sorry," he said, his voice filled with genuine contrition. "Was I doing it again?"

"Always," Verret replied across from him, his thin face pinched. *He's mellowed since last I saw him.*

"Verret, you've changed," Terian said, breaking his own silence. "Before I left, you would have gotten fed up enough to draw a sword on him by now." Verret looked over at Terian, unexpressive. "Have you grown more patient in my absence?"

"More fond of Grinnd, I would think," the healer—his name was Dahveed Thalless—said with a smile of his own, "or didn't you hear about how Verret has spent the last couple of years?" Thalless had hair that was dyed a wild red color; it marked him as the lowest of the low class of Sovar, something Dahveed took exceptional pride in displaying—in spite of his high position in Saekaj.

Terian shrugged. "I've heard very little, being away as I was." He looked from Dahveed to Verret. "What? Did the two of you engage in that long-suggested deviancy while I was away?"

Verret raised an eyebrow. "I was sent to the Depths."

Terian felt his own brow rise in surprise. "You?" He looked to Grinnd, who was studying the game board with exaggerated interest. Terian lowered his voice. "But … it wasn't for deviancy, was it?"

There was a moment's quiet. "No," Verret replied calmly. "It was for denouncing Dagonath Shrawn and his puppets, the tribunal, for having not even a thin shade of the Sovereign's greatness yet using his name in their every proclamation."

"Oh." *Crossing Dagonath Shrawn was foolish indeed*, Terian thought but kept to himself. "Typically, that would land you in the Depths for life, would it not?" Verret gave a slight nod. "I presume they haven't changed the law while I was away, since Guturan cautioned me at holding my tongue and my opinions to myself while I'm here ..."

"No, they have not changed the law," Verret snapped, looking back at Terian impatiently. "But the Sovereign has returned, and your father brought my plight to his attention. He immediately set me free, rectifying the wrongs done by Shrawn and his overbearing vek'tag calves."

"Ah," Terian said and looked back at Thalless, who was still wearing an impertinent smile on his face. "So why would Verret be indebted to Grinnd?"

"I visited him in the Depths," Grinnd replied, finally making his move, sweeping the little piece of soapstone up in his massive palm and placing it on a space across the board. Verret ground his teeth at the sight of Grinnd's move, which caused the big man to grimace in contrition. "Went and saw him every couple of days in the mines, helped him tunnel and break rocks."

"Sounds like fun," Terian said with a hint of sarcasm.

"Hard labor keeps you in a good humor," Grinnd said with a nod and something that was probably intended as sage wisdom. He caught a scalding look from Verret. "Well, it keeps me in a good humor."

"Probably because you were allowed to leave whenever you wanted," Verret replied thinly. "Those of us who had to continue laboring into the night and who were forced to sleep in the rock piles, bereft of female companionship, did not find much good to keep humored about."

"Now, now," Dahveed Thalless said with a little smile from where he stood near Xem, "I imagine that without female companionship, the rocks were scarcely the hardest thing you had to deal with in the Depths."

Verret opened his mouth to make a reply but shut it as the door to the study opened and Amenon Lepos entered in full armor, another man trailing just behind him. The follower was unfamiliar to Terian, but he walked in his father's shadow, only a step or two behind, yet quietly. He wore no armor, but the sash around his shoulders marked him as a wielder of magics; upon further study Terian recognized the runes as those worn by druids, users of nature's magic.

The druid had a cloak of his own, as did the others—*ready for travel, I suppose*—and an exceedingly serene feel about him; he exuded an expressionless calm that put him at odds with the other druids Terian knew. *He's nothing like Niamh, that's certain.* Terian felt the twinge of sadness at the remembrance that he hadn't even had a chance to say farewell to the red-haired elf before he'd left Sanctuary, and he immediately tried to push her memory out of his mind.

"I believe we're all acquainted here," Terian's father announced as he walked behind his desk, "with the exception of Terian and Bowe," he nodded to the druid. "Bowe Sturrt, this is Terian Lepos, my son and heir. Terian, Bowe is our magical transport."

Terian gave Bowe a curt nod and received a calm inclination of the head in respect in return. Terian looked back to see both Grinnd and Verret on their feet at attention with the arrival of Terian's father. Dahveed was similarly off the wall, standing straighter. Only Xemlinan remained slack against Terian's father's desk, but he watched every move Amenon made with careful attention.

"We have a mission, sir?" Grinnd asked with some eagerness. Terian felt something entirely different at the thought of what might be coming.

"Indeed," Amenon said without preamble. "Information has fallen into our grasp that must be acted upon with utmost haste. We will be leaving immediately for Kortran, the city of the titans, upon completion of this meeting, and will likely not return for at least a day, possibly more."

There was a simple nod of assent and agreement from everyone in the room, though Amenon seemed to pay it no heed, gathering his thoughts and watching none of them. *Figures*, Terian thought, *he doesn't have to care about any of their opinions.*

"We have a fugitive from the Sovereign's justice," Amenon went on after a moment's pause, "a heretic who has been on the run for some time. We've been sold a piece of information that he has found refuge in the city of the titans, hiding under their very noses unnoticed, much like a rat would do in one of the hovels of the poor."

"Only one solution for a rat problem," Verret said with a cold edge to his voice.

"I quite agree," Amenon said, "as does the Sovereign. However, he wishes us to extract a piece of information from the prisoner, and so we shall, by any means necessary. If he parts with it immediately, we will leave his corpse to rot in Kortran. If he does not, he will return with us and enjoy our hospitality until he surrenders that which the Sovereign desires."

Terian watched the assemblage as they nodded idly along. *Torture. He means torture.* Terian blinked, and he tried to bury his growing unease deeper within. *We're going to torture this poor bastard until he tells us what we want to know.*

"Any questions?" Amenon asked, giving a quick look around the room. "Very well." He shot a nod to Bowe, and the druid began to cast a spell.

He's not even really allowing time for a question, nor for doubts, nor for us to do anything save agree with him and go along. There's no time to even grab anything, though I suppose Father expects we'll all come to his meetings prepared. Terian felt his grimace deepen. *Prepared for missions that involve capture and torture.* His hangover felt suddenly worse.

He said nothing, though, and the intensity of the druid's magic kicked up, filling the study with a teleportation whirlwind that carried them away, off in the gale of a magical tempest to a destination far, far from where they had been standing only a moment before.

11.

Terian squinted his eyes against the brightness of the Gradsden Savanna. In contrast to the snows of Reikonos that he had left only a day earlier, it was miserably hot. The scent of the heavy grasses swaying in the delicate breeze hardly compensated for the oppressive warmth and humidity. The horizon shimmered in the wafting heat, and in the near distance he could see the beginning of mountains. *And the gates of Kortran, I hope.*

"You look like a newling venturing outside Saekaj for the first time," Thalless said to Terian with a grin. His healer's robes looked cool and light in the oppressive midday sun, and Dahveed himself seemed to be taking the dramatic shift in temperature from the warrens of Sovar to the open savanna much better than Terian would have anticipated.

"It's the heat, the humidity and the flies," Terian pronounced, swatting at a fly larger than his thumb and knocking the fat thing out of the air. "Actually, I can swat or curse the flies. It's mainly the heat and the humidity." *Though should I run across one of the oversized animals that inhabits this land, I'll be cursing them as well—as I run away.*

"It does have a way of making a body long for home, doesn't it?" Thalless wore a wide grin, seemingly untroubled by the terrible weather conditions.

"For the first time in a long time, yes," Terian said. "I was here a few months ago and I'd swear it wasn't this bad back then." He struck another fly. "But then again, maybe I'm misremembering."

"The skywatchers say that the sun shifts," Grinnd spoke up from behind them. "I was reading a book about the movement of the stars through the seasons, and they speculated that it changes position as the winter comes to us, and the southern lands grow hotter for some reason." Terian shot Grinnd a quizzical look and was met by a shrug in return by the beast of a dark elf. "It's all very fascinating."

"Reading is an unseemly hobby for such a dull warrior as yourself, Grinnd," Verret said. "You should stick to breaking rocks and smashing skulls."

"A man needs hobbies to balance himself," Grinnd said, slightly affronted. "There is more to me than just my muscles, after all. A true warrior sharpens his mind and his sword, as both require use in battle."

"Is it just me," Terian mused, "or does 'sharpening your sword' sound like a euphemism for sex?"

"You'll have to forgive my son," Amenon said after a moment's pause in which no one said anything. "He seems to suffer from a near-terminal case of needing to speak every insignificant thought that springs to his mind, even when best they remain unshared."

Terian felt his cheeks burn with the dark navy of his embarrassment. "Or maybe unlike you I simply feel a need to talk about things I enjoy in my life. I suppose that would take feeling an emotion for you to understand."

Amenon sent a scalding look his way, and Terian actually felt himself quail before it. The others, if they thought anything of it, were wise enough not to comment.

The party continued on across the savanna in silence, and Terian fell to the back of the pack. A few minutes later, Dahveed joined him at the rear, his white robes swishing with the calm exertion of his steps. "I find it strange to see you here with us, Terian."

"Why is that, Dahveed?" Terian asked, listening to the gentle tapping of the blades of long grass brushing against his armor as he walked. "Because my father can't stand me, I can't stand him, and yet here we both are, together again in misery?"

"No, that's easily understood," Dahveed said with a shake of his head. He reached out his hand, letting the tall tops of the long grass, their seed pods extended, brush against it as he passed through them. "Your father had need of an heir, you had nowhere else to go, and money was offered. That's simple."

"I didn't *need* anywhere to go," Terian said, almost growling. "I'd found a life in Reikonos."

Dahveed's expression was purest amusement. "I heard about that. You cannot tell me that you, raised in the manner you were, would ever have been happy simply being an idle guardsman scraping by in that human city."

"There are more than just humans there," Terian said, avoiding the obvious point that he had no refutation for.

"There are," Dahveed agreed. "I have been there myself, you know. But that's a minor point to quibble with when the greater accusation I just leveled had more to do with you consigning yourself to doing less than you're capable of."

"I always do less than I'm capable of," Terian said with a grin. "It keeps expectations low and allows me to slide right on by doing what I want to do instead of more things that I'd have to do."

Dahveed nodded sagely, a strangely puckered grimace on his face. "So I've heard." He looked sidelong at Terian. "But I had thought you had changed in the wake of your admission to Sanctuary. I had heard rumors—rumors only, I suppose—that you had decided to stand up and become a person to be counted—not a low, slagging wretch drifting through his life like you were when you left. An officer of the guild, intent on fulfilling the great purpose set by the Guildmaster."

Terian felt his lips purse and the warm wind ran through the cracks in his armor as a trickle of sweat ran down his back. "How do you know about Sanctuary's purpose?"

Thalless laughed as though this were the greatest joke he'd heard, his robes swishing and bright red hair shifting in the hot wind. "I didn't know it was a secret."

"It's not," Terian said, shifting his attention to the mouth of the valley visible on the horizon. "It just isn't ... widely circulated." He felt his head dip, as though shame were forcing it down. "Guilds aren't renowned for having greater purposes. They're a step above a mercenary band; treasure hunters, beast killers, explorers—we adventurers are a fractious and self-interested lot."

"Indeed," Dahveed said. "I thought it most peculiar when first I'd heard the news. Terian Lepos, the wastrel, officer of a guild that professes to fight against the darkness?" A wide grin split the healer's face. "I thought perhaps I had heard it wrong." He raised his hands for effect, then clasped them back together again in front of him. "But, no, I heard it again and again, in whisper and rumor, circulating among those who would know. I pondered it for a piece, truly I did. And suddenly it did not seem so strange to me."

"Why is that?" Terian asked.

"Because the one thing you have lacked since the day you left was something you could truly believe in."

"I believed in what I was doing in when I was still in training at the Legion," Terian said, but it didn't even sound like his own voice.

Thalless laughed, loudly—too loudly for the wide, grassy savanna, and he drew a stern look from Amenen. "Your lying needs practice."

They walked on, and Thalless said no more. Terian did not press him, either, but not for lack of interest. *A part of me wants to know what he has to say; the other thinks it's all foolishness.* He felt a sourness build within him. *He hasn't known me in years.* The bitterness grew as he said the words in his soul. *No one does. Not anymore.*

If they ever did.

12.

They crept through the outer gates of Kortran under a spell of invisibility cast by Bowe. They made their way down a rocky path, one that Terian had trod only a few months earlier. He didn't know it well enough to know the curves, but they kept to the shadows cast by the boulders as they hid in the lee of the trail. They made their way in short bursts, Verret at the fore and scouting carefully the way down. He paced them by a hundred feet on the wide-open trail and signaled every few minutes when a patrol came in his sight. Always he hid before they saw him, and the rest were forced to cover. There was no shortage of boulders in the road—small stones to the titans, no doubt—and they hid truly and well from the few of the enormous beasts that they encountered on the way down.

Terian caught a look at a titan as it passed. Massive, it stretched into the sky the height of twenty men stood on end. The ground shook as it went by, sending vibrations up his ankles and knees. The shadow of the ledge above him helped keep him concealed, and Terian's face sweated inside the heavy metal of the helm covering the sides of his head. He kept his hand still, though, not quite ready to make a motion yet, even though the titans had yet to look back.

"We're like mice to them," Grinnd said quietly, prompting Xem to nod along with his statement.

"Xemlinan," Terian's father said in a low, commanding voice, "join Verret at the fore on scouting detail. We'll halt outside the city until the fall of night." He looked skyward. "That seems likely to be about six hours or more from now, and we'll need a quiet, out-of-the-way place to stay hidden until we can pass through the streets unseen."

"We could just use an invisibility spell and go now," Grinnd suggested.

Amenon did not glare at Grinnd, but the dismissal in his tone was hard as iron. "Those spells are notoriously unreliable. This mission calls for minimal risk of discovery." He looked at Terian with a knowing glance. "Should we be discovered, they will hunt for us high and low, and their guard shall increase in the days that follow."

Terian nodded along with his father. "It's true. It happened when last I was here, a few months ago. Someone penetrated their defenses, and they were on guard at the very least on the night after it. I wouldn't be surprised if their vigilance carried them through at least another month."

"We shall keep our presence to the shadows," Amenon said quietly. "No engagement with the titans unless it can't be avoided. As much as I'd enjoy matching my steel against these beasts in the name of the Sovereign, we shall keep our focus on our mission, on our orders, and leave the desire for battle to another occasion."

"Such as after we've killed the traitor?" Grinnd suggested.

Amenon let the faintest smile show. "Perhaps. Perhaps then. But only then, once we have finished our duty." The smile faded, as though swallowed whole into an abyss. "And in this matter, as with all others I undertake in the Sovereign's name—I will not fail."

13.

Time marched along surprisingly quickly. They found a cave further down the path, the discarded bones of small animals littering the ground. "Looks like someone of our stature has camped here at some point," Verret observed.

"You don't think it was a titan, do you?" Grinnd asked, looking around the darkened cave, surveying the castoffs, the garbage left behind by someone who had long since vacated the small cavern.

Terian snorted. "You saw them. You think they could fit in here?"

Grinnd gave him a wry look. "All it would take is a good grasping hand." He gave a glance to the mouth of the cave. "I expect they could fit a finger in for a good poke that'd end a man. Or woman."

Terian let a faint smile cross his features. "Most women I know enjoy a good poke." He cocked his head to the side. "Though not necessarily in the end."

"The women say differently," Xem murmured under his breath. "At least from you."

"Enough childishness," Amenon said with sufficient quiet menace to shut them all up instantly. "We'll sit here, quiet, until the hour of darkness." He met each of their gazes in turn. "Strictest silence. Let there be no chance that our voices give us away."

They did indeed sit in silence, occasionally rummaging through small pouches on their belts for preserved foodstuffs. Terian chewed on a hard lump of jerky that he had purchased long before he left Reikonos. The salt was heavy in the thing, overpowering any other spices that might have been used when the meat was dried. He gnawed on it, let the faint, smoked flavor cover his taste buds, and listened to the sound of water dripping somewhere behind him.

The rest of the party did not make much noise. Grinnd could be heard breathing, just barely, and he sat still, as if he had merged with the wall, his eyes open but staring straight ahead. Terian realized he had not moved in several hours, and would have been concerned but knew the warrior could be intensely quiet and still when he desired to be.

Bowe seemed to be in some sort of meditative trance, his hands held out to either side, palms open. Terian watched him as he sat there, his long hair tucked over his shoulder and his face serene. He gave no sign that there was anyone around them, or that he was anything other than content to be sitting in the dark, in a cave, his eyes closed but not sleeping.

Xem was perhaps the twitchiest of them, a knife drawn from his scabbard and clutched in his hands. It was ornate and well decorated, with a skull on the pommel grinning back at him. When Terian met Xem's eyes, he saw something that he hadn't seen from the gentleman of Sovar before, a kind of fear or pain that quickly vanished when he realized that Terian was looking at him. He fidgeted once more, tucked the knife back into his belt, and sat still for a time after that, making no noise.

Nightfall came on a few hours later, filling the cave with darkness like the slow rise of floodwaters. Terian kept as near to motionless as possible, but compared to his father, he failed horribly. Amenon was a statue of himself, not meditating, not fidgeting, simply sitting as still or more so than even Grinnd. The movement of his eyes in the dark, flicking from each member of his party to the next was the only sign he was even still alive, though Terian recognized the determined look in his father's eyes. It would be a bad time to raise his ire. Hours of introspection had not left him with an overabundance of desire for a verbal sparring match with his father in any event. *I just want to move, to swing my sword, to throw a Lockjaw curse at something that will feel it.*

"Come," Amenon said after the cave had become totally enshrouded with the rise of night. He stood, slowly and quietly, his armor making only the slightest noise as he did so. There was a faint glow of torches somewhere outside, fires burning so that the titans could see in the dark, their eyes as pathetic at seeing through the blackness as a human's. *We are the rulers of the night*, Terian thought, *just as Yartraak always intended it. It is our birthright, the dark, and we knights who tread in the shadows are the ones to walk in both worlds.*

They walked out of the cave, the rough stone path echoing with the clatter of metal from the ones who wore plate boots. It was quiet enough outside that Verret motioned them forward, no sign of any sentries to block their passage. A ring road circled the bowl of the valley, and as they crossed it Terian took only cursory notice of the surface being made of solid wood. They descended into the city, which was laid out in a pattern before them, down in the bottom of the valley, stone buildings from one side of the natural bowl in the land to the other.

They reached street level, leaving the ramp behind as they ran for cover in the shadow of the nearest house. They stuck to the dark spots on the street, veering carefully away from the illuminated zones where torches cast their light. The whole of the town had a powerful stink, stronger than any other town he'd been in. He wondered at it for a moment, then dodged when a window above him opened on the massive house that they were walking along the front of. Something was thrown out the window and splashed onto the wooden street magnifying the foul stench. It took Terian only a moment to realize it was a chamber pot that had been emptied.

"Holy Sovereign," Xem said, nearly gagging. "No wonder the place smells so powerfully bad."

"Aye," Grinnd said with a wary look, barely visible in the shadow in which they were hiding, "their turds are as big as you." He smiled broadly and looked over at Verret, chucking a thumb at the scout. "And they look like him."

"Silence," Amenon said, only once, and a pall fell over the group, as though someone had stolen their voices. Terian looked around at each of them, all serious now. *If this were Sanctuary, Vaste would still be cracking wise, filling the air with his japes.* He felt a hardening in his heart and his resolve. *Just as well, then; base foolishness has no place in a mission such as this.*

They followed Verret's lead. The scout seemed to have a map either in his mind or close about his person, because he never once came back to them for directions and never seemed to doubt his course. Terian wondered if he'd simply missed seeing his father give Verret a map to lead them to their destination or if the man was operating from some instinct that he was unaware of. *No ... Father would never allow him to simply drag us along without purpose.* He watched as Verret took them down an alley as black as any day in Sovar, following the lead. *No, he's been told where to go.*

They slid up to a house that was a towering thing, a multi-story creation that had some ornate finishings around the edges of the stone building. They crept to the door. Even before they attempted to open it, Terian wondered if it was barred. *That would make this a short trip.*

Verret halted them next to it. The nearest lamp was down the street a long ways, but a lantern glowed in the window, casting a pale light for them. Verret held up a hand calling for silence, then motioned for them to each take up position by the door and gestured for Grinnd to open it. They all lined up, Amenon first behind Grinnd at the edge of the frame. The big warrior reached under the crack between the ground and the door and hooked his arms underneath it. He started to pull, keeping his exertion quiet, even as the strain began to show on his face. It grew a deeper blue, navy, as though he were holding his breath while pulling with all the force in his muscles. Terian saw a crack appear in between the frame and the door, and it grew wide enough for Verret to squeeze in, which he did, then his hand popped back out and motioned for them to follow. Amenon went first, with Xem only seconds behind him. Dahveed and Terian followed, while Bowe brought up the rear as Grinnd shut the door very slowly behind them.

They found themselves in a wide, open room with a hearth roaring with faint flames that still stood taller than Terian's head. He stared at the massive logs within the fireplace and wondered from whence they had come, remembering tales of massive forests south of Kortran in the mountains that spanned the expanse between the titan city and the Ashen Wastelands of the dragons to the south. There were no signs of giants in the room, nor of any living things at all, just a mighty staircase in the corner with steps taller than a man.

"How did you find this place, Verret?" Terian asked, approaching the grey-clad scout as the man drew his sword. Terian heard the others unsheathe their blades. His eyes fell on Grinnd, who carried two fat swords with blades as wide as his thigh, but shorter than the average bastard sword.

Verret's long, thin, curved blade matched its master in two of the dimensions. If he leaned over, he'd just about look like it. "I studied the map of Kortran that your father gave me and noted the location that was given to us." He tapped his head. "It's all in here, now, along with an exit route, should we need it." His eyes flicked to Bowe. "Though I suspect we'll just teleport once we're done."

"I didn't see you look at a map," Terian said, more for conversation than anything.

"I only need to look once," Verret replied, his long, white length of hair swaying behind him as he took the lead again, keeping close to the wall at their left. He looked ready to make a circle around the perimeter of the room, which was shadowed, the dying fire the only source of light. Terian was the first to follow him this time, and they clung close to a rock wall. There appeared a buckle in the wood under the stairs, and Terian realized after a moment that it was a hole, only barely concealed. He started to point to it but Verret nodded once, sharply, to stop him.

It was going to be a tight squeeze, Terian realized, looking it over. Verret halted a good thirty feet away, behind a well-placed bucket that was large enough for all of them to hide in plus a few others. *That's a blind hole that we're going to have to charge into.* Terian's eyes tried to pierce the darkness within. He looked back and saw his father doing the same, peering at it. Verret waited until Amenon gave a gesture to move up, and they all slowed their pace to the quietest speed possible, tiptoeing along. Loud snores echoed through the house from upstairs; Terian was certain that if a titan was moving around up there, it would be obvious. *So we're being quiet for the sake of this heretic. This mysterious heretic.* He tried to remember the face from the sketch on the poster his father had brought.

They reached the stairs and filtered into two lines, each taking a side of the hole. Because it was so near to the wall, only Verret and Dahveed went to the left, placing their backs to the wood and pushing themselves into the corner where the stairs met the wall. Verret stood closest to the hole, staring across at Terian, who was just behind Grinnd and Amenon in the line on their side. Amenon was still, resolute, and Terian could tell he was listening. There was no sound to be heard, though, all noise drowned out by the terrible snoring from above.

Terian stood with his back against the wall, the hard wood and his weight pushing his armor against him even through the light padding he wore to cushion it. He could feel the spikes on his pauldrons dig into the grain of the wood as he pressed against it, leaving indentations. The smell that permeated all of Kortran was present here as well, the stink of the titans, and the smell of footprints that had trod in those filthy streets. It was so thick he could nearly taste it over the salty remnants of the jerky he had eaten hours ago. He saw his father make the hand sign to move and he did, careful not to butt up against Amenon in front of him but to follow a respectable distance behind. Thalless shoved a hand past Terian and cast Nessalima's light, forcing Terian to look away just briefly before turning back to see Grinnd and his father already down on their knees, grappling with a rustling figure wrapped tight in a bedroll.

"Well, that was anticlimactic," Terian said, pausing just behind the two of them. They surged to their feet, the struggling figure firmly grasped between them as Amenon reached back and hauled off, punching the man wrapped in the bedroll squarely in the face. He slumped, unconscious, and Grinnd delicately wrapped his arms around the man and hoisted him on his shoulders.

"So that's Sert Engoch," Verret said, not sheathing his sword but keeping his voice to a whisper.

"I'm not certain," Amenon said, coldly dispassionate. "Let's have a look at him, Grinnd."

The big warrior brought the limp body down and Dahveed brought his hand closer, the soft glow of the Nessalima's light spell illuminating the face of the possible heretic. The dark elven features were impossible to deny, and they looked plump, every bit the same as the ones on the poster, and possibly even a little fatter.

"Remind me to hide out among the titans if ever I feel compelled to run away as a heretic," Dahveed said with wry humor, "as this fellow doesn't seem to have suffered much in his life as a fugitive."

"Their scraps are enough to fill a table for us," Xem said with quiet awe. "What do you suppose they eat?"

"Their own dead," Grinnd said, causing every head to swivel to him. The imperturbable warrior shrugged, keeping the body of Enoch, the heretic, perfectly balanced as he did so. "A variety of the large animals that live here in the southern lands. Dragons, when possible. Elves occasionally, or whatever of our smaller northern kind comes this way, but that's more of a lesson; we're far too insubstantial to make a meal for them." He wore an expression that told Terian instantly that he was not lying, that he'd read it somewhere reliable.

There was a sort of deep quiet, and Bowe turned to Amenon. "Shall we leave, my lord?"

"We have our duty to tend to," Amenon said stiffly. He waved a hand around the room, at the little piles of things, a few small tomes. "Take everything. The Sovereign will want to know what he knows." He waved a hand at the inert body lying over Grinnd's shoulder. "We need to return our prize to Saekaj." He gave a nod to Bowe, who began to cast a teleportation spell. "So that we can begin the arduous—and painful—last moments of Sert Engoch's life."

14.

They were in a little room in the basement of Terian's father's house, in the farthest reaches. It was square and big enough to hold the entire team, plus their prisoner, who was strapped to a table, still unconscious, with a little room to spare. The smell of fear was heavy in the air, and to Terian's mind it wasn't that far different from the scent in the streets of Kortran. *A dungeon. He's had his own dungeon built.*

As if he was reading Terian's mind, Xem, who stood next to him, shrugged. "When you've got to torture as part of your job and you don't want to have to travel to the palace or gaol to do it …" The slow, audible breathing of the prisoner was the only discernible noise of note, and it overcame all the quiet, ambient sounds that the team was making.

"I remember this whole room being a coal bin when I was a child," Terian said, looking around the dim, dank room, lit by a single candle.

"Your mother has fresh firewood brought down from the surface every day now," Amenon said, stepping into the room while letting the door squeak shut behind him. "It's better for her constitution than that black dust and the thick, heavy smoke."

"Also, it freed up all this space for your very own torture room," Terian said with a ring of sarcasm. "Because no manor in Saekaj is really complete without a place to wring the screams out of your enemies."

"Indeed," Amenon said with a total lack of irony, "it seems that the men who built it do quite the booming business. Though I hear most who have one use it to keep the servants in line, set an example for them." He clinked his hand against the chains that secured the heretic to the table. "I had to make sure I got chains adaptable enough to fit any guest we might have, from trolls all the way down to gnomes." He smiled, and it was horrifying to Terian's eyes. "They were very accommodating."

He's being ghoulish just to unsettle me, Terian realized. *He's taking my taunt and throwing it back in my face.* "Do you enjoy torture because it's part of your duty to the Sovereign, or would you do it gladly even outside of your work?"

Amenon's face grew impassive, and his hand clinked against the metal table more quickly now. Any amusement that had been present a moment earlier was gone. "We have a task at hand." He looked over the entire crew, huddled around the walls. "Less is more, I think. All of you save for Terian may go. I have every confidence that your efforts today will please the Sovereign, when I make my report to him." He nodded once and they began to file out.

"Lucky me, I get to stick around for the blood and beatings portion of the show," Terian muttered under his breath. Xem gave him a sympathetic look as he exited. "Save me a drink," he said as Xemlinan walked out.

"You'll be conducting this interrogation," Amenon said without preamble as Grinnd, the last to leave, shut the door behind him with a clank. There was a small stand just to the side of the table, covered over with a small white cloth. Terian's father pulled the cloth off delicately, revealing all manner of instruments beneath. There were short ones and long ones, but the commonality was that they all had points on them, in spite of the hooks and claws that some seemed to sport.

Terian raised an eyebrow. "I don't think I'll need those."

Amenon let just the faintest hint of a smile show. "Good. I worried that perhaps your long absence would cause you to forget what a dark knight can do to bring pain and terror."

Terian let his face twist naturally with the hard emotion that bubbled up from within him at his father's words. "I trust if ever I forgot, you'd remind me in the most painful way possible. You know, like you did yesterday." He took a step toward the inert body of Sert Engoch, heretic. "Time for a rude awakening." He pulled his gauntlet off and brought his fist down on the man's cheek, hard, rocking his head back and causing his eyes to snap open.

"Oh, good, you're up," Terian said, burying the tentative feelings that were worming around inside deep within. *I will not fail this most basic of tests now that it's been laid in front of me.* "I thought maybe I'd have to start gutting you while you were still sleeping."

The heretic's expression showed only a moment's worth of fear before it became straitlaced. "I have long expected this moment to come. Gutting me would be a sweet end to what I'm certain will be a long and tedious process that I have prepared for." He gave a nod as he looked around the room. "Very well then, go on with it."

Terian took his helm off by grasping one of the points. He set it gently on the ground and shook his long hair to let it breathe. He could feel the sweat causing the strands to stick together and ran his gauntleted fingers through to loosen it up where it was matted.

"I don't think you understand," Terian said, looking to his father, not the prisoner. "I'm not here to torture you to death because you're a heretic." He leaned an armored elbow rather uncharitably into the soft space below Engoch's sternum. "The Sovereign wants information that you possess," Terian said, and pressed down, causing Sert to grunt with pain as the small, jutting spike on Terian's elbow joint penetrated the skin, "and you're going to share it with me."

Engoch's face was at peace, his expression staid. "No, I shall not."

"Yes, you will," Terian said with a calm assurance and just a tinge of sadness. "The only question before us is how much blood you'll lose, how many bones will be broken, and ultimately how much suffering you'll experience before we're done." He leaned over to look Sert in the eyes, and the heretic's pupils were dilated and fixed, trying to remain centered. *There's fear in him yet. He'd have to be afraid to hide in that hole in Kortran.* "You must know we have healers. I can cleave you limb from limb and then restore you, drain you nearly dry of blood and then replenish it, kill you and bring you back to life time and again." He adjusted his elbow so that it no longer drove into Engoch's sternum. "You will, eventually, tell me what I want to know. The only question is how much you'll suffer before you do it."

Engoch watched him for a moment, his eyes no longer fixed and staring straight ahead, but instead looking at Terian's for brief glances, then darting back to where they began.

"You know I'll do it, don't you?" Terian said, leaning over him, almost conversational. "You're a heretic, so you've studied magic? Some of the process of it?" Engoch gave only the faintest of nods. "Then you know about dark knights. Who we are. What we do. What defines us." Terian did not wait for an answer. "Let me tell you something about me, make my introduction." He eased off Engoch and took a few steps away, beginning a slow, loping walk around the torture chamber. His father stood by the door, watching him with narrowed eyes, assessing him. "My name is Terian of House Lepos, and I'm a failure of the worst sort." He didn't look at Engoch as he circled the man. "I left my house to the shame of my father just after I became a dark knight—after the ritual, you know," he glanced and saw Engoch watching him, but the heretic turned his gaze away upon seeing Terian look back at him, "and I joined a guild out in the wide world outside Saekaj. I failed at that, too, though. I'm a disgrace as a son, and every woman I've ever cared about has run screaming away from me."

He hooked a slow arc around the table and ended up by Engoch's face again. "I have failed at nearly everything up to this point. Guildmate, lover, son. The only thing I've never failed at—the only I've ever been good at—is being a dark knight. Fighting using the spells darkness has bestowed on me, the weapons that make me a knight of the shadows." He dangled a hand over Engoch's face. "And now I have a second chance. To not fail as a son. As a subject of the Sovereign. And all it will take is me using my skill as a dark knight." He twirled his finger around the face of Engoch in a slow circle, bringing it lower and lower. "What do you think, Sert?" He felt the hoarseness creep into his tone. "Is there enough at stake for me?" His voice got coarser, and lower, and he took a long breath as he leaned over the heretic. "Do you think I'll fail this time?"

He touched his gauntleted finger to the pale, damp blue flesh of Engoch's chest and the heretic screamed, a short, sharp shriek that was followed by breath after excited breath, drawing frightened panic out of the dark elf. "I will tell you ..." Engoch croaked, "...

everything I know." His breath came in hurried gasps, one after another.

Terian didn't smile, and there was no satisfaction as he touched his cold finger to the inside of his gauntlet, left it dangling, pressed against Engoch's chest. He said nothing, felt nothing, and simply stayed there, still as a statue, as the heretic began to speak a long, breathless tale that flowed right over Terian's shoulder and into ears behind him. He stood there all the while, though, unmoving, finger still poised to deliver his first torture.

Engoch, meanwhile, only cried the same word, over and over again, as he reached the end of his tale.

Aurastra.

15.

"That was excellent work," Amenon said as they reached the door to his office and his father shouldered it open. "A bit more talkative and less action-focused than I would have employed, but undeniably effective."

Terian walked without any spring in his walk; his father seemed to have boundless energy. "Yes. Now that you've gotten what you want from him, I suppose he can die. Or go to the Depths, or whatever."

"Indeed," Amenon said, easing behind his desk where a stack of parchment awaited him. He ran a finger over the topmost piece of paper before picking it up and crumbling it before tossing it into the hearth. "His final fate remains in the hands of the Sovereign."

Terian hesitated as his father went to the next piece of parchment in the stack. "What Engoch was talking about, these books that he was declared a heretic for reading …"

"Hm?" Amenon looked up after balling up another parchment and tossing it into the hearth where it began to crackle and smoke. "Oh, yes. Trifling details. We recovered the volumes from his rat's nest, and he's confessed to what they've told him, so barring any sort of disposition from the Sovereign to the contrary, I believe this concludes our business with him."

"I didn't know that the Sovereign cared enough about heretics to send his elites after them," Terian said, trying to word his statement as carefully as he could. *Best not to raise his ire if I want an answer.*

"He generally does not," Amenon said without looking up. "But this one was one of the Sovereign's own librarians, who escaped in his absence. I suspect it was a personal grievance in addition to being, most probably, an area of wounded pride for the Sovereign." He paused. "I sometimes forget—you have not stood before him in the past, have you?"

"No," Terian said, standing his ground near the edge of the desk. "He was gone long before I was born." *Which you should know, being my father.* He left that unspoken. "If he took affront to this Engoch stealing his books—"

"And knowledge," Amenon said, tossing another piece of paper into the fire. The stack of correspondence that had accumulated while he was gone was now down to half the size it had been only moments earlier. "The Sovereign has plans, strategies. Whatever business he had with this Sert Engoch goes beyond simple heresy. You should know that by what he told us after you tortured him."

Terian flinched. "I didn't even hurt him."

Amenon looked up, watching him carefully. "But you would have, and he knew it."

Terian kept his gaze locked on his father's. "I would have."

"I will speak to the Sovereign about this Aurastra," Amenon said, glancing back to the desk and its contents. "Though I confess I am not familiar with it."

"It's a dwarven village," Terian said. "Close to the northern reaches of the Dwarven Alliance, far up in the mountains. Mining town, about three weeks beyond Fertiss."

Amenon narrowed his gaze at Terian. "Indeed. Then it would appear that there is something of interest in this … Aurastra, something that the Sovereign will want to get his hands on."

"I'd be interested to know what it is," Terian said as Amenon crumpled the last of the parchment and tossed it into the fire.

"No, you wouldn't," Amenon said, rising from the desk and walking toward his son. He laid a hand awkwardly on Terian's shoulder. "We don't wish to know the secrets of the Sovereign unless he desires us to assist with them. Then, and only then, do we take information. Even then we take as little as possible." He drew Terian a little closer, the better to look him in the eyes, unflinching. "We serve the Sovereign, but believe me, you do not want any more of his secrets in your mind than the bare minimum necessary to do his bidding." Amenon's grip on Terian's shoulder loosened, and Terian felt it grow slack as his father clinked a gauntlet against the small, un-spiked area on Terian's pauldron. "They would weigh you down."

Terian looked up and met his father's gaze. "What would you have me do now?"

"Nothing," Amenon said, and his reserve was slightly lessened. "You have done adequately well this day, and so the night is yours. I would advise sleep, but I doubt you shall heed that advice, so I shall only say that I desire for you to return by the break of day, in case I have need for you."

"Very well," Terian said stiffly, and his father clinked his hand against the pauldron once more before leaving, without another word.

16.

Terian found himself lying on the bed, listless, staring up at the ceiling of his room. It was beige, a plaster construct built over timbers brought in from the forest above. All the facades of the houses of Saekaj were built like this, not made of the cheap and plentiful dirt and kiln-fired mud and clay of Sovar homes. Saekaj homes were the showpiece of opulence, of surface materials, just as the diets of their residents were. The lessers ate the food of below. Terian could barely remember the taste of fish from the Great Sea, so long had it been since he'd had any of the Sovarian delicacy. It was considered a poor meal in Saekaj.

There were noises of House Lepos all around him; the creak of floors as servants crossed them going about their work. It was a distinctive noise, far different from the sounds his father made when he was about. His armor was heavy, and the thunk of metal boots on the wood was audible even through the plaster.

Terian's room was not small; it befit an heir of Saekaj, the furniture finely crafted by artisans who were masters of woodworking and metallurgy. Knobs of burnished bronze, one of the rarer metals found in the Depths, were knitted into the front of his dressers and the nightstand. He ran a bare hand against the crafted wood headboard of his bed; it had not changed since he was a child. House Lepos had known prosperity all the days he had been alive, but the difference was between the affluence of his youth and the accumulated wealth that had come to them now. *Father has saved his monies all these years, in spite of Mother's puffery, her best efforts at making us look wealthy by spending copiously. Now our fortunes have grown along with our incomes.* He spared a thought and a bit of disturbance at the realization that he had included himself in that assessment by saying "our." *But truly, it is ours, if I am heir.*

There was a sound in the foyer below, the clunk of the door being opened, and then a squeak of a door hinge unmitigated by oil, unnatural and piercing. He listened for more, and the familiar clatter of metal boots on wood floors came to him and he sat up, bringing to mind the times when he was a child and had awakened to find his father arriving home at an unanticipated hour. He quickly put his armor on, knowing that if he showed up unprepared that he would be dressed down for his lack of preparation and formality, and stepped out onto the second floor balcony.

He could hear the hushed voices below and looked down. His father was there, speaking quietly into the ear of his mother, his dark blue face buried beneath her pale white hair, whispering in her ear. Terian could not hear her and wondered at what his father might be saying. It could be the idle pleasantries a man and woman long married might express, or news of a political nature. *It could even be that he simply does not wish to wake the entire household, though that seems unlikely.*

His father looked up at the squeak of a floorboard under Terian's weight, and there was a subtle hint of a smile that rounded the corners of his mouth. "Ah, good," Amenon said, and walked straight past his wife as though he had finished. "I had thought that you would be out this evening."

"No," Terian said carefully, a little guarded. "I didn't ... feel up to it," he lied, just a little.

"Walk with me," Amenon said as he ascended the stairs, and Terian moved aside for him to pass. He followed his father up the stone stairs to the top of the house to the study, where another small mountain of parchment waited on the desk. Amenon gave a look of disgust. "The vultures circle day and night, as though none of them can make a decision to dip or dive without the Sovereign's approval to keep them safe, as if that were any sure guarantee of absolution for whatever failures they might make." He picked up the first. "Slave reports, as though I give a damn." He crumpled it and threw it into the fireplace and pulled the next piece of parchment off the stack. "The disappearance of fishing trawlers in the Great Sea." He pulled two now after tossing the last, putting one in each hand and holding them up like pictures to be shown to Terian. "Army logistics reports, the whispers of the Sovereign's spies about Pretnam Urides's curious preference for much older women, and the six-month sales of wildroot dyes in Sovar."

Terian cleared his throat, hesitant to speak. "I ... assumed that Dagonath Shrawn would handle the non-military reports for things like commerce."

Amenon did not look up as he tossed the parchment into the fire. It crackled and made a hissing, popping noise as the air filled with the smell of smoke. "He does. Shrawn is tasked with all the civilian oversight of Saekaj and Sovar."

"Yet you still get reports on things like wildroot dye sales and fishing trawler disappearances?" Terian asked. *Why would he burden himself with such inconsequential matters?*

Amenon paused then looked up, a slow smile spreading across his face. "I do. I even read them occasionally, though I tend to focus on more important civilian oversight matters than some trifling reports about dye consumption." He leaned over the desk toward Terian. "Can you imagine why?"

Terian only pondered it for a moment. "If you're going to take Shrawn's place at some point, you'll have to take over his duties."

"Correct," Amenon said and brandished three pieces of parchment. "The Sovereign has made certain that I receive everything—or almost everything—Shrawn does, in case Dagonath were to meet an unfortunate end." He smiled and threw these as well. "Not that he will—at least not at our hand—but it pays to be prepared in case the House of Shrawn makes an unfortunate misstep. The Shuffle goes on, after all."

"Indeed," Terian said quietly. *Moving to the manor house across the way?* He shook his head without saying any more. *It feels almost ridiculous, like a folly to even give voice to the thought. Winning the Shuffle, though …*

"Don't dwell too deeply on those thoughts," Amenon said, not looking up from the parchment stack. "Dagonath Shrawn has inhabited his manor house for nearly five hundred years, and I daresay it will take some great event to displace him from it. Still, the House of Lepos will continue to serve in the exceptional manner the Sovereign has come to expect of us." Finally, Terian's father came to a piece of parchment that he held differently, not pinched between his fingers but cradled in his hands. "Enemy troop movements. Spy reports about enemy strengths and dispositions. These are the things that matter, that I can deal with, that I enjoy." He placed the parchment back on his desk with utmost care and shoved the remainder off his desk onto the floor. "The rest are a waste of my time; I spend hours combing them for only the occasional tidbit of useful information." His eyes gleamed. "So I have a duty for you—a duty that the Sovereign compels you to undertake."

I very much doubt that. But Terian bowed his head slightly, deferentially. "You wish me to comb through these reports for you and keep an eye out for anything of consequence?"

"I do," Amenon said, nodding. "I shall train you to look for the things in the reports that are seconded to me. Things that will catch the eye of the Sovereign. After that, you will take the job of reading through this ..." his hand waved to encompass the paper now strewn over the floor next to his desk, "... this ceaseless drivel, looking for the kernels."

"How will I know what are kernels and what is ... drivel?" Terian circled the last word for a moment before landing on it, finding none better and knowing his father would approve of having his own words parroted back to him.

"I will teach you in the coming days," Amenon said. He sat heavily in his chair, which squeaked under the weight of the man and his armor. "Also ... I come bearing news from the Sovereign himself."

"Oh?" Terian tried to express some enthusiasm but found he couldn't muster it.

"He is well pleased with our capture of Sert Engoch and with the information drawn from him. He orders the interloper's death and told me to make special mention to you of his pleasure in the fact that you were able to get Engoch to talk so willingly and quickly." Amenon folded his mailed fingers one over another. "He had anticipated it taking a day or more to break Engoch."

Terian almost felt the need to laugh, but the thought of Engoch in chains drained that desire out of him. "I can only assume that living in a hole in the wall in Kortran was exceedingly bad for the man's nerves. Else he wanted us to know what he knew. There is no other real explanation for the ease with which he broke and told us everything."

Amenon nodded slowly, reflective. "I cannot deny my shock in seeing it happen so quickly as well. You were compelling, to be sure, but my assumption is that there were other factors at play, as though he wanted it to be known so that he could get it over with as quickly as possible." He turned sideways in his chair, wheeling it around with a hard squeak and looking sidelong out the window behind the desk. "That could be the sort of thing to compel a man to hasty speech, the idea of months spent dwelling on a possible fate while giants stomped on the boards above your head and you ate whatever crumbs from their table you could snatch." He turned his gaze back to the fire. "Whatever the case, he spoke the truth that the Sovereign wanted to hear, needed to hear, and he is pleased with our work." Amenon looked back at Terian, roughly satisfied. "With *your* work. He is also pleased that House Lepos has an heir once more."

Terian nodded once and looked away. "Yes, well, it is … good to be … home." There was a grain of truth in there, somewhere.

"Our little operations group grows," Amenon said, looking back at the fire. His mailed fingers tapped on the desk. "The Sovereign has decided to try something different." Amenon looked up. "Do you recall Sareea Scyros?"

Terian felt an unpleasant pucker to his lips. "I do. She was of an age with Ameli." His eyes fell down to the desk. "There was that time—"

"Yes," Amenon said without emotion. "She was the first woman to go through training at the Legion of Darkness here in Saekaj."

Terian blinked thrice. "I ... I had no idea she had ... the Sovereign let a woman enter training to become a dark knight?" He took a sharp breath. "I didn't think the Sovereign allowed women into the military."

"He hasn't," Amenon said, waving him off. "He made an exception because I asked it of him, and because she asked it of me. She was tested, told she had the disposition to be a holy knight, and found herself quickly put aside, relegated to low-status work of some kind or another—secretary, scullery maid, concubine. Her family is not terribly well off, by Saekaj standards, having their house by the gate. I intervened because she asked, because of—"

"Of course," Terian said, cutting his father off.

Amenon raised an eyebrow at him, but continued, seeming to take no offense at the interruption. "She did exceptionally well. As well as you, in fact."

Terian felt the rough desire of his muscles to propel him into a run, to lift heavy objects, to bleed physical energy out in some manner. Instead he remained standing in his father's study, at near attention. "Good for her. Long have I seen female holy knights of other races do very fine work, surpassing in many cases their male counterparts. I quite like the thought of the Sovereign changing his backward views on this—" Terian watched his father's countenance darken, "You know what I mean; no offense intended." Placated, Amenon turned back to the fire. "It feels as though we've been misusing precious resources, resources that could have been directed toward making the Sovereignty stronger—"

"Well," Amenon said, interrupting Terian, "you shall have your chance to evaluate her strength for yourself. She'll be joining us, our group, going forward."

Terian raised an eyebrow. "The Sovereign has—"

"The Sovereign," Amenon said, raising an eyebrow and staring at the fire, "is sending her to us to evaluate her performance. She has seen no combat, like much of our army at this point, and he wants my assessment before he allows the next class of the Legion to contain more female entrants to the profession of dark knight. We will keep a careful eye on her; as well you may know, the Sovereign's specific concern is that women combatants will be quicker to show mercy, something that our army has never considered as a virtue, unlike those weak elves and pitiful humans."

Terian raised an eyebrow at him. "I can think of one elven female paladin who's less likely to show mercy than any ten male dark knights I know."

"I do not criticize the Sovereign," Amenon said archly, giving Terian a look of favored superiority. "That said, the effectiveness of female knights in other armies cannot be denied, and I am pleased that he is considering this proposal. I do not believe that Sareea will disappoint him. Or us."

Terian gave a mild shrug. "I haven't seen her since she was a girl, so I suppose I wouldn't be able to judge the way you have."

"Oh, but you will," Amenon said, and turned his chair about with a screech. "You and the others will offer your assessment as well. She will be the most watched part of our team as we continue our operations over the next few months."

Terian gave a nod of concession. "As you will it, it shall be done." He knew that the gesture was wary.

Amenon watched him, as though trying to detect any bit of sarcasm. "Very good. Go on. Morning will be here to greet us with all its woes, and you have much reading to do tomorrow, after our meeting in the morn." He waved Terian away with his hand. "Enjoy your sleep. From now on you'll be awakened in the middle of the night to deal with missives and reports, so you might as well take advantage of your last night of rest." With that, he turned from Terian and looked to the parchment below the edge of the desk, stooping to retrieve it.

Terian walked out of the study, the slow, thumping cadence of his boots against the floor lulling him into a natural rhythm. "Sareea Scyros," he muttered to himself, remembering a knock-kneed girl in a muddied dress, skinny around the neck and arms, which were all of her that was exposed by Saekaj standards of modesty. *I haven't seen her since ...* There was a bitter taste in his mouth, and he shook his head as he walked back down the stairs toward his room, the lamps filling the room with the sweet fumes of the oil.

He did not find sleep easily, tossing and turning in the night as he recalled the circumstances of their last meeting, the faint light of the lamps from under the door continuing to menace him as he sweated into his sheets, feeling sick all the way until morning woke him out of a sleep he didn't even know he'd entered.

17.

Sareea Scyros was not skinny any longer, nor was she a little girl in a dress. She wore the armor of a dark knight, flat plate that hid whatever womanly attributes she might be carrying underneath it. She had spikes shorter and more utilitarian than Terian's mounted on her shoulders, gauntlets and boots. Every angle still had a sharp edge, though, her helm looking particularly vulture-like where she carried it under her arm. The woman herself was all hard edges as well. Red eyes surveyed the study and the men it held, and while her face was hardly contemptuous, there was no warmth on it at all. She was severe at least, Terian concluded, and not quite the angular girl he had met in earlier days.

"I welcome you to our group on the direct order of the Sovereign," Amenon said, standing before his desk, the rest of the team assembled around with an air of vague discomfort. It took Terian only a minute to pin it down, his mind stuck in the lethargy of sleep deprivation. He was also sweating, in spite of the cool cave air. *They have never worked with a woman before, save for the occasional healer or wizard. Even women rangers are terribly uncommon in Saekaj, and women are barred from being warriors here.* He shook his head to try and clear it from the fatigue. *I forgot how strange that was to me when starting with Sanctuary all those years ago; Niamh, Cora and Raifa cleared me of that prejudice quickly enough.*

"I am honored to do the Sovereign's bidding," Sareea said in clipped, efficient tones. There was a little bit of longing there, especially around the words "Sovereign" and "bidding." Terian kept tired eyes upon her, resisting the urge to close or rub them. He felt a cool droplet trickle down his spine from the back of his neck and another make its way down his forehead from his hair.

Dahveed Thalless stood next to him, his fingers steepled beneath the overlarge sleeves of his healer's robes. "Are you quite all right?" His voice was placid, but the barest hint of amusement overlaid his words.

"Fine," Terian grunted tersely. He kept his reply low.

"Don't mind Terian," Xem said leaning across Dahveed to speak so that he didn't interrupt the crosstalk between Amenon and Sareea, "I believe he's now suffering the consequences of his evening of dire responsibility and seriousness."

"Ah," Dahveed said with wry amusement, "most of us suffer when we are irresponsible and overindulge. Our dear friend, always doing things backwards, now suffers when he acts responsibly and doesn't indulge at all."

Amenon turned his head slightly to look at them and all of them fell silent, quieting instantly, though for Dahveed it came with a smile that was not short on irony. Once his look had its desired effect, Terian's father turned back to Sareea. "I feel certain that you will bring honor upon your house and your Sovereign by your service."

"May it ever be so," Sareea murmured, and the rest of them said it as well, a low intonation that reminded Terian of the time he'd stumbled into the ceremony of a sect worshipping Mortus. He brushed off that comparison.

"We remain ready to serve at the Sovereign's bidding," Amenon said, and the group of them relaxed. Verret, in particular, looked stiff and at attention after all the talk of the Sovereign and his bidding. *Months spent in the depths in the Sovereign's name will do that to a person, I suppose.* "Today I expect you all to remain close at hand, whiling your time away until you are needed, as I have a few inklings that we may have use for our abilities yet before the close of the day."

Terian felt himself speak in acknowledgment just as the rest did, a faint murmur of "Yes, sir," that was not quiet out of lack of conviction but hushed in respect.

"Go on, then," Amenon said. "Go to the basement if you desire to remain here, otherwise find your stations in town where you can be easily fetched if necessary."

"I shall be at the Healer's Union," Dahveed said with a nod and turned up the cowl of his white robes. "If anyone finds they've lost a limb and has sudden need for my skills."

"Why should anyone lose a limb here?" Grinnd said, a pinched expression on his broad face.

Terian looked at Sareea out of the corner of his eye, and she caught him and looked back with fierce red eyes. "I can think of a few causes offhand."

"Come, my friend," Verret said, clasping a hand on Grinnd's shoulder and steering the big man toward the door. His queue snaked down his back as he steered the warrior out of the study. "We can surely find something to do in the cellar. Perhaps tend to the cleanup of the mess that Terian must surely have left taking apart our prisoner yesterday."

"Surely," Grinnd said with true enthusiasm. "Labors of the hands make the mind free."

"You'd need a mind to make that work," Verret replied.

"That will be a great disappointment for them," Amenon said, watching the two of them go, Bowe following not far behind after giving a short, curt bow from the waist to Amenon which was returned by a simple nod of the head. "To find the cellar rooms already in good order, no sign of blood to scrub or flesh to pick up." He settled himself on the edge of his desk. "Not that Guturan would have let a mess linger overnight …."

"I shall see you later," Xem said to Terian with a nod and a half-smile. "I will await your order at my establishment, sir, should you have further need of me." He bowed deeply to Amenon.

"The Unnamed is a little far for a messenger to go and fetch you in case of emergency, isn't it?" Terian asked, looking at Xemlinan with all seriousness. *Wouldn't want him to raise Father's ire*, Terian thought, finding himself a little surprised at the consideration.

"Not that one," Xem said with a smile. "I just bought the Jaded Eye this past month."

Terian blinked. "That fancy ale house and inn off the square here in Saekaj?"

"Indeed," Xem said with a smile. "One cannot remain stagnant, always treading water in the same unmoving pool, after all."

"Sure you can," Terian replied. "Fish do it in the Great Sea all the time."

"And are destined to be the meat and bones in some poor family's stew," Xem said.

"Many's the time you've been the bone in some poor woman's—"

Amenon cleared his throat loudly, cutting Terian off. *Just when I was starting to feel a bit of myself,* he thought and felt the trickle of sweat growing on his forehead, beads falling down his brow and into his eyes. "Fare thee well, Xemlinan," Amenon said with a nod.

Xemlinan took the meaning plainly, bowed to Amenon once more, and departed without ceremony, shutting the double doors to the study behind him.

"Thank you for remaining, Sareea," Amenon said.

"You did not order me to depart," she said, voice still hard like cavern rock. "I will remain until you do so."

Amenon lifted himself off the desk and studied her carefully. "Will you follow my every order?"

There was no hesitation. "Without question."

Amenon nodded and took a slow, meandering path around his desk, filled with pondering steps. When he arrived at the other side he paused and looked down at the desk, and Terian caught him looking at the little red gemstone on the far side. He looked up and caught Terian's gaze before turning it back on Sareea. "Very good." He looked her straight in the eye and spoke into the quiet. "I'd like you to kill yourself."

Terian did not have a chance to speak before the sword was drawn. His eyes went wide even as Amenon made no move, did not flinch, merely stared on. Sareea's blade was curved, fearsome, broad at the top of the arc like a scimitar Terian had seen an elvish sea captain carry but with a much broader blade. The inside of the curve was serrated, lending it a savage look, and the crossguard was simplest metal. She reversed her grip in a half a heartbeat, just as he surged into motion.

He reached her as the blade finished running over her throat with a stroke so light he would have sworn it was cutting through the air itself. Deep purple blood spurted out from her throat, running down her dark armor as her red eyes failed to so much as register surprise. He caught her as her legs gave out and he helped cushion her fall.

"Son of a—" Terian jammed his hands against the wound, her glassy eyes staring up, staring past him. He looked at Amenon. "Are you going to do something?"

Amenon said nothing, merely watching, as still as if he had been carved into place. "Usually they hesitate quite a bit more than that."

"She's dying!" Terian yelled and turned his attention back to her. She stared on, straight ahead, at Amenon, though her glassy look was already fading. Terian felt heat simmer through him unrelated to the sickness he was already experiencing. "Were I her, I would swiftly reverse my condition unto you with a spell, rip the vitality right out of your body to make you feel the pain of—"

"Which is why I did not even bother to test you," Amenon said coolly, watching the proceedings as though it were nothing more disturbing than watching a vek'tag being slaughtered for dinner. "For it would have been a shame to have to reverse your own spell back upon you. Keep in mind she slit her own throat first; by your logic the smartest thing to do would have simply been to not run the blade across your own neck."

Terian looked down; the red eyes were empty now. They stared at Amenon no more, instead looking to the dark wood ceiling, the glow of the fire somehow barely reflecting in them now. "This is despicable, even for you."

Amenon arched an eyebrow at his son. "You grow soft or forgetful, and I know not which. Life and death are games, mere states that we have authority over. They are a simple enough matter to cure and control with the magic at our disposal." He clapped his gauntlets together once and called out, "Dahveed!"

The doors opened and Dahveed Thalless walked back in, his white robes trailing. He knelt next to Terian and Sareea, and closed his eyes, concentrating on an incantation that he did not even speak aloud. A moment later the light gathered in his palms was released, blurring Terian's vision as a sharp intake of breath could be heard from Sareea in his arms. Another few moments, another spell, and he watched the dark blue skin close around her wounds, knitting them shut.

Sareea said nothing at first then once her gasping was done, she turned to look back at Amenon. He did not say anything. Terian heard the slow rattle of metal against metal, and before he could stop her, she held a wide dagger in her hand. It came across her throat again, and this time the spatter covered Terian and Dahveed, turning the white robes of the healer a deep indigo. Terian tried to stop her, grasping her hand, but the damage was well done. Her throat was opened once more.

"Quite the devotee here," Dahveed said with a certain amusement, and his energy gathered once more, white light glowing in his fingers as he touched Sareea with his fingertips. There was no reason for it, Terian knew, but the healer did it anyway, as though to impart his life-gift back to her.

Terian turned his glare back to Amenon, who watched still, impassive. "Would you have her do it again?" Amenon did not answer.

Terian's grip on her arm was strong, anchoring it in place while Dahveed, on the other side, maintained a looser grip. *She's going to—*

Sareea bucked, knocking Dahveed aside. Terian looked down to see her eyes afire, and her hand snaked at him with mailed fingers extended. He ducked his head and she knocked his helm asunder, narrowly missing his eyes. He twisted her arm in his grasp, forcing her body down while moving her shoulder until he heard it crack from dislocation. She did not cry out, instead driving her free hand up toward his face. She caught him across the cheek with an ineffectual punch that did little more than anger him. The next hurt slightly more, and he ducked his head so her third blow hit him in the forehead, on the bone, where it ached only slightly. He drove his shoulder into her back and heard her bones crack further, though she still did not cry out.

"Enough," Amenon said, and Terian let his grip grow weak. "I no longer wish you to kill yourself, Sareea Scyros."

"I hear you and obey," came her muffled voice from where her face was pressed into the floorboards. Terian pulled his weight off of her and stood, getting to his feet while listening to the bending metal of his armor as he took a step back. He watched her warily, tempted on the one hand to offer her assistance, on the other hand knowing it would in no way be taken as anything other than a suggestion of weakness. *She is no longer a little girl, that is certain. To slit one's own throat is madness, to do it without even a thought is the sign of a truly deranged mind.* She came to her feet, a little slower than she might have, but giving no obvious sign that her shoulder was wrenched out of its proper placement. Her expression was cool, no sign of rage, but she was covered in her own blood from front to back. Terian knew she must be feeling sick from the resurrection spell but she hid it well, expressing nothing whatsoever.

"Very good," Amenon said with a nod. "Very good indeed." He looked to Terian. "Not you."

"I assumed as much," Terian said.

"Tell me, Sareea Scyros," Amenon said, watching her. "How did they teach you to handle the matter of someone blatantly disregarding an order given by an instrument of the Sovereign?"

Terian felt the tingle run over his scalp. "You can't possibly mean—"

"Death," came the whisper from behind him, and Terian did not manage to turn faster than the full weight of Sareea slammed into him. "Death to all those who disobey the Sovereign, and to disobey his own instruments is to disobey him." Terian heard it all even as he slammed face first into the floor of his father's office. There was a weight on his back, and his neck. "All you need do is give the order."

Terian's hand was pinned, unable to reach behind him but ineffectually. He grasped at her, landed a hand on the plate metal that surrounded her thigh and squeezed at it. There was only the sound of metal against metal, a light scratching that was nearly lost in the sound of blood pounding in his ears. He looked up enough to see Dahveed, standing warily to the side, still covered neck to hem in Sareea's blood. Terian shifted his gaze to his father, who looked down impassively, watching the spectacle as though there was not a woman straddling the back of his only son. *Dammit, I'm his heir.*

"The order is given," Amenon said, and Terian felt a chill run through him far beyond the queasiness he had felt all morning.

There was barely even time for him to register the blow before it broke his neck. He shuddered once, felt his whole body go slack, his breathing dissipate, and then he simply died.

18.

Eighteen Years Earlier

"All these girls are skinny," Terian said with a chuckle as he stared at Ameli's peers. She was standing in the midst of several other girls, but she turned to wave back at him.

"Thin girl, thin purse," Amenon said. "Or so the conventional wisdom goes when searching for a bride."

Terian let his hand fall on the hilt of the training sword he carried with him everywhere he went now. It had only a dull blade, but to him it was the weight of responsibility that made it so important. "I don't know why, but I don't quite subscribe to that philosophy."

"It's because your mother is thin," Amenon said, with a hint of a smile. "And you know she is wealthy."

Terian nodded. "True."

They stood in the small yard of the school Ameli attended, a few dozen parents and siblings of the girls knotted toward the back of the courtyard. The whole place was stone with wood trim where possible, a clear attempt to demonstrate the wealth and prestige of this particular school. Terian knew it was only open to the most elite of elite. *And that is why Ameli is here.*

Terian's eyes fell on the thinnest of girls, who was standing next to Ameli. "Isn't that …?"

"Kahlee Ehrest," Amenon agreed, his voice soft and low where no one could hear him. "Her father was the one who gave me the idea to send Ameli here. Nothing but the finest for our family."

Terian nodded stiffly. *Damned right.*

There was an officiator making a slow path toward the front of the courtyard, where a dais sat, but he was taking his time. Terian felt the itch and annoyance at watching the man's slow progress. He wasn't old, just slow. *Does he not know the aggregate value of the time he is wasting here? The parents are some of the most powerful people in Saekaj, and he's just loafing along like they're the poor waiting for their daily ration!*

"Fuming will not make this go any faster," Amenon said, and Terian could hear the lightness in his voice—a surprise in and of itself.

"But Father," Terian said, lowering his voice to a whisper, "this man clearly has no respect for his audience. He treats this as though it is some matter of little consequence that can simply be dealt with at leisure."

"Most do," Amenon said, looking sidelong at him with a twinkle in his eye. "Those outside the top manors know not what goes into acquiring them. The time, the effort, the single-minded focus. This man takes his slow walk because in this moment he is more important than every other person in the room—and it is the only time he will ever feel this way. Let him have his moment." Amenon smiled. "For we have all the rest."

Terian felt his father's words trickle down into him, pondering the wisdom of them. *He knows this man is milking this moment, and he lets him have it. Curious. I would think he would land upon him like a blade on the back of the neck of a true traitor.*

There was a noise from ahead as the officiator reached his dais. The pudgy, round fellow blinked as he locked his eyes on the disturbance. Terian followed his attentions to where every eye in the room rested.

Firmly on Ameli, Kahlee Ehrest, and another girl standing next to the two of them.

"You are a fool, Sareea Scyros!" Ameli's voice broke over the crowd, silencing the hundred quiet conversations that had sprung up in the courtyard.

Terian felt his father bristle next to him. *This is shameful. A public dispute with some unnamed, unknown soul? Ameli would have been better off feuding with Kahlee Ehrest; that wouldn't look nearly as bad.*

"I am no fool," the girl said in reply to Ameli, in a voice low and cool, like ice on glass. "And you are making a spectacle of yourself in front of everyone."

"I don't care!" Ameli gave this Sareea a firm, double-handed shove that knocked her off balance. Terian watched the girl fall backward, landing in a wet patch of clay. Her face showed only a hint of shock that faded quickly.

"Ameli." Terian's father's voice crackled with quiet menace, silencing everyone in the courtyard. Every head turned to look at him, without exception.

"It was not my fault, Father!" Ameli said. To Terian's eyes, she looked as though she were regaining her senses. Her eyes widened as she took in the scene around them, the realization that she'd embarrassed herself before the entirety of the audience sinking in.

"She was firmly in the right, Lord Amenon." Kahlee Ehrest said, her white dress hanging off her skinny shoulders and clinging to her thin figure. She drew nearly every eye in the room, pulling them to her through the volume of her voice, which Terian noted was curiously directed. *She's had experience controlling a room, drawing their attention to her. Of course.*

"Thank you, Kahlee Ehrest," Amenon said. *He calls her by her full name to make her aware that he knows who she is, but denies her the respect due an adult by doing so.* "I think I can handle my own daughter's behavior without your counsel." He turned a burning eye on Ameli. "Come with me." He looked to the officiator. "You will wait on us."

The officiator stood stunned, mouth slightly ajar. "Of course, Lord Amenon."

Without waiting for a reply, Amenon strode out of the courtyard. Terian watched Ameli, and she followed moments later, her head down and avoiding every eye in the room—all of which were on her. As the low buzz of conversation sprung back up in the courtyard, Terian looked at the girl who had been pushed—*Sareea, wasn't that her name?*

She was no beauty, that was certain. Her face was all harsh lines, though her lips were full and dark. He caught her eyes trawling the room, studying the reaction to the scene that had just played out. She saw him watching her and stared back, giving him just the hint of a smile—barely enough for him to know she was doing it.

"YOU WILL CONDUCT YOURSELF IN A MANNER THAT BEFITS YOUR FAMILY!" Amenon's voice crackled from outside the courtyard, and the sound of a hand slapping a cheek was followed by a sharp cry from Ameli. Amenon's voice was lowered upon his next comment, and Terian did not hear it.

He did fix his eyes on Kahlee Ehrest, though, and caught the darkening of her cheeks. Her embarrassment and shame was obvious. Terian did not take his eyes off her as Ameli made her way back into the courtyard. He saw her turn her gaze on his father, saw the emotion shine from beneath a face that had long been taught not to show itself truly. Terian recognized it for what it was, though, having seen it all too often on Ameli's face.

Anger.

19.

Terian awoke in the dark, in his room once more, the shock of his own breath in the cool air not making up for the sweat that coated him, covered him. The sheets smelled of whatever fever afflicted him, a sick feeling that was not likely to depart any time soon. "He had her kill me," he said in realization.

"Oh, indeed," came a voice out of the dark, and suddenly a lamp hovered in his vision, illuminating a dark blue face in the darkness. "I am rather surprised you didn't see it coming, though. How long have you been gone again?" Dahveed's ironic smile was still there, and his robes still bore their bloodstains.

"Not long enough," Terian said with a grunt.

"Now, now," Dahveed said, and Terian realized the healer was sitting in a chair at his bedside, "he's not that difficult of a man to figure out. He simply wants his every order followed, and every action to carry with it the appropriate amount of honor to the Sovereign." Dahveed's smile grew broader. "Is that really so hard?"

"Apparently," Terian said, sitting up in bed, feeling the squeak of the frame under the feathered down, "for a free man, it is."

"There are no free men in Saekaj or Sovar," Dahveed said seriously. "An important lesson to remember if you'd like to avoid having that terror of a woman separate your head from your shoulders in the future."

Terian's hand fell to his throat. "She didn't …?"

"By the Sovereign's grace, no, she did not," Dahveed said. "That would have taken me a bit more time to repair. I believe she smashed the bones in the back of your neck to a fine powder, though, and the bones in the back of your skull for good measure." The healer's nostrils flared and he leaned forward. "You should remember where you are if you wish to avoid invoking your father's displeasure in the future."

Terian let himself stare at the far wall, the sick feeling not even beginning to subside. "I haven't given a vek'tag's anus about my father's displeasure in years. Why start worrying about it now?"

"Because you're under his roof again now, I would think." Dahveed settled back once more, and there was a soft whooshing of the fabric of his robe against the wooden chair. "Different country, different house, different rules. Surely you're a bright enough lad to realize that."

"I question how bright I truly am at this point, Dahveed." Terian leaned back and felt the soft pillows awaiting him against his neck. He turned his head just a little, to look at the healer, and lowered his voice. "Was it always like this?"

Dahveed raised an eyebrow. "In your father's house? Yes—"

"No," Terian said and looked up at the ceiling as though he could see through the boards above into the third floor and through the ones above that to the study at the crest of the house. "I know it's always the same here in the House of Lepos. I meant Saekaj. Sovar. The invoking of the name of the Sovereign seems to be at a fever pitch, and I don't remember it being this way when last I left—"

"This is treason," Dahveed said warningly and twisted the little flame at the base of the lamp. After a moment, the flame grew brighter and the shadows around them grew longer.

"Sorry," Terian said.

"It's quite all right," Dahveed said. "I just wanted to be sure you remembered it before we went further. The flames of the Sovereignty's nationalism are growing by the day, stoked by the Sovereign's own return. Before, in his absence, the words were said but the meaning was not there. 'In the name of the Sovereign!'" Dahveed said it loudly and without irony and his words echoed off the walls of the room. "After he left, after Shrawn and the tribunal took their place—his place—the flames died for a piece." Dahveed mimed the action of turning down the lamp's wick. "Only the dedicated preferred the Sovereign to the weaker grip of the tribunal. Only a true fool like Verret would be mad enough to give voice to those thoughts, especially given all that the last hundred years have brought us." He began to lift his fingers, one by one, to illustrate his points. "The lifting of the laws set at the end of the last war that confined our entire race to these underground pits, the relaxation of the death penalties for those who dared to speak a single word that could be interpreted as disloyal—"

"That's enough for me," Terian said. "I can feel it in the air down here, in the chill. There's an atmosphere of suffused ... I don't know, goose-stepping. Like everyone's in a hurry to do their assigned tasks. It's always been bad, but not like this."

"Pride and fear," Dahveed said. "Pride in the thought of our nation ascendant once more, fear from the thought of the punishments that might come each of our ways for any perceived disloyalty." He held his hands a short distance apart from each other. "The twin motivators, working hand in glove with each other to assure that the dark elven people all march to the same song." He gave a long sigh. "And that tune is whatever one that the Sovereign finds to be prettiest. As it has always been."

Terian looked at Dahveed, measuring a response. "Where does that leave us?"

Dahveed smiled bitterly. "The same place as ever. Marching to the music. Because the alternative is too unpalatable to bear."

Terian stared into the distance to the darkest corner of the room, as though he could see into the shadows there, see something watching or waiting for him within them. "Maybe I don't want to march to the tune."

"Because you'd prefer to dance?"

Terian let out a disgusted noise. "I never prefer to dance. I'd rather just ignore the music and hope it goes away."

Dahveed turned down the wick and the flames that lit the room grew fainter. "I'm afraid that the music that drives us forward doesn't abate simply because we wish it to, any more than the Sovereign will simply …" he smiled faintly, "… disappear into the darkness because we wish it. No, these changes, this difference … it is here to stay." His face grew placid, calm, with just a hint of unease. "After all … what can two men do against the entire Sovereignty?"

20.

"You will read all of these missives," Amenon said as Terian seated himself at the small table in the corner of his father's office. It was piled high with parchment; at the top, he could see a report on the amount of fish sold in market the day before. "You will look for threads of interest that call out to you, keep watch for ongoing concerns, anything that may be of interest to the Sovereign, and generally try to make yourself useful." He glared down at Terian. "A sarcastic response to that last point would be unwise."

"What am I looking for?" Terian asked, lifting the first parchment and finding a prisoner report from some guard in the Depths that talked about the number who died from labor-related injuries and fatigue in the last day.

"Interesting points," Amenon said.

Terian stared down at the fish sales report. "I may have to look deep for anything interesting."

Amenon waved a hand at him. "Now you see why I have assigned it to you."

Terian squinted, the dark elven text much more complicated and looping than normal elven or human letters. It was more intricate script, with more characters that one had to memorize and understand, a separate one for every elementary concept. After an hour, he was rubbing his eyes. After two, he wanted to burn all the remaining parchment. After three, he was still only halfway through and wondering how his father had sorted through a similar stack in minutes the day before.

"Anything yet?" Amenon said from behind his desk, a book in his lap and cracked open to the middle. Terian could not tell whether it was a spellbook, some practical guide to unknown skills, or perhaps a fictional account of some soaring love story between a paladin and a warrior of the sort he'd seen others read before. *Doubtful on the last; fiction of that sort doesn't tend to make it onto parchment even here in Saekaj.*

"Fishing production seems to be down again," Terian said.

"Ah, yes," Amenon said. "They've been griping about that for some time, but it's hard to maintain output when the boats keep disappearing."

Terian looked up from his reading and met his father's gaze. "The Great Sea is an enclosed cavern."

Amenon raised a white eyebrow. "And?"

Terian pondered it for only a moment. "So where do they go? It's not as though the Great Sea has some plethora of exits. It's buried deep in the earth, it's a cave room with one entry and one exit—"

"Above water, yes," Amenon replied. "There are more beneath the surface, I am told."

Terian thought about that for a beat. "So you're suggesting that these fishermen decided to abandon their jobs and swim into unknown cave exits?"

Amenon took a breath to say something but stopped, watching Terian shrewdly. "No. I wouldn't suppose they would do that, especially given that work on a fishing boat in the Great Sea is one of the most sought-after jobs in Sovar."

"So then they're sinking, right?" Terian said, leaning his head back against the wall. "If they're not finding any sign of the boat."

"A fair assumption," Amenon said.

"Have you not sent anyone to look into this?" Terian asked.

Amenon turned back to his book. "Why should this matter?"

Terian thought about it. "It just should." *Because the poor will starve, you ass, but if I tell you that, you'll either laugh me out of the office or kill me. Possibly both.*

Amenon sighed. "Pray tell, why should it? Explain it to me." There was a shrewdness about him, about the look he gave Terian, something that prickled the dark knight's senses.

Terian held up the parchment in his hand, gathering his thoughts as he read it again. "This is not the first report of this sort you've had?"

"Not the first, no," his father said, still watching him carefully. "But you have yet to answer my question. Why is it important?"

Terian thought about it, reasoning it out. "Our bean crops, mushroom crops and wildroot are not up to the task of feeding the entirety of Sovar without some sort of fish or bones to help fortify the pottage."

"Go on," Amenon said.

"It creates a slow, desperate trickling down of starvation as the fish supply decreases," Terian said. "Not everyone in Sovar can afford the fish, but—" He blinked. "It's like a chain—"

"Yes," Amenon said. "Go on."

"Food riots in Sovar would be an unpleasant prospect at best, would they not?" Terian asked.

"Any act of insurrection is beyond unpleasant." Amenon's countanance darkened, a thundercloud of anger settled in over his features. "I doubt anyone has forgotten what happened the last time such a thing occurred. It did not go so well for either side, and it would be best to avoid such unpleasantness in the future. Desperate, starving people do desperate things."

"So we should look into these disappearances, right?" Terian waited, but Amenon had looked down into his book as though the lesson was over and nothing of interest was left to be said.

After a moment Amenon looked up again, his face drawn. "You should indeed. Even so small a thing—" *Probably not small to the people who have lost families,* Terian thought, "bears a closer look when the stakes are so high. Assemble the team and investigate these losses." Terian started to stand, but Amenon stopped him with a sour smile. "After you've finished your reading for the day."

"I will," Terian said then paused. "Wait … you said for me to do it? On my own?"

"Indeed," Amenon said, not looking up from his book. "This is a test of your leadership ability. I put this matter in your hands to determine your capability." He looked up one last time and favored Terian with a look that was deep, burning, and filled with unyielding suggestion. "Do not fail me."

21.

Terian walked down the steps one at a time, the weight of his armor especially heavy. *I have to lead the team on this one. Lead. A team. Urk.* The clomping of his feet against the steps made a maddening noise.

He reached the landing; the smell of the mushroom gruel was heavy in the air. He wrinkled his nose. *Never will get used to that.* He turned at the landing and looked down to the floor below, where a straight-backed Guturan Enlas waited for him.

"Guturan," Terian said in faint acknowledgment.

"I would have your attention for a moment, Lord heir," Guturan said stiffly, his scratchy voice nearly cracking.

"Oh, you would, would you?" Terian could feel his frown deepen, unrelated to the smell. "Go on, then." He stared down at Guturan, folding his arms and listening to the metal clink at the joints as the pieces of his armor rubbed together.

"We have received an invitation for a ball to be held at the House of Shrawn on this very eve." Guturan's face was as stiff as his posture, his mien as neutral as if he were delivering an order for a meal to the cooks in the kitchen. "You are expected to attend."

"I'm busy," Terian said and resumed his downward journey. The thump of his boots rang out and echoed. "Send Dagonath

Shrawn my insincere regrets that I'll be unable to attend his self-congratulatory, highbrow *veredajh*." Terian smiled.

Guturan hissed. "Society events are hardly a—" Guturan made a guttural, throat-clearing noise. "To say such a crude thing is a very great insult to the House of Shrawn, and an ill reflection on your own house."

"As though he'll even hear about it," Terian said.

Guturan stuck an arm out, iron hand landing hard on Terian's breastplate and halting his descent. "There are spies in the House of Lepos that report directly to Dagonath Shrawn," Guturan said nearly silently, "and you are a fool if you do not assume every conversation in this place reaches both his ears and the Sovereign's."

"Oh, come on," Terian said with a shake of his head.

"He will hear of this," Guturan said quietly with a deep seriousness. "Know it to be true and curb your tongue accordingly."

Terian looked down the stairs into the main room; a few servants milled idly about. *Truly?* He shook his head. "Either way, I'm not going to Shrawn's ball. I have not the time; there are things I need to attend to on the order of my father."

"Master Amenon!" Guturan called out, his gaze still fixed upon Terian, his arm still in place to halt his movement.

There was a rustle above and Terian heard his father's voice call down. "Yes?"

Only Guturan could get my father to step out of his study to speak with a mere servant. "Master Terian wishes to decline Dagonath Shrawn's gracious invitation to his ball. Do you want me to send notice to Lord Shrawn to that effect?"

There was a pause and Terian looked up. "Sovereign's grace, no," Amenon said, and there was irritation in his voice. "Terian, you will attend. Your investigation of that other matter will have to wait. Send word to Shrawn that he'll be there, Guturan—and thank you for bringing this to my attention." His father's head disappeared over the railing and back into his study.

Terian looked back to Guturan, who wore a smile of deep satisfaction. "You're a boil on my arse, Guturan."

"I am tasked with keeping this house running smoothly," Guturan said, "and that means ensuring that the heir of Lepos is esteemed in the proper social circles. I will not have the House of Lepos lose face in the Shuffle because of elementary mistakes made by a spoiled brat who keeps trying to throw himself into the gutter."

"But it's so much fun in the gutter," Terian said. "You meet a great class of people there; better than the ones at Dagonath Shrawn's *veredajh*, anyway." Terian watched Guturan's face twitch with outrage, and he pushed past the steward's arm to continue downward to his room, where he shut the door so he could stew quietly while he awaited his fate.

22.

Terian waited in his room, staring at the dark walls and pacing to and fro as the hour drew nearer. He suspected a servant or two would be along shortly to groom him in preparation for the ball, and he felt his stomach turn over at the thought of his evening ahead.

When Guturan showed up, he had given over to pacing the room. His boots tread lightly on the woven rug that sat in the center of his room, the smoke of the candle carrying a strange vanilla scent that seemed more appropriate to the outside world than the darkness of Saekaj. "What is that?" he asked Guturan, pointing to the candle.

"Imported from Aloakna," Guturan said without missing a beat. He stared at Terian, assessing him. "Yes, this will do nicely."

"An imported candle from Aloakna will do nicely?" Terian asked. "For what? Covering the moldering scent of fear in the basement torture chamber?"

"Your armor," Guturan said, unamused. "It will do nicely for the ball."

"I get to go to Dagonath Shrawn's ball in my armor?" Terian ran a finger over his smooth chin. He'd run the razor over his stubble in anticipation of what he suspected was coming. "Perhaps this won't be so bad after all."

"Soldiers of the Sovereign are expected to attend formal events in their battle garb," Guturan said with an appraising eye. "But your helm must remain off your head at all times indoors."

"I remember the particulars of etiquette from my schooling, Guturan," Terian said icily.

"Do you?" Guturan asked with a faint trace of a smile. "I can never tell." His expression straightened. "Your hair will have to be dealt with, of course."

"Dealt with how?" Terian asked as Guturan snapped his fingers so loudly it echoed in the chamber. A retinue of servant girls opened the door, and he could hear the giggles cease as they did so. Their faces were dipped low, bowed heads on the lot of them, but the smirks remained. "Oh."

"Also ..." Guturan said. "I think a bath is in order."

"*What?*"

Terian was scrubbed quite against his will, though he did not fight it too hard. A tub of heated water was brought in, and in that moment he knew Guturan's careful survey of him was all a sham. *Guturan stepped in here already knowing what was to be done with me—to me*, Terian thought as a serving girl ran a scrubbing brush with bristly needles down his back. "What the hells is that made of, exactly?" He glared at the serving girl, who barely stifled a giggle. "Discarded sword blades?"

"I think the hilt might be," Guturan said lightly, moving around the room while the serving girls did their worst to him. *At least it feels like their worst.* "There are expectations of an heir of your station at this event, and we should cover them swiftly."

"Is there still dueling?" Terian asked. "I seem to remember some dueling taking place at balls I went to when I was younger. I was always so crestfallen that there was an age requirement for that sort of thing ..."

"You will not duel," Guturan said sharply. "It is beneath your station. Only lesser nobles squabble like children among themselves. Higher houses already have all they need; there is nothing to be gained from dueling with your lessers."

"What about with one of Shrawn's kids?" Terian asked. "Seems like it could be fun—"

"You will not duel," Guturan said again, and this time there was no mistaking the fury with which he said it. "Your father has given explicit instruction in this matter." He straightened and continued in his leisurely orbit around the tub while one of the serving girls probed Terian with the brush in a manner that he had once paid a girl from Reikonos good money for. This time, though, he jumped, drawing Guturan's gaze again. "Besides, all of Shrawn's children are either too young or too old to duel with you. His eldest son in his current family is only sixteen and still in training at the Commonwealth of Arcanists; his elder two families with previous wives are all in their third century at youngest and also out of his line of succession—and thus unworthy of your time and effort." Guturan leaned over the edge of the tub. "You have a purpose and these people are aimless curs. You will not duel. Are we clear?"

"Yes, *Mother*," Terian said under his breath. Guturan's eyes narrowed, but he did not comment.

When Guturan started his slow circling of the tub once more, he was silent for a few moments before speaking. His voice was much gentler this time. "Perhaps Mistress Kahlee will be there."

"That's not exactly a selling point for me, Guturan," Terian said as the serving girl working on his front took the bristly brush far too low for his liking. "Augh!" He sent her a daggered look, which she ignored. "She essentially told me to throw myself into the Great Sea when last I met her in the square. Which I actually planned to do tonight, before you told me I was going to be forced to enter the Realm of Death instead." He paused for effect. "Actually, the Realm of Death is probably less frigid."

"You prefer physical combat to social gatherings?" Guturan said, and there was a hint of curiosity in the way he said it.

"By fathoms," Terian said. "The threats are obvious in physical combat. In social combat here in Saekaj, I find the swords and daggers much less obvious but no less deadly."

"True enough," Guturan said, and he'd finally stopped his slow circling of the tub. "That's enough scrubbing, I'd say."

"Are you sure?" Terian asked. "Because I've still got some skin left on my—" The servant girl ran the brush between his legs drawing a sharp cry from him. "Oh, no, wait; there it went."

Guturan stood there with a sly smile as two serving girls approached the edge of the tub in their drab, barely-dyed green dresses. "All this is mere preparation, heir of Lepos. For you are correct in your assessment of the social arena of our city." His smile disappeared. "And the flaying you have received here is nothing compared to the one you will receive should you fail and disgrace the family in the eyes of your father." The smile came back, but it was a smirk. "Develop thicker skin, m'lord Terian, because for this—and every one of these events for the rest of your life—you will need it."

23.

The vek'tag carriage pulled along the wide loop of Shrawn manor's entry road. The ride was smooth, Terian noted as he ran a gauntleted finger over the sharp points of his helm. He held it in hand, watching tentatively as the carriage crawled up the drive toward a portico that was growing closer outside his window. It was an affectation only the wealthy had; a protection against the drips that came inside a cave.

The smell of food and perfumes wafted through his window and happy chatter greeted his ears as he traced his fingers over the points of the helm. He sighed deeply, draining his lungs and leaving himself tired. His armor felt as if it weighed tons, the dread within him magnifying its heaviness by factors. He pulled his finger back from the sharp points of the armor, unable to take his eyes off the helm he had worn for more than half his life.

Is it really worth it? He shifted his gaze out the window as the carriage shuddered to a halt. *Is any of this—these sacrifices, these impositions—worth it? What does it truly buy me?*

The door to his carriage swung open as a servant appeared at his door. Terian took little notice of the stiff man in the long coat who held the door for him unblinking as Terian stepped out. He carefully placed the helm back on his head. He felt the weight of it increase, too, though he knew it was all in his mind.

He stood under the portico, looking across the sea of women in black with only the occasional spot of unfashionable white to break the monotony, and the men of Saekaj in the uniforms he knew belonged to the civilian oversight or the armor of the Saekaj Militia. A few, all of them younger men, were dressed as dandies. They wore long suit coats that were cut differently than the one worn by the servant holding the carriage door. Wooden buttons adorned their coats, and fancy hats were coupled with long dueling canes in their hands.

Terian watched two of the dandies clack their canes together before being scolded sharply by a man in military garb. It took little more than five words and a cross look to have them both blushing, deeply ashamed. He watched the scene with little interest as he threaded his way through the crowd to the front doors of Shrawn's manor.

Everything was wood, opulence on full display. *Shrawn has been in his position for much longer than Father has been in his, and the accumulation of wealth makes it obvious who is first in that department.* Terian stepped into the room without fanfare. Some of the lesser noble houses had people to announce the entry of guests into their parties.

In the House of Dagonath Shrawn, if you needed to be announced, you were clearly too unimportant to be worthy of notice.

Terian paused in the door. He was in a foyer that stretched up a wide staircase. It was a pale imitation of the Grand Palace but made in the image of the Sovereign's house and with his permission. *Only Shrawn could possibly be so bold. The Sovereign would have denied anyone else—and by denied, I mean killed.* The wood paneling alone was several fortunes, more gold and silver than most houses in Saekaj would see in ten generations. *The view from the top is grand indeed, eh, Shrawn?*

"Terian," came a soothing, quiet voice from his left. He turned to see Dahveed grinning at him with a small aperitif in his hand. He made his way through the small crowd with lithe steps that kept him from so much as brushing the tightly knit conversational circles that filled the room.

"Come to save me, Dahveed?" Terian asked, taking his eyes off the healer to look around the small room. To his left there was a grand ballroom of mahogany and oak, filled to the brimming with people. No dancing was taking place, though surely that would come later.

"Perhaps I've come to save myself," Dahveed said, slipping next to Terian and clasping a hand lightly on his shoulder. The faint smell of chicken wafted from the healer, whose long, dyed red hair was blazingly obvious in the midst of the sea of black and white and grey. "Apparently a lowborn healer is expected to attend these functions but fairly shunned when he actually shows up."

"Even if that lowborn healer is the head of the Healers' Union?" Terian asked, raising an eyebrow. "And one of the three most powerful spell casters in all Saekaj?"

Dahveed popped the appetizer into his mouth with a smile. "Few know that. It is a well-kept secret."

"I wonder why?" Terian asked.

Dahveed shrugged lightly, clearly unconcerned. "Reasons of birth, I expect. I care not, so long as my privacy is protected. Imagine the toadying and currying of favor that would sweep my way if the truth were known. Why, I'd never be able to attend one of these functions again."

"I have a hard time believing that would pain you overly much," Terian said.

"Oh, but it would," Dahveed said. "They serve the best food here." He cracked a grin.

Terian couldn't even manage a lackluster laugh for that one. "What am I expected to do here?"

"What is one expected to do at any party?" Dahveed asked. "Talk. Mingle. Perhaps dance if the opportunity presents itself."

Terian froze. "Dance?"

"A strange concept, I know," Dahveed said. "But you were raised in Saekaj, not Sovar, and have walked in the outside world. Surely you're familiar with music and dancing."

"Yes, I'm familiar with music and dancing, Dahveed," Terian said with a frown. The healer smiled insufferably at him. "I didn't know I was going to have to—"

"It's a ball," Dahveed said.

"It's in Saekaj," Terian said bitterly, "where music is largely outlawed because the echoing hurts the Sovereign's ears or something."

"This is the House of Shrawn," Dahveed said, "where the ordinary rules do not apply because the Sovereign gives his grace leave to suspend them from time to time."

"Well, damn," Terian said.

"I wouldn't worry about it, if I were you," Dahveed said. Now he was smiling thinly. "Do you anticipate being asked to dance?"

Terian ran through the thought in his mind. The crowd moved in a flow, seeming to swell as conversational circles grew larger with the steady trickle of new arrivals. Perfumes hung as thick as the air of food, and Terian caught glimpses of a steady run of servants bringing more trays out to a long buffet table that took up a full wall of the ballroom. "No," Terian said finally. "There are only five or six houses that would even be of a station to tender such an invitation to me, and only one I wouldn't be able to refuse bluntly without insulting them."

"The House of Shrawn, of course," Dahveed said.

"Of course."

"I believe his eldest daughter in his line of inheritance is only fifteen," Dahveed said, "so you're probably safe."

"She's sixteen, actually," came a voice from behind them, "but I've already warned her away from you, so you need not worry."

Terian turned at the deep voice, already knowing what he would find there. The speaker was a man who had been long familiar to him—indeed, his face was familiar to everyone in Saekaj and Sovar. He wore a suit unlike those sported by the dandies, and cut from an entirely different cloth than those worn by the civilian overseers of the city. He carried with him a cane that Terian knew for a fact was not used for anything so crude as striking another in a duel. His coat hung loose, and his belly fell over his belt.

"Dagonath Shrawn," Terian said, bowing his head slightly. *I should bow lower; this is probably an insult.* But he couldn't seem to make himself do it. "How lovely to see you again."

24.

"Now, now, Terian," Dagonath Shrawn said, his jowls hanging loose in an amused look, "I'll forgive your rudeness because I'm certain you've been gone from Saekaj long enough to forget the little politenesses we expect here."

"Yes, of course," Terian said, almost atonally, "forgive me my rudeness. It's been a while since I've been in company so polite as this; I'm much more used to fighting my way through dens of snakes rather than smiling my way through them." Terian heard a sharp intake of breath from Dahveed and stifled a smile. *This could be fun, I suppose.*

Shrawn smiled. "Den of snakes? Why, and here I thought I was hosting a *veredajh*." Shrawn's smile grew broad as Terian felt his fade. "Although, if you are looking for an actual one of those, my boy, I would suggest talking to Lady Grensmyth. I'm told she has a circle of servants willing to debase themselves in quite spectacular ways to afford her, her husband, and whatever manservant they have an interest in that week a filling for their more perverse appetites."

Terian felt the chill. "You're awfully bold essentially admitting to the Heir of the House Lepos that you have spies right under his nose."

"Lad," Shrawn said, "I have spies everywhere, not just under your nose. I find it helpful to remind everyone from time to time that you cannot whisper a word in this city without it finding its way back to my ears. You'd do well to remember that in the future."

"Or I could just dismiss all my servants," Terian said, jaw tight. *He's so damned smug.*

"And that would trouble me for the five minutes it would take to slip fifteen more in the next group you hired," Shrawn said. He clapped Terian on the shoulder. "Come now, let's talk about more pleasant things. I could scarcely believe it when I heard you'd returned to us. Leaving as you did, the rift with your father. Not many men have the mettle to come back after shrugging their responsibilities the way you did." His face grew more satisfied. "It's hard to step back on the path laid out for you after you've veered so badly off it."

"Not as hard as you might think," Terian said, trying to keep his jaw in place as though it were iron.

"Indeed," Shrawn said, and Terian could feel his grip tighten on his shoulder as he leaned in. "Excellent work convincing Sert Engoch to give up everything he knew. And so quickly! The Sovereign is quite pleased, you know."

"Well, you know," Terian said, applying only the thinnest layer of sarcasm, "I work in the name of the Sovereign."

"Truly," Shrawn said, leaning back out. He was more mysterious now, though still self-satisfied. "Then perhaps you should go ... pay your respects."

Terian stopped short of rolling his eyes. "I wouldn't trouble him by knocking on the door to his palace just to present my lowly self."

"Nor should you," Shrawn said, "under normal circumstances. Fortunately ... tonight's circumstances are not normal."

Terian could feel the jaws of the trap closing, but he could not see the teeth of it. "I get the sense you're pushing me toward a cliff's edge, Shrawn, so why don't you just cut the ground from beneath me and be done with it?"

Shrawn laughed lightly. "Is paying homage to the Sovereign of your land so dreadful a burden? Your protestations amuse me, true though they somewhat are. My, ah, lording over of you is entirely predicated on knowledge I have that you do not."

"Obviously," Terian said. *Though it's not really obvious because Shrawn is too busy being an officious prick to plainly say what he's manipulating me towards.* "If you want me to go to the palace, let me say this: I am not so far removed from Saekaj that I have forgotten all etiquette. For example, I do remember that those who knock upon those doors without invitation tend not to have a happy result laid upon them in return."

"You misunderstand." Shrawn gestured toward the back of the ballroom, where a shadowed alcove in the back corner was filled with an impenetrable darkness. Terian felt a slight shiver as he looked at it. "You need not go to the palace to pay homage to Master of Saekaj and Sovar." Terian glanced back just in time to see the insufferable grin upon Shrawn's face, magnified at what was probably his obvious discomfort, "for he is here, in this very room, watching us at this precise moment."

25.

"Well, isn't that a surprise," Dahveed said, rather dryly to Terian's ears. "Admittedly, I don't know the Sovereign as well as others, but I had never thought parties an area of interest for him."

"He is here at my invitation," Shrawn said, a little too obsequiously. "Though of course his reasons are his own."

Dahveed inclined his head. "Of course."

Terian felt the faint dread he'd experienced earlier return in full, calamitous force. The smells of the food tables in the distance now seemed rotten to him, rancid, and the perfumes that had smelled somewhat appealing, bringing to mind the scented whores of Reikonos, were now foul and bitter. The hum of conversation was muted by the rushing sound of the blood in his ears and Terian had to steady himself.

"Lad, you look positively sick," Shrawn said with great glee. "Go pay your respects to the Sovereign. I am certain that meeting you is one of the reasons he accepted my invitation, and wouldn't it be a shame to disappoint him?"

"You think I'm going to embarrass myself, don't you?" Terian said, feeling the anger replace his fear. "You're steering me toward this sure that I'm going to cock it up somehow and make a disgrace of myself in front of the Sovereign."

Shrawn laughed. "I think I've known you since you were a child. I think I've watched you since you were a suckling babe. I think I know you better than you know yourself, and I think your house is so desperate for an heir that if you had failed to return they'd have dressed a shrieking, rabid vek'tag in your clothing in order to fill that gaping hole. I know not what will happen in the next few minutes, not to a certainty. But I know you, and your capacity for missteps and ill-spoken words, and I find favorable the odds that, given enough time with the Sovereign, you will bury yourself in a grave deep enough to push your entire house in behind you." The corner of his mouth turned up in a smirk. "The real you—the one that's been off the path for nearly twenty years—he never stays hidden for long because your bizarre conception of what's right drives everything you do, and you have never learned to contain or restrict that foolishness." Shrawn laughed lightly. "And it will bury you, eventually."

Terian stood there, listening to Shrawn's lengthy pronouncement. "You think you've got me all figured out, don't you?"

Shrawn's eyes were unblinking, but now the amusement faded into something much more ... sinister. "I know you, and the path you're on, and it tells me everything I need to know about where you'll end up." He bowed his head, lower than Terian had when he'd greeted him. "Enjoy the party, and don't forget to pay respects to the Sovereign. He's waiting."

With that, Shrawn disappeared into the crowd as if he'd wisped into smoke and vanished. Terian caught a glimpse of him halfway across the room a moment later, glad-handing another guest and talking with a smile on his face that seemed wholly insincere.

"Well, now that you've drunkenly stumbled halfway into the Depths," Dahveed said, "perhaps you should go greet the Sovereign and try to avoid going the rest of the way."

"I haven't drunkenly done anything," Terian said with more than a little bite. "But I surely could use a drink right now."

"I doubt that would improve your situation in any measurable way."

"I have my doubts that I'll be walking out of this party under my own power regardless of what I do," Terian said darkly. "You heard Shrawn—"

"I heard the idle chatter of a man who doesn't truly know you," Dahveed said.

"He knows me," Terian said. "He knows me well enough to know that I'm an insufferable bastard, especially around people trying to lord their power over me. He knows me well enough that I'll bristle if the Sovereign says anything that steps on my sense of absurdity or right and wrong." Terian brought a hand up over his eyes. "He knows me well enough, Dahveed. Well enough to smell my imminent demise from across the room."

Dahveed seized Terian by the shoulder and pulled him around, looking into his eyes with a seriousness that was out of character for the good-humored healer. "Then prove him wrong. Show him that you have changed. That you have control over your mouth, a brake on your actions. This is a necessary thing for the heir of House Lepos; it won't do to have you trying to strike down everyone in your path with word or axe. Prove him wrong." With that, Dahveed let loose of him and faded into the crowd as Terian stared numbly at the space he'd occupied before turning to look at the shadowed alcove across the room.

He moved stiffly, an unnatural walk that felt as though his joints were all frozen in place. *What do I say? This is the Sovereign of*

Saekaj and Sovar! What can I say that won't sound like idiotic platitudes or idle arse kissing? With each step his mind grew blanker, his mouth grew drier, and his feet carried him closer to the dark alcove where the shadows hung thick.

He felt a strong hand on his arm and paused, wondering who would dare. He needed to see nothing more than the blue hair to realize. "Kahlee?" He watched the surge of irritation run across her face. "I'm a little surprised."

"Imagine how surprised I am," Kahlee said, removing her hand and holding it apart from her body, as though it were contaminated. "Are you going to speak to the Sovereign?"

"I am," Terian said, his voice sounding strangely choked. "Shrawn told me he wants to speak to me."

"Fathoms and Depths," Kahlee said softly. "Keep your tongue in line, fool." Her head shook, strands of light blue hair falling to and fro as she did. "Lest you find it on the buffet table being served to fat old Lord Freitoth."

"Keeping a civil tongue was uppermost on my mind," Terian said, "given that if I don't, said mind will be disconnected from the rest of me by the swing of an executioner's axe."

Kahlee's eyes flashed. "I know you well enough, Terian, or I did before you left. Any civil tongue you had was torn out long ago by—"

"Yes, thank you," Terian said abruptly. "I remember it well."

Kahlee's voice softened. "Just … don't be a fool. Ameli would hate it if you were to be killed for something so idiotic as speaking your mind to the Sovereign."

"I'll just try to forget I have a mind for a few minutes," Terian said. "I'll pretend I'm someone stupid, like Tolada."

Kahlee's brow wrinkled in confusion. "Who?"

"Never mind." Terian turned his eyes toward the alcove again then back to Kahlee. "What are you doing here? Society party and all that? Doesn't really seem like your sort of soiree."

Kahlee stiffened, and for the first time Terian realized her dress was indeed somewhat formal and vastly different from the servants clothing she'd worn in the market. "Not all of us have the luxury of abandoning our families, Terian. I'm here to do my duty."

Terian felt a low rumble of amusement. "You have your hair dyed like a servant's, you're as thin as a beggar, and you go to the market by yourself dressed like the hired help. I can't help but feel you've bucked more than few familial expectations yourself."

"There is a line between disagreeing with someone and leaving them," Kahlee said, without a trace of amusement. "Here, allow me to demonstrate." With that, she turned and left him standing in the middle of the ballroom. He did not follow, but he did watch her retreat. *I don't mind thin at all ...* He wasn't too proud to notice she looked back once, but only quickly.

Once she was well out of his sight, Terian turned back to the alcove. *Duty. My duty. Family honor. These are the things I need to remember going into this. Not the sight of Kahlee walking away—though I can't imagine what harm that would do—NO! Duty. Family honor.*

With a sharp breath, Terian eased on through the crowd, skirting the edge of conversational circles that moved to let him pass as he threaded his way toward the dark alcove. *Maybe he's not in there.* Terian kept himself from laughing out loud. *And maybe a bounty of ten million gold pieces will fall into my lap so I can leave this hell and start a new life in Aloakna free of worry.*

There was a gap between the last group in conversation and the wall, a gap that was sizable and not at all accidental. *Everyone knows he's here. Guturan must have known, too. Why wouldn't he have said something to prepare me ...? Oh, right. Because he's smart enough to know I might have run as fast as I could to the Unnamed and buried myself in a bottle of Reikonosian whiskey.* He gave it a moment's thought. *But would I have? Really?*

Or would I be standing right here, ready to face the darkness?

He stared into the shadowed alcove and knew that the tentativeness must be present on his face. He willed himself to relax and then stepped up to the edge of the darkness. "My Sovereign ...?" He listened expectantly, hoping deep inside that he would not hear any answer.

"Terian Lepos," came the slow, raspy, dragging response. "Son of my left hand, Heir to the second-most honored house in my land. I look upon your face for the first time." Each word came slowly and sounded oddly snakelike in the hiss. "You have done ... well."

"Thank you, my Sovereign," Terian said and bowed deeply. "Thank you ... My Lord Yartraak. I bow before your darkness."

26.

"Do you see the difference in this city since I have returned?" Yartraak said from within the shadows. Terian could see the inky blackness stirring in the alcove.

Terian tried not to look in at him. *The God of Darkness. The actual God of Darkness. The Sovereign. Gone for a hundred years back to his realm, hiding his face and licking his wounds after leading us to ignominious defeat in the last war. Gods,* Terian thought, realizing the blasphemy of such a simple thought, *if only he'd go back!*

There was a smell that hung in the air, something strong and oily. The ambient noise of the party continued behind him, hushed voices speaking irrelevancies while he paused, then looked into the face of the deity of their nation. *Well, I look into the darkness that contains his face, somewhere.* "I see … people moving with purpose, my Sovereign."

"During the interregnum of my absence, the people languished," Yartraak said. "The Sovereignty folded in upon itself, losing all the territory we had amassed over thousands of years, retreating into the borders of Saekaj Sovar and the uplands above us."

Do I throw Dagonath Shrawn to the wolves by agreeing with him here? It would only take a subtle push. "Naturally," Terian said. "No leader could fill your ... uh ... shoes. You know, if you indeed do wear shoes."

A rasping chuckle came back at him. "I do indeed wear shoes. Made from the skins of my enemies, but shoes nonetheless." Terian heard a deep breath being drawn and wondered if it was his own. "Do I detect a subtle attack at Dagonath Shrawn in your words, Terian Lepos?"

"I don't think it was all that subtle, my Sovereign." *Well, shit, that can't even be written off as a slip of the tongue.*

The rasping laugh came again. "The impetuousness of youth gives your tongue a quicksilver edge. Your father, wiser, more mature, would have gone about it much differently but still driven the same point home."

Terian felt a surge of boldness brought on by the Sovereign's laughter. "What's the point of holding back? You left the Sovereignty in the hands of Shrawn and we shrank while the humans and elves took our territory."

"You might exercise more caution, given that your father has had control of my army during that entire time."

Terian cleared his throat, fighting back the urge to grit his teeth. "Subordinate to the orders of the tribunal. It wasn't as though he could march off and strike through the humans to reclaim what was rightfully ours. Yours," Terian amended. "Rightfully yours."

There was a brief silence from the darkness. "You are blunt to a fault, Terian Lepos. But this is a fruitless discussion, a sifting of old ashes rather than a kindling of new fires. You have returned, and to a city that is once more on the rise. Our army is growing again. Our predations are small now but soon to grow in intensity and boldness. You rejoin us at the cusp of the rise of the Sovereignty to claim our rightful place as the rulers of all Arkaria." There was a pause. "And you sit in the line of succession of the second-most powerful noble house in our land. Tell me, young Terian—do you feel the weight of responsibility upon your shoulders?"

"More and more by the day," Terian said.

"Good. That is as it should be. Your burden was once shirked. You left the path laid out before you in favor of one given by ... that false, thieving, accursed knave who sits atop your former guild."

What? Is he talking about Alaric? Terian kept his face free of any emotion. *Does he even know the man?* "You mean—"

"Do not say his name," Yartraak said. "Forget it, and forget him. Your old comrades do not exist for the purposes of our discussion; best you cleanse your mind of all memories of those days. Focus your thought and attention on your duty and the bright future I see ahead of you ... Lord Terian."

Terian knelt. "As you wish, my Sovereign. I will exert all my energies toward my father's orders ... and your will."

"Excellent." There was a stirring in the darkness. "One other thing ..."

Terian's eyes darted up from where he knelt. "Anything, my Lord Yartraak."

"Your ... evening entertainments," Yartraak said. "It would be exceptionally wise to keep yourself within the bounds of decency. Lest you give your friend Lord Shrawn some additional material with which to convince others of your ... failings."

Terian stared into the darkness and felt his mouth open slightly. The words slipped out before he could pull them back. "Would my spending every evening satiating myself with eighteen whores convince you I am an unworthy heir to the House of Lepos? Or are you concerned with my performance of the tasks you set before me?"

There was a silence broken by a deep, rasped breath. "My concern ... is that a man with so much power at his fingertips, keeps said fingers preoccupied with his duties rather than the pursuit of every leisure that his body compels him toward. If you require satiation, find yourself a mistress." Terian's eyes widened. *At least he didn't say ...* "And find yourself a wife as well." *There it is.* "I may not have interest in these standards, but your fellow members of society do, and staying within the bounds of their societal conventions is not only expected, it is required for one in my service."

There was a long quiet, and then Terian heard a scraping of what sounded like claws on a wood table. "Now, go Terian Lepos, and heed my words ... and soon enough, we shall meet again."

27.

The oily scent that had hung in the air around the alcove lingered as Terian bowed and started back toward the fringes of the crowd of partygoers. His head was swimming with the thoughts of what had taken place in the conversation. *Find a mistress and a wife? No pressure, you just got told what to do by the Sovereign.* His vision seemed to darken, the party ahead under a shroud that he was sure only existed in his mind. Candles and hearths still burned, after all, shedding the same light as he'd seen by before he'd walked to the alcove.

Yet, somehow, the room seemed dimmer to his eyes.

Terian cut a path through the circles of conversing guests, ignoring the stares and murmured comments. The low buzz of conversation was louder now, with voices raised to reach his ears in an attempt to pull him within the bounds of each circle.

"Heir of Lepos is favored by the Sovereign—"

"The House of Shrawn is on the decline, you think?"

"The House of Ehrest will replace them in that seat by year's end—"

"An heir disinherited once will always be in danger of being cast out again—"

He steamed past each of them, not rising to the bait laid out in his path. *Fools. Fools and attention-seekers, trying to cross my path in any way possible. And me, unable to duel.*

Still, his way remained clear, the crowds moving aside and throwing only ill-timed jibes at Terian as he passed. Until he reached one soul who did not move. He was dimly aware of a steel-hued, armored figure in his path, but it took his eyes an unfocused moment to discern what he was seeing.

"Sareea Scyros," Terian said, sighing as he came to a halt. "I should have known you'd be here."

She cocked her head at him, an almost playful trace of a smile perched on her lips. "It is a gathering of the most powerful people and houses in Saekaj. I could scarcely be elsewhere, could I?"

"I think you may have an overinflated opinion of your house's importance," Terian said, and he moved to pass her.

She put out an arm and he stopped, giving her a searing look of annoyance. "Perhaps I'm just calculating and shrewd enough to play the role of importance while I'm securing it for myself. After all, if one acts like a pauper one's whole life, one can scarcely be expected to rise to the nobility."

"A grain mouse could try to act like a vek'tag, but that would hardly make it one," Terian said, and made to pass her by again. She stopped him once more, and he fired her an even more irritated look as he sighed in annoyance. "Do you intend to block my passage all evening, or will I be allowed to go home at some point?"

"According to your father, you're not to leave until a reasonable interval of time has passed," Sareea said, still smiling.

Terian froze. "Gave you those orders, did he?"

"He did." The smile never wavered. "And I'll see they're carried out at any cost—but you already know that."

There was something chilling about the way she said it, so bereft of any emotion, so matter of fact, as though she were simply a party guest having a conversation about some trifling detail. *I don't want to fight her. At least, not here.* "How long is a 'reasonable interval of time'?"

"I'm glad you asked," Sareea said. "Your father was very specific—at least one hour after speaking with the Sovereign. Anything less would seem rude by its very nature. Leave within a half hour, and it would seem rude to the Sovereign to dash out after speaking to him, as though you were affronted in some way. Leave in the half hour after that, and it would be rude to your host and his guests, as though you only came to speak with Sovereign." Her smile remained in full force, cold and yet light. "As though they were insignificant to you."

Terian held his tongue for only a brief second. "They are insignificant to me."

"I know," she said, and her smile broadened, "but best not tell them that." She leaned closer and whispered, "It's against the rules, you see."

"What rules?" Terian could hear the disgust in his own voice.

"Why, the rules of polite society," Sareea said, and now her lip quivered as though her smile were going to break even further out of control. "This is entirely a society of rules. We have rules for everything—where you can live, what you can do, who you can speak to, how you can speak to them, who you can touch, who you can sleep with," her expression changed not a whit. "Only a fool fails to notice the rules in this country, and all fools end up in the Depths sooner or later." She let that statement hang between them as her nostrils flared and she drew a deep breath. "You don't strike me as an utter fool, Terian, though you do some very foolish things at times."

"Oh, really?" Terian asked and kept his anger under wraps. "Such as?"

"Did you really think your father was going to let me stay permanently dead?" Her smile trod the line close to a sneer but stopped short.

"Personally, I wouldn't have risked it if I were you," Terian said, "but I suppose I know him better than you."

"You know nothing," Sareea said. "This is how the game is played."

"I don't see a game," Terian said.

"Then perhaps you are a fool indeed," Sareea said as the crowd bustled around them. "This is all a game, every bit of it. The rules are part of it. Sacrificing things of worth is never done pointlessly, it is always done for a reason. Your father knows how to play this game well, which is why he is now sitting at the left hand of the Sovereign. He calculates. He weighs the odds, weighs the alternatives, considers his actions to greatest effect. Why would he pointlessly kill a new knight sent to him when he can find use for her?"

"Oh, I don't know," Terian said with a sneer, "but I've seen him do it before." He made to brush past her but this time she interposed her body against his, their armor clacking against each other's as she leaned close and whispered in his ear.

"You've seen him make calculated sacrifices," she said, "seen him do things to profit himself and his house. You've watched with the emotion of a child while he put aside emotion to make choices that vaulted him upward. Your father is not a fool, and you would do well to remember it. My resurrection after my sacrifice was as assured as him ordering me to kill you afterward." He could feel her hot breath on his neck, on his ear as her warm whisper carried past his cheek.

She's crazy. She just smiled back at him, motionless, with that same slightly unhinged smile of cold pleasure. "You're putting your faith in the wrong man," he said. "Or to put it in your words, when the calculation turns against you, when you are no longer of service to his plans, your resurrection won't be assured. Only your death."

She never flinched. "That's part of the game here."

Terian leaned closer to her, and his every word came out with burning heat. "This isn't a game to me."

She did not stop smiling. "Then that is why you will lose." With that, she removed her arm, and he passed her by, not taking his eyes off of her.

28.

What. A. Witch. And I don't mean the kind that casts the good spells, either. Terian's anger burned blindingly bright as he threaded his way through the crowd, avoiding hip checking guests out of the way only because Guturan's command about not dueling was echoing in his head. The smells of the buffet table grew strong as he approached, drawing him like a beacon of comforting light in the dimness of the ballroom. *I don't know why I'm coming over here; I'm not even hungry.*

The scent of chicken and fish from the surface, along with beef and pork was nearly overwhelming. *The strongest smell in our house is that mushroom mess that my father eats.* He swept along the edge of the buffet table, passing fattened party goers, gorging themselves on the House of Shrawn's culinary treats.

Terian found himself lingering next to a tray of chicken drizzled with some thick, creamy cheese sauce. He took a breath and the smell was almost intoxicating in its richness. *A far cry from what I was eating in the boarding house on my guard pay.* A steward brushed past holding high a tray of crystal glasses filled with some wine of foreign import, and Terian grabbed one in his gauntleted fingers as it passed, slugging it down before placing it delicately back on the tray.

"Another, sir?" the steward asked.

"I'd better stop at one," Terian said, turning his attention back to the buffet. He grabbed one of the aromatic chicken and cheese creations and slipped it into his mouth. It was rich and warm, a flaky crust undergirding the little hors d'oeuvre. The whole thing seemed to dissolve in his mouth, spreading the flavor all over his tongue. *That's more delicious than anything I've eaten since I left Sanctuary.*

"It would appear you've found your way to the best company in the room," came a voice from Terian's left. He turned to see a man in a fine grey coat bearing a long black walking stick. It was no dueling cane; this one was actually used for walking, he could tell by the scuffing at the tip. He stared at the man who carried it, blinking at him. *I know his face, but damned if I can remember his name ...*

"You don't recognize me," the man said. "That doesn't happen very often, but I suppose you've been gone a long time. My name is Vincin Ehrest."

The third most powerful man in Saekaj. "Of course I remember you," Terian said with a quick bow of his head. "Kahlee's father."

Vincin Ehrest let escape a small chuckle. "I'm not often remembered by my daughter, though I suppose she does catch a few more eyes nowadays with the blue hair."

"I simply meant that I know her," Terian said. "I'm sure we've met on countless occasions in the past, you and I."

"Undoubtedly," Vincin said, nodding as he turned his attention to the chicken canapé that Terian had just taken a bite of. "At these events it's impossible not to run across the same people over and over. The same conversations, the same recurring themes discussed in infinite detail. 'Do you remember that time that Madame Yoilotte leaned over the buffet table and it collapsed under her weight?' "He shook his head. "It would be hard to forget such an occasion, though it doesn't stop it from being brought up every single time."

Terian stood there at attention, taking the man's story in. "I suppose it would be rather hard to forget the sight of a plump woman crashing through a buffet table."

Vincin Ehrest laughed. "She was married less than a month later. Her weight was taken as a sign of her prosperity, and the fool who married her has only his own idiocy to blame that she ate through her dowry." Terian shook his head but said nothing. "We live in an idiotic society, do we not?" Vincin asked.

Terian stiffened. "The Sovereign is wise in all his ways—"

"I'm not talking about the Sovereign," Ehrest said, waving a hand at him dismissively. "I'm talking about the toadying, the favor currying, the 'throw your neighbor under the vek'tag carriage for a chance at taking his home in the Shuffle' attitude that pervades our society."

He speaks the truth but ... he could be trying to ensnare me in treason. "I would agree with you, provided you lay the blame where it belongs—on the people who engage in such ridiculousness, not on the Sovereign." Terian smiled.

"Of course, of course," Vincin said. "You can't blame the source of the river if the stream gets contaminated down the way. All this is the result of the people of Saekaj growing fat and indulgent, drunk on the smell of their own excrement. The Sovereign of course guides us, leads us in paths of discipline and strength." *He says it fairly convincingly*, Terian thought. "No, my gripe is with the people who carry the competition to a ridiculous extreme."

Which the Sovereign encourages. "Of course. Though since I must confess having been absent for the last few years, and never present during a time when the Shuffle was going on, I don't really know what you're talking about—"

"Naturally, my boy, quite naturally," Vincin said, taking stock of him. Cool purple eyes were surveying him. *Does he see I'm indulging him or is he just trying to decide if I'm marking him as a traitor in my head?* "I forgot that you're young. I'm an old man, and I've seen ... much. But of course, you would not know. Let me give you an example—Lord Tiskind and his Lady were recently found by the Saekaj militia to have orchestrated the murders of the entire House of Jernarr."

Terian raised an eyebrow. "Well, that's ... shocking."

"Indeed," Vincin said. "Of course, the Jernarr were several houses ahead of them in the line, so the murders allowed them to be brought a step closer to favor."

"Until the truth came out?" Terian asked, reaching idly for another bite of the chicken. The smell was wafting at him.

"Oh, no, the murders had no effect on their rise in standing." Vincin wore a sliver of a smile. "I believe they got a mild admonishment, but the House of Jernarr had recently fallen into disfavor and were expected to be Shuffled down sometime soon anyway. This merely hastened their downfall and made it a touch more ... permanent."

Terian realized his hand had frozen in front of his mouth, the chicken canapé held mere centimeters from his lips. "You're joking."

"Oh, no," Vincin said, shaking his head. "The message was clear, of course—do whatever you wish to those who have entered disfavor. I wonder how long it will be until a full-scale war between the houses breaks loose." He turned his head and Terian realized for the first time that his hair was a silver-white rather than the clean white of a young man. *How old is he?* Terian noticed a hunch in his back, the slight stoop of age. "That should be an interesting bit of business, don't you think? House warring with House, blood in the streets of Saekaj?"

Terian did not answer, still holding the canapé in front of his mouth. "I don't ... imagine that will be much good for anyone."

"Oh, but it will," Vincin Ehrest said, shrugging slightly. "See, it will be good for determining which houses are on the rise, which ones have power—and which are on the decline. Nothing lasts forever, not even here in Saekaj." He tilted his head slightly to Terian. "It's in the wind, as they say on the surface, and in time it will come blowing our way." He smiled. "It was nice to speak with you, young man. I think I like you. You still wear your emotions on your face, unlike so many." He clapped Terian on the shoulder and Terian noticed the veiny hand, wrinkles beginning to manifest themselves.

"I don't—" Terian said, almost stuttering, "I mean, I don't mean to—"

"It is not a mark against you, son," Vincin said, letting his cane click hard against the floor as he started away. "It's a mark in your favor. Take it as the compliment it was intended." With a last nod of his head at Terian, he disappeared into the black and white sea of party guests.

29.

"It sounds as though you had quite the time," Dahveed said to him, cutting the silence in the carriage.

"Oh yeah, it was a ball," Terian said as the carriage rattled and thumped its way down the long passage. Terian glanced out the carriage window and saw only a small stream of traffic outside. It was the early hours of the morning, hours after the ball had ended, and they were descending. He'd seen Sovar's gates pass on his left a short while earlier, the lower chamber already buzzing with activity the way he'd once seen a hive of bees stirred.

And just as likely to sting if we don't solve this food problem, Terian thought. He blinked, trying to keep his mind focused on the task at hand.

"So, you spoke with Vincin Ehrest at some length?" Dahveed asked, spoiling Terian's attempt to keep his thoughts on their destination.

"Yes," Terian said with a sigh. *Dahveed won't let this journey pass in silence, I suspect.* "He seemed ... how do I put this without overstating it? He seemed very critical of the Shuffle and all the fruits it has produced of late."

"Hrm," Dahveed said with his usual knowing smile. "Hard to believe that the number three man in Sovar would find fault with a system that has allowed him to ascend so high."

"I think House Ehrest has actually waned," Terian said. "Weren't they number two until my father came along?"

"Oh, yes, you're quite right," Dahveed said, looking unsurprised. "How could I have forgotten?"

"You didn't," Terian said. "You just wanted to see if I remembered."

"I can hardly be faulted for testing you now and again," Dahveed said. "After all, it is a complicated game that is played in Saekaj; it's hard to keep track of the rise and fall of so many houses, especially so many that are of little import to the overall picture." He tapped the bridge of his nose idly. "Though you'd be surprised how much of a role they play in the overall scheme of things."

"No house ascends on its own," Terian said, stating an oft-spoken proverb, "and none descends entirely of its own efforts either."

"House Lepos was the first to break that mold," Dahveed said, "if you recall your history."

"I recall," Terian said tightly. "We never needed allies before."

"Your father has a few now." There was a bump in the carriage as Dahveed spoke, and Terian braced himself in the seat.

"I'm sure they're very helpful to him," Terian said, looking out the window. The iron gates of the Depths peered at him from his right, forbidding and tightly shut. Guards wearing the black, boiled leather of vek'tag skin armor watched the carriage as it passed. *Even the symbol of House Lepos does not spare us from their wary eyes. And wary they should be, guarding the entirety of the Sovereign's criminals and undesirables.* Stone towers flanked either side of the gate, and Terian knew without looking that the guards atop them were staring down at their carriage as well.

"They are vital to him," Dahveed said, breaking Terian's musings about the security measures of the Depths. "They provide a variety of services, up to and including keeping an ear to the ground throughout Saekaj and Sovar to keep him apprised of things that Dagonath Shrawn might not want to pass his way."

"If you say so," Terian said, turning his attention back to Dahveed. The healer sat with one foot up on the bench, looking as comfortable as he was casual, his healer robes draped over him and his sash around his neck. "Seems to me if we could climb to the top of the heap without them, it hardly makes sense to pick up clingers-on once we're there."

"I haven't spoken with your father in depth about the subject," Dahveed said, "but I have to imagine it's a different game once you reach the number two house. Before it was only a question of climbing. Now it becomes about trying to climb while maintaining your current foothold. Many a bold misstep's been made while seeking purchase on higher ground."

"I wouldn't know anything about that," Terian said, looking at the dull metal of his gauntlet. He let out a slow breath. The one sip of wine he'd had at the ball had done little for him but make him crave more. *A craving I will keep under control.* He watched his gauntlet shake slightly at the thought of drink.

"I suppose not," Dahveed said with that same aggravating smile as the carriage rolled on. The thumping increased as they kept going along the path until Terian felt the carriage slow as it wended its way through a series of turns. Terian stuck his head out the window as the cavern widened ahead of them, the tunnel giving over to a massive clay beach. He could see the ruts where the fish wagons parked themselves near the docks.

Water lapped at the edge of the clay beach, making a curious, echoing noise that somehow overcame the dullish roar of the fishmongers and fishermen. Terian had been here before, long ago, and remembered the roar being louder. It was subdued now, the air laden with dankness and fear, as well as the smell of fish.

"Now that's an aroma I haven't forgotten," Dahveed said with good humor. "Puts me in the mood for a fish bone stew."

"I suspect you could afford a whole fish now, Dahveed," Terian said, looking over the docks. Countless wood-plank tendrils stretched out into the blackness of the Great Sea. The cavern ceiling was barely visible overhead, the width of the massive chamber stretching off into a distance too far to see.

"I probably could, but I'd take the bones just for the sake of nostalgia."

"You sound like my father with his gruel," Terian said absently as he stared out at the colorful garb of the fishermen. *No pretense here, no black and white pride keeping them from using the wildroot dyes.* Terian took a breath and it was like a nose full of the Reikonos docks, a place he had rarely gone in his time in the city. *Quieter, though.*

"Most people would take that as a compliment," Dahveed said, strangely indifferent.

"Do you take it as an insult?" Terian asked, still transfixed by the sight of the boats at the end of the docks. There were more of them than he could count. Hundreds, perhaps.

"I don't worry much about such things," Dahveed said. "I am but a simple healer, and effrontery to my ears passes lightly and without consequence. No, I worry more about the real blades that come my way, not the verbal ones."

"I doubt you see many of those these days," Terian said.

"Not since the last war, no," Dahveed said with his usual amusement. "But I expect any day now that will change."

"We're here," Terian said as the carriage ground to a halt. Terian opened the door before the driver could get down to open it himself, prompting a look of consternation from the driver—*at his "failure,"* no doubt. Terian brushed past the man without saying anything, making for the latticework of docks that lay ahead. Fish carts passed him, half laden or empty, the men pushing them muttering forlornly about days gone by. The smell of fish nearly took his breath away.

"You can see the change undergone in this place, can you not?" Dahveed said, catching up to him to walk alongside. "The men with their stooped backs, downcast eyes."

"Sounds like all the men of Sovar," Terian said. *No, that's not true. There is a difference here.*

"These were not like all the men of Sovar," Dahveed said. "These were men with work and purpose and little enough supervision breathing down the back of their shirts. To be a fishermen in the Great Sea was to live at least in the Middles, if not closer to the Front Gate. They were men as close to free as you could get down here." Terian realized Dahveed was whispering. "There were tunes whistled from their lips on every occasion I've had to visit down here—and I've made quite a few."

"You do enjoy the smell of fish, eh?" Terian asked as he took his first step onto a wooden dock. It creaked with his weight and gave him pause for just a moment. A whole market and web of docks ahead of him belied the idea that this one plank would drop him into the water that waited mere inches below.

"I enjoy the smell of freedom," Dahveed said. "Which is why I avoid the surface farms most conscientiously."

Terian paused and looked back. Dahveed wore a tight-lipped smile and his eyes glimmered for just a moment. *You do enjoy treading close to that treasonous line yourself, don't you, Dahveed? It seems like I'm drawing these sentiments to myself of late, as though people can sense my reluctance to embrace this world.*

"I think I see Grinnd and Verret waiting up ahead," Dahveed said, nodding toward a fisherman's boat in the distance.

"Then I suppose the rest will be nearby," Terian said, turning back to look in the direction Dahveed had been pointing. Sure enough, under a bright red sail, he could see the outline of Grinnd's muscled form, chatting amiably with a sea captain in bright green vek'tag silks that were showing more than a little wear.

"The rest are very nearby," came a soft voice at his side. He felt the clank of armor lightly tapping his and looked to his side to see Sareea Scyros watching him, her white hair and lively eyes at odds with the dispassionate look on her face. "You should do a better job of watching your back for threats."

"I'm on a dock in the Great Sea," Terian said. "What threats need I be concerned about? Some angry fishmonger upset at my father for not conquering new waters for him to trawl?"

"You never know," Sareea said in a throaty whisper, leaning to speak into his ear. "After all, you're the width of a silk strand away from someone who has recently killed you, and you never saw my approach." She pulled away from him, and he did not deign to look at her as she took up position next to him as he resumed his walk. The cool cave air prickled his skin. *Or is that something else?*

"You have a report for me?" Terian asked. "Or were you just malingering in hopes of ambushing me for your own entertainment?"

"My own entertainment?" Sareea asked, amused. "All I do, I do for the Sovereign—and of course for the greatness of House Lepos."

"And your own, presumably?" Terian asked.

"Somewhere down the line," Sareea agreed, but in the way she said it, Terian caught more of her amusement than truth.

Terian steered his course over the docks, the clunking of his boots and Sareea's keeping time with their march. As he weaved around a right turn onto a quay, he realized that Xemlinan was waiting in the shadows of an upturned crate. The smell of fish was stronger here, and it made Terian's nose curl. Sareea wisely said nothing, and Dahveed did not speak either. The clunking of the boots on the dock was all the sound Terian heard until he got close enough to hear Grinnd's enthusiastic tones.

"Report?" Terian asked as he closed in on Grinnd. The big man was still in conversation with the sea captain, nodding along with something the captain said. He turned at Terian's voice.

"Ah, you're here," Grinnd said with his usual smile. *It's unseemly for a warrior to be so damned friendly and happy.* "I've got quite a lot to report, actually."

"Almost all of it sap and silliness," Verret said, lurking in the shadows near Xemlinan's upturned crate.

"Almost all of it interesting," Grinnd corrected, not backing off his smile. "Twenty-seven boats have gone missing in the last three weeks alone."

"Is that a lot?" Terian asked. "Comparatively speaking, I mean?"

"They typically lose one per year," Grinnd said, "and there are almost always survivors. Not a single survivor has turned up from these, so—yes, it's a lot. There were more before that, but the harbormaster wasn't keeping a tally until the numbers got high enough to catch his notice."

"A real 'big picture' sort of fellow," Xem said with a dose of irony. "Clearly concerned about the well-being of those sailing from his port."

"I got the sense that he didn't care about much of anything so long as his quotas weren't affected," Verret said with an air of irritation. "I would recommend to your father to have that one sent to the Depths and replaced by someone more competent—and less drunk. The man is clearly a traitor by his dereliction of his post."

"Tell my father yourself if you feel that strongly about it," Terian said. *I don't really want to be responsible for some poor, sodden bastard getting that treatment.*

"The disappearances happened all over the Great Sea," Grinnd said, apparently unfazed by Verret's diatribe. "No one specific area that the ships were fishing. Most of the fleet is sticking close by the shores at present, and fish yields are dropping by the day."

"Getting messy," Xem said. "I'd say it's a mess best left to someone else, but since your father assigned us this duty ..." He sighed. "What now, Terian?"

"We go out on the sea, I guess," Terian said, unblinking. "Figure out what this is for ourselves." He looked to Grinnd. "What are you thinking?"

"I am but asking questions of these people, my friend," Grinnd said with a warm smile. "I leave it to smarter men than me to draw conclusions."

"Grinnd," Terian said, "there aren't many smarter men in Saekaj Sovar than you. You have a working theory, yes?" He waited for Grinnd to nod. "Out with it."

Grinnd took a deep breath and sighed, tapping his big fingers on his dark-plated armor as he adjusted the swords across his back without any apparent thought. "The disappearances are quite vexing. My first instinct might run to pirates."

"Pirates?" Verret said, turning his head to look at Grinnd as though the warrior were mad. "On the enclosed, buried Great Sea?"

"Aye," Grinnd said, "it was but a working hypothesis that I quickly rejected. The men who know the Great Sea tell me that there aren't any coves or grounds where any such pirates might be hiding. And the difficulty of maintaining a ship, overpowering crews—it just doesn't sound feasible given that secrecy would be of the utmost importance. The moment that secrecy ended, the Sovereign's own wrath would descend upon the pirates, and the Great Sea offers little in the way of hiding places. In addition, these fishing trawlers are not exactly prizes."

"Thank you for walking us through your thought process on how you ruled out what isn't responsible," Verret said. "Perhaps now you might share what you believe is happening—"

"There are several theories—" Grinnd said.

"Cut to the chase," Terian said. "Most likely culprit."

Grinnd took another deep breath. "Sea monster, I think."

There was an air of quiet among the group. "This is your theory?" Verret asked, incredulous. "A sea monster? Some great threat hiding beneath the lapping waves?"

"Yes," Grinnd said, nodding sagely. "I think that's it. Some transplanted beast that belongs outside of these caves, in the open water, where the diet can include larger sea life. I think whatever it is that's doing this, it's ill suited to this environment and forced to feed on our people because they're all it has. The fish that live in the outside world cannot survive down here without some specific adaptations—"

"Blather on, man of science," Verret said. "This is all preposterous."

"Preposterous as it may sound," Grinnd said with a light sigh, "I believe a large aquatic creature from one of the freshwater lakes—perhaps even Lake Magnus—has been introduced into the Great Sea, and it's eating the only thing it can reasonably find to subsist on—the fishermen."

Verret started to speak again. "This is—"

"Preposterous, yes," Terian said, stroking his chin. "You've said that. Grinnd, assuming you were right, how would we even go about rooting something like this out?"

"We would have to take a fishing trawler out," Grinnd said, "and attempt to locate the creature—which I suspect would not be hard. It's doubtless hungry, having not had anything venture out far enough to become fodder for it in a week or more. Once we found it, we would have to kill it—and then preferably bring it back for study—"

"Find it and kill it," Terian said, his eyes falling on the blackness of the water extending in front of him. "It's destroyed every boat that's come its way."

"None of these fishermen were armed, I should point out," Grinnd said. "That put them at a significant disadvantage. They were probably plucked and eaten while trying to swim to shore." He paused. "We'll need to dispense with our armor in case the boat is destroyed."

"I like this idea not at all," Xem said. "Actually, why am I even here? I'm no use at fighting sea monsters. Never done it before. If you need a bit of thieving done, though—"

"We all go," Terian said, studying the dark waves. It felt as though he could see motion beneath them, as though they were teeming with life just beneath the surface. "No armor, like Grinnd said. It'll just weigh us down if we end up having to go in. But we carry our weapons, because they'll be our salvation if we run across this thing."

"It eats boats," Bowe Sturrt said from behind Terian. He turned and realized that the druid had been sitting there in a meditative position, legs crossed before him on the docks, his hair stirring as he turned his head to look at Terian. "No wreckage. What can weapons do against such a beast?"

"There aren't any currents in here," Grinnd said. "Doubtful it eats the whole boat. Probably enough to reduce it to wreckage, which fails to wash ashore due to the lack of currents." He blinked, almost embarrassed. "That's just a theory, though. It's probably susceptible to magic and blades."

"'Probably' is thin armor with which to gird ourselves," Sareea said quietly.

"We have a job to do," Terian said. *She's right. But how can I return to my father and tell him I didn't do this assignment he ordered me to look into because it didn't seem safe?* He almost laughed. *Nothing we do is safe. That's the hallmark of our jobs.* "We go. Grinnd, we'll need a fishing trawler."

"This kind gentleman has already has volunteered his." Grinnd nodded at the sea captain he'd been speaking to. The green-robed man bowed. "Though he did emphasize that it's a very easy craft to steer and row, without any necessity for himself or his crew to come along."

Terian looked at the green-clad captain, and saw the fear in the man's eyes as he bowed low again. "Fine, he can stay here. It's a long cave anyway, it's not like we're going anywhere but directly out to sea and back when we're done." He glanced around. "Take off your armor if you can't swim in it, just in case." His gaze came around to Sareea. "You can stay here if you'd like."

She cocked an eyebrow at him. "And give you the opportunity to tell your father that I did not come along on this assignment which he gave to us?" She reached for the clasps that anchored her breastplate to her backplate. "Unlikely."

"I was just giving you the option," Terian said, removing his helm. "All right, crew—we've got some rowing to do." He turned his eyes toward the dark waters again. "Best get ready."

30.

Terian stood at the fore of the ship. He could almost feel his body shivering in the chill of the cave air. It wasn't as cold as Reikonos in winter, but he'd grown used to the fires burning in the grates, the heavy blankets when he slept. *Sanctuary. I'm thinking about Sanctuary again.* He cursed quietly and heard the words echo softly over the black water of the Great Sea.

The sea air was different down here. Musty, with a curious odor to it that reminded him of the smell of his laundered smallclothes when they were drying on the line. The lapping of the waters at the bow of the boat was quiet compared to the grunting of Grinnd, Verret, Sareea and Xem manning the oars. Grinnd was outpacing them all, having taken the whole of the left side to himself and powering the boat with swift, sure strokes.

"All this labor is warming me," Xem said, mopping his brow with a vek'tag silk handkerchief. He had removed his fine shirt, as had Verret and Grinnd. Sareea sat behind them both, eyes fixed on a point directly ahead, seemingly empty of any interest. She, too, had removed her shirt, which he thought curious. It didn't feel warm in here to him. *But I've been gone from this place for so many years that I've grown used to the out-of-doors.*

Terian tried not to stare at Sareea. None of the others seemed to be giving her much of a look. A bare chest on a woman was an unusual thing in common company. *It's not modest,* Terian thought. *But a bare chest on a soldier is quite common, and I suspect she's aiming to play to that angle.* His eyes danced over her once and then returned to safer ground. *She's not all that remarkable or different from the men, anyhow, I suppose. Certainly not like the ladies of the brothels with their pushed-up breasts. Probably helps her fit in with the soldiers during training—though I wouldn't want to cross her.*

"Anyone need a break?" Terian asked, looking over them. Dahveed and Bowe waited at the back of the boat, next to the till. Dahveed had his hand on it, steering, a peaceful expression on his face. Bowe had resumed his meditation, eyes closed. "Sareea?" Terian's eyes found her again as she continued to pull on the heavy oar, working it as her shoulder muscles showed with the effort she put in. "Do you need me to take over for a spell?"

"I'm quite fine, thank you," she replied, her voice as placid as if he'd asked her if the caves were still cold and dank. Her eyes were unmoving, still on a flat line in front of her, gazing past Xem and Verret in front of her along a straight line.

"I could use a break, now that you mention it," Xem said, pulling his oar one last time before dragging it back in with a sigh. "Light of the sky, that's exhausting."

"I'll spell you for a bit," Terian said, making his way down the center aisle separating the benches on the trawler. It was a small boat, only twenty feet long and narrow enough for only one person to sit on the benches on each side—barely. Grinnd was hanging off into the aisle on his side.

Terian made his way to the middle bench, sandwiching himself between Verret in front of him and Sareea behind. He fell into an easy rhythm, pulling at the same time as they did. He glanced at Grinnd to see if the big man was moderating his pace. He was, a pleasant smile on his face as he pulled lazily upon the oar.

Terian found he lost his breath after a few minutes of pulling, the effort working a far different set of muscles than his usual swordplay did. Verret was gasping in front of him, pulling in a frenzied hurry now, sweat trickling down his spine. Terian watched as Verret strained, then strained some more trying to keep up with the pace set by Grinnd. When Terian glanced over to the big warrior, he appeared undisturbed, but his oar was moving with a speed that Terian could scarcely believe.

"All right, that's it!" Verret slammed his oar down and it rattled across the Great Sea, echoing. "Now you're just showing off."

Terian glanced at Grinnd, who appeared startled, as though he'd been jarred awake. "What?"

"Never mind," Verret said and pulled his oar back into the boat. "Slow down, fool, lest you put us into a slow spin on the water." He stood and grabbed his shirt, cursing loudly as he stormed toward the back of the boat.

"He seems agitated about something," Grinnd said, mystified. "I suppose I should go see what's wrong."

"That could take a while," Terian said.

"Hmmm," Grinnd said with consternation. "I suppose I could sit in the middle of the boat and row both sides ..."

"I'll take over for you," Sareea said in an empty tone. "We won't make as much progress, but we won't drift in slow circles, either."

"All right," Grinnd said, and Terian could sense his hesitation. The smell of dank air was heavier now that they were out to sea. "I'll see if I can assuage his hurt feelings—whatever might have caused them." The entire boat creaked and rocked as Grinnd made his way toward the stern of the boat.

Terian kept his eyes forward as Sareea took up the seat next to his and began to row. He let his breaths flow in and out as he rowed, ignoring the aches in his arms.

"You're going to continue to play the game of not looking at me, aren't you?" Sareea said quietly, but he could hear that familiar amusement.

"Just trying to be polite," Terian said, keeping his eyes forward. "I wouldn't stare at Grinnd or Verret with their shirts off."

"And if you did, we'd all worry you were a deviant," Sareea said. "Still, I'm not Grinnd or Verret. You can stare if you want. I don't mind."

Terian glanced at her, careful to keep his eyes on her face. "I'm fine, thanks." He turned his head back to face the bow.

"Ooh, it's almost entertaining to watch you fight your own nature," she said. "I've heard about you."

"About my fine talent for japes and my finer talent for good conversation?"

"I've heard both and I think they need work," she said. "I've heard you've visited every cheap whorehouse in the land looking for places to deposit your yearnings."

"That's a vicious and ugly rumor, spread by the people who know me best," Terian said. "So what?"

"It doesn't have to be that way," Sareea said.

Terian felt a creeping sense that he knew what she was about to say. "Why? Because you'd gladly offer yourself instead?"

Sareea was quiet for a moment. "I see you've had this proposal before."

"Once or twice," Terian said, keeping his eyes fixed straight ahead. "But strangely, I get the feeling that it's never because of my rugged good looks or sparkling personality."

"Of course not," Sareea said. "You could have both of those things and it would be only an added bonus. It's all about power."

Terian stared at the dark horizon, trying to determine where in the muddy bleakness the Great Sea met the cave. He couldn't see it. "Well, at least you're honest about that. The flatterers always get my bile."

"I could be a balm to you," Sareea said. "Could soothe those aches you need taken care of." He still did not look at her. "And having a mistress is much more socially acceptable than visiting the whorehouses of Sovar. It's practically a requirement of polite society."

"Another fine reason why I dislike our society."

"Which is a funny line of argument coming from a man who visits whorehouses," she said.

"An unmarried, unattached man who visits whorehouses." Terian felt the first stirrings of heat in his cheeks. *Maybe it is warm in here.* "There's no one who cares other than the prissy faces of Saekaj social circles who have too much idle time to fill and not enough juicy gossip for their continuous blather."

"I'm not judging," Sareea said. "Merely offering a more ... palatable alternative."

"What makes you think I'd find you—" He whirled around to look at her and found her turned to face him, her oar on the ground and her bare chest right there to greet him. "... palatable?" *Well, that's not bad.*

She waited a moment before responding. "I think you'd find me ... energetic. A worthy consort for the Heir of Lepos."

He turned back to his oar, picked it up and continued rowing, but with more fervor this time. He could feel the slight breeze on his face from the motion of the boat. He heard Sareea mimic his motion across the aisle. "I think I'd find myself quite ill at the notion of being socially acceptable at the cost of being with a woman who has no interest in me."

"Oh, and I suppose the whores you visit find you fascinating."

"When you've got a sack full of gold on your belt, they certainly act like you're the most interesting man in the land," Terian said, feeling the heat fade from his cheeks. A cold settled on them.

"I don't see a difference in the arrangement I propose," Sareea said. "I'm merely allying myself with power instead of asking for petty coin. I'm already in the favor of your father—"

Terian let a low sigh. "I know you're doing this for the wrong reasons, but I don't think you're aware of the consequences. My father would never consent to a marriage—"

"Between us, I know," Sareea said. "Assuming you even wanted such a thing, I'm a social inferior who is already in the service of your house." Terian looked over at her, alarmed. "I told you—I know how the game is played," she said with a smile. "I harbor no illusions about what our dalliance might bring in terms of long-term benefits. I suspect I can convince you of my short-term worth, though, and that has its own rewards."

"Uh huh," Terian said. "Some trade contracts of lesser import thrown the way of your house. A job in the customs office with a fat stipend for one of your relatives. Better standing at the next ball." Terian shook his head. *Predictable.*

"Those are the sort of things your father can toss as easily as a bone to a dog," Sareea said, and he could hear her rowing still, with the same steady rhythm. "Yet to us dogs, they are everything."

"This is obscene," Terian said. *I'm not sure if it's my sense of propriety that's offended, but something is definitely breaking inside me right now, because I'm feeling ill at this suggestion. And that takes some doing for me.*

"But you feel good about throwing gold to a girl from the Back Deep who's selling her body to you for a night for much less reward." That got him to turn his head, and his cheeks were burning again. Sareea did not even look at him as she rowed, but she wore a placid smile. "It's interesting, isn't it?"

"What?" Terian heard his voice crack, unintentionally.

"The little lies we tell ourselves to explain our own hypocrisies." She rowed, and he saw a bead of sweat trace a slow line down her forehead to her temple, tracking its way down her dark blue skin.

"You think I'm a hypocrite?" Terian asked. His voice felt stronger. His anger had faded, replaced by a sort of gut-level weariness, wrapped in a feeling that something horrible was about to happen, completely unrelated to where they were.

"I think your attitude toward using women is hypocritical," Sareea said. "The thought of using me with my full knowledge and consent to the barter bothers you, but using a woman in far more dire straits does not." She smiled as she turned her head to him. "Does that not strike you as the worst sort of hypocrisy?"

Terian made no reply because he had no immediate reply to make. The gentle quiet of the oars hitting the water in time was interrupted by Bowe's deep voice somewhere behind him. "It comes."

Terian blinked and held fast his oar. "Wait, what?"

"I hear something," Sareea said, suddenly still. Terian could hear the drip of the water off his oar into the Great Sea in the silence. All were still on the boat, still as death.

Then, in the dark, in the quiet, he heard it too. A rippling in the water, something beneath the surface making its way ... up.

31.

"Brace yourselves," Terian said, pulling his sword from the scabbard on his belt. He felt nearly naked in only his underclothes. *The sword helps, but armor would be better. Until I sank to the bottom with it weighing me down. I can't believe Father never got me a set of mystical armor like—*

Something jarred the boat, hard enough that Terian had to brace himself against the bench in front of him to keep from falling. There was something else added to the dank smell now, something worse than fish: deep, like blood but heavier. He listened and heard the water rippling as though a stream were flowing nearby. He cast a look around and saw nothing but the Great Sea in all directions, the sea and water that was beginning to churn off the bow of the boat.

"That way!" Xem shouted, pointing off the left side of the ship. Terian stood, still hunched enough to brace himself on the bench, and readied his sword. He could see what Xem had pointed to, the same spot in the water that looked as though a tornado was moving beneath the surface.

"What foul beast is this?" Grinnd said from somewhere in the back of the boat.

"It is your overdeveloped sense of drama," Verret snapped back at him, "run completely amok and split loose of any semblance of common sense to ground it."

"I would have said sea monster, myself," Dahveed said with a calm Terian most certainly did not feel. "But I think I'd find Grinnd's sense of drama a welcome departure from my expectations."

A quiet fell as the churning water burbled. Bubbles broke to the surface with pops as though the water were boiling. It held its place, just off the bow, waiting.

"What the hells is it?" Xem asked. Nervous tension shot through his voice, and his hands grasped his daggers and held them in front of him as though it were going to leap out of the water for him to strike.

"I'm afraid we'll find that out soon enough, whether we want to or not," Dahveed said.

The bubbling stopped, and silence reigned. *Where did it go?* Terian wondered but kept his question to himself. *It was just sitting there, and now it's gone?*

The boat bobbed from the water's disturbance, and Terian could feel it gently swaying back and forth beneath his legs. He waited. Xem was frozen at the front of the ship, staring into the dark waters with a look of horror. Sareea stood directly across the aisle from him, her curved sword now drawn as well.

She caught his eye and nodded at him. He wondered at her meaning but had no time to decipher it before something bumped the boat.

It was a gentle bump, one that jarred Terian only slightly. His breath caught in his throat as he kept his balance.

The lapping of the waters at the hull grew more insistent—a steady, maddening sound as though the sea were trying to slowly consume the boat.

Another thump drove Terian to his knees. Angry screams of the wooden hull, tested for its strength, filled the air. A few cracks followed as timbers met their match, and a trickling noise of water streaming into the boat washed over them.

"Not good," Verret said. "This boat is not going to make it back to shore like this—"

"I don't think this boat was ever going to make it back to shore," Terian said and turned his eyes toward Sareea again. Her gaze met his and she nodded again, just once. In agreement.

The boat rocked again with the full snapping of planks this time, and Terian was thrown against the side. Something broke through the bottom. Tall and dark, like a mast sticking out of the middle of the ship, it writhed.

Terian stared at it from where he lay. Water was pouring in from the hole it had made. He could feel it wetting his back, his hands. He started to force himself back to his feet but the ship was jarred again.

It's a tentacle.

He realized it with a certain amount of shock. He'd seen the squids brought into the Reikonos market. Little things, most of them, no more than a few feet long for the biggest of them.

Except ...

There had been one. He'd heard about it, years ago, and had gone to Reikonos with some other members of Sanctuary to see it. Niamh had carried them there on the winds of a teleportation spell. It was the talk of all the land. A sea beast so large that it hung as tall as a titan across a beam planted at the docks. People were crowded around it in amazement, teleporting in from as far away as Oortrais, Pharesia and Fertiss.

A squid bigger than a giant.

Terian felt himself groan in pain and anticipation. The boat lurched as the tentacle moved. It slid down and withdrew, shaking the boat as it did. Water gushed in through the hole it had made at the bottom of the hull.

"This is all wrong!" Grinnd said. "That looks like a saltwater squid, but this is fresh water—"

"Save the analysis for after it kills me, please," Verret said, his voice muffled. Terian looked back to see his face buried in the deck. Dahveed was the only one still on his feet.

"Should we go overboard?" Sareea asked, and he fixated on her. She was watching him.

"I don't know," Terian murmured. *It's so big. How do we fight that?*

"You're the leader," Sareea said to him, so softly that no one else could hear her. She was looking in his eyes, whispering, and she wore no shirt to cover her …

Terian felt his fear dissolve, replaced by a flash of lust, then a hard sense of reality crashing down on his gut drove even that out of him. *I'm failing. I can't fail. If I fail, they die.* "Everybody out of the boat before it sinks!" he called. "We need to kill that thing, now!"

There was not even a pause before he heard the sound of bodies hitting water. Terian vaulted over the edge himself, though his feet had already been nearly up to the knees in the deepening water. "We'll need to submerge—" he started, and felt air fill his lungs even though he was not taking a breath.

"You can now breathe underwater," Bowe's calm voice reached him. He glanced back and saw Bowe hovering above the sinking ship, the water a foot below his feet. His hands were moving in a frenzy, and at the end of each motion he indicated another member of the crew. *Casting Breath of the Aquatic spells. Sovereign bless you, Bowe.*

I should have ordered those as soon as this menace appeared.

"Let's see what we're dealing with," Sareea said, and he watched her pearl-white hair disappear underwater. Her feet broke the surface for a second before dipping below with her.

"Let's go," Terian said, feeling far behind. *She's leading right now. Leading me. I need to get moving, get my mind moving. I was an Elder of Sanctuary, for the gods' sakes—and I'm being led by a newly graduated dark knight. What is wrong with me?*

Terian dove without waiting to see if anyone else followed. The depths were dark, scarcely any light penetrating them. He felt a tickle in his vision and he could see. *Eagle Eye. Bowe, you are truly an indispensable man.*

He could see Sareea swimming beneath him. The dark, rocky bottom of the cave was visible now, covered over with some thin lair of algae.

Something was moving, something big.

He could Sareea swimming toward it. *She's fearless, that one. Or crazy.*

Or both.

He followed her, his strokes of middling effectiveness. Something passed him on the right, and he realized it was Grinnd. He was paced a moment later by Verret.

Terian swam faster, flailing his arms and legs while maintaining his grip on his axe.

Grinnd and Sareea reached the beast at the same time. Its tentacles swept upward around its center like spikes driven in a circle around it. It aligned itself to use the tentacles as a fence between it and its foes, and Terian knew with horrible certainty that this thing was a predator of the worst sort.

It's ready for us.

A flash of something cut through the water leaving a hard trail behind it. It streaked over Terian's head and snaked between an open space of tentacles to strike the beast in its oblong head. Terian watched the tail of the spell drift slowly downward, dissolving as it went, and he realized it was a burst of ice.

Whatever my father is paying Bowe, it's not nearly enough.

The monster swayed with the strike of the ice, tentacles flailing in clear anger. One of them shot at Sareea, another at Grinnd. Terian felt bubbles escape his mouth as he drove his muscles to take him down.

Grinnd met the tentacle with the blade of one of his swords, and dark blood stained the water. It went cloudy and opaque, as though a well of ink had been dropped into the Great Sea. Terian watched the edge of the tentacle continue to flail, a four-foot section of it severed. It drifted out of sight as the beast pulled the rest of it back toward itself.

Sareea cleanly dodged the one flung at her. She managed no counter blow, spinning in the water to reach the inside of the squid's defensive perimeter. She plunged her sword toward the bulbous head, but the tentacles moved as one and it shot upward as though it had been launched.

Sareea spiraled down like she had been caught in a whirlpool. Terian watched her legs spin until she seemed to catch her bearings and reorient. By then, he was almost upon a tentacle of his own.

He bore his axe in front of him. Verret was alongside him now, aiming for another tentacle, and Grinnd was only just behind them. Another streak of ice pelted the creature but from closer this time.

Ugly monster. Terian swept his axe back to strike, feeling the resistance of the water as he pushed through. He struck the tentacle that came at him squarely in the middle.

And the axe hung in place.

The tentacle pulled back as though he'd burned it. It dragged him along with it holding the handle of the axe as though it were a rope that would pull him back to the clay beach. The strength of the beast was astounding, and Terian could feel the tug of the water's resistance to his passage as though it were trying to rip him free of his weapon.

This is not going to be as easy as I'd hoped.

A flare of ice blasted the squid in the side of its head. It was a dome-shaped monstrosity, pointed and almost phallic. Terian ripped his axe free of the indentation he'd made in the creature and swept it into the beast's head, trying to cut his way in. He made only a thin mark before the squid blasted upward again, knocking him asunder with the sweep of its tentacles.

Terian spun in the water, tossed and disoriented. Up and down became meaningless, concepts he felt he'd once learned but now had forgotten. His head spun with the rest of him and a sudden nausea crept in. His breakfast crept up his throat and he tasted the bile and nastiness of it through the water trying to force its way into his nasal passages.

This was the worst idea in the history of terrible ideas. Who fights a sea monster in the middle of the sea?

A moron, that's who.

It lingered above him, hanging between him and the surface of the water. He could see it rippling, tentacles moving in time like a dress being spun at a ball.

Something swept by him in a flash. Terian's head was still swimming while he was holding his position in the water. It took only a moment for him to realize that it was Verret.

Verret swam with long strokes, long sword in one hand and his legs carrying him upward in powerful scissoring motions. Terian could see the underside of the creature, where some aperture waited to spit hard water out and send it upward again.

He watched Verret's approach almost helplessly, trying to marshal his own limbs to work to push him up as well. After a moment he managed, using his legs to propel him toward the surface.

Verret had a long lead, though, and Terian was moving slowly. Sareea and Grinnd passed him, and another blast of ice came from somewhere above, the trailing edge looking for all the world like someone had made a long pillar of frost with which to stab the creature.

Terian watched them move toward it, and he saw the bottom aperture of the creature open at Verret's approach. Something bothered him about it, something tickled at the back of his mind.

It was not until he saw the teeth that he knew what he had feared.

The tentacles pushed upward in a solid motion, driving the creature down toward Verret, who was still swimming up to meet it. The dark elf did not have time to react to the beast's motion, and it came straight for him.

It was a mouth that had opened, and Terian watched it shut again upon Verret's torso. Teeth shredded through the man, ripping him solidly in half. His upper body disappeared, followed by his lower body in the next motions.

Blood darkened the waters around the mouth, a black cloud hanging beneath the sea monster.

But before it disappeared it the mist of the blood, Terian would have sworn its face was creased in a bizarre, twisted grin.

32.

He wanted to scream, wanted to yell, but the water would come flooding down his throat so he did not. He tightened his grip on the axe handle so that his knuckles cracked. He could feel the pressure of his grip and wished for his gauntlets so he could sink those taut, metal fingers into the skin of the creature.

I want to hear it scream. I want to hear it cry.

It shot through the cloud of Verret's blood still hanging between it and the rest of them. It snaked toward Grinnd with three tentacles and each one of them met an end so vicious that Grinnd might have been hacking off his enemies' heads for the fury with which he treated them. His motions, so normally relaxed and languid, looked merciless.

Grinnd flung himself at the head and buried his swords into it as another blast of ice, larger this time, spiked into the creature and drew blood. Sareea swept through the hole in its defense created by Grinnd and buried her blade several inches in its skull.

The sea monster shook but showed little response to all that was happening to it. The remaining tentacles still moved in a light, swirling dance.

Terian shot toward the head as the creature turned to place its mouth toward its attackers. He did not halt as it opened wide to devour him, and he swept the axe in and hit it squarely in the soft tissue above the teeth.

Three of the pointed things broke free and fell out of the mouth with a swirl of cloudy blood. The monster recoiled from him, dragging Grinnd and Sareea along with it as it tried to escape.

Terian felt a solid jet of water push against him, expelled by the thing's mouth. He felt it and pushed back, swimming against the current it made. This time he did not spin, though he felt it try to push him away.

You won't get rid of me that easily, you son of a bitch. I'll see you hanging on the docks for what you did to Verret!

Grinnd attacked again with a mighty blow that opened a wide gash in the squid's skin. It split open and Terian saw Sareea plunge her blade into the hole that Grinnd had made while the warrior sliced another on the top of the bulbous skull.

The monster jerked with its remaining tentacles. They flailed in the water loosely, like it had been struck by lightning. Terian paused, and watched, preparing to defend against whatever next blow it might strike.

Sareea's sword split the skull vertically as she pulled it free. The blade glowed with blue, cold fire. *The most powerful spell a dark knight can wield—the Cold Flame of the Darkheart.* Her face was lit by the light of the blade and he could see a cruel satisfaction in the twist of her lips.

The squid jerked one last time and began to fall, loose tentacles hanging in the water like leaves drifting down from a tall tree.

Terian watched it fall wordlessly. He and the others—the survivors—kept watching until it vanished into the depths of a crevasse, swallowed up by the darkness that had borne it.

33.

Seventeen Years Earlier

"There is no greater triumph," the voice of the instructor intoned, "than to follow the will of the Sovereign and defeat his enemies for him. In the time that Sovereign is gone, his tribunal is his voice in these lands, and to obey their command is to please the Sovereign himself greatly."

Terian listened as Cidrack Urnetagroth spoke. His low voice echoed over the Legion of Darkness class, the faint whispers of two students in the back row not nearly enough to distract him from Urnetagroth's lesson. The aroma of candles burning in the darkness was enough to distract Terian from the smells of his class, the blood and sweat after a day of exercises.

"Excuse me, Cidrack," came a familiar voice from behind them. Terian turned, his eyes falling on his father standing at the entrance to the classroom. "I hate to interrupt." Terian could tell from his father's tone that he did, indeed, not wish to.

"By all means, come in, Lord Amenon," Cidrack Urnetagroth nearly fell over himself bowing. "Your presence is no interruption at all. What humble service may we provide for you?"

"I have come for my son," Amenon said, the sloped brow and the slant of his eyes showing the rarest of moods—joviality. "If his absence will not be too much imposition, I should like to take him home early for the day."

"By all means," Urnetagroth said, bowing again. "Our exercises for the day are complete, and he is at your disposal."

"Excellent." Amenon made a come hither gesture to Terian, who was already scrambling to his feet, the sweaty smell of his well-worn training armor wafting up at him as he moved. *I won't be sorry to be rid of this armor once I've graduated; it smells like it's been worn for eighteen generations. Which it probably has.*

"Attention!" Urnetagroth shouted, and Terian stiffened to attention with the rest of the cadets. Urnetagroth brought his hand sharply to his breast then saluted in a gesture that was instantly carried out by every single cadet in the room. The sound of steel gauntlets clanging against breastplates echoed in the small classroom. When each finished, they held stiffly at attention, Terian included.

"As you were," Amenon commanded, with just a trace of amusement. "Thank you, Cidrack." Instructor Urnetagroth bowed his head once more, but remained at attention until Terian and Amenon had left the room.

"That is respect which cannot be bought by any merchant," Amenon said as they walked under the arching gate of the Legion of Darkness. Terian glanced back to see others peering out the windows at them. *Not every day that the foremost graduate of the Legion comes back to visit these hallowed halls, I suppose.* "Try to pay in coin for it even in that whorish city of Reikonos, where any virtue is up for sale for the right price and you'll fail to find it cheap—if it all."

"Yes, Father," Terian said. His mop of hair was still damp from the afternoon sword exercises, and as he walked he felt the place on his leg where some idiotic fourth year had tried to force the dull training sword into a chink in the armor. Terian had rattled his helm for him, loudly and forcefully enough that he'd stopped before doing much more than causing an ache.

"I suppose you're wondering why I've come to get you early," Amenon said once they were through the gate and into the city. They passed through the square in silence, and it was only on the other side of it that his father spoke. The midday crowds had receded from the madness of morning, and now only a faint stream of servants, buyers and pedestrians remained.

"Of course, Father," Terian said, nodding. He walked in step with his father as best he could, his shorter strides forcing him to hurry along.

"I had some time, and I wanted to show you something," Amenon said with a mysterious smile.

What could that be? Terian wondered—but he did not ask.

They went in silence until they reached the manor. Upon entering, Amenon nodded to each of the servants holding the doors for them. "This way," he said to Terian, gesturing toward the stairs.

"Are Ameli and Mother here?" Terian asked, hesitating by the staircase.

"No," Amenon said with a shake of the head. They ascended together, their boots echoing through the silence of the manor. Terian halted at the door to his father's study. "Well," Amenon said with that same hint of a smile, "go on."

Terian paused and waited for his father to nod once more, then turned the knob of the door. It opened silently, and he pushed hard against the stone doors to make his way into the study.

Standing before him was a suit of armor, dark and beautiful. Spikes jutted high from the shoulders, and the helm was crowned with spires that reached half a foot higher than the crest of the helm. The metal was shaded and looked nearly black in the darkness. Terian stared at it, openmouthed.

"What do you think?" Amenon asked.

"It's ... amazing," Terian said, looking at it. "The perfect armor for a dark knight."

"It will be yours," Amenon said. "When you complete your training and have finished your sacrifice."

Terian felt a ripple of hesitation. "The sacrifice ..."

"Yes?" Amenon asked, and there was a change in his voice.

"What is it?" Terian asked. "No one will tell me."

"Nor should they," Amenon said stiffly. "And nor will I. The soul sacrifice is the binding and defining ritual that marks us as dark knights and as true servants of the ethos of our kind. While I cannot speak to its particulars, you will face it before too much longer—and I am certain that you will be equal to the test." He straightened. "Which is why I have already procured this armor for you."

Terian stared in awe at the armor. *It truly is beautiful.* "I hope I do not fail you, Father."

"You have lived up to every one of my expectations thus far," Amenon said stiffly, and Terian saw a hint of a smile as his voice loosened. "I could not ask for more. Continue to do what you have done, and I have no doubt you will find yourself wearing this armor soon enough." He leaned toward Terian and gave him the hint of a smile. "Just be willing to do everything that is asked of you, and you will never find yourself in a place where you fail my expectations."

"I will, Father," Terian said, and he kept his hands at his side to keep from touching the armor covetously. "I will not fail you so long as it is within my power to keep from doing so."

34.

"We swim down and recover the body," Grinnd said. They were on the surface now, swimming and sputtering and treading water. "We drag the thing up and cut it open and pull Verret's remains out. From there, you can patch him back together and cast the resurrection spell—"

"I'm afraid that's not possible, my friend," Dahveed said. He was treading water next to them, calm, slow, motions keeping him afloat. "He's gone, Grinnd. Even assuming we could recover him, without a boat I couldn't do the work of stitching him back together. I'm sorry." He did sound genuinely contrite.

An uneasy silence settled over Grinnd. "I want to maim that thing further."

"I can't stop you from doing that," Dahveed said, looking at Terian. Terian caught the implication—*But you can.*

"We need to get back to shore," Terian said. "It's several miles of swimming."

"I want to rip that thing up," Grinnd said, and Terian caught him taking a breath to submerge.

"Belay that," Terian said, and Grinnd looked at him with a fury that was utterly out of place on the warrior's face. "We return to shore. Now. If the master healer of Saekaj says he can't bring

Verret back, then he's truly lost. We're not. We get back to shore and make our report. Immediately."

Grinnd let a long, furious sigh that made it look as though he were restraining a rage about to be turned loosed on Terian. "Yes sir," was all he said.

"Easier to walk to shore, I think," Bowe said, hovering above the dark waters once more. With a wave of the druid's hands, Terian felt lightness surge through his body and lift him from the waters. He dripped, dark spots falling back to their home on the surface like the rains of the Perdamun.

I failed. Verret is dead. Terian ran a hand over his face, mopping the water off of him. *And that thing—*

"The shore is this way," Sareea's light voice said, jarring him out of his thoughts. For once, she looked unamused. She started off in that direction, and after a moment Terian followed. *Still leading me.*

Terian looked back to confirm that they were all still with him. Bowe stood as stiff and straight as if he'd not been in a battle at all, but was on a parade ground somewhere doing nothing more than standing at attention. Grinnd sulked and it was a sad thing to behold. Terian watched the warrior as he slunk, head down, expression still burdened by fury. Grinnd cast frequent looks back at the water behind them, muttering so low that Terian could not hear him.

Xem, on the other hand, was leading the way, ahead of even Sareea. He cast furtive looks back, and Terian wondered at why until he remembered he had not seen Xemlinan at all during the battle. *Hiding? Is he now ashamed?*

Dahveed clapped a strong hand on Terian's shoulder, startling him. It was wet and made a suctioning noise that sounded disturbingly like something being eaten to Terian's ears. "Is that the first man you've lost under your command?"

"We lost others in Sanctuary," Terian said, and the world seemed shadowed around him, a bleakness as the spell of the Eagle Eye began to fade. He hesitated. "But never directly under my command."

"It is a hard thing sending people to their deaths," Dahveed said, and the weight of experience rang through his words.

"If Verret were here, he'd say we did our duty to the Sovereign," Terian said, letting his voice harden. "That any losses necessary to the mission were simply the price we pay for our service. I can't see him quailing before the sacrifice we made."

"He might have said things differently knowing it was him that was being sacrificed," Dahveed said in a hushed voice.

"No, he wouldn't have," Grinnd said from behind them. Terian turned to see the warrior stalking along, arms swinging at his side as he walked with a fury. "Terian has the right of it. Verret would never back down from paying the ultimate price. You're talking about a man who did his time in the Depths still praising the name of the Sovereign. This is the way he would have wanted it." Grinnd sent a searing glare at Dahveed, who merely bowed his head in acknowledgment. "And I won't ever believe anyone who tells me differently."

With that, Grinnd brushed past Terian to head to the fore. Terian watched him go, watched the warrior break even with Sareea Scyros and then outpace her.

"He doesn't like the sound of truth," Dahveed said. "I've seen many a man falter when the pain starts. Suddenly they don't believe as hard in what they'd professed. A dark and jagged-toothed end to all your days? I can't imagine anyone staring into the mouth of that without a moment's consideration for what they're doing. It'd take a man rooted deeper in conviction than any I've ever met to meet that fate without a second thought." Dahveed turned to him with a smile. "Have you ever met a man who lived with such certainty?"

Terian stared at Grinnd's retreating back. "I can think of only one."

35.

The ride back to Saekaj was long. Terian scarcely noticed the bumps save for the last one when the carriage parked under the portico of his father's house. The door was opened before he could gather his thoughts and do it for himself. He stepped out and adjusted his armor. His underclothes were barely dry from the swim, and they had a hardness about them like they'd crusted over.

The stink of the Great Sea was still upon him as he stared at the front door to the house. He could taste bile and dank water on his tongue, as though he were about to vomit up its depths right there on the walk. *Compose yourself, fool. This is a message to be delivered. That MUST be delivered.*

Duty.

He took his first step, then another, and another. The door was opened for him by the coachman, and Terian found himself standing in the foyer, imagining his still damp clothes dripping upon the floor. They did no such thing, but he still felt as though he were staining the place by his mere presence.

"Ah, good, you've returned," Guturan said, passing through the room from the kitchens. "Your father awaits you in his study."

"Does he?" Terian asked, more musing than serious.

"He does," Guturan said, the meaning of Terian's words passing him by. "He waits with great anticipation."

"I doubt it," Terian said, taking a faltering step toward the stairs. "He knows it's me coming, after all."

Every step was a lengthening nightmare that felt like years. Terian let his feet land softly against the rug stretched over the stairway, heard every clank of the metal boots on stone as he ascended. *So why does it feel like I'm climbing down to the dungeons? I didn't know Verret, not really. Haven't known him in years. He was just a hardass on my father's team, not a friend of any sort.*

His death does not warrant my own.

Does it?

Terian reached the heavy stone doors of the study with shocking alacrity. He stood before them, cowed. His eyes took them in, and he could smell the faint scent of the fire burning within. He raised a hand to knock and hesitated. *What do I fear more? What he'll say? Or what he'll do?*

He brought his hand down and struck the stone cleanly.

"Come." The voice of Amenon Lepos was crisp and clear. *He has no idea.*

Terian entered the study, not bothering to close the door behind him. He made his way to the center of the room, standing before the desk. The fire crackled off to the side, the sound of words burning. *So many words. So many empty words. How many empty words have my father and I exchanged? Well, at least these will be full ...*

His father looked up at him, taking him in with one good appraising look. "Did you solve the problem?"

"Yes," Terian said. "But—"

"There are no 'buts,'" his father said crossly. "Either you have completed the task set before you or you have not."

"I have completed the task set before me," Terian said.

"Very good," his father said with a nod. "Then I have another matter to discuss with you—"

"And Verret is dead." Terian heard his voice crack like a whip turned loose on a vek'tag.

His father, for his part, raised only an eyebrow. He crumpled the parchment he held in his hand, let the crackle of the paper fill the air. "How did he die?"

"Not well," Terian said. His every syllable was flat. "He was shredded by a sea monster of some sort."

Amenon appeared to ponder this. "We have never had any such creature in the Great Sea before."

"No," Terian said. "We have not."

Amenon sat there, his armor giving him a look of stiffness that Terian suspected was reflected below the surface of that armor. "A mystery, then. It either snuck in from the depths of the earth and chambers below ... or was brought there by someone." He stood, staring into the fire. "A matter for another time," he said abruptly, and tossed the parchment into the fire. "We have other things to discuss."

Terian blinked. "Like Verret?" His voice was hoarse, and it came out accusing.

"There is nothing to discuss as relates to Verret," Amenon said. "Are there any remains to be sent to the Depths for composting?"

"What?" Terian almost choked. "No, there was nothing left—"

"Then we will have a standard sending ceremony for his family in a few days," Amenon said. "As befits a man of his station."

"A—sending ceremony?" Terian asked. *I cannot believe what I'm hearing.*

"You know he was of far too low a station to have been laid to rest in the Tomb of Heroes—even assuming there had been anything left of the man," Amenon said. His tone was all business, and his eyes were back to studying the next piece of parchment.

Terian started to argue, started to protest, started to say, *You've known him for a hundred years and he's followed you everywhere you've asked.* But his gaze fell upon the red gem upon his father's desk and he went silent. *Of course.* "The path of duty," he said.

Amenon looked up at him from where he sat, face inscrutable. "Sacrifices must be made in the name of the Sovereign."

Terian laughed, but it was a mirthless, joyless sound. "I actually thought you were going to be angry with me." He focused in on the red jewel. "I should have known differently."

"I will never fault you for doing what needs to be done," Amenon said. "Even when the cost is high."

Terian started to turn his back but stopped halfway. "I should have known."

"Yes," his father said. "You should have remembered. There is no sacrifice too great to be made in the name of duty. Or family."

Terian snorted. "Or at least some of them."

"We have another matter before us," Amenon said coldly. "Vincin Ehrest stopped by this morning."

Terian let out a sigh but still felt every muscle in his body tense. "I hope he wasn't here to complain about our conversation last night."

"He mentioned that the two of you spoke," Amenon said. "But it was not the purpose of his visit." Amenon leaned forward. "He had a much ... grander reason for being here."

"Is that so?" Terian listened with half an ear. *He really doesn't care that Verret got eaten. Not a bit. Just another sacrifice in the name of duty.*

"He proposed an alliance," Amenon said, causing Terian's interest to perk up.

"An alliance?" Terian stared unblinking at his father, the heat from the fire causing him to blink suddenly. "His house and ours?"

"Indeed," Amenon said with a slight smile. "The second and third most powerful houses in Saekaj working together."

"I can't imagine Dagonath Shrawn being too happy about us playing nice," Terian said with a shrug. "In fact, I'd think he'd take measures to break us apart as quickly as possible. Which shouldn't be too difficult, absent a—" The realization hit Terian as squarely as an axe blow to the forehead. "You son of a bitch. You said yes, didn't you?"

"The arrangement is made." Amenon showed only a flicker of acknowledgment at the insult leveled in his direction.

"And I have no say in the matter," Terian said then let out a curse that blackened the walls of the office.

"Are quite finished?" his father asked, coldly.

"Oh, I don't think I've begun," Terian said. "Which of his unfortunate offspring gets to bear this particular burden on their side?" He watched, but Amenon said nothing, looking at him in return. "It's Kahlee, isn't it? Light of the sky, Father, have you seen her hair?"

"Somehow I doubt that subtle problem of appearance much matters to you," Amenon said. "I know it doesn't concern me."

"Well, you're the only one in polite society who doesn't care, I suppose," Terian said. *Other than me.* "This is ridiculous."

"No, this is Saekaj," Amenon said, without a hint of emotion. "It is how things are done here. Now … will you do what is expected of you, or shall I have a carriage take you back to the surface to make your way on your own?"

He's never threatened me like this before—or with that before. "Am I just a playing piece to be moved around your board?"

"You are right now the single most valuable weapon in my arsenal," Amenon said and stood, drawing himself to his full height. "You are the Heir of House Lepos, and since you have returned, you have wavered, you have made half measures, you have given me less than your full support and respect. For every moment of triumph such as this endeavor or the torture of Engoch, you show me pitiful emotion that has no place in our house and sentiment that puts my soldierly instincts into the mind of cutting my losses."

Amenon made his way around the desk to look Terian in the eye. "Even now, you practically weep over Verret as though he were some dear compatriot you have known all your days. I served in the war with him, kept him from death for his stupidity, have shepherded him and rewarded his loyalty in kind. I feel none of those things that you do. His was a sacrifice. A sacrifice for his duty, a sacrifice for our house, which he pledged himself to serve. Sacrifice is expected as a leader and as an heir." He drew his sword. "You know the lengths that I am willing to go to in order to make sure my house is kept in order, that we maintain and grow our influence. In this maneuver, we are finally about to take on an ally that is worthy, that is close to our equal. I will not have this alliance dragged down by an heir who will not do what is needed— what has to be done!" With that, he slammed his sword down into floor and it reverberated through the house. "If you want to leave, now is the moment. Walk freely through that door, leave my house, leave this city, and never return. Your commitment to this family is about to be tested, and I no longer have use for the weak of heart as my heir."

"Well, you don't have another," Terian said, glaring at his father with sullen eyes.

"I will find one, if necessary," Amenon said with coldest fury. "I will make one, if need be. It is long past time that you decide your course and stay upon it with whole heart."

Terian stared back at him. "You'd set Mother to the side so you could have a new heir?"

Amenon's eyes were dead. "I will do anything it takes to make certain that our house continues with the strength that is required to maintain our position."

He'll do it. The thought came without a moment's hesitation. *He'll set her aside and find some new young thing. This is a man who's never had a mistress, but he would put her aside for the position of his house in a moment to fulfill the expectations. Without doubt.* He could have read it all in his father's eyes had he not already known it to be true.

"I am not in the habit of being kept waiting." His father's fingers rested lightly on the hilt of his sword, still stubbornly standing upright where it had been driven into the floor. "Your decision is needed, and swiftly. Slow action is the province of the weak."

"I am not weak," Terian said, his voice a low, scratchy noise. "I am not ... weak." He opened his mouth and shut it again to prevent himself from saying the same thing once more. "I will do ... what is expected of me. Without fail."

His father did not waver, did not move, not for a long moment. "Very well." He pulled his sword from the floor without resistance and slipped the red-tinged blade silently back into his scabbard. "I will make the necessary arrangements. You have ... done right by your house. I can ask no more of you than that."

Terian felt his lips pucker in a curious way, but no words were forthcoming. He inclined his head slightly, as close as he could come to a bow of his head and started to turn.

"It will get easier," his father said, and Terian looked back to find him examining the parchment. "It will get easier to make these decisions. Let your pride and your will go and bury yourself in duty, and your life will become quite simple indeed. Soon enough, you'll be running things yourself." He looked up. "Go on."

"Yes, Father," Terian said, and bowed his head again. A sickly feeling had taken root in his stomach, and he tottered out the door on legs as unsteady as ever they'd been when he was drunk.

36.

When the knock came at his door, he was unsure what to expect. It was loud, formal, and to Terian's ears, had the ring of Guturan Enlas all over it. "Yes?" Terian croaked, his voice sounding as foreign to him as music in the depths of Sovar. His face had been buried in his hands, and the hard wood of the chair in the corner of his room was upon his backside. The ache was beginning to set in.

"Your betrothed is here to see you, Lord Terian." Guturan's reply was crisp and certain, and formal as he'd ever heard the steward.

"I'll be ... down in a moment," Terian said, lifting himself up from his chair. A daze was upon him, a thousand thoughts bombarding him from every direction.

"She is here, Lord Terian, and would like to speak with you in the privacy of your chambers."

Terian blinked. "Is that ... proper?" His words sounded weak and foolish to his ears.

"Quite so, sir," Guturan's voice came from behind the door. "Do you need a moment to prepare?"

"Send her in," Terian said, and no sooner had the words left his mouth than the squeak of the door handle and the hinges echoed through his chamber. He stood at stiff attention, as though he were still in training and the Commandant of the Legion of Darkness were coming to inspect his barracks.

Guturan's arm was all that was visible of him, snaking past Kahlee to hold the door open for her. She was not attired in the dress of a servant, not today. She wore a full black gown, less formal than the ones he had seen on the ladies at Shrawn's ball, and her hair was shorter, falling only to her shoulders. It still bore the blue tinge of the wildroot dye, though part of it was covered under a large bonnet.

He bowed, feeling stricken. "My lady."

Kahlee glanced back at Guturan, who shut the door without any of the squealing or squeaking that had been present upon its opening. She turned back to him once it was closed. For a moment, she stared at him, her face telling him nothing about what she was thinking. It lasted for all of a second. "Are you going to be this foolishly formal in our marriage as well, or can we get back to the business of speaking to each other without the stupid airs?"

"I think *we're* actually the stupid heirs at this point," Terian said.

"Droll," Kahlee said with a shake of her head that highlighted her lack of amusement.

"I strive to be, when possible," Terian said, but he did not feel any levity.

"It rhymes with 'troll' for a reason," Kahlee said with a dark irritation in her eyes that was unlike anything he had seen from her in the past. "You and I are to be wed in a little over a month, as befits the tradition of our people."

"Oh, good," Terian said. "I wouldn't want a long, lingering engagement. It always struck me as something like a sickness—best not to happen at all, but if so, make it mercifully short."

"There's that trollery again," Kahlee said. "I'd ask you to hold your jokes off until we're through this, but as this entire wedding is nothing more than a rather elaborate jape at my expense, yours added to the mix seem nothing less than appropriate."

Terian blinked. "You're not the only one dissatisfied with this union."

"Bear your dissatisfaction in silence," Kahlee said archly, "or to me in private. In public, I will not criticize you as my fiancé or my husband, and I will have you do the same." There was an air of danger in the way she said it. "Do you understand?"

"I guess I see who's going to be carrying the sword in this relationship."

Kahlee's eyes swept the chamber and then came back to rest on him before she took steps toward him. She looked up at him and smiled. "Oh, my sweet husband to be. Of course you will be in charge of our household." She leaned her head upon his shoulder, and nuzzled in close to his ear. "Don't be a fool," she whispered. "Shrawn has ears everywhere. Even now, surely he is hatching a way to drive a wedge between us—and our houses. Do not be fool enough to let your words give him the dagger with which to make the split."

Terian stiffened, and she raised her head off his shoulder to look him in the eyes. *She's right*, he realized. *Shrawn will be trying to find a way to split us. We're the single greatest threat to him at the moment.* "I will ... of course speak of you in nothing but the most glowing terms, betrothed."

"Very good," Kahlee said and brushed back to arm's length from him. "Although this was not a union of our choosing, you know me and I know you. I will do my duties to you as your wife and I expect the same from you as my husband."

Terian felt his mouth suddenly go dry. *Gods. Our primary duty ...* He saw a very subtle flicker in her eyes as she nodded. *She knows. And she's willing to 'do her duty' anyway. There is something so absurd about this ...* "I would never doubt your commitment to this alliance and to our ..." Terian coughed, "... marriage."

There was another flash of emotion on Kahlee's face, something deeper. "I expect we can come to accords on all that needs to be managed and handled?"

"Such as?" Terian felt as though he'd been smacked by the tentacle of the sea monster, full in the face with all force.

"Where we shall live after our wedding is the foremost among the questions," Kahlee said coolly. "The wedding itself will be planned by our mothers and we will have little say in the matter."

"I suspect the question of where we'll be living after the wedding will also be similarly settled by our fathers," Terian said. "I don't think ... they'll leave much in the way of choices up to us."

"Perhaps not," she said. "But there is the matter of our courtship, however short it may be. There are rules to be observed, formalities that need to be taken into account."

"Of course." Terian nodded. "Whatever you need of me, let me know."

"I think this will do it for now." She nodded to him in return and stepped close to him, kissing him on the cheek. Her breath smelled faintly sweet, as though she'd taken a chew of mint before coming to see him. "We will likely see each other every day for the near future. In a week or two we will be expected to begin ... other activities related to the courtship." Her face was blank, and Terian could see the hints of displeasure. "It would be considered a very positive sign if we were able to meet certain ... expectations ... before the day of our wedding. A very good sign indeed, and the mortar which would ensure that the alliance between our houses remained strong." She spun very quickly away, moving toward the door, which opened for her. She glanced back only briefly. "I will see you tomorrow, betrothed." With that, she vanished through the door.

Terian did not answer her back. Still floating within his head were the last thoughts she had left him with. *Duty. Our primary duty ... the only one that matters to our fathers right now.*

To produce an heir.

37.

Two Months Later

The smooth burn of Reikonosian whiskey left a trailing fire in Terian's mouth and down his throat as he swished it for a moment before swallowing. It was a powerful flavor, but the alcohol overrode anything else he might have sensed from it. The heat after it went down surged into his nasal cavity and felt as though it were lighting his nose hairs on fire.

He leaned back against his chair, eyes focused on the bottle that had been left on the stone table in front of him. "I'm going to need another one of these, Xem."

Xemlinan was only a half dozen paces away at the bar. The two of them were the only ones in the Unnamed. Terian could hear the crowds of midday Sovar moving outside, thronging down the street. *Probably going to make their gruel in the communal ovens. That could have been my life if my father hadn't gone and ascended to the so-called good life.* He sniffed, the fiery aftertaste of the whiskey still burning. *I might have been able to choose my own destiny then.*

Xem approached, his cloth shoes whisper-quiet on the bare floors of the Unnamed. "You look like a man who's had his first marital quarrel." He pulled the stopper out of the bottle with a soft pop and poured into Terian's glass with only a gentle sloshing.

"What? No," Terian said, looking at the amber liquid in the crystal glass in front of him. "No quarrels. We get along as well can be expected, I suppose. She's yet to dig in her heels on anything." He blinked. *And I've been the very model of politeness. Which is surprising.* "She's been fine," he said. "No complaints from me."

"Ah, Terian," Xem said, still standing over him. "Then why are you sitting in my bar in the middle of the day drinking? Hmm?" He leaned over, and Terian could see the concern spread over Xem's features. "This is the act of the old Terian, the one who left Saekaj. The thoroughly unserious dark knight who had all the hope burned out of him. This is not the new Terian, the married man and adjutant to his father. That fellow doesn't drink, remember?"

"He drinks a little," Terian said, meeting Xem's eyes. "Very little," he conceded. "Perhaps one glass of something on social occasions and never at home." He held up a hand in front of his eyes and watched it blur. *It didn't take much to make me woozy now, did it?* "What happened to him, Xem?"

"Everyone has to grow up sometime, Terian," Xem said, and started a slow retreat back to the bar. "The path you're on doesn't allow for much frivolity or stepping outside the lines. You have responsibilities now. Your days of disillusionment with the way our land works are over." He smiled. "You're part of the system you hated before. Welcome to the other side."

Terian blinked. "It happened so quickly and yet so slowly. It doesn't feel like it was that long ago that I was in here after my soul sacrifice, drinking everything you had to give me."

Xemlinan's face grew drawn. "That was a hard day. The first many, I know. But for duty's sake—"

"Don't talk to me about duty," Terian said, and he cradled the glass in his hand, and smelled a faint, oaky aroma. "Not today." He took the whiskey back with a single slug.

"Fair enough," Xem said and eased around the bar.

Terian watched him from across the room, mulling his thoughts as he moved the glass in a slow circle. He watched the liquid slosh in time with his motions, casting about in a slow circle. *Do I say something to him? What would I even say? Yesterday I was fine, in fine form and humor, and today I'm bleak as a Saekaj day. Nothing happened.* The liquid cast along in that same slow circle. *No missions, no deaths—not since Verret—nothing of note since the wedding. Just a slow grind of work, work and more work. Reports enough to bury me.*

"Don't you have work you should be tending to?" Xem asked, as if he were harmonizing with Terian's own thoughts.

"Done for the day," Terian said, looking at the dark liquid in his glass for a beat before he drained it. "My father gave me leave to go home to my wife." He chortled. "To work on my primary duty."

"You don't sound happy to be doing that," Xem said. "Not as happy as I'd expect you to be. Do you miss the ladies of the brothels now that you're acting respectable?"

"Not really," Terian said, a little surprised to realize it was true. "Things are fine in that arena."

Xemlinan let out a sigh. "Leave it to you to be in the midst of what most around here would call a most bountiful life … and still be wracked with dissatisfaction."

"Does this look like the face of a man dissatisfied, Xem?" Terian looked up at him and pasted a fake smile upon his lips.

"It looks like the face of a man trying his hardest to appear a fool."

"I don't have to try very hard."

"You have a beautiful young bride," Xem said, "the favor of your father, more gold than you can spend—"

"And less to spend it on, now that I have responsibilities," Terian said.

"—you don't want for the finest food, you have a plum job if ever there was one," Xem said, as though he were ticking off the points on his finger. "Oh, and last I heard, you're favored by the Sovereign as well. Or was that another god hiding in that cloud of infinite darkness in the back of your wedding?" Xem let air out through his lips. "Never heard of him going to anyone else's wedding, that's for sure."

"Indeed, Xemlinan," Terian said, "You have spoken truly and I cannot refute a single point you have made. Why, I seem to have the world by the ass." He lifted his glass. *So why can't I sleep at night?* But he did not dare to say it.

Xem watched him carefully, as if trying to see if he was being disingenuous. After a moment he gave up and shrugged his shoulders before turning back to organizing bottles behind the bar. "I can't even tell when you're being serious anymore. It used to be easy because it happened so rarely."

"Nothing is so rare as a man who gets everything he wants in life," Terian said and flinched a little as he said it. He kept his eyes on Xem to make sure he did not see. *Of course, I haven't gotten a damned thing I wanted out of my life…*

"It almost sounds like you appreciate it," Xem said. "When you say it like that, anyhow." He put a bottle up on a high shelf as there came the sound of the door opening.

"I'll work on that," Terian said as his eyes went to the door. A stranger came in wearing a long cloak with his cowl pulled up over his head. He was tall for a dark elf, though not as large as Grinnd.

Terian watched him with practiced disinterest, waiting to see if his cowl would slip to reveal his face.

"Hello, stranger," Xemlinan said, putting on his best faux smile. "What can I get for you?"

"A bottle of Reikonosian whiskey to match my friend's in the corner," came a hushed voice from beneath the cowl. Terian squinted at the dark cloak. The voice sounded ... familiar, and his mind raced to place it. Raced, and failed, the swimming sensation behind his eyes hampering his ability to think.

"Are we friends?" Terian replied, the answer coming as naturally to his lips as drawing a sword came to his hand.

"I would regard you as a friend, Terian," the man replied. He faced Xemlinan, waiting as the bartender reached behind him and pulled down a bottle of whiskey as the stranger placed a gold coin on the bar. "Whether you would still do the same is really more up to you."

"Perhaps if I knew who you are," Terian said. "I'm not in the habit of befriending empty cloaks, and the problem with the damned things is that they're a nice disguise to hide behind."

"Indeed," the stranger said, and Terian caught a hint of a nod to Xem, whose face showed slight surprise at the identity of the stranger before he nodded in return. With a slow, careful walk, the stranger turned toward Terian and made his way across the Unnamed, metal boots clicking quietly against the stone floor. "Which is probably why I find them so helpful."

"If you want to hide your face, sure," Terian said, peering toward the shadowed cowl the stranger was wearing. "Which is kind of a cowardly thing to do."

"Discretion is the better part of valor, I'm told," the stranger said, pulling the chair across the table from Terian out with a screech against the floor. "And I did not come here for a fight, so I wore a hood." The voice ...

Terian blinked, and he knew.

The stranger sat down across from him and slipped the cowl back. His helm covered most of his face, but not nearly enough. *Not nearly enough, not in Sovar.* Pale flesh peered back at him, and a single, solitary grey eye was visible through the slitted helm.

"Hello, Alaric," Terian said and raised his glass. "So nice to see you."

38.

"You know," Terian said, staring at the little of Alaric's face revealed through the helm, "humans are who come into Saekaj and Sovar are put to death immediately."

"Yet here I am," Alaric said, lips moving under the helm. "Would you like to run and fetch the militia to have me arrested?"

Terian sighed deeply and stared at his glass. "I really don't have the energy for all that activity. I'm amazed you made it through the gates, honestly. I figure they'll get you on the way out."

"What makes you think I came through the gates?" Alaric asked with the thinnest veil of amusement over what Terian could see of his expression.

Terian watched him. "What are you doing here? I doubt it's for the Reikonosian whiskey, since that's considerably easier and cheaper to get in Reikonos."

"Perhaps I'm here for the ambience," Alaric said. He glanced at Xem. "Or to speak with Xemlinan here. He's quite the conversationalist, you know."

Terian glanced at Xem, who shrugged. "It's a burden of its own kind to be known far and wide for your conversational skills."

"Meaning you're a chatty spider in the gossip web," Terian said darkly, feeling his lips curl at Xem. "I trust my father doesn't know you're an information broker?"

"Of course he knows," Xem said, expression nearly blank. "It's one of the reasons he saved my life."

"I doubt he'd be enthused to know you're treating with outsiders," Terian said, shaking his head.

"Why, Terian," Xem said with a curious smile, "what use do you think an information broker would be to your father if he only treated with the people of Saekaj and Sovar?" He shook his head. "None. Your father's eyes are focused outside these caverns, and he needs eyes outside of them as well."

"Alaric doesn't have an eye to spare for my father, I know that much. Are you an ear, Alaric?" Terian said, glancing back to the paladin. "Because personally, I think you're an ass."

"I am many things to many people," Alaric said, and Terian's skin prickled at the amusement he could hear in the Sanctuary Guildmaster's voice.

"Yeah, well, if you're here to talk to Xem, let me get out of your way," Terian said and made a motion to stand.

"But I haven't had my drink with you just yet," Alaric said. There was the firmness of a command in how he said it that made Terian bristle again.

"Just pretend we toasted to old times or something," Terian said, pulling his cloak off the back of his chair and draping it over his shoulders. "It'll probably be better than any actual conversation we could have."

"Why is that?" Alaric said and took a sip of the whiskey in his hand straight from the bottle. "Do you not have exciting news to tell me about the wonderful events in your life of late?"

Terian sent a searing glare at Xem, who busied himself behind the bar. "But of course," Terian said, fighting back the grimace. "I suppose you've heard that things are going marvelously. That I'm my father's adjutant, helping him handle his affairs. Oh, and I'm married now, to the most eligible woman in Saekaj, so there's that bit of excellent news."

"I congratulate you on your nuptials," Alaric said, and raised the bottle toward him. "May your marriage be filled with much happiness."

This is Saekaj Sovar; that sort of shit doesn't happen here, he thought but did not say. "Thank you. Did you just come here to catch up? Or did you have an ulterior motive?"

"I came to see you," Alaric said, studying him.

"Not to talk to Xem?" Terian gave a slight nod. "Now we get to the truth of it."

"When have we ever not gotten to the truth of it?" Alaric asked.

Terian gave a faint laugh that was all the funnier from the sensation of the alcohol working on his mind. "When do we ever get to the actual truth of things, Alaric? You kept us Sanctuary officers on a thread all the time. You work in darker mystery than even the Sovereign does, and to much less defined purpose."

"I have clear purpose," Alaric said. "And you know very well what it is."

"To protect the people of Arkaria from impending threats and doom and forgive me if I just go to sleep right now," Terian said, blowing air between his lips. "You always acted like there was some great evil hanging over our heads at all times, waiting to strike down and smite us." Terian threw his arms wide. "It gave you this larger than life presence, as if you were working toward anything other than building a bigger guild so you could increase your purse and your influence, just like everyone else in Arkaria."

"You think I was false in my profession of threats existing outside our walls?" Alaric asked. He did not look offended. Just calm.

"I think you overstated it in order to get your officers to fall in line," Terian said. "I think you either played overly grandiose or you actually believed it, and I don't really care which. Your intentions don't mean shit to me. You intended to run a happy household, but when it got unruly and pruning became necessary, you didn't want to do what had to be done, and you landed on me like a rock giant on a gnome for letting the wildfires burn out the rot. You lectured me about laws keeping us in check." Terian sniffed. "Well, there's one of us in this room that's violating a law right now, and it isn't me, and it's probably not Xem." He hesitated. "This time, anyway."

"Terian," Alaric said, "when last we spoke I talked to you of the importance of keeping intentions restrained so that moral drift doesn't carry you away down the river to an unrecognizable place."

"Yeah, and I told you I don't care," Terian said. "You know what's changed? Now I'm in a place where the rules are a little more flexible surrounding things that need to be done. See a problem, solve it. Whatever it takes."

"And you feel good about this?" Alaric asked. There was disappointment in the way he said it, and it prickled at Terian.

"I feel like I know where I fit in," Terian said. "And that counts for a lot. I have a wife. I have a life. I have power at my fingertips to help shape things in the ways they need to be shaped."

"Does your father dictate the way things need to be shaped?" Alaric asked. "Or do you?"

"My father, you," Terian said airily, "what does it matter who shapes them? At least now when I'm being told what to do I'm being well compensated for it. I'm not scraping along. I'm doing just fine without you."

"Perhaps we're not doing as well without you," Alaric said.

"I figured you'd have promoted Cyrus Davidon to officer by now," Terian said, shaking his head. "He's capable. Earnest. Annoyingly earnest, but capable. He could be your new golden boy. He seems like he'd be easily convinced to buy into your bullshit for a while."

"Cyrus is on a recruiting mission to grow our strength even now," Alaric said, "and he's doing well at it. But that's beside the point. He is not you, Terian."

"I'm not me anymore," Terian said, a little flip and a little resigned. "I'm not the same person I was when I left, Alaric. I've grown. I've faced new challenges, walked a different path."

"And do you find this path to your liking?" Alaric asked, watching him.

"I'm good at it," Terian said. "Better than I was at the one you'd set me upon."

Alaric stared at him, watching carefully, keeping that sole eye on his as though he were reading through to Terian's mind. Terian tried to keep his face immovable. "I suppose that's what matters, then," Alaric said and stood slowly. His armor clanked as he did so.

"It matters to me," Terian said.

"And that counts for more than anything else," Alaric said, seemingly agreeing. Terian caught a hint of something else, though, a sort of disagreement too subtle to even protest. "I wish you well in your new path. In your new life."

Terian set his jaw. "Thank you." He hesitated as Alaric turned to leave, the whiskey bottle left behind on the table. "Good luck with your … rebuilding." He felt a twinge of guilt that he shoved away.

Alaric paused at the door to the Unnamed and rested a hand on it before pushing through. "If ever a day comes when you lose your way ... I hope you will find the road back to our door." Without waiting for a response, Alaric pushed through and left.

Terian stared behind him, trying to drum up a response. He found none.

39.

Terian felt the cool sheets against his skin, the smells of the night and the body pressed against his. The alcohol still gave his head a gentle, swimming sensation as he laid his head against the pillow.

"You had a bit to drink," she said.

"I'm not drunk," he said, running a hand over his forehead, which was slick with the sweat of his exertions. He tilted his head to watch as she got out of bed, putting on a vek'tag silken dressing robe and knotting the belt.

"I wouldn't care if you were," Sareea said, tilting her head to look back at him with a half-smile. "This is not about sobriety, it's about release. It's about what you need." She ran a hand over his bare chest. It tickled.

Terian let out a slow breath. "I need a damned clue."

"Oh?" Sareea asked, retreating toward the corner where a chamber pot waited. "Are you still mulling the origin of that sea monster?"

"It didn't just swim into the Great Sea," Terian said, staring at the ceiling. "Someone put it there. And it wouldn't have been easy to do, either."

"No, nor does it seem likely it were possible when it was as fully grown as the thing we encountered." She was squatted down, but he could feel her eyes still on him. "So it would have to have been brought in when it was small, yes?"

"Yes." Terian ran a finger over his lips idly. "But why?"

"There was a time that someone spread wildroot dye over the gates of the greatest manors in Saekaj," Sareea said, standing up and gathering her robe about her. "When they caught the responsible party, it turned out to be a teenager from near the gate. He had no reason for doing it but that he hated those who had what he did not."

"So you'd chalk it up to resentment?" Terian said, and looked over at her. She stood, standing aloof as she spoke. "I wish I could. I'm in the midst of looking for deeper connections, darker reasons."

"You mean to suggest someone intended the thing to eat those fishermen?" Sareea asked, eyes narrowed. "To what purpose?"

"Start insurrections in Sovar?" Terian spoke aloud, letting his thoughts fall out. "Starve the people out a little at a time? I don't know."

"Both of those would be an end of some sort," Sareea said.

"Pretty horrible ends," Terian said, "for lots of people."

"Yet some would profit by it."

"That's a fairly ghastly way to look at things," Terian said.

"But true," she said, thin smile still turning up the corner of her mouth. "Do you not see it?"

"Maybe I don't want to see it." He yawned. "It's pretty horrible way to look at the world, to think someone would put a beast like that in the Great Sea just to starve out the poor."

"Saekaj is filled with men and women base enough to do something of that sort if the advantage was apparent," Sareea said. "Would you not do it yourself if you had to?"

"No." Terian sat up in bed, his disgust outweighing his fatigue. "I have to go home."

"Very well," Sareea's arms crossed in front of her chest.

Terian slid over to the edge of the bed and fished on the floor for his underclothes. "I thought I had a dark mind, but you coming up with this—"

"Don't play the innocent," Sareea said, and he heard a ripple of laughter from her. "As though you can't see the profit in it yourself for someone who might want to stir animosities in Sovar."

"Rioting in Sovar benefits no one," Terian said as he grabbed his rough cloth pants off the floor and struggled into them.

"It benefits someone," Sareea said. "You just have to be—as you put it—ghoulish enough to see it."

Terian paused, tightening the cord of his belt. "I don't think I want to be that ghoulish."

"Then you're missing the point. There are dozens who would benefit from upheaval in terms of power consolidation. The army alone has grown by leaps and bounds since the fish supply has dwindled." She spoke and a thin satisfaction fell off her words. "There's an advantage right there for your father—he has more soldiers and more power because they're guaranteed to eat and their families get a larger stipend than if they were aimless poor."

Terian paused in bed, his hand over the edge and clutching his undershirt. "You're not accusing him, I hope."

"I would support him if he'd done it," Sareea said, though she sounded hollow. "He has my loyalty, remember? I'm just pointing out that you're not thinking it through because somehow it offends your sensibilities."

"He wouldn't do that," Terian said, shaking his head. "Even he's not that much of a—" He stopped speaking, and closed his eyes. *He's that much of a monster and more.*

So much more.

"I doubt he would have sent us to kill the beast if he'd gone to the trouble of unleashing it," she said. Her voice was hovering somewhere in the darkness that surrounded him now that his eyes were closed. "But I am impressed at your naiveté. It's almost as if you have enough optimism to want to blindly believe no one would do such things. A peculiar trait in a man who's made a soul sacrifice as dark as the one that was required of you—"

"Don't...mention that in my presence again." His eyes were open now, and he stared straight up at the dark ceiling. He looked right, and knew the danger was radiating off of him. He caught her gaze and saw whatever emotion she was sporting—amusement again, he thought—slip beneath a stony facade.

She bowed her head slightly. "As you wish, my lord."

"I have to go," Terian said, rolling out of bed and finding the heavy plate of his greaves with his toe. He cursed.

"Would you like me to help you put your armor back on?" she asked coolly.

He stopped short of telling her to go to hell and held his tongue. "Yes," he said after a minute, and he heard her dutifully fishing around below him.

He stood there, still and silent, as she helped him re-dress, one piece of armor at a time. When he was finished, she gave him a perfunctory peck on the cheek. "Come see me again whenever you wish," she said with her customary coolness.

He started to snap a reply, the rawness still burning from their conversation. A sense of unease settled over him, and he kissed her cheek in return, tasting the faint hint of sweat as he did so. "You know I will," he said, speaking the truth, because no other words he could summon to mind seemed to matter.

40.

The door to his house was opened for him, and Terian stepped inside without waiting for the servant's greeting. The air seemed especially damp in Saekaj today, and he shuddered under his coat as the chill crept over him.

"My son," Olia said, greeting him from where she sat in a chair in a recessed alcove under the curve of the stairwell.

"Mother," Terian said tightly.

"Your bride was inquiring about you earlier," Olia said, somewhat brightly for her. He studied her lined face; it had seemed less worn of late, and she occasionally even smiled.

"Is my father still here?" Terian asked, glossing right over her words. *Kahlee can wait.*

"In his study," Olia said, and her brow slumped into a frown. "What is it?"

"Just need to discuss some matters of state with him," Terian said, heading for the steps and climbing past her. "Typical things, nothing urgent."

"Of course, dear," Olia said, and turned her head back to whatever she was doing. "Shall I have Guturan send you up some lunch? You missed eating with the rest of us."

"I'm not hungry right now," Terian called back, already halfway up the third floor stairs. "Maybe later."

Terian halted in front of the study doors. He hesitated then knocked boldly. *No point in holding back now.*

"Come in," his father said.

Terian entered, taking care to shut the door behind him. Amenon looked up from behind his desk, which was curiously bare of parchment. "You're back earlier than I would have expected," Amenon said.

"Concluded all my other business," Terian said. He saw a hint of tension in Amenon's jaw as he spoke, but it faded. "I had a thought."

Amenon stared at him, lips slightly puckered in distaste. "Is it one I even want to hear?"

Terian faltered. "It's about the monster."

Amenon sighed in resignation, then waved a hand as if to shoo Terian away. "It's done, let us put it behind us—"

"Someone put that thing in the water," Terian said, taking a step forward. "I know you don't want to talk about this, but it killed Verret, so we should at least discuss it—"

"It happened months ago," Amenon said, looking at the cold surface of his desk.

"Two months," Terian said. "Two months in which we've yet to discuss it."

"There have been more important matters to attend to."

"Verret died killing that thing," Terian said, feeling the fury rising within.

"He died doing his duty," Amenon said with a quiet sigh. "If it hadn't been this, it might have been something else. People die in our line of work, Terian. Don't be a child about it."

Terian resisted the urge to chew his lip the way he had when he'd addressed his father as a child. "Did you put it there?"

Amenon's eyebrows arched downward and the souring effect on his expression was immediate. "No." His answer didn't come out quite as a growl, but it was obvious that there was anger behind it.

"Do you know who did?" Terian asked. He stood resolute, in the middle of the room. *I won't retreat on this, even though I can see how much he wants me to just leave.*

"I have my suspicions," Amenon said, standing without warning, armor clanking as he did so. "But this is a foolish path to go down. We take what gain from it we can and we are thankful. It is not our place to probe deeply into the realms of unfounded speculation—"

"Unfounded speculation about who turned loose a monster to starve Sovar?" Terian asked, and the hints of fury started to break loose. "That killed countless fishermen? That killed Verret? Why wouldn't we want to know who did this thing? This foul thing—"

"Because!" Amenon leaned over on his desk, knuckles of his gauntlets slamming hard into the surface before his voice dove into a whisper. "Because, you fool, it was in all likelihood Shrawn."

"Shrawn?" Terian lowered his voice to match his father's. "But why? Why would Shrawn—"

"Because of power," Amenon said. "And because of revenge. When the last food uprisings happened in Sovar, Shrawn was in charge. No good came of them, not really, and the sting is still felt to this day. The Sovereign is now returned, and he looks upon his diminished dominion, and he wonders who is to blame. His fingers are now on the yoke, though, and—"

"And if Sovar experiences food riots now, with him in command," Terian said, "he blames the people and not Shrawn." Terian his fingers under his helm's edge and pulled it off his head, letting a rush of cool cave air into his sweaty hair. "What a bastard."

"You must admire the cleverness of the stratagem," Amenon said, voice low. "He is already feeling the heat of the Sovereign's ire for the territorial losses we experienced in the aftermath of the last war. The Sovereign's eye is fixed on his strength, on building the army, on preparing to reassert ourselves as a power to be feared. He pays no attention to events within these caves, and until something dramatic catches his eye, this will continue. Riots in Sovar will awaken him in the most shocking way possible to the idea that even with him at the helm, Saekaj Sovar does not run flawlessly without continued attention."

Terian closed his eyes tightly. "And if a whole lot of soldiers and innocent people in Sovar have to die to show the Sovereign how 'weak' he is—"

"It's not about weakness," Amenon said, hissing as he whispered. "It's about strength. About realizing that even as strong as he is—the God of Darkness—he cannot put his fingers around everything at once. And he will be more forgiving toward those who have erred in the past, presumably."

Terian thought about it in the cold silence for a moment. "Why would you not say something about this? Why not throw it before the Sovereign and let Shrawn look even weaker than he already does?"

Amenon watched him carefully. "If I had even one ounce of proof, I might do exactly that. But Shrawn is far, far too clever to have left any loose ends." He leaned forward on the desk and lowered his voice further. "I sent Xemlinan after a smuggler named Boultres Tarrin who regularly runs illegal goods for Shrawn through hidden tunnels into both Saekaj and Sovar. Word reached Xemlinan that he had brought in something especially difficult several months ago, something that required a large, strong, glass container the size of five men. Shrawn had it manufactured by the glassblowers of Aloakna and shipped across the Bay of Lost Souls to the human city of Taymor. From there it traveled under guard to the shores of Lake Magnus where it was met by an acclaimed trio of monster hunters from the Bandit Lands.

"It remained there for a fortnight," Amenon continued, "then came into the possession of Boultres Tarrin, who brought it into the Waking Woods through a series of rough paths that only he knows. Xemlinan had a man inside his convoy, and this man knew all of the illicit goods in the convoy—gold, silks, powders, dusts and spices—save for those in one wagon in the caravan. When the goods came through the tunnels into the city, that one wagon was left to the attention of Tarrin himself and two other men. How they got it into the city after that is a matter of mystery to us, but what is not is that a fisherman saw a man fitting Tarrin's description along with five others charter a boat with a heavy cargo to take them out into the Great Sea. That boat did not return that night and was found adrift later, every last one of the men aboard missing save for Tarrin himself.

"It was the first to disappear," he finished.

"That's quite the scheme," Terian said. "But if you know where Boultres Tarrin is, you could have him brought into the torture chamber—"

"Tarrin is hanging from a tree in the Waking Woods," Amenon said calmly, "tarred from head to toe so that his body holds together for as long as possible as an example to other smugglers."

"Shrawn had him killed?" Terian said. "He moves fast, to have him tried—"

"He was not tried," Amenon said with a slight smile. "He was killed in the act of being caught, you see. He was tarred and hanged after the fact."

Terian nodded. "And the monster hunters? The glassblowers? The smuggler accomplices?"

"All dead," Amenon said. "Or missing and presumed dead. Several of the glassblowers were found floating in the Bay of Lost Souls; I would assume the rest will wash up eventually. The dockworkers who handled the shipment in Taymor are also mysteriously gone. The monster hunters have disappeared—they, of course, could have actually gone back to the Bandit Lands, though I very much doubt it as Shrawn is far too much of a completionist to let that particular detail go unattended when he has wrapped up so many others." He rubbed his palms together once and then pulled them apart as though he were washing his hands. "So there you have it. A conspiracy, murder, scheming, all in the name of helping Dagonath Shrawn to maintain his position by making himself look slightly better in the eyes of the Sovereign."

"How many people died to accomplish that?" Terian asked.

"Half a hundred," Amenon said with a light shrug. "Perhaps a few more, perhaps a few less. Does it matter? He failed to accomplish his aim, after all."

"Are you truly so coarsened that the means he used to reach that end matter little enough to you?" Terian asked.

"How coarse I am to death is of no consequence," Amenon said with a sigh, once again looking tired. "It was done regardless, and not by me."

But you would have done it if you could have gotten the advantage from it, Terian thought.

"Consider carefully what you are thinking in this moment," Amenon said, and Terian watched his eyes narrow. "It is obvious and written on your face. Consider whether taking it to its natural conclusion will make you a greater servant of your family and your Sovereign than letting it be."

"It's 'anything it takes' at this level, isn't it?" Terian asked flatly.

"It always has been," Amenon said, looking weary again, "and you know that."

Terian felt his head bow. "It never ends, does it? The wheel just keeps spinning and we have to constantly run to remain atop it."

Amenon sighed and seemed to grow stronger. "That is the very nature of the Shuffle. Favor and disfavor are as obvious as the position of your manor. But it is a wheel that we run upon, and all it takes is a slip to fall beneath its grinding weight." He gazed at Terian. "Thus far we have escaped that fate, but remember that it is never more than a turn away."

"What do we do?" Terian asked. "To make sure that—"

"We do what we have always done," Amenon said and reached out to touch the ruby resting on his desk. "We provide the exemplary service that the Sovereign requires." He looked up at Terian and for the first time he truly saw the weariness in his father's eyes, the bone-tired essence that he realized had been there all along, beneath the surface. "Without fail."

41.

Terian entered his room to find Kahlee in the corner reading a book by the faint light of a lamp. She looked up as he entered, but she did not smile. The smell of the burnt lamp oil was faint but present, and Kahlee herself wore a bedding gown, ready for sleep. The blue had begun to grow out of her hair, the dye's effects fading. She wore a look of indifference at his entry and closed the book with a heavy thump as he shut the door noiselessly.

"Wife," Terian said as he unfastened his breastplate.

"Husband," she replied with little interest.

"My mother told me you were asking after me earlier." He removed his gauntlets one by one and laid them upon the dressing table.

"I was merely being polite," she said crisply. "I know you were at the Unnamed and visiting your mistress afterward."

He halted, his left hand caught halfway out of his gauntlet. "Does this displease you?"

"It does not surprise me," she said. "How I feel about it other than that is irrelevant."

"It's relevant to me," he said, removing the other gauntlet slowly, as though it might rattle and drown out her reply.

"Ours is an arranged marriage," she said, "a matter of duty, and thus my feelings are also irrelevant—even to you."

"I see," he said, beginning to remove his boots, taking care not to make excess noise by kicking them off. "Then I take it your feelings are not greatest enthusiasm and pleasure."

"Your sense for these things is exceptional," she said acidly. "I have one task before me, one task that our ridiculous and suppressive society levies upon me, and you are wasting your seed with a mistress before I have even borne you one child." She let out a disgusted noise. "Not that I care for myself, you understand, as the thought of bearing your offspring is a dose of water straight out of the morning chamber pot—but I have my duty, and I would not fail my house in this matter."

Terian blinked. "Bearing my child is like drinking from a full chamber pot?"

She did not flinch away when answering. "And only slightly less likely to result in some form of plague being introduced to my body, based on the murky inkpot in which you dip your quill."

"Gods," Terian cursed, slipping his helm off and placing it on the corner table.

"I hope you keep your blaspheming tongue in your head outside of our chambers," Kahlee said thinly. "Lest the Sovereign find you out and disgrace us all."

"Most of the time I do," Terian said. "But about my other activities—"

"I have no interest in discussing them further," Kahlee said with another noise of disgust. "You know what you are doing, I know what you are doing. We need not delve into the details of your wanderings. Just realize that I am not a fool."

"I never thought you were," he said quietly. "But much like everything else in this city, there are expectations—"

"That you must follow?" Kahlee let out a sharp, barking laugh. "I can scarcely believe this comes from Terian Lepos. You have made a life of defying convention and expectation—but apparently only when it suits you." She cocked her head. "Now you're making a life from obedience that would make a tame vek'tag's carapace show a blush. Is it mere enrichment that causes you to fall into line with the other good soldiers? Or did the idea of a wife and mistress under your power suddenly make you appreciate the ways of Saekaj that you so recently denounced?"

"Oh, maybe I'm just a hypocrite," Terian said and felt a resignation deeper than that which he'd seen on his father's face. "Maybe I'm tired of bucking conventions and trying so hard to fight against the expectations levied on me. I mean, look where it landed me last time—in a cold room in a human boarding house, scraping a living by guarding a warehouse against the predations of ruffians and street urchins. When I rebelled here, in my father's house, it got me killed by one of his loyal servants." Terian felt his shoulders heave in a shrug. "Why fight it? I'm here, aren't I? I made my choices that led me to the dead end in Reikonos, and I made the choices that brought me back here, where I have gold in my pocket and a wife who hates me." He took a breath and an absurd grin broke upon his face. "One of those is easier to live with, but I'll cope with both somehow."

Her lips were pursed in utter disgust, as though she were about to spit on him from across the room. She started toward him, and he did not flinch from her, waiting to see if she actually would spit on him. She did not, and when she reached him she took his hand lightly in hers. As her soft skin brushed against his, he was acutely aware of his calloused, rough, dry hands against the softness of hers. She pressed the back of his hand to her lips, but the fire still burned in her eyes. He let another sigh. "We don't have to—I don't want you to be saddled with a burden you don't want from me—"

"I have a duty," she said simply and kissed his hand again, harder this time. "I have one duty, one duty in this loathsome place. I may not love you, but I love my family."

He started to clamp his mouth shut but words escaped anyhow. "That's a piss poor reason to have a child with me."

She froze for a moment before she lowered his hand. "It is the *only* reason to have a child with you."

He felt a sickness in his gut at her words. "Then don't. It's not good enough."

She glanced down. "Perhaps you're not the only one who has grown tired of bucking expectations."

He pulled away from her and removed his breastplate and backplate, hanging them on the carved wooden figure just to his side. He stared at the smooth, rounded head of the carving, a face as blank as the one he felt like he wore even now. "It isn't right."

"It is law," she said from behind him. "Law laid down by our fathers, by our society. It's their will, and it's the one thing that will keep our houses together against any storm."

He thought about the sea monster again. *Shrawn will do anything to protect his position. Anything. Destroying an alliance seems like a natural thought for him.* "I get the feeling the storm is coming, that's certain."

"Then we'll need a strong boat," she said, and he felt her light touch on his shoulder.

Maybe it would be better to drown, he did not say. *Maybe it would be better to let our houses sink, to defy expectations, to thwart my father and let the wheel roll on without us.* He felt the air rush out of his lungs in an uncontrolled burst as he thought of Sanctuary, of the lounge, with fresh kegs set out and a roaring fire to sit beside with companions—of Niamh, and her natural red hair, without a hint of wildroot dye, of Curatio and his stoic pragmatism, of—

He cut it off in the middle, and came back to himself to feel her hand still upon his shoulder, her fingers kneading into the muscles there. *Duty.* "I suppose we will," he said, and placed his hand upon her own. He could feel her skin against his, and it felt colder than the air around them.

42.

The hammering at his door fell in the very early morning hours, jarring Terian out of a sound sleep. He could feel Kahlee stirring next to him, and cleared his throat in the cool night air. "Yes?"

"Lord Terian," came Guturan's voice from behind the door. "Lord Amenon requests your immediate presence in full armor."

"Okay," Terian said, cotton-mouthed from the whiskey he'd had hours earlier. "Did he say why?" His eyes slid in the dark toward Kahlee's form and saw her head off her pillow, listening into the night the way he was.

Guturan's answer came after a pause. "There is a disturbance in the Back Deep of Sovar, Milord. Your father has been summoned to deal with it."

Terian saw Kahlee's eyes widen, he suspected in direct response to his own. He fought his way through the sheets to the edge of the bed and let his unclad feet hit the rug, the small fibers digging into the skin as he hurried to dress.

"Do you think it's an uprising?" Kahlee asked from the bed.

"I don't know," Terian said, slinging his underclothes on at a rapid pace. He jumped into his pants both feet first, sliding his way into them before throwing his shirt on. "I kind of doubt it's a *veredajh* that's gotten out of control if they've called Amenon Lepos to come running to the Back Deep."

Kahlee held her tongue for a moment before responding, giving Terian time to start fastening plates into place. "How bad could it be? If it is an uprising?"

"I don't know," Terian said. "I think the fish supply has returned to normal, so I'm not sure what it is, exactly." He held his tongue before saying anything more. *But if it's an uprising, you can bet Shrawn is behind it somehow.*

Kahlee got out of bed as Terian put his breastplate on and began to fiddle with the straps. "You have servants for that," she said, draping herself with a robe.

"Yes, and I'm sure Guturan would have thought to send them in—if Guturan wasn't panicking right now," Terian said, trying to get the straps to fasten.

"How can you tell he's panicking?"

"Because he didn't send in the servants," Terian replied, almost mumbling as he fastened the last strap. He grabbed his helm and slid it carefully onto his head before securing his axe on his back. "Go back to bed."

"If it's all the same," Kahlee said, sounding a little irritable as he reached the door, "I'll likely join your mother in the foyer to await your return."

Terian stopped at the door, hand on the frame, holding himself back. He shot a look over his shoulder. "Why?"

Kahlee stood with her arms crossed over the cloth robe. She was straight-faced, without an eyebrow out of place. "Because it is expected."

Terian felt a hint of chastening in the way she said it and tried to decide how to respond before ultimately giving up and throwing himself through the door without uttering the one that came to mind. *So long as it's not because you love me.*

He nearly collided with his father in the hall but dodged narrowly. "Guturan woke you," Amenon said without prelude.

"You didn't think he'd let me sleep through this, did you?" Terian said, falling in like a shadow, a step behind his father. "Is it an uprising?"

"Too soon to tell," Amenon said stiffly, "but suffice it to say there is some act of rebellion taking place at present. Arms have been raised, hostages taken—all in a communal house. Some of the residents of the home have fled, some from neighboring homes have taken up arms and joined the troublemakers."

"I notice you didn't say 'insurrectionists,'" Terian said.

"No reason to start a panic," Amenon said, "and loose use of words like that is sure to set fire to the tinder of gossip throughout Saekaj and Sovar."

They burst out the front door to the waiting carriage, Terian sliding in just behind his father before shutting the door himself. The driver lashed the vek'tag into motion and they stuttered down the drive over the rutted roads. The sound of running water drew Terian's eyes out the window of the carriage to the chimneys in the rock overhead, where water sluiced down from the ceilings. "Not a great day for this."

"How's that?" Amenon said, and looked past Terian. "Light of the sky! A torrent from above? What would you care to wager that the Back Deep is already under an inch of water and rising?"

"All your money and none of mine," Terian said. "You didn't get word that it was flooding?"

"No," Amenon said, stiffly again. "I had suspected my messages of late have been somewhat compromised, but to see water flow of this sort with my own eyes and not receive a single word of warning ..." His brow creased, and adopted a dark expression. "Someone shall be flayed for this."

"Sounds like fun," Terian said, shaking his head. The noise of falling water was a dull roar, but something else seemed to reach his ears, something faint. He sat against the carriage's hard seat, shifting in his armor as the sound grew louder. It was almost a chattering, something on the order of the sound of Shrawn's ball, but with the noise of the water to give it depth.

He took a deep breath through his nose and caught the scent of the vek'tag, the earthy, deep aroma of the spiders pulling the carriages. The carriage pitched in a sudden, jerking slowdown, and the driver yelled ahead, shrieking at the vek'tag to stop.

Terian hit the side of the carriage with a spiked pauldron, chipping wood from the surface as he cursed. He stuck his head out the window once he'd righted himself, and the cool cave air came through his facial slit. "Son of a bitch."

"What is it?" He could hear his father scrambling to look out the other window.

The square of Saekaj was filled with a crowd—servants, women and men standing from end to end. The houses had emptied, and people in nightclothes were thronging in the streets. Hands were being wrung, and Terian could hear the shrieks of children and the high, fearful tones of women and men. "They think it's started. The big one. They think Sovar is rising to destroy them." He looked over the crowd, packed tightly in the streets, blocking access to the square, to the roads that would carry them down to Sovar, where they could conceivably quell the panic already in the streets. Before his eyes, Terian watched a bulky woman in fancy nightclothes faint dead away in the middle of the lane, her companions useless to prevent her fall.

"I think the tinder has already been lit," Terian said to his father, staring at the chaos on the streets of the upper city. "And the gossip has already spread in a way far beyond what we could have hoped for."

"Indeed," Amenon said ruefully, "and these fools have no idea that by their mere stupidity, they may be allowing the very thing they fear the most to grow enflamed enough to consume them—and us—in the fires."

43.

It had taken three hours to reach Sovar. Three tense, terrible hours in which Terian and his father had hung out the open doors of the carriage, screaming profanities at the nobles clogging the streets of Saekaj. After the square they were aided in this by Sareea, who hoisted herself into Terian's side of the carriage after elbowing her way through a knot of men carrying dueling canes. She showed little remorse in her blows, Terian thought as he watched her, and when one of the dandies spoke against her she silenced him with a punch followed by a Lockjaw curse.

The down slope of the tunnel to Sovar was a steady flow of running water. The carriage slid every few feet, going diagonally until the driver managed to straighten it back into the ruts. It bumped over the hard rock and slowed when it hit clay and sediment. Amenon's expression grew blacker and blacker as they descended.

When they reached the gates of Sovar, the army was already visible in the streets. There were guards on the corners and not a civilian in sight. Helmeted heads dominated the avenues, columns and formations filling the plazas and squares around the Front Gate. As they followed the road, lines of soldiers moved aside for them. The running water was not so bad here, at least not until they reached the slope in the Mids that led to the Back Deep.

The straight-line street they took was a disastrous, sloping waterfall. Pooling water was visible at the bottom, and Terian cringed as he kept his head out the window. He could see an entire regiment of the army marching along the cross streets, a show of force so blatant he wondered if the message was anything less than obvious.

Terian glanced up at the windows and cloth walls of the buildings to see faces staring down at him, peering from the cracks. *I think they get the message. Otherwise they'd be out here.* "Not exactly the full-scale uprising they think it is in Saekaj, is it?"

"Perception may veer wildly from reality but when the perceivers help control reality, it's best not to let the misperception linger too long," Amenon said darkly.

Their progress halted at the bottom of the hill. Water stood in the streets like a small-scale version of the Great Sea, dark water that barely revealed the sandy roads beneath it. "We walk from here," Amenon pronounced. Sareea dismounted out of the carriage before Terian could even remove himself from his seat. She pushed him aside, making no attempt to be gentle, her armor clashing with his as she made her exit. The splash of her boots on the ground coincided with a surge of annoyance that flushed his face.

He followed her out, but she was already trailing his father on her way down the street. "Find the commander in charge," Amenon said, and Terian watched Sareea immediately veer toward the nearest cluster of soldiers, a patrol of four standing on the nearest street corner. They straightened to attention as she approached, and Terian watched her speak in quiet tones to the patrol leader.

"She is quite the find, isn't she?" Amenon asked.

"She's quite *something*," Terian said.

"Hrm," Amenon said, his strides long and making dramatic splashes with every step. "I should think you'd be singing her praises, given that you've made her your mistress."

"Wouldn't want to compromise my ability to lead with any sort of emotional attachment," Terian said, as seriously as he could. His father glanced back at him, as though trying to see if he were speaking in jest. Terian gave no sign.

"I see," his father said and nodded once, sharply. "An admirable attitude. Still and all, the two of you seem to have handled things well enough thus far. Do not give me cause to change my opinion."

Terian rolled his eyes. *The man spreads warnings even when they're unneeded; I know full well what happens if she and I become a problem. One of us gets the axe, possibly literally. Hopefully it'd be her, but I wouldn't care to lay all my gold on that bet.*

"The commander is this way," Sareea said, returning to them. The splash of her boots in the standing water sent beads of water onto Terian's armor, prompting a flash of annoyance in his head. "He's set up a field headquarters in one of the buildings ahead."

"Very well, then." Amenon broke into a jog, and Terian fell in behind him, Sareea keeping pace at his side.

The water made for slower going, and Terian could feel the drag against his feet. *This will be like a fight in a swamp. Clearly I've been neglecting my physical fitness.* He glanced at Sareea, and saw the light of humor in her eyes as she watched him—*she's got a jest on her mind about how our exertions together have clearly not conditioned me for this. Predictable.*

They passed two blocks of buildings, thin structures of wood framing with cloth pulled over them as a facade. Some of them had real walls, made of plaster or slabs of stone. Banners dyed wild colors hung off the shop fronts, which blended with the residence houses here in the Back Deep.

Ahead, Terian saw a figure in a white robe lingering outside one of the houses. He was next to another, a large man in armor. Dahveed and Grinnd. Terian looked up and saw Bowe sitting in a careful knot with his knees crossed, hanging in the air.

Where is Xem?

"Hello, General," Dahveed said with a sharp bow. "We have a situation unfolding."

"I gathered as much from the urgent missive," Amenon said, slowing to a walk as he approached. "And the Third Army being deployed here in Sovar."

"Aye, sir," Dahveed said, a little more formal than Terian was used to from him. "They have the building surrounded. We have other forces in route from Saekaj—"

"This doesn't even look to fit the description of a small-scale insurrection," Amenon said, frowning at the building across the way. It was silent, absolutely silent, the cloth walls of the upper floors not even moving. Drips of water fell from the porous ceiling above. "Why haven't we stormed the building and killed everyone in it?"

"There could be innocent people in there," Terian said quietly.

"Best not to take chances with these things," Amenon said without looking back, "lest you allow some marauder to survive."

"They have a wizard," Dahveed said.

There was a stark silence for a moment. "That ... changes things," Amenon said.

"Indeed," Dahveed said, his hands crossed in front of him and hidden in his robes. "I should mention, just for the sake of it, that they do have women and children in the building."

"That's a shame," Amenon said with no more interest than he'd shown when water had begun to splash on his armor. *Bastard*, Terian thought. "The good news for us is that they've chosen to deploy their wizard at a moment when his fire spells are going to be of minimal effect. Everything in this place is soaked."

"Would it matter if it wasn't?" Terian asked. Amenon shot him a look. "I wasn't criticizing, just pointing out that we have a task in front of us regardless of the weather."

"It matters," Amenon said, not removing his glare. "Very well. I'll consult with the commander while you lot make plans to storm the building. We need to make sure that wizard does not escape. Bowe," he glanced up at the druid, "make ready to kill him at distance if need be, understand?"

"He will not see the spell that kills him," Bowe said quietly.

"We do have other spell casters en route," Dahveed said. "I have the Commonwealth of Arcanists and Gathering of Coercers sending several of their instructors to assist us—"

"They will be hours in arriving," Amenon said abruptly. "Saekaj is in utter chaos at the moment. We cannot afford to wait for wizards and enchanters. We do this now. If necessary, we burn the building with the wizard in it." He gave one last look at each of them and then shouldered his way through the door into the army headquarters.

"That may not be enough to stop the wizard," Bowe said through slitted eyes that Terian could barely see from below. "I will ensure he does not escape."

"What else is inside?" Terian asked. *If we're going to do this, best to do it right.*

"No idea," Dahveed said, and Terian could sense his discomfort. "We only know there's a wizard because he hurled a spell at us."

"He could teleport if things get dicey," Terian said. "Just disappear out of here."

"No, he couldn't," Dahveed said. "The Colonel in charge of this regiment brought with him an iridescent sphere that prevents teleportation out of Sovar. The wizard—and any others within those walls—are trapped."

"Trapped means dangerous," Sareea said. "Like a cornered rat, they'll strike at anything."

"And a cornered wizard means their strikes are somewhat more effective than tiny claws and teeth," Dahveed said.

"Will they be expecting someone to come from the air?" Grinnd asked, breaking his silence.

"Depends on how much of a veteran their wizard is—hell, how many veterans they have in total," Dahveed said. "Anyone with any experience serving in an army knows that when you bring spell casters into a fight, the rules change dramatically. Assume they know we'll come at them from all directions, including above."

"Army moves in and seals off the ground exits," Terian said, staring at the building across the street. It looked to be in shambles, just another dilapidated shanty home in Sovar that had probably seen its best days centuries earlier. "We crash through the plaster wall there," Terian pointed to indicate one of the solid walls, "but also come in through the second floor simultaneously with three floaters through that cloth wall," he gave a nod to Bowe, "and try to get this wizard before he causes any damage. He goes down, we mop the rest up."

Amenon reemerged from the door of the headquarters, the sharp spikes jutting off his armor cracking against the plaster frame and dislodging grey powder. "I heard the gist of what you are proposing and I approve. Grinnd will lead the way on the ground,

I will follow with Dahveed behind me. Sareea, Bowe and Terian will strike against the second floor."

"How soon will the army start to move into position?" Terian asked as he felt the effects of Falcon's Essence take hold, pulling his feet above the surface of the water.

Amenon paused, and turned his head toward the house in question. Soldiers were visible in the back alley next to it, moving slowly.

"They'll hear them," Terian said. "With the water filling the streets, there's no way to move silently in that—"

"We go now," Amenon said, and started across the street. "Make your attack on the second floor in fifteen seconds." He drew his sword as he went, Grinnd and Dahveed trailing behind him.

"Son of a …" Terian muttered and then shook his head. Drips from above were pelting his armor like a lightest rain. He glanced at Bowe, who stared at the building across the street, and then at Sareea, who seemed to be casting him a *What are you waiting for?* look. "You heard the man. We have an appointment to keep in about ten seconds. Let's move."

44.

Terian's axe shredded through the thick-spun cloth, some cheap threading manufactured from low quality vek'tag silk castoffs. He could hear Sareea's blade doing the same next to him, and they burst through into the dwelling and into a world of shouts and screams.

Most of them were coming from downstairs, Terian realized as he plunged his axe into the chest of a man carrying a short blade sword. The look of shock was muted as dark blood ran down the man's chin, pouring from his lips like the water rushing down the slopes of Sovar.

Sareea was already sweeping forward into the room as Terian pulled his axe out of the man's chest and let him fall. *Traitors are supposed to bleed to death anyway.*

A trio of screams from below hurt Terian's ears and he cringed. One of the shouts of agony degenerated into cursing, and he recognized the voice as Grinnd's, the loudest of the three. Another was a little higher, more accented—*Dahveed.*

The third was his father's.

He broke toward the outline of a stairwell ahead but was halted by a hard gauntlet slapping him in the chest. "Go up," Sareea shot at him as she pushed him back. Bowe flew past him in her wake, and Terian froze, watching the two of them descend. Another scream penetrated louder than the others, and he knew from the sound of it that Sareea had dealt with someone—and quite harshly.

Terian steered his course woodenly toward the stairs up to the third floor. His feet were still drifting above the old planks that made up the floor.

He's not dead. He's not. He's fine. The screams below were fading as he stepped into the open stairwell and looked up to the floor above. He could see nothing looking back down at him save for the beams of the ceiling above. With a quick motion, he squatted and jumped as hard as he could.

He felt his feet catch firmly as the spell prevented him from falling once his upward momentum was arrested. He leapt again and came over the railing of the third floor of the building with his sword at the ready. There was only one man waiting for him there, a scrawny runt of a dark elf, thin fingers extended in front of him. "Wait!"

Terian buried the axe in his shoulder and it cut down through the collarbone until it lodged. The man cried out, and blood dripped down his ragged tunic, dyed green. He fell to his knees, the axe still buried in him.

"When I pull this weapon out, you'll have about a minute to live," Terian said, keeping a snug grip on the handle. His eyes took in the rest of the room. There were ratty little bedrolls on the hard floor, a handful of possessions scattered about the room. The whole place stunk, the chamber pots full to the brimming.

"Please," the man said, and blood was dripping from his thin lips. "Please."

"You have women and children in here?" Terian asked. He looked up, trying to see if there was a stairwell to the roof. The planks looked rotted and there were countless gaps. *Not sturdy enough for people to live up there, or they would, sure as shit.*

"No," the man said, and his body shuddered. "We're not ..." His voice sounded far away, like it was fading. He looked up at Terian, looked him straight in the eyes with dark pupils that appeared to be getting larger by the moment. "... monsters."

Movement behind him caused Terian to rip his axe free and bring it up in a defensive posture as he spun toward the stairwell. Sareea stood there, watching him, looking grim until she broke into a faint smile.

"What happened?" Terian asked, glancing to the fallen rebel he'd pulled the axe from. The man made a faint choking noise, his thin frame rattling as it tried to cling to a life that was already fleeing.

"Wizard caught our team with an ice spell as they entered," Sareea said. "Froze the standing water and their legs within it."

"Huh," Terian said, still watching the skinny rebel. The man reached out toward him with those long, thin fingers. They touched his boot, smearing dark blood on the toe where the spikes jutted. "Are they all right?"

"They'll be fine," Sareea said. "Is this the last one?"

"Seems that way," Terian said, glancing around the room. "They had most of the resistance stacked up on the first floor, then?"

"Where we were most likely to hit, yes," Sareea said. "And nobody up here?"

"Their leader," Terian said with a shake of the head. "We should ... attend to the rest of our team."

"Right," Sareea said, already descending. She paused, just for a moment. "What are you doing?"

"The sentence for a rebel is death," Terian said, and stared down at the man. "Death by bleeding, if it happens in the course of resistance. I'm just watching the sentence carried out." He shot a look around the room. "The man's near dead, I'll bring him with us." He reached down and grabbed the skinny body with one hand, laying it over his shoulder, spikes on his pauldrons burying themselves into the man's guts.

"Why not leave him for the army?" Sareea asked, still paused on the stairs.

Terian hesitated. "Because I want to watch him die. Did you kill the wizard already?"

"Couldn't be avoided," Sareea said, and she broke into a faint smile. "We could resurrect him, though, if you'd like to make him suffer—"

"We'll leave that to my father," Terian said, heading toward the stairs. Every step gave way to a creaking noise, the weight of his armor making the floor seem as though it would give at any moment. "Let's collect the bodies from the second floor and toss them out into the street for disposal."

"Aye," Sareea said, descending below where he could see her. "I wonder if they'll tar and hang them as examples?"

"No," Terian said, pausing just before he reached the edge of the staircase. He checked to make certain that Sareea could not see him. The body on his shoulder was drawing its last breath, one last, dying gasp, a rattle, and then it went quiet.

He glanced around the room, the empty room—where water dripped in from the ceiling above, splashing in the corner in a strange pattern that looked like hair. Hair bereft of substance, hair that was colored in the exact manner of the wall behind it, like a lizard Terian had once seen that could blend in with whatever it was pressed against.

The colorless hair hung there, the barest outline of a head visible with it, only a couple feet off the ground.

A child.

Terian held up his finger and placed it on his lips, then spoke low as he tossed the body over the edge of the railing, hoping its landing would keep Sareea from hearing his words. "Stay quiet, stay hidden until the army is gone. Do not make a sound until they've left."

He looked around the room, wondering how many of them there were, hiding, invisible from the spell the wizard had surely cast upon them. He would have guessed at least five, maybe ten. Maybe more.

"What are you doing?" Sareea called up from below.

"Hurt my shoulder throwing that corpse over the edge." He stepped into view and looked down the stairs to see her standing there, the body at her feet. "Too much desk work. I think I'm atrophying away."

She cocked her head at him and smiled faintly. "You need more exertion in your life."

He smiled back, but there was no warmth in it. *Say what you have to.* "I trust you'll help me with that." Without another look back, he descended the stairs toward her. The thin, bony face of the rebel he'd killed stared back at him with hollow eyes.

45.

"Utter foolishness," Amenon pronounced as the carriage made its way back up the tunnel toward Saekaj. "An insurrection not even in name, nor half measure." The bumping of the carriage along the tunnel road jarred Terian's tense body. Sareea sat next to him, aloof as ever. Dahveed was in the seat next to his father, who had his helm off.

"You would wish for a more dramatic and troublesome rebellion, then?" Dahveed asked with some amusement. His head rocked slightly as they hit a rut in the road. "I suppose we could send down a few more wizards, perhaps some enchanters with the instruction to make a true mess of it."

"I think that the mess we had was quite enough," Amenon said with a slight smile. "That wizard acted with far more craftiness than I would have expected from Sovar trash. Any idea who he was?"

"I don't know the wizards as well as the head of the Commonwealth of Arcanists might," Dahveed said with a shrug. "I could have him come down to the Depths to try and identify the body on the rot pile, if you'd like."

Amenon hesitated for just a moment, lips pursed. "Do so. I do not wish to let this matter go to rest without investigating all possibilities."

"The Third Army will be tied up in Sovar for quite some time, yes?" Terian asked, trying to control his voice.

"At least a week to allow tensions to dissolve, I would think," Amenon said, his face pinched in contemplation. "It may not have been an actual rebellion or riot, but I see no reason to let it spark another before we have a chance to dampen Sovar's enthusiasm for one."

"I'd be surprised if their enthusiasm wasn't already dampened," Terian said, looking out the window to see the thin sheen of water making its way down the slope. It was only a trickle now, compared to what they'd faced on the way down. "Among other things."

"A week will see the Back Deep dried out," Amenon said with a nod. "When I was a child I saw many a harsher flood than this. The ground will accept the water, and it will make its way down to the Great Sea after a time. Such is the way of things there. This is normal."

Normal to see your home turned into a flooded bog with water in the streets. Terian kept himself from grimacing. *I suppose hanging out nearer the Front Gate in the Unnamed, I had no idea how bad it got down in the Back Deep.*

"What I'm curious about is what prompted this particular uprising," Sareea said.

"Do rabble need cause to rise?" Amenon said, staring out the window.

"No, but seldom will you find a man willing to toss himself into death without good cause," Dahveed said, his eyes canny.

"The one I fought looked underfed," Terian said, thinking about it. "I haven't seen any fishing production reports in the last couple weeks."

Amenon looked over at him, eyes focused in the distance, as if staring through him. "You're quite right. I hadn't noticed." He tapped a finger on his chin. "Now that I think on it, I haven't seen production reports for wildroot or mushrooms in at least a few weeks, either."

"Starvation has been the cause of more than a few desperate maneuvers," Terian said.

"It's not quite reached starvation levels," Dahveed said, "but there are some who are most certainly getting close."

"You knew this was a problem?" Amenon snapped.

"Whispers and secondhand rumors," Dahveed said, holding his hands up. "Until this visit, I had not been to Sovar in a few weeks. Too busy attending to other matters."

"If they are edging close to starving," Amenon said, "Shrawn is holding back information from me."

"And you didn't notice?" Terian asked.

"Did you?" Amenon spat back at him. "I've been dealing with the upsurge in training reports for the fourth, fifth, sixth and seventh armies."

"I haven't read those," Terian said. He could feel the sharp surprise. "I didn't even know we had seven armies now."

"We have ten," Amenon said, looking at him through narrowed eyes. "And you did not know because I had set you to watching the civilian side of Saekaj and Sovar, not the army. You were supposed to keep an eye on things here for me."

Terian stared at his father, keeping his jaw from hanging open. *We haven't had ten full armies since the last war.* "I am sorry, Father," he said, trying to choose his words carefully. "I assumed you were holding back the reports since you prefer to filter what I receive."

"I expected you to—" Amenon paused, cocked his head to listen. Terian turned his head as well, and could hear some commotion outside the carriage.

"Lord Amenon!" came a shout from outside. "Lord Amenon!" Terian rose from his bench to look out into the tunnel. The dark cave was lit by lanterns suspended from the walls, casting illumination over the seeping floor. The ground was a muddy, rocky mix, and even with the vek'tag pulling the carriage, it was moving more slowly than a man might run.

Out of the darkness behind them, Terian could see a man sprinting up the slope. He wore the livery of the Third Army, draped in the boiled leather and bearing a metal helm as befit an officer. He was a far cry from the runners typically used to deliver messages. This was an officer, a curious choice to send after the General of the Armies of the entire Sovereignty.

"Stop," Terian ordered the carriage driver, and he could hear the vek'tag at the front of the carriage receive the driver's shouts and curses. "Sareea, with me," Terian said. He heard her move behind him as he jumped from the carriage.

There was a line of other conveyances behind them, carts and the sort. If their drivers were irritated at the inconvenience of the stop of traffic, they were wise enough to say nothing to Terian as he waited just behind the carriage, Sareea at his side, sword drawn. He held his axe loosely in his hands as the officer chasing them huffed his way up the slope.

"Identify yourself," Terian said, moving to intercept the man as he closed on the carriage. Sareea was right there with him, and he could feel her tension without looking at her.

The officer pulled himself upright, fired off a sharp salute, and eyed Terian with a genuine fatigue. "Apologies, my lord. I bring a message for Lord Amenon that I must deliver to his ears only."

"I bet," Terian said, holding up his axe. "And they send you, a fat, slow officer rather than a thin, fast messenger boy?" He raised his axe. "I think—"

"Terian, hold." His father's voice washed over him from behind. "This is Colonel Harsmyth's adjutant, I doubt he's some assassin in disguise." Terian glanced at his father, who stood at the door to the carriage and motioned them forward. "Come. Deliver your message."

"Yes, sir," the adjutant said, breathless. He worked his way up the last few steps. Terian and Sareea flanked him the whole way. He carried the sweaty air of a man who'd been running, a brisk smell. "I come with a message from Colonel Harsmyth."

"I figured that much out," Amenon said, looking at him with narrowed eyes. "Out with it."

"Colonel Harsmyth requests your immediate return to Sovar," the man said, nearly gasping. He slumped, placing his hands on his knees. *He's more winded than even I would be*, Terian thought.

"Did the Colonel give a reason for this request?" Amenon asked, almost hesitant.

"He did, sir, but he asked me to please wait to tell you of it if at all possible until you are far removed from any ... prying ears." The adjutant spoke the last part of the sentence with an apologetic hesitation, as though he had done some great wrong he needed to hide.

Amenon showed little reaction to that which Terian could read. "I'm afraid I'm going to need to know before I turn around."

The adjutant swallowed hard. "Of course, sir." His voice was little more than a whisper. "We have had a problem."

Terian could feel the blood run out of his face. *They found them. They found them—dear gods, they found them and now I'm in for all manner of hell—*

"One of the squads of the Third Army, sir," the adjutant said, talking over Terian's racing thoughts. "They—" He faltered.

"They what?" Amenon snapped. "Out with it, lad. I'll not have you mince words here in front of my staff. Get on with what you mean to say."

"One of the squads has ... rebelled," the adjutant whispered. "Killed their Lieutenant ... and struck out against their fellow soldiers. They say ..." He swallowed again, as though the words might disappear into his throat by his actions, "they said they would not be bound by the laws and rule of a Sovereign who would starve and kill his own people."

46.

"I don't see the problem," Terian said as they rolled through the near-empty streets of Sovar. Soldiers ran in clusters here and there, but the citizenry were still indoors. "So a squad went stupid and decided to revolt. That's hardly—"

"That is the beginning of the end of everything," Amenon said, cutting him off. "And you should know it."

"Patience, my old friend," Dahveed said, but his expression was pinched. "It might not be as bad as you think."

"A squad going renegade and starting an insurrection?" Amenon said with barely contained fury. "I can think of nothing worse."

"An entire division going renegade," Terian said. "A whole army. All the armies." An overwhelming sense of silence greeted him. "It's a squad. A squad of what? Four people. Three of them lost their minds and did something incredibly stupid. It's not like we weren't just in a situation where we watched several civilians and a wizard do exactly the same thing."

"This is the army!" Amenon said with a low growl. "My responsibility! The single line that stands between Sovar's overwhelming numbers and the elite of Saekaj! If there was panic in the avenues over the idea of a revolt in the Back Deep over one building of starving idiots, imagine the panic when they realize that some of their protectors are joining this revolt!"

Terian shook his head. *This is madness. The army is from Sovar; to expect them to be immune to the events down there simply because you feed them better and pay them better is naiveté at its finest. And also ridiculous.* He set his eyes on his father, on the man's stare, which was blank and now focused out the window nearest him. *It's not going to stop him from agonizing over it, though.*

There was little water running down the slope into the Back Deep now, and Terian could hear the wheels of the carriage against the floor as they rolled. He sat there, tapping his gauntleted fingers against his greaves softly as he waited. The slope leveled off, and he heard the sound of the wheels lapping through the water again.

"A squadron should be easy enough to kill," Sareea said, nearly whisper quiet in her assessment. "They won't escape."

"I have no doubt," Amenon said abruptly but more gently than he might have if Terian had suggested the same. "But this is a problem again of perception. Three men out of the thousands in the Third Army alone is an insignificant number in the scheme of things. Yet our people will only hear alarm, and if there are insurrectionists still hiding here in Sovar, they will receive a message of hope."

"I don't know how much hope they're going to get from three guys," Terian said dourly, "especially after they meet their end."

"You don't much deal in hope, do you?" Dahveed asked him, with the oddest smile.

"This is Sovar," Terian said, shooting him a smile, "hope is for the upper chamber."

Dahveed made a low chuckling noise that did not sound particularly genuine. "Hope is wherever you find it. Different people find hope in different things."

"I would find great hope in knowing that this incident was confined here within the Back Deep," Amenon said. He retrieved his helm from the seat next to him as the carriage came to a stop. He kicked open the door and was out of the carriage in seconds.

Terian followed, giving only a brief pause to see Dahveed shrug at him. Sareea once more beat him out of the carriage, but this time he found he cared much less.

The slow churning walk back to the army field headquarters was in silence, and Terian spent it looking up at the buildings to see if eyes were still staring out at him. They were. Squadrons were still on every corner, but there was a tension among them now. *Probably wondering if one of their own is going to turn on them.* Swords rattled in scabbards everywhere, and the smell of extinguished fire lingered. *I suppose the poor missed their daily time at the communal ovens. Going to be a cold dinner tonight.*

Amenon burst through the door of the army headquarters without preamble or announcement. This time, Terian followed him into a building that had been carved into the cave bottom. The first floor walls were all stone, with planking laid atop them to build the second floor. Terian eyed the planks of old wood and wondered if they had been replaced since the building had been built. *Questionable.*

"General!" A half dozen dark elves in full armor snapped to attention as Amenon entered. Even if Terian had not known his father well, he could not have missed the displeasure that had crept into his usually controlled expression. The lines radiating out from his eyes and cutting deep trenches into his forehead were evidence to any moderately talented observer that the man was angry. *His legend alone should warn them all that saying the wrong thing right now would be a foolish error indeed.*

"Explain the situation to me, Colonel," Amenon said. Terian could see his jaw lock tightly into place when he finished speaking.

A man dressed in dark blue steel armor from head to toe stepped forward and saluted again. "My Lord Lepos, we received word of a squadron that had killed their Lieutenant in the wake of our action here. Rumors reached us—"

"Rumors from where?" Amenon's words came out tightly wound, the sound of fury coiled around discipline, close to being unleashed.

"We have spies here in Sovar," the Colonel said, face barely visible under his helm. He hesitated and removed his helm to show the face of a man who had probably been in the army for several centuries. "Three of them came to us, three that live around an intersection a few blocks from here. Hundreds witnessed the altercation that started the incident. The Lieutenant in question gave orders to move to reinforce our position here and was subsequently attacked by his own men. They shouted their reasons for said action rather loudly, according to our spies. This was later confirmed by our other witnesses, who claim that the rebelling soldiers said—"

"That they would not follow a Sovereign who starved his own people and killed them?" Amenon asked, expression curiously neutral.

The discomfort on the Colonel's face was obvious. "Yes, sir. That is what was said."

Amenon took a slow breath that was visible even through the slits of his helm, nose flaring. "Where are these insurrectionists now?"

"Dead, sir," the Colonel said with a sharp bow of the head. "Three squadrons overwhelmed them. We have already resurrected the Lieutenant who was killed and sent for the bodies of the three soldiers to be disposed of." The Colonel lowered his voice. "I acted swiftly as soon as it became apparent—"

"Yes, thank you, Colonel," Amenon said abruptly and turned from the man. Without another word, he brushed past Terian and out the door into the street. Terian followed with a wordless salute to the Colonel, who slumped in immediate relief as soon as Amenon was out the door.

"It doesn't sound too bad," Terian said as he exited the building. The splash of his metal boots as he tread through the water was muted compared to the sound of troops formations moving through the streets. Officers bellowed orders that rung out through the artificial canyons made by the narrow streets of the Back Deep.

"Doesn't sound too bad?" Amenon whirled on him. "You are … such a fool. Such a little, little fool." Flecks of spittle flew from Amenon's mouth. "Shrawn has spies everywhere. He has already heard, surely. The leap from his mouth to the Sovereign's ears is as certain as the movement of gossip from one noble lady's mouth to another's ear. This could be the end of us."

"The end of us?" Terian asked, feeling his skepticism set in. "You think he's going to completely annihilate our house for this foolishness?"

"I am the General of the Armies!" Amenon shouted, bellowing loud enough that it echoed down the street. He lowered his voice. "It falls on me. All of it. Whether I was here or not, whether I was supervising the Third Army or not." A hand came up as he pushed his teeth together in a horrible grimace. Terian could see his neck muscles bulge and tense beneath the gorget, threatening to burst it.

"I just don't see it being as bad as you think it is," Terian said. "I recognize that you need to do everything you can when you're the number two house to be able to protect yourself and your reputation, but this is a hiccup. Armies cannot exist without soldiers defecting, failing to follow orders—"

"Weak armies suffer from that," Amenon said, low and with menace. "The Army of the Sovereign marches true. It exists on a foundation of unquestioning loyalty and brutal discipline that leaves every member in absolute certainty that loyalty will be rewarded and disloyalty will result in death. It's very effective in that regard." He stepped past Terian and slammed his fist into the rock wall, breaking chips off of it. "We ... do not ... fail. Ever."

What do you even say to that? Terian stared as his father, who was now staring at the wall he'd punched. *Everyone fails. The Leagues fail people out constantly. You can't have ten armies without*— He blinked. "When did you expand to ten armies?"

"What?" Amenon asked, frowning at Terian as he looked back over his shoulder. "Recently. Since the Sovereign returned. We were fixed at two before, but—" He bowed his head. "You think this springs from our accommodation to rapid growth?"

"Well, gods, father, how many new recruits did you bring in to make this happen?" Terian asked. "A five-fold increase in the size of the army?"

"We pulled from the Saekaj militia first," Amenon said, "then from the nobles of Saekaj as well as the existing enlisted men to help form the officer corps. Once we had the bones in place, we expanded enlistments in Sovar. Where before they had been capped, we ... loosened things somewhat. Took a few men from the Depths."

No wonder your army had a problem, Terian thought, watching his father warily. *You've sifted down to the dregs, thrown them into the field and found them ... wanting.*

"Lord Amenon!" Terian turned to see a man approaching on the back of vek'tag. He watched with surprise—vek'tag were normally used for pulling wagons, not carrying a single passenger. The spider moved quickly and surely, and the rider seemed to have a good grip on the beast. "I bring a message from Saekaj."

Terian turned to look at his father. His mouth was open and his tongue was pushing at the side of his cheek as though it were about to burst out, as though he were putting all his unspent fury into it. "Very well," Amenon's reply came hushed. "Deliver your message."

The man on the vek'tag slid off the side, keeping his grip on the reins. He wore silk clothing, and when his boots splashed into the water Terian knew they soaked through. "I bring a message from the Sovereign, Lord Amenon. He requests and requires your presence and that of your heir at the Grand Palace of Saekaj immediately."

47.

The Grand Palace of Saekaj was carved out of the farthest wall of the cavern, fine stone work covered in gold and lit with braziers and torches to project light upon its surface. Terian had heard countless people over the years whisper about the Sovereign's hypocrisy for making his palace a beacon of light, but so far as he knew, no one had ever whispered a word of it to Yartraak's face.

The carriage rattled as they moved under the portico. The cavern was still seeping, droplets of water falling from above. Terian stepped out onto the cobblestones fired in the kilns of craftsmen and laid end to end to make proper roads in Saekaj. The cave's dank smell was nearly unnoticeable here, replaced instead by the scent of incense burning from the braziers. Terian wondered if the Sovereign had ordered the expensive oils burned, or if that was something Shrawn had begun in his absence.

Terian glanced at his father. Amenon's shoulders were slumped as he got out of the carriage, but he straightened his back and raised his head as he stood under the portico. He appeared to be composing himself, preparing for whatever was coming. He did not so much as look at Terian as he stared at the intricately carved doors to the palace. They swept slowly open, pulled by unseen servants as Terian stood with his father staring into the open door.

This can't be as bad as he thinks. The loss of face in front of the Sovereign concerns him more than it would anyone else.

On the other hand, he didn't get into the number two manor in Saekaj without taking things like this into consideration.

"Come along," Amenon said, starting his walk at a fast clip. His legs moved swiftly, and as they entered the palace the smell of the air changed: still incense, but something far different—a deeper aroma now, something that caused Terian's nose to curl. *I don't remember that being here before.*

"This way." A servant stepped into their path, a broad-shouldered, expressionless dark elf with white hair and blank eyes. He made a motion with his hand gesturing them onward then began to move into a hallway to the right of the foyer. Everything was covered in deep, rich woods, lit by lamps that flickered with more illumination than was common even for the streets of Saekaj.

Terian followed his father, who followed the Sovereign's servant. They entered an antechamber that Terian vaguely remembered from some ceremony or another he had attended in his youth. *The Sovereign's throne room lies beyond.* He stared at the wooden double doors, carved in a style that would not have looked out of place in Sanctuary. He drew a sharp breath at the thought of Sanctuary. *This is not the time to be thinking about that place.*

The doors cracked open, and once again unseen servants pulled them wide for Terian and his father to enter. A long, sweeping room lay beyond. It stretched like the Great Hall of Sanctuary, and Terian cursed himself again for thinking of the old guildhall. Sconces held metal lanterns on either side of the wall, but they burned darker than the other lights, as though they were burning on the last of the wick.

The room's floor was all wooden, opulence stretching as far as Terian's eye could see. The walls were paneled as well, and the blatant show of wealth made Terian think of the throne room as possibly the largest dance floor he had ever seen. That thought forced him to stifle a smile, keeping his lips in straight, unmoving lines, though he felt one corner of his mouth quirk upward.

"Good of you to join us," the Sovereign's voice rasped from the throne at the far end of the room. It was massive, carved out of grains of wood both light and dark, mingled together in a stunning display of craftsmanship that would not have been out of place in shops of the finest Reikonosian artisans. Here, in Saekaj, it was unparalleled.

"My Sovereign commands and I leap to obey," Amenon said, sweeping low in a bow as he continued to cross the distance toward the throne. The room was easily several hundred feet long, and even at their quick pace, Terian and his father were still a great distance from the throne.

Terian could see other shapes in the gloom around the throne. The Sovereign was not covered in darkness as he had been at the ball. Here he was only slightly shrouded in the dark, his figure showing upon the throne. He was nothing like the shape of a dark elf, nor an elf, nor a man—nor like anything Terian had ever seen. Long, thin legs of grey flesh stretched out from the bottom of the throne. His torso was angular and stretched to a thin middle, and bent at the center of the chest as though he had a second waist there. His long arms were almost stick-like, and three-fingered claws rested upon the arms of the throne. His head was shrouded in shadow, but the outline of horn-like protrusions around where Terian suspected a mouth might be were visible, and a third horn seemed to spring from the top of his head and swept forward, curving to match the other two. *He'd be a difficult bastard to kiss with those things protecting his face; I wonder how his harem handles it?*

"You have not seen my true form before, Terian, son of Lepos?"

As they approached, Terian guessed the Sovereign was at least ten feet tall, if not taller. *Taller than Vaste.* "No, my Sovereign." Terian bowed low. "I have only been in your presence when you were shrouded in darkness. I apologize if my eyes offend you by trying to glimpse your greatness—" *The bullshit just flows out of me when I'm in his presence. I wonder if I should worry about that.*

"Curious eyes do not concern me," the Sovereign said as he stood. His body moved in the oddest ways, and Terian could not help but stare as he moved. "There are more troublesome matters at hand." He moved his face into the light cast by a nearby lantern for but a second, and Terian caught an impression of ridged flesh, as though wrinkled but not by age. He recalled an elephant he had seen once in Reikonos, and remembered the grey skin that bore wrinkles as natural to it as blue pigment was to his own.

"I bring news of the suppression of the insurrectionists in the Back Deep," Amenon said, clearing his own throat. *Is he nervous?* Terian wondered. It took only a second to answer his own question: *Who wouldn't be?*

"News has already reached us of the events in the Back Deep," Yartraak said, stretching taller. Terian looked up, and then up some more. The Sovereign was much taller than ten feet; at least fifteen as he currently stood, and he seemed to be stretching before Terian's eyes. He shot a look at his father, but Amenon remained silent, head bowed. "Not only was there an insurrection by civilians, but a squad of the Third Army has killed their officer and made their own revolt."

"Yes, my Sovereign," Amenon said.

The Sovereign waited, as though he were expecting Amenon to say something else. "So it is true? You do not deny it?"

"Why would I deny a truth to my Sovereign?" Amenon said, and Terian had never heard his father sound so lifeless. "Three Sovar rats joined our army and when their loyalty was tested, it failed like gnomish steel."

The Sovereign stood before them, and in the shadows next to the throne, Terian saw movement. Dagonath Shrawn stepped out from behind the arm's rest on the right, leaning on his staff and bearing a thin, satisfied smile.

"This is grim news indeed," the Sovereign said. "Disloyalty in your army, Amenon?"

"It has happened, my Sovereign," Amenon said. "That much is plain."

"I'm sorry," Terian said, feeling a certain amount of anger bubbling up within. "When was the last time you actually saw that army, Father?"

Amenon's response was immediate, a blazing fire in his eyes as his head snapped around to look at Terian. The message was obvious: *Shut up!*

Terian waited, looking back to the Sovereign, whose head was slightly cocked. Terian wondered if it was in curiosity. "Lord Amenon, that is a valid question."

Amenon's teeth gritted together so obviously that Terian could not miss them. "It has been ... some months, my Sovereign. There are ... many armies at this point. I make inspections of each as often as I am able."

"Perhaps running the army is too great a responsibility for you," Shrawn said, speaking at last.

Amenon did not answer, but Terian saw him fire a searing glance at Shrawn. "Perhaps it's too great a responsibility for any one man," Terian said, drawing Amenon's look back to him. "Especially when we're drawing our candidates from Sovar while you're doing all you can to starve them out and foment insurrection in the lower chamber."

There was a deadening silence that settled over the room as Terian realized the full weight of what he had said. His father wore a stricken, wide-eyed look and did not bother to turn to send Terian any message. "My Sovereign, forgive my son for his foolish and wagging tongue. He knows not what he says—"

"Is this true?" The Sovereign's calm voice echoed in the throne room. "Is it true, son of Lepos, that you know not what you say?"

"I think the better question, my Sovereign," Terian said, letting the anger boiling within him find its outlet in his calm, controlled words, "would be to ask Lord Shrawn why he went to great expense and effort to import a monster into the Great Sea that killed our fishermen and helped to starve the people of Sovar."

There was another long silence. "Do you have any proof of any of these accusations?" Shrawn said, looking surprisingly cool.

"Of course not," Terian said, with more confidence than he felt. "You are not so foolish as to leave alive anyone who could speak to the truth of that particular scheme."

The Sovereign stood silently and then nodded. "Excellent."

"Yes, I—" Terian started, then cut himself off. "I apologize, my Sovereign. I don't think I quite take your meaning." *Please, I hope I don't take his meaning. If he means what I think he's saying, we're screwed.*

"I ordered Lord Shrawn's actions," the Sovereign said quietly. "I ordered him to cut production of mushrooms in the Depths, to find a way to slow the fishing of the Great Sea. The rats of Sovar are in need of culling, and our armies need strength. There was to be no way to trace his actions back to us."

"Why?" Terian asked, focused on the tall shadow of the Sovereign's figure. "Why not just do it and take credit?"

"Because," Yartraak said, "the people must believe that I am working toward their ends. Insurrectionists will always be about, looking to blight our order with their chaos. But only a fool would give these malcontents true and just cause for their pathetic visions. They are a blight on our people that must be wiped out. This winnowing would help us to separate the weak from the strong and grow our strength by wedding the willing of Sovar to our cause. Desperation makes men willing, and this starvation has created more willing servants of your Sovereign than any ten years of normalcy could."

Terian could feel his tongue flapping uselessly in his mouth, licking the back of his teeth. *This is truly monstrous.*

And if I say one word in recognizance of that obvious fact, I will die.

To the hells with it. He started to open his mouth. "I—"

"Obviously you operate with the greatest wisdom, my Sovereign," Amenon said, cutting across Terian before he had a chance to speak his mind. *He's just going to glaze over this whole thing*, Terian thought. *Just let it slip.* "To grow your strength while eliminating your enemies is wise indeed."

Terian felt his face struggle to remain neutral, the sudden dread seeping in at the gut-level. *Say anything and I'm dead.* He caught a glance of warning from his father and let the disgust settle in his belly. *Fine. I'll just eat it and deal with the indigestion of this later.*

"It was a rather brilliant stratagem," Yartraak said, "but I have a problem now. My most loyal army commander has professed that he is not up to the increased challenge I have handed him."

Amenon straightened. "My Sovereign, it is not that I am not up to the challenge. I am willing to undertake any challenge you set before me—"

"I have set this one before you and you have failed it," the Sovereign said. Terian could see his eyes moving behind the veil of shadow, hints of red glow lighting them in the darkness. "The numbers are too great for you to manage, to be able to keep closest watch upon without letting details of loyalty—something of utmost importance in my army—slip out of your sight. No," he said slowly, "I think we have reached the threshold for your talents, my friend, and it is not in overseeing the entire army. I think a new candidate needs a chance to prove whether they are equal to the task you have failed at."

"My Sovereign, I ..." Amenon began, but his voice drifted off mid-sentence.

"Do not think I will be swayed in this," the Sovereign said, and an air of unrelenting harshness came to his voice through a hissing noise. "Your own son displays more aptitude for bringing hard, fearsome truths to me than you have demonstrated. If there were even a whisper of possibility that Shrawn's plan were true, you should have brought it before me knowing that I would want to be informed."

"It was rumor only," Amenon said, rather weakly to Terian's ears. "I had no proof, not a hint of it. I did not wish to waste your time with mere whispers of dubious certainty—"

"And that is why you are not sitting in the most favored seat in all Saekaj," the Sovereign said. "And it is why you are about to lose your position to General Grennick."

Amenon bowed his head, but Terian could see the shock. "Grennick." He said the name in resignation, complete and utter.

"Grennick will be the General of the Armies," the Sovereign said, hard voice lashing them across the room. "This will, of course, require some additional ... recalculations."

Amenon's head came up and Terian saw the dazed look on his father's face, something he had never seen there before. "My Sovereign?"

"The Shuffle, Amenon," Yartraak said. "The manor you have inhabited this last century—it is time to move ... down."

Terian felt the heat in his face but said nothing. *The Shuffle ... we just got moved down ... that's never happened ...*

"You have disgraced us both this day," the Sovereign said. "You have played me false, underestimated and failed to inform me. You have let a pernicious element into my army unchecked, and I see no other alternatives. You will move to ... number twelve."

Twelve. That's not so bad. We're still on the main road. Last in line there, but still, not quite as far back as the square—

"Your wisdom is unquestioned," Amenon said, but his voice was dull and bereft of life. "I will make my preparations."

"Perhaps it's been so long you might have forgotten," Shrawn said, and Terian locked eyes with the elder dark elf, "but you bring no furniture with you, not even that which you might have used your wealth to purchase. Your clothing and personal possessions are all that come with you to number twelve." *Rub it in, you dirt bag son of a bitch.* Terian stared him down and Shrawn smiled. *Your day will come.*

"I have not forgotten the ways of the Shuffle," Amenon said, his voice coming near to cracking. "I have not forgotten any of our ways."

"Oh, good," Shrawn said. "I had thought perhaps your ascent had been so rapid that you had never felt the halting of momentum." The sound of amusement peppered his reply. "I simply wanted to prepare you for the sensation of falling."

Terian heard a noise of gentlest amusement from the Sovereign. "Return to your old self, Amenon. You do neither of us any favors by feeding me only what you think I wish to hear."

"I will not refrain from telling you every rumor that comes to my ears henceforth," Terian's father said, his voice bereft of any emotion.

"Though I think you'll find it somewhat harder to get an appointment to do so going forward," Shrawn said, almost gleefully.

"I place you in charge of the Eighth Army," the Sovereign said. "Now go, and disappoint me no further."

"My Sovereign," Amenon said, partially turned to leave. "The special operations group you've had me assemble for you …"

"Oh, yes," the Sovereign said. "You will continue in that same capacity, unless you prove incompetent to keep their loyalty." Terian felt the heat of Yartraak's red-eyed gaze fall on him. "Then, perhaps I might turn to your son to carry out my orders with them." There was the sound of a breath being drawn, louder and different than the breathing of any creature Terian had ever heard. "You impress me with your bracing honesty, Terian Lepos. Show your father what he has forgotten. Guide him back to my good graces with your straightforward fearlessness of speaking your mind. Learn from his experience. Now, go, both of you, and claw your way back to my attentions." The Sovereign waved a three-pronged hand at Terian, then Amenon, and bid them go.

Terian bowed once, sharply, at the waist, still holding his tongue as he watched the Sovereign seat himself once more. He turned his head to avoid staring at the peculiar way in which Yartraak moved and fell into step beside his father. He tried to slow his pace to walk behind him, but when he did, Amenon sent him a tired look. "Walk beside me," his father said, voice almost a whisper. "For we are linked in the eyes of the Sovereign now; your fortunes rise as mine fall and are the only thing that have saved us from falling farther."

Terian felt a sudden pain in his chest, in his guts. "Father, I—"

"Say no more," Amenon said, waving him off. "We have preparations to make. A house to move." His father's face looked hollow, beset with worry. "A defeat to manage." His voice was soft, quiet—and Terian knew his father spoke a truth he had never before considered.

48.

"These are grim proceedings," Kahlee said to Terian as they stood outside the old manor house. The drip of the cavern ceiling had slowed, a mere trickle here and there to mark the end of the flooding waters. Terian wondered how the Back Deep was afflicted, if it was still under inches of water. He gave that only a moment's thought, though, with his wife standing at his side. "To see this house—our house—humbled so ..." Kahlee's head fell, and her jaw stuck out slightly. The faded blue strands of her hair, the white beginning to show through the dye, fell over her eyes.

"It's happened before to your family," Terian said, numbly. Guturan Enlas was shouting orders at the servants. The entire avenue was in motion, with clothing being shuttled back and forth between manor houses by the help. Everyone else was being shuffled up, the House of Lepos was being shuffled back. *Number twelve. A crushing fall indeed.* Terian turned his eyes toward the direction of the square, where the manor houses ended at numbers eleven and twelve, and turned into smaller homes built in rows. *Still, it could be worse.*

"But I wasn't there to see it," Kahlee said, turning to look at Terian. She brushed bluish strands of hair out of her face and laid her hand upon Terian's arm. He heard the click of her fingernails against the armor. "My father has invited us to remain here, to stay with him as he moves up."

"I think my father would see that as an insult," Terian whispered. He cast his gaze down the cobbled drive to where Amenon stood by the gate, standing sentinel upon the exodus of House Lepos from the manor they had inhabited for over a century. He did not turn his head, nor watch anything, merely stood, dead-eyed, as servants moved into and out of the gates. "I don't think he's tasted this sort of defeat before. I don't know if he's prepared for it."

"There is no preparing for it," Kahlee said, matching his motions. They both stared at Amenon as Olia approached him, hands shaking. She spoke to him, too softly for either of them to hear, and he did not react. "Your father has ascended his whole life, moving from victory to victory against incredible odds to become not only the foremost dark knight in Saekaj and Sovar but also the head of the army. To be thrown down so harshly over something he had so little control over ..."

"The Sovereign doesn't see it that way," Terian said, lowering his voice and his head. He stared at the cobbled stones on the drive and at the edge where they met the hard stone and rocky gardens. "He views it as something he gave my father dominion over that failed. When it happens that way, the blame goes to the man in charge. There is no flexibility in his worldview." Terian sighed. "And in strictest terms, he's right. My father is in charge of the army, and in the Sovereign's world, there is no room for a failure of loyalty in the army. Too much rides on their loyalty being unquestioned."

"All hail the Sovereign," Kahlee said out loud, loud enough to catch the attention of two servants passing by. She exchanged a look with Terian, a subtle glance that told him she was lying, lying full and fair. As if to prove his point, she leaned in to speak in his ear. "If the rumors are true and there really are ten armies, there is no possible way that one man could oversee legions of that size. There are Colonels, Majors and Lieutenants in the chain above that squadron who are far more deserving of punishment than your father."

Terian leaned in to his wife's embrace, and whispered in her ear. "And every one of them is now dead." He waited until she recoiled, staring into his eyes, her own wide. He watched her throat bob as she swallowed. "Not by his orders," Terian said, and caught a hint of her muscles relaxing. "The new General of Armies issued them after he took charge. I saw the couriers running down the street with guard squads and executioners following behind." He pursed his lips. "It was a tense moment, until we were sure they'd passed us by."

"You thought it would fall upon—" Kahlee's mouth hung slightly open.

"When you earn the Sovereign's disfavor, can you really expect any less?" Terian asked with a gentle smile. *He tried to starve out his own people in some ill-designed scheme to increase the army's enlistments. Killing his generals when they piss him off is hardly shocking behavior from such an … individual.*

"I suppose not," Kahlee said. The stream of servants had grown smaller. One passed him now with the portrait from his father's study in hand, the ornate frame gripped tightly as he paraded it past. Terian stared at the subject, at his sister Ameli, her face, as the painting passed him. A sideways glance told him Kahlee was doing the same. "You never talk about her anymore."

Terian gave that one a moment. "Would you? If you were me?"

"No." There was a pause, followed by hesitation. "I suppose I wouldn't."

Terian nodded because there wasn't anything else to say.

Guturan Enlas appeared out of the front door a moment later, straight-backed, hands clasped behind him. "I have very nearly gotten all of the trinkets and other assorted minutiae out of the manor. Little enough remains now that you should prepare your father to move on your way."

"I'll work on that," Terian said, sensing a hint of acid on his own tongue. "And what about you, Guturan? Are you coming with us or do you stay with the manor house?"

"I stay with the manor house, of course," Guturan said a bit quickly. "Though I suppose you did not know that, having never experienced the Shuffle."

"Well, I'm experiencing it today," Terian said, stifling the snap of anger he felt ready to burst out at Guturan. "Perhaps next time, things will be different."

"Things are always in motion, Lord Terian," Guturan said, remaining oddly stiff in his delivery. "For the good of some and the ill of others, things must always remain fluid. The Shuffle keeps the old blood of Saekaj always fresh, lest it become coagulated and still. For one to rise, another must fall; always remember that."

"Do you doubt I'll ever forget it after this humiliation?" Terian asked, nearly growling. He felt Kahlee's hand land on his arm, avoiding the spikes on his armor.

"There is no humiliation in being beaten by a superior foe," Guturan said, cocking his head almost quizzically. "We would not consider it an embarrassment for a suited dandy with a dueling cane to be killed by a titan in single combat, would we? We would simply say they were ... overmatched." He let the thin hint of a smile filter through. "The last century has let much old blood settle in Saekaj. Now that the Sovereign has returned, the veins must flow again ... and sometimes that means opening them so that the old blood can drain out."

"That's funny," Terian said, feeling more than a hint of fury. "Sometimes when you let the blood out, you kill the body." He felt his wife's hand on his arm, restraining him. He did not resist her, instead taking her hand in his and moving toward the gates to the manor.

"Lord Terian," Guturan called after him, as he was halfway down the drive. Terian turned back, and saw the servant's smile had disappeared. "He was simply overmatched."

With traitors like you advising and serving him, I don't doubt it. "You should be careful when you bleed someone," Terian said, looking back at Guturan. "You just never know exactly how much is going to drain out before it stops." He turned his attention back to his wife, who met his gaze with a thin smile and a nod. Together, they walked toward the gates where his father waited, now moving, slowly, Olia's hand in his, toward where they would pass from the only home Terian had ever had in this place.

49.

Sixteen Years Earlier

"He was completely overmatched," Terian said, feeling the beat of his heart, pulse racing, chest fit to burst with pride as he told the story. "Bereneck Dorrnd is the top of the class at the Legion, and I cut through his defenses in training as though they weren't even there, afflicted him with the Lockjaw curse, and took him to the ground." He felt the smile break over his face. "It was beautiful, Ameli. You should have seen it."

"I just have," Ameli said, and Terian watched her stifle a yawn. "You've described it in intricate detail. I feel as though I was there. And bored." She cracked a grin of her own. "All this fighting, you know it tires me. Because I'm a delicate little cave cress, according to the dictates of our society."

"I get the sense you're mocking me," Terian said, raising an eyebrow. "And our society."

"It provides such rich opportunity," Ameli said. She was not so small anymore, he reflected. Lately it seemed she grew a few inches every week. She was over his chin now, but that sparkle in her eyes had yet to give way to any hint of maturity. "I am provided of no self-restraint in expressing myself. You, on the other hand, have nothing but restraint in that regard."

Terian felt his smile evaporate. "I recognize the bounds, Ameli, and I stay within them."

"You recognize that speaking your mind and letting fly with the jests your heart desires to make would wreck your considerable ambitions," she said, with just a hint of sadness. "I have no ambitions to wreck, you see, so there is no reason for me to contain my wicked wit. What's the worst that can happen? I'm not wed to someone in the House of Shrawn because I am possessed of a sharp tongue?" She clapped her hands on her cheeks. "Oh no! Sovereign forfend!" She laughed, her sarcastic delivery echoing in the sitting room they occupied.

Terian felt his back straighten. "I wish I had your lack of care."

"Come, Terian, you have a wonderful wit," she said, running a hand along his sleeve in encouragement. "You have shared it with me, when you knew no one was listening. Now your stifle yourself, and it saddens me so to know that such choice comments go by the wayside, unappreciated by anyone …" She laughed. "I'm sorry, I can't even keep up the pretense of seriousness. Terian, Saekaj and Sovar are ripe for mockery. Saekaj, especially, with its elite 'No one may enter' policy."

"That's not true," Terian said, and he felt a burning in his cheeks. "Father did."

"And no one else," she said, shaking her head at him. "You need more than one example in two million to prove a point, brother mine. Otherwise you're talking exceptions, not rules."

"And you're breaking rules," Terian said, feeling the anger cloud his face, "and hoping that being a part of this family will allow an exception if ever you get caught."

"Smooth change of subject," Ameli said, unruffled. "But we both know I don't say anything bad enough to get me into trouble."

Terian started to respond but didn't. *No, we don't know that.*

"I see that look on your face, the one that screams doubt," she said impishly. "Do not fear for me. I'll be fine. Father will protect me, after all. He can't have his daughter sent to the Depths for treasonous talk. Especially not for the extremely minor crime of saying inconvenient things."

"It's only minor until it lands you in the composting heaps," Terian said. "Then it's—"

"Major," she said. "And smelly!"

He flinched from her statement, closing his eyes and bowing his head. "I hope you're right," he said finally, looking up to see her still wearing that same impish smile. "I wouldn't care to—"

"I wouldn't care to hear whatever blasé sentiment you're about to throw my way, brother," she said. The smile stayed firmly in place. "Now, let's not get weighed down by your unhappy thoughts. What can we do to while away the evening? Skulk in the markets and laugh at the dandies?"

Terian gave a slow nod. "If that is what you wish." He forced a smile. *I do hope you're right, Ameli. For running up against the dark side of the Tribunal's anger is not a fate I'd wish on anyone, let alone my own sister ...*

50.

"There were no bodies," Grinnd said to Terian in a hushed voice. They stood together in a small room in the new manor house with Dahveed. There was little light, but that mattered hardly at all. Terian strained his eyes to keep watch on Grinnd's expression as the large warrior delivered the news. "The commandant of the Depths—a friend, I might add—said they sent no bodies for composting save the insurrectionists that we killed."

"No soldiers?" Terian asked, blinking in the dark. He looked over at Dahveed, whose red hair looked near black in the darkness. Dahveed shook his head, almost as though he were anticipating the answer.

"None," Grinnd said. "Not a one. I saw the bodies of the ones we sent—the wizard and the others. But no sign of the soldiers that rebelled against their Lieutenant. Nor of the Lieutenant himself—"

"He was resurrected," Dahveed said pensively. "I cast the spell myself rather than wait for them to bring a Union mage down from Saekaj or summon an army one away from other duties. Came back to life rather shocked at what had happened."

Terian wanted to reach for his sword, pull it and bury it in the wall nearby. "Shrawn. He planted traitors in the Third Army and forced this whole insurrection scare. Then he tattled to the Sovereign and took my father out at the knees."

"Perhaps you can bring it up to him?" Grinnd asked, voice hushed but urgent. "Help restore your father to grace?"

Terian felt a bitter sigh creep in. "I don't know that it'll do any good, but I'll mention it the next time I get a meeting with him. Probably in about twenty years, based on my house's current level of disfavor."

"You could knock upon his gate," Dahveed said. "He might receive you favorably."

"And I might tell him what I think of his and Shrawn's depopulation scheme," Terian said and felt the seething rage bubble up in him again. "I came within inches of getting my head separated from my neck in there. I can't see how the Sovereign could possible think that my brand of 'honesty' would be any good for him if he actually heard it in its unfiltered state."

The door opened abruptly, and Kahlee breezed in, a proper black and white dress of a fashionable cut layered around her. "I can't see it doing you or your house much good either," she said, "getting yourself killed."

"And there's the voice of reason that tells me to save my own skin," Terian said. "It's odd to me to have to look outside my own skull for that perspective."

"M'lady," Grinnd said, bowing low, his armor squeaking as he did so. "I did not realize you were listening or I would have kept my traitorous musings to myself—"

"I heard no traitorous musings," Kahlee said with an eyebrow raised. "I heard only the talking of men loyal to both their Sovereign and their general. Men of such quality as these are hard to find and impossible to replace."

"Kind of you to say, Lady Lepos," Dahveed said. "Yet still, we should be careful to confine such conversations to only the quietest, most out of the way places."

"Terian!" Amenon's voice echoed through the house. Terian looked up, as though he could see through the ceiling that separated him, on the ground floor, from his father somewhere above. The new manor was considerably smaller, only two floors and a basement. *The grandeur is lacking*, Terian thought.

"If you'll excuse me, gentlemen," Terian said, giving Dahveed and Grinnd a nod each. "And my lady wife."

"I excuse much from you," Kahlee replied with feigned disinterest and a roll of her eyes.

"Don't expect that to change anytime soon." Terian opened the door and stepped into the dim foyer. It was smaller in scale by an order of magnitude than the last manor, and wood was replaced by plaster on many of the surfaces. The floor was a quarried stone tile, with only aged wood kept for the upper floor and one choice room. The whole place had a sense of being drafty, the dank cave air not kept nearly as at bay as in their old house.

Terian made his way up the stairs and into the office that his father had claimed. It backed into the cave wall and was dimmer and smaller than his previous study. Not even the faint light of the phosphorescent ceiling shining from outside was there to break the monotony, and the fireplace was miniscule compared to his old one. A lone piece of parchment sat upon his father's desk. Terian pulled up the chair across from him and sat, staring at Amenon.

The older man looked ... old, Terian had to concede. *His defeat at the hands of Shrawn has sucked the very life from him.* The lines were set around his eyes, and he had the look of a man who needed sleep.

"What is it, Father?" Terian asked.

"I find myself completely ill at ease without Guturan here to manage my affairs," Amenon said, blinking, head turning to take in the empty surface of his desk. The only thing on it save for the lone parchment was the red gem that had graced his previous desk.

"Guturan was a traitor who was reporting everything you said and did back to Shrawn," Terian said. He had a vision of the butler in his head, and imagined him skewered on the tip of his sword. *Now that's a fun thought.*

"Yes, I know," Amenon said, nodding, "but he was very efficient."

"At betraying you."

Amenon sighed. "Forgive me, my son."

Terian's ears perked up. *He's never said he was sorry to me for anything, ever.* "For what, Father?"

"Everything I have done in my life I have done for my house, for my family," Amenon said, the weariness upon him. "I raised my star so high so that I would be able to shine all down upon you and your mother. Once you left, I was left with only her. Now you have returned as my star wanes and done what you can to save us from the fall."

"Father," Terian said. "Grinnd investigated in the Depths. There were no bodies sent to the composting pile for the traitors who rebelled. Shrawn planted them. He created the incident that resulted in your fall."

Amenon stared straight ahead. "Yes. Of course. Shrawn."

Terian watched him carefully, but there was little life in his father's motions. "What do we do, Father? How do we bring this before the Sovereign?"

Amenon blinked. "Bring it before the Sovereign? Why would we?"

"So that he can know the truth of the matter—that the army is still loyal!" Terian said.

"The Sovereign will commend Shrawn on his excellent scheming," Amenon said, staring into the distance. "In the Sovereign's view, I will have failed by allowing Shrawn to find purchase in the army at all, let alone to perpetrate such a scheme."

Terian felt his jaw drop slightly open. "What madness is this?"

Amenon blinked once more and looked straight at him, and a muted, whisper of a chuckle came out. "It is the Sovereignty. All blame lands on the responsible. I should have seen Shrawn's scheme coming. Since I did not, it makes me weak, and deserving of being 'reshuffled.' Do you not see?"

"I see cowardice and treachery rewarded," Terian said, setting his jaw. "I see the worst virtues being held up above strength and honor—the things that will win wars."

"Cunning and treachery can win wars," Amenon said, settling his gaze to look at the wall past Terian's shoulder. "Ambushes, sneak attacks, these are all weapons in the arsenal of war—and politics. I see now that I was unready to fight in that arena. My ascension to the number two house came too close to the end of the Shuffle and the Sovereign's exodus; I was ill prepared for the resumption. I became complacent, thinking that merely serving was enough to maintain my house in its position. Oh, to be sure, I spoke the words about being steps ahead of others, but I did not understand how deep it went until Shrawn's scheme closed its fearful jaws upon me. Clever, Shrawn. Very clever." Amenon's words echoed, as though he were talking to Shrawn himself, there in the room.

"Father," Terian said, trying to catch his father's gaze and failing, "what do we do? How do we … regain our position?"

Amenon blinked, and looked at him. "Regain our position? I built my reputation on flawless service, and now that reputation is sullied forever. Whatever you do to rebuild that reputation, Shrawn will always act to sully it again. Should he strike now, we would, I think, be finished." Amenon made a clucking noise, drawing his lips together. "He will act soon, I suspect."

"What do we do?" Terian asked and thumped his hand on the desk. It was an old wood, and it made a cracking noise even from Terian's minimal strike.

"We wait," Amenon said after a moment's pause. Terian stared at his father, at his lifeless eyes, as they stared into the distance. "We wait for an opportunity to serve the Sovereign, to prove our worth."

"But you said Shrawn will be acting against us even now!" Terian exploded. "What do we do about him?"

"There is nothing we can do," Amenon said, and his voice was so gentle Terian wondered for a moment if this was the same man he'd known all his life. *No ... he's not*, he realized after a moment. *This man is broken. His strength is broken. He's not the same man who ordered Sareea to kill me, he's not the same man who struck me down in our first meeting after my return.* Terian clenched his teeth together. *This is a man who has seen his better days pass him by and is now ready for death.*

He stared into the face of his father, and Amenon stared into the distance, at the wall behind Terian. Terian felt a chill as the realization slowly crept up his spine. *And he will wait here—helpless, hopeless—until Shrawn brings it to him.*

51.

The sound of his gauntlet slamming hard against the iron door of Sareea's apartment made Terian self-conscious, as though it were loud enough for them to hear it in Reikonos. He waited, nearly holding his breath, until the screech of the metal bar that fastened it shut unlatched and the heavy thing swung open. The smell of sweat hit him in the face like a punch, and he blinked as he stared at Sareea in her nightclothes, eyes slitted as she looked out at him.

"Thought you were going to keep me standing out here all night," Terian said, making to move past her. She did not budge from the doorway, though, and stood there giving him the full weight of her dead gaze. "What are you doing?" He stood fast, when she did not say anything, and the slow realization washed over him like the waters the ocean he had seen in Reikonos. "You're done with me now, aren't you?"

She stared at him with the dull eyes, and he saw a flicker. "You know I'm climbing. And you—and your family—are not."

"I suppose all those gifts of influence and deals that benefitted your house are unnecessary now?" Terian asked, shaking his head slowly. *I forgot where I was. What I was doing. Who these people are.*

"They were appropriate for the business we were conducting," she said, still icy. *Like she doesn't know me at all.* "So don't think I'll be handing them back, because the rules of society say I needn't."

"You certainly know how to play by the rules of society." Terian felt pressure in his mouth and bit his lower lip for a second to hold it in. "But you don't know a damned thing about loyalty, do you?"

"I know enough about loyalty to keep your secrets," she said, with the ghost of a smile.

"My secrets?" Terian said, nearly scoffing. "I don't have any secrets. Not from Shrawn, anyway."

"Of course you do," Sareea said, almost amused. "Like, for example, those innocent souls you left under the invisibility spell during the insurrection." He snapped his head around to look at her, caught the corner of her smile. "Yes, I knew about them. They got safely away, not that you bothered to check. Now they're gone without a trace, and no one knows—except me, of course." She smiled wider. "And by the rules of our society, as your mistress, it is not only my prerogative but my duty to keep that secret."

"You know the rules," Terian said, staring at her in a cold fury. He watched her glistening eyes, and knew she was entertained by the whole exchange. *She thrives on this, lives for it.*

"That's why I'll win," she said, and Terian started to turn away from her. "Wait."

"Why?" Terian asked, ready to leave her behind. "So you can lord it over me that my house is too far in decline to be worthy of your notice now?"

"No," she said, "so I can give you one last warning before you depart."

He shuffled slowly around to take her in. She was standing in her nightclothes the way any other woman he'd ever known would, arms crossed and folded. She looked feminine like this; but he'd seen her in her armor, when the sharp edges matched those of her face. "Oh, boy. This should be good."

"You should decide whether you want to play by the rules," she said, and the glister was gone from her eyes. "Your heart's not in it just yet. You play at it, but you don't commit. Shrawn is fully committed to playing and winning by any means necessary."

"Are you going to be his mistress now?" Terian asked, folding his own arms.

"Perhaps," she said, and arched an eyebrow. "I have offered my loyalty to his house and he has accepted it. It remains to be seen whether he will have uses for things other than my sword."

"Well, I wish you the best of luck with his," Terian said bitterly and turned away from her. As he descended the stairs toward the street below, he could hear her door slowly closing behind him. He did not bother to look back as he left, and he suspected—knowing her as he did—she did not either.

52.

Terian had scarcely entered the foyer when he sensed the change of atmosphere in the manor house. He paused at the threshold, with only one servant holding open the single door for him as he trod on the worn purple rug. It was not on par with the one they had left behind, that much was certain.

There were hushed voices in conversation somewhere nearby. He could hear the whispers, the sound of urgency fueling the words, but could not distinguish the meaning. The smell of his father's gruel still hung in the air, the one constant from the old manor to the new, and an oddly comforting thing in this new house.

A door opened with a bang and Terian turned his head to see his mother standing in the open doorway to the kitchen. "My son," she said quietly.

Terian stared at her. *Something is not right.* "What is it?"

"Your father …" she said, causing his heart to pulse, "… he wishes to see you in his study. Urgently."

Terian hesitated only a moment before breaking into a run, legs pounding in a jog as he made his way up to the second floor. His metal boots rang out against the wooden steps, and the pit of uncertainty grew in his stomach as he made his way up.

He reached the door and halted, stopping himself before bursting in. *He's in too much of a state right now; I'm actually worried about him. Almost forgot my manners.* He rapped sharply on the door and was rewarded with the echo of his knock in the foyer.

"Come in, come in," his father said, and Terian had the door open before he'd finished speaking. Amenon looked up at him as he entered. "Glad you're back from your ... errand. All is well, I take it?"

"If you define well to include the shedding of former allies in roughly the same way a dog sheds water after a dousing, then yes— all is well."

Amenon stared at him, and then curled the side of his mouth. "She did not wish to attach her carriage to your horse, then?"

Terian stared evenly at him. "To put it mildly. But I don't consider it much of a loss."

"Yet I suspect it stings all the same," Amenon said with a quick nod, "but no matter. We have, at this very moment, a way to take our first step back to grace."

Terian paused, considering his reply. *Please, don't let this be some madness afflicting him.* "How?"

Amenon picked up a long page of parchment. "This ... is a mission from the Sovereign for our band."

Terian nodded, staring at the page. "Our band is down by two at present. And Xemlinan has been of little use lately."

"No matter," Amenon said, shaking his head, "because this is a mission that we could handle between just the two of us."

Terian waited for the other boot to drop. "The particulars?"

Amenon shifted in his chair, pushing it back from the desk. "You recall our friend Sert Engoch?"

Engoch? "That poor bastard I scared the living hell out of in your torture chamber?"

"The very same," Amenon said, pacing around his desk with the enthusiasm of a much younger man. "You recall the name of the town that he made mention of?"

"Aurastra," Terian said. "Dwarven town. Kind of isolated—"

"Correct," Amenon said, eyes shifting wildly. "The Sovereign has asked us to deal with a matter in Aurastra. There is a mine that has been excavated. Something was found within it that has the Sovereign concerned."

Terian listened without speaking. *If this something has the God of Darkness concerned, it's probably worth worrying about.*

"He has assigned the task of carrying a barrel of some elven creation called Dragon's Breath to the mine," Amenon said, "where we are to light it where it will explode and seal the mine shut, thus preventing any further excavation."

"Won't they just be able to dig it out again?" Terian asked.

"Apparently not," Amenon said, almost dismissively. "Something about destabilizing the tunnel and thus keeping it from being dug out—I confess I don't fully understand the details, but the Sovereign is set upon this. His message addresses this mission in the most strident tones." He waved the paper. "It is written in his own hand! He has trusted this to us, and we must carry it out immediately."

"All right," Terian said, feeling almost like he was conceding to it rather than hurrying to carry out the Sovereign's orders. "I'll assemble the team."

"With haste, Terian," Amenon said, a thin smile splitting his face. "With haste. This … it could be our chance to rise again."

Terian smiled, but faintly. "We won't fail, Father." He turned to leave, but a thought cut through him as he did so. *Unless Shrawn has planned for us to … and then, based on your current disposition, we'll likely charge blindly into it ... and end ourselves in the process.*

53.

The light of the teleport faded to reveal snow-capped peaks on all sides. The wind howled around them and the bright light of a winter sun shone down blindingly. Terian flinched from the light, brighter than anything he'd seen in weeks.

"It takes adjusting," Amenon said. He wore a dark cloak over his armor, bound tightly around his shoulders. "After acclimating to being underground again."

"Aye," Terian said in simple acknowledgment and pulled his own cloak tighter around his shoulders. He had a very fine one that tucked under his pauldrons to keep from shredding on his spikes.

"A brisk day," Grinnd said with a smile. Terian cast a look at the big warrior. *He'd strip down to bare chested and roll in the snow if we let him, the crazy bastard.* Terian's eyes alighted on the heavy barrel that was strapped to Grinnd's back. *But not today. Not with that on his back.*

"It'd be nice to have Verret with us for this one," Xemlinan said, shielding his eyes from the sun. Green pines stretched toward the heavens a little ways off from the portal, but not nearly close enough to shade them. Snow covered the branches and boughs in thick clumps like fluffy tufts of white cotton brought down from the slave fields. "He was always better in the open air than I."

"We have Bowe to aid us," Amenon said, brusque, all business—*like he's returned to form*, Terian thought. Their feet already hovered above the snow, the result of the Falcon's Essence spell that had been cast upon them before they had even left Saekaj. "We must leave no sign that we were here." He looked around the circle of them. "Clear?"

"It sounds as though it is just another mission in that regard," Dahveed said, eyes dancing in the sunlight. He had his robes wrapped tightly around him and another cloak for protection from the elements. "Always in the shadows, we dark elves."

"Aurastra is a day's hike in this direction," Terian said, staring at the morning sun overhead. He pointed northwest.

"The Sovereign's will waits for no man," Amenon said abruptly. "Let us be on about it. Bowe, keep us in the air." Without waiting for acknowledgment, he was off.

They headed off over a nearby peak, treading up impossible cliff faces and threading their way through thick forests by brushing between tree branches. Terian heard countless pine needles scratch lightly against his armor as they walked twenty feet off the ground through snow-covered pines. They kept silent, the exertion of their legs and the gravity of their mission quieting them. Even Dahveed did not seem predisposed toward conversation, preferring to keep his hands inside his robes as he walked along in line with the others.

The sun crawled across the sky as they made their way over the ground, far from any road. The scent of pine was heavy in the air, along with the brisk smell of the mountain wind. A creek burbled nearby, and they followed it for some time, the chorus of the waters playing along with the thoughts that ran through Terian's mind.

I live in a land of horror, where slaves are kept and no man is free. Where the Sovereign rules all and does so with an unbreakable fist. Our own god smiles down upon us from the palace, and he is a merciless enemy when opposed, yet for some reason he likes me. Me, of all people. Probably hints he's not a great judge of character.

A branch whipped toward him, released from where it had caught on Grinnd's barrel, and Terian drew his axe in time to catch it on the blade. It splintered and broke, the remainder of it whipping past him. The end scraped his helm before it fell, down to the snowy ground below. *And then there's Sareea ...*

I should not have expected loyalty from her, not in return for the minor rewards of position my family gave her. He sighed. *Kahlee, on the other hand ...* The sun seemed blinding overhead. *I live in a land where mistresses are strangely venerated, and exchange is expected in return for keeping one. Well, I kept one, and she was the first dark knight of her kind. Why am I surprised when she stabbed me while I was down? I should consider myself lucky she didn't spill my little secret ...*

He cursed under his breath, drawing a look of amusement from Dahveed. "It's not that bad of a walk," the healer said.

"I didn't say it was," Terian replied. *I was foolish to expose myself in that way. Foolish to even consider letting myself not do the hard things, the necessary things. Sareea was right. I'm not playing this game in a way that will enable me to win, and if I'm not going to do that, I should damned sure quit before I get myself and my family killed.*

"Down there," Amenon called as they reached a peak. The air was thin, and Terian felt himself fighting harder for breath. He looked down into a valley below. Snow covered it, rocks and trees breaking the white monotony with faint strains of grey and green.

A village rested in the center of the valley, snow-covered huts and buildings introducing lines of brown barely visible under the snow. Chimney smoke wafted upward in columns and clouds, breaking the fading light of day and the distant horizon.

"How far down do you reckon that town is?" Xem asked. He was huffing now that they'd stopped, gasping for breath.

"A good hour's hike," Amenon said, looking up at the orange sun dipping behind the peaks across the valley. "Enough time for the sun to set and conceal our purpose."

"As much as I like the darkness," Terian said, "we do need to find the mine that we're supposed to destroy. Any idea where it is, exactly?"

"On the far side of the valley," Amenon replied, and pulled a crumpled piece of parchment from under his cloak. "The dwarves burrowed under that peak looking for gems and metals, and they found something ... else." He stopped suddenly, as though he'd thought the better of what he was going to say. "Let us go." He started down the mountain, following the slope but closer to the ground this time.

What did they find, Father? Terian wondered. *What could possibly worry the Sovereign so?* He watched the team get ahead of him, Xem falling into line last of all, leaving Terian at the rear, still up on the peak.

What does a god have cause to fear?

54.

The darkness was nearly as complete as any day in Saekaj or Sovar. The sun had retreated below the horizon long before Terian and the others had reached the bottom of the valley, and now the sky was deep purple and heading toward blackest night. The village was nestled quietly before them, no sign of activity within its borders. The smell of dinner was heavy in the wind, the scent of some animal roasting on a fire wafting through the cold, crisp mountain air.

"Keep to the shadows," Amenon whispered, so quietly that Terian barely heard him at the back of the line. They were moving slowly now, hovering only inches off the snow. "We need to cross the main thoroughfare unseen."

"Might want to wait until darkness has finished settling," Dahveed suggested. "It shouldn't be more than an hour or so."

Terian could see the gears turning in his father's mind. "An hour's wait to remain undiscovered is not … unreasonable," Amenon said.

They settled in quietly, staring at the edge of the village through the pines. The mountain loomed above, watching quietly over them. Terian stared into the dark, trying to see through the gaps in the houses. Snow drifted from the trees above, falling here and there in drifts blown by the wind. Terian felt the cold wind finding the gaps in his helm and chilling his cheeks.

Dogs barked in the distance, faint yelps here and there in the village, falling silent every now and again. The whole place was still save for the whipping of the wind and clouds of smoke piping from the chimneys.

Once the night had claimed the land for its own, Amenon rose from where they had waited. "Come along," he whispered, his voice hushed as they moved forward out of a thicket that had frosted over in the winter.

The squeak of a hinge caused Terian to freeze as though he'd had snow dumped down the back of his armor. He hesitated only a moment before snaking behind a tree, pressing his armor against the bark. He watched Grinnd do the same against a nearby pine while Dahveed went prone, finding cover behind a bush. Bowe had disappeared, as had Amenon. *An invisibility spell. But where's—*

Terian saw movement to his side and craned his neck around the tree to see Xemlinan caught in the open, frozen in the middle of the snowy ground, his black silk clothing obvious against the white background.

A dwarf came around the corner of the nearest house, whistling lightly to himself as he trudged down into the snow. It came to his waist, and he trod a path that had already been partially cleared. The crunch of his footfalls was the only noise in the night save for a barking dog, and his sure steps carried him toward where Xem waited.

The dwarf's head was down as he walked, oblivious to the dark elf just in front of him. Terian could see Xem's eyes wide, and his head turned slowly, as though it were stuck. *He can't move now or he'll be heard and seen, but if he stays still there, he'll be seen in a matter of moments—*

Terian looked to the ground just below him for a stone, a stick, something to throw as a distraction. *I have to get Xem out of there before the fool makes obvious our presence—*

He felt a jarring sensation down his spine as his muscles straightened. *He's trying to get us caught. Because...*

Because...

Shrawn.

Terian felt the icy clutch of fear and turned his gaze back to Xemlinan, who waited, his hand on his dagger. Terian saw his muscles twitch, and he started to cast a spell, then stopped himself. *What if he's just a fool caught in the middle of a daft moment?*

The dwarf had come close enough now to be within inches of Xem, and Terian held his breath. *I'm not like the others. I can't lash out blindly at a friend just because I've been betrayed before, or else the Sovereign and Shrawn win. Xem has been loyal. Xem is not a fool. He is indebted to my father—*

He is—

The dwarf paused in his shuffle, and Terian could see the dim awareness on his face that something was wrong, that something was lingering in front of him. *Are his eyes weak? Dwarves can see in the dark, can't they?*

Can he see Xem?

The dwarf said nothing for a long moment, staring into the dark, his jawline twitching as he squinted. *He doesn't know what he's seeing? Maybe he sees something but can't figure out what it is?*

Xemlinan was mere feet away, and Terian found his breath caught in his throat. *Don't move, Xem.*

Terian clenched his jaw as the dwarf leaned forward slightly. *Don't move. Just... don't... move.*

There was a long pause and a desperate silence. The dwarf seemed to pull away slightly, his face slackening.

And then there was a flash as Xemlinan drew his dagger and struck at the dwarf. The dwarf recoiled at the sudden motion and threw up a hand. The blade caught him across the palm on a thick leather glove, and he cried out in pain as he stumbled.

Xem moved toward him, pursuing the kill, but it was too late. The dwarf shouted into the air, loud enough to call for oblivion.

"DARK ELVES! DARK ELVES IN THE VILLAGE! DARK ELV—"

The slash of Xemlinan's dagger across the dwarf's neck ended the cry. A rattle of doors and the sound of alarms being raised across the village echoed through the valley. Cries of "Dark elves!" rang forth with the thunder of boots and the clatter of weapons.

"We're buggered," Grinnd said, hoisting his sword and snugging the barrel closer to his back. "They'll be coming, now."

"Time to fly," Terian said, turning to look at Bowe. "Get us out here."

"Hold," Amenon said, and the wind kicked up a bitter gust that found every crack in Terian's armor. "We shall not fail."

"We were supposed to complete the mission and escape unseen," Terian said, gesturing with his arm toward the village. "There are a hundred dwarves heading toward us at the moment that will make that nigh impossible."

Amenon unsheathed his blade, and the glow of the red in the night caused the chill to seep into Terian's bones. *Surely he doesn't mean to—*

Amenon turned toward the town, eyes narrow and cold, his blade clutched tight in his hand. "We kill them all."

"Father, this is a town of dwarves—women, children." He extended his hand outward. "We can't just—"

"We can." Amenon's voice was heavy and hard like steel. "We will. Make ready for our foes as they come to us." His words came steady and sure like the way he had been before, but there was a cold and furious edge that Terian had not heard since the night he had ordered Sareea Scyros to cut his own son's throat. "And we will leave none alive."

55.

This is madness. The thought echoed over and over in Terian's head as he dropped the axe blade again and again. A dwarf caught it in the middle of his skull and the bone was split open, dashed out in streaks of red on the snow. The smell of it sickened him, but he controlled his stomach's urge to empty its contents and buried his axe into the chest of a dwarf coming at him from the side with a pitchfork.

"They're breaking!" Grinnd's shout echoed over them, crackling against the peaks that surrounded the valley. He let out a mighty bellow that sounded over the field of battle and then cleaved a dwarf in half with a blow from his sword that would have split a log in two.

Terian felt something sharp at his back, the screaming pain of a hatchet hitting his armor and slipping into the crack at his waist. He wanted to scream but controlled it into a grimace then spoke words under his breath while pointing his hand at the red-haired, red-bearded dwarf who had sunk the wood cutter into him. He tore a scream from the dwarf's throat, a bloody scream that caused the man to fall in pain, blood seeping out of his side onto the snow.

"Not so much fun when someone turns your own harm back upon you, is it?" Terian asked, tasting blood from what the dwarf had done to him. He knew if he checked under his armor, the wound would be healed, flawless skin peeking from beneath the broken chain main. The blood remained, however, as did the phantom sensation of pain.

"You're all making this far too easy on me," Dahveed said calmly from behind them. "I never truly get a chance to exercise my skill when I'm with you."

Terian turned his head slightly to see the healer with a long, thin-bladed short sword in his hand. There was only the body of a single dwarf at his feet, and he sighed as he looked down at it. "Looks like you're practicing one of your skills," Terian said.

"But not one that the Leagues would encourage me to practice, if you can believe it," Dahveed said with a shake of his head. "As though a healer's sash would protect me on the battlefield; dogma would have me go unarmed, as though preventing the wound from happening is somehow less glorious than healing it afterward."

"You're in charge, why not change that?" Terian asked, fending off the strike of two dwarves with a strike that took off an arm at the elbow.

"Dogma is not so easy to change as you might think," Dahveed said, and Terian could hear the healer's smile in his answer. "And just because I'm in charge of the Healer's Union in Saekaj, don't assume I have much power over our direction."

"You blathering fools!" Amenon said, and Terian turned his eyes to his father. Amenon was covered in blood, cutting through a dwarf with his red-bladed sword, which glared as though it were drinking in the blood of his foes. *Like legend says it does.* "This is a time for battle, for proving ourselves to the Sovereign!"

"It would appear Grinnd's pronouncement about their breakage is somewhat optimistic," Terian said. He blinked, looking around. "Where's Xem?"

"I don't see him," Dahveed said, glancing about. "Is it possible he's dead?"

"By these earth diggers?" Grinnd struck down three dwarves wielding mining picks. "If he is, it should be of shame for falling to their pitchforks and pickaxes!"

The throng of dwarves was growing thin, their numbers slackening as Terian watched a few of them run. A blast of lightning followed by balls of fire blazing through the air struck down a few of the fleeing number. Terian turned to see Bowe standing over a stack of dwarven dead, a curved-bladed scimitar gripped in one hand while magic flew from the other.

The smell of smoke drifted under Terian's nose, the scent of something burning coming from the corpses of Bowe's victims and pines set aflame by stray magic. Terian counted three trees and a nearby house that were engulfed, flames rising around them.

"Set the village aflame, Bowe," Amenon said, unyielding. "Let us track the stragglers—and Xemlinan, if we can."

"If?" Terian asked. "Why can't we?"

"No footprints," Bowe said in his slow drawl. "He has the Falcon's Essence and could have gone in any direction."

"That treacherous son of a bitch," Terian said. "He landed us in all manner of hell on Shrawn's orders then abandoned us to the flames." He turned his head to look at the burning house before them. "Literally."

"Burn it all," Amenon said, sweeping forward through the flaming forest. "We have work to do."

"Keep the flames away from me," Grinnd said in warning, dodging around a tree as he advanced toward the town. "Just a suggestion, given my cargo." Bowe did not answer, but he did nod—the only concession to show he was listening.

Terian advanced into town with the others. The single street was quiet, a few stragglers running here and there. Bowe cast flame and lightning, striking them down. Terian watched as a female dwarf hurrying on stubby legs burst into flames, and he turned his head to avoid looking. *This is madness. Damn you, Shrawn, for pushing us into this. If I ever catch Xem ...*

A fireball struck a nearby house, gusts of flame bursting out of the window, and Terian flinched away from the heat. "Perhaps we should search the houses," Terian said hesitantly. "Keep from wasting Bowe's magic." He turned to see his father's reaction.

Amenon did not flinch. "This town must burn. We must leave no sign."

"Blackened corpses are a sign," Terian said. "Usually a bad sign."

"I am going to run low on magical energy soon," Bowe said, more calmly than Terian would have in his position. "Anything we can do to limit the waste would speed our task's completion."

"Very well,"Amenon said grudgingly. "Terian, Grinnd, search house by house. If there are survivors within, kill them. If there are too many, signal Bowe to burn them." He raised a hand at a dwarf crossing an alley between houses as he strode forward. The dwarf fell, clutching his throat. Amenon strode to his side and drove his red blade into the dwarf's skull as casually as if he were sheathing it. "Hurry; we still have a mission to attend to. This is all distraction and foolishness born of sabotage. Dahveed and I will circle the village and make certain we can track down and kill any fleeing survivors." His eyes narrowed as he looked to Dahveed. "Keep an eye out for footprints in the snow."

Terian saw Dahveed raise a skeptical eye. There were countless footprints, running in all directions, forward and backward. "I will do all that I can." The healer ran down the street, his blade still in hand.

"Come on then, Terian," Grinnd said. Terian saw the warrior's heavy expression; there was no joy in it. "We have a task. You take the left side of the street, I'll take the right."

"Aye," Terian said, drawing a sharp breath. The sick feeling in his belly persisted. He cut left, running toward the first house at the end of the street.

It was a dwarven hovel, a stone mortared little building with a straw roof thatched tight against the elements. There were no windows to allow him to look inside or the occupants to look out. The door was wood and probably barred, Terian reflected. He stood just outside, paused, waiting for a beat—listening. He heard movement inside and kicked down the door. It broke open, shattering upon the impact of his boot.

He stood in the entry, staring into the darkened dwelling. A fire burned in the hearth, and his gaze shifted to the dwarven children huddled next to it, a teenage girl standing before them. Her arms protected them only slightly, her body sheltering them. She was not a dwarf but a human, and fear was written all over her face.

Terian clutched at his axe as he stared in. The smoke from the hearth wafted over him, a gentle smell of home, and he felt a trickle of sweat bead and run down his forehead as he stared into the house. The girl stared back at him, light hair and fair skin overshadowed by eyes wide with terror.

Terian felt his jaw quiver, and he hefted his axe.

Duty.

56.

Sixteen Years Ago

"This is the day," Amenon said with great relish. Terian could see the pride warring with something else on his face. "You have never yet disappointed me, my son." His expression wavered, just for a second. "Hold fast through this day and I will be as proud of you as any father has been of any son, ever."

"Yes, Father," Terian said, standing almost at attention. They were in his father's study, and Terian could feel the nerves ripping at him. He glanced at the suit of armor standing just before the desk; a beautiful, dark-metal axe now leaned against the figure that the armor was placed upon. He almost reached out and touched it but stopped himself before he did so. *Not yet. Soon. So soon.*

"The soul sacrifice is the single most important ritual for a dark knight," Amenon said, and Terian pulled his eyes off the waiting armor and back to his father. He chuckled. "Though I suppose I don't need to tell you that." He clapped Terian on the shoulder. "You've been waiting for this day nearly as long as I have."

"Yes, Father," Terian said, and he felt the quiver of excitement pass through his body. *I mustn't fail now. I am the best in the Legion; whatever comes my way this day, I am better prepared to handle it than any other student.* He'd heard the whispers, of course. Gossip about the soul sacrifice was forbidden in the Legion—but that didn't stop it from happening.

Amenon nodded once, sharply, his eyes dancing all over his son's attire, inspecting it for the proper look. "Your mother and I will be there with you the entire time. As will your instructors and classmates. I know it is tremendous pressure—"

"I can't fail you," Terian said, with a nod. "The pressure is good. It will ensure that I complete the task set before me with utmost speed and with a skill worthy of the best of dark knights."

Amenon nodded once more, emotion filling his features. "I could ask no more of you." He looked toward the window. "All we need do now is wait for Guturan to let us know that all is ready, and we can go to the garden to begin."

Terian did not speak for a moment. He tried to come up with something to say, something that would express the fear and excitement fighting among each other in his heart but failed. *This is the moment I have been waiting for all my life. For as long as I can remember. This is my moment of triumph.*

There was a knock at the door to the study. Precise and measured, the flutter in Terian's stomach told him it was Guturan before his father even called out, "Enter."

"Your guests await you both, my Lords of Lepos," Guturan said, holding the door open with a sweeping bow.

Amenon smiled once more upon Terian, a smile of encouragement and strength, and Terian returned it. The world seemed to blur around him, and he led the way down the stairs. Each of echo of his boot on the steps felt as though it were symbolizing his rise. *I am not descending to this ceremony; I am rising to be a dark knight.*

The most fearsome dark knight in the land.

Like my father before me.

When they reached the foyer, the servants swept open the doors. The smell of Saekaj's dank air flooded in over the incense that burned in the foyer. Terian could see the guests waiting outside, chairs arranged on the lawn. He knew a dais waited outside, off to his left where he could not see it. He looked at the visible guests—nobles, dark knights of note and renown, and a few of his peers.

He cocked his head—Kahlee Ehrest sat close to the middle, next to her father. Her face was a mask, her cheek twitching as she turned, along with all the other guests, to look at his arrival.

This is my moment.

Terian paused for a single beat at the threshold of the manor house. He kept his gaze centered on the steps ahead. *I cannot trip now. I cannot look foolish at this moment. Not this moment.*

This moment I have been waiting for.

When he reached the center aisle he turned, crisply, walking in a timed march that would have impressed any of his instructors from the Legion. *Discipline and duty be my guide. Whatever task I am to perform, let me carry it out with grace and alacrity worthy of my house and name.*

He was halfway up the aisle before he looked at the dais. Cidrack Urnetagroth stood waiting for him at the top of a small rise of stairs, along with another figure in a black cloak. They blocked his view of something beyond—something that looked almost like an altar.

A ritual, after all.

Terian felt his father's hand land on his shoulder, and he paused to look back. "I can go no further with you," Amenon said. "From here you walk the path on your own."

Terian nodded. He had known this moment was coming. He felt his father's hand leave his shoulder, the weight of the gauntlet carrying all the hopes and dreams that had been instilled in him since the day he had learned to walk and speak. The weight of the countless conversations that his father had had with him, telling him of his purpose and destiny.

I will not fail him.

Every step was made with leaden legs that carried him forward toward that dark destiny, toward the fearsome armor awaiting him at the completion of the ceremony. He took the stairs carefully, staying focused on Urnetagroth and the black-cloaked figure. He took a deep breath and tasted the bile from where he'd lost his breakfast from nervousness earlier.

"Come forth, Terian Lepos," Cidrack Urnetagroth said, intoning as though he were a priest of some sort. "Come forth and face your test."

"I am ready," Terian said, a little stiffly. He had rehearsed this answer a thousand times, simple as it was, for this was the point that his knowledge of the soul sacrifice ceremony ended. From this moment forward, it was all a glorious exploration off the edges of the map, and the shudder of nervousness hinted at the grinding fear within him.

I cannot fail. I must not fail.

"Follow," Cidrack said, and the black-cloaked figure moved aside as well. Terian's eyes fell upon the altar behind them, and for the first time, he realized that there was something upon it. *I must not fail*, he repeated to himself.

Someone upon it.

Her white hair spilled over the edges of the thin stone altar. Her mouth was sealed shut by a cloth rag stuffed into it, and her hands were bound in chains.

I must not fai-

Ameli.

Terian felt the pull and dragged himself toward her unbidden. He surged to her side and saw her wide eyes, open in fear like an animal sensing its doom. He ripped the cloth free of her mouth and stood above her, breathless and suddenly faint. "Ameli!"

"Terian!" Her cry burst free of her mouth and she struggled against the chains that bound her. "Terian, let me free—"

Cidrack brought a hand down upon her cheek that rocked her head to the side. Terian spun upon the instructor and slammed into his armored form with his shoulder unthinking. He heard a great crack followed by an agonizing pain in his arm but did not care. He took the dark knight to the ground with his clumsy charge, and felt the sharp edge of his armor cut through his tunic. He raised a fist to strike Cidrack Urnetagroth squarely in the face—

"TERIAN!" Amenon's shout silenced everything in the vicinity. Terian froze, hand raised to slam Urnetagroth squarely in his exposed nose, the weakest point available to him, but he lowered his arm. His fingers, however, did not unclench. "This is the task before you," his father said.

Terian dragged himself to his feet, ignoring Urnetagroth. "To do what?" It came out in a huff, emotion dripping with every hard breath. "To ... to ..." He dragged a finger loose of his fist and pointed at the altar. "To ... her?"

Amenon stood at his place in the aisle, his eyes thin and severe. "No sacrifice is too great in the name of Sovereign."

Terian opened his mouth, but no words came out, his jaw quivering in outrage and disgust. "Sacrifice ...?" He glanced back at Ameli. "She's a ... sacrifice?"

"We are all sacrifices, if need be," Cidrack Urnetagroth said, rising from the ground. His cheeks were flushed, and Terian gave him a glare that made the dark knight take a step backward—though out of caution or fear, Terian did not hazard a guess. "This is our place as servants of the Sovereign."

"Terian, help me!" Ameli said. He looked back at her, still pinned to the altar. Her cheek was bleeding, her eye already swelling shut where Urnetagroth had struck her. "Please!"

I will not fail. The words echoed in his head, mocking.

Terian stood, frozen, in the center of the altar, eyes locked on his father. "You cannot ask me to do ... this."

"Darkness requires sacrifice," Urnetagroth said. "The Sovereign requires obedience."

Terian glanced back at the black-cloaked figure. "Are you a healer?"

The black-cloaked figure shook his head, slowly.

"He is a necromancer," Urnetagroth said, and Terian turned back to look at him. "There will be no resurrection from this. She is your soul sacrifice, the price you pay to embrace the darkness and rise a knight of the shadows." He stared down with the coldest eyes Terian had ever seen. *I never noticed that about him before. How did I not notice that in the last four years?*

"I don't want to be a—" Terian cut himself off before the last word, looking back to his father. "This can't be the price. Not everyone has a sister—"

"You are the only son of a most powerful house," Amenon said from his place in the aisle. His face wavered, and Terian saw shame begin to peek through his facade. "More is required of you than others. Now ... remember your duty." He clenched his teeth, and Terian had a vision of dark fangs gnashing him to pieces.

Duty.

He turned back to the altar. The necromancer stood before him, just to the side, hands extended. A dagger lay upon them. "This is the instrument of sacrifice."

Terian stared at the black blade. He eyed it then turned slowly to Cidrack Urnetagroth.

"Any sacrifice but the one placed before you will result in your death," Urnetagroth said warily.

Terian stared at him through lidded eyes. *Maybe I want to die.* He glanced back at his father. Saw him move his head to urge Terian forward. *My sacrifice must be greater than others?*

You son of a bitch.

The crowd was hushed behind him, and Terian felt the world pull away from him. He stood upon the altar, and even Urnetagroth stepped back.

The necromancer waited, dagger in his extended hands. "Take this ... and perform your duty. I will handle the rest."

Terian stared at the dagger as though it would leap out and strike him down.

Duty.

Finally he reached out, and took it in his hands. Dimly, he could hear Ameli sobbing.

"Terian, no ... Terian, please ..."

He closed his eyes, trying to block her out.

"Terian ..." The rattling as she fought against her bonds nearly blotted out her pleas. The faint smell of her perfume filled his nose.

I must not fail.

The chains shook with a fury once more. "Terian! Please, Terian! Please don't!"

He opened his eyes. Now she was still, eyes seeping quiet tears. "Please."

He brought the dagger down straight and true, plunging it into her heart.

He felt the blade break through the bone, his hands latched hard to it. There was a gasp of her breath in shock at the strike. He could smell the faint perfume that she had worn—the sweet, sickly scent of cave cress—over the sweat and stink of fear.

There was a burning blast of light before his eyes, a flash as magic ran through the dagger and into his hands. It sounded like the crack of thunder he'd heard when he'd gone to the surface, the roar of a mighty river of blood rushing through his ears.

He looked away when he saw the light leave her eyes, the purple irises relaxing as the skin around the edges went slack. She was looking through him now, and he turned to see the necromancer holding a red gemstone in his fingers. It glowed with light, then faded to a luster.

Terian stayed there, hunched over Ameli's form, as the sound of the roaring blood subsided, replaced by thunderous applause.

Strong hands clapped him on the back. Cidrack Urnetagroth's hands. Still he remained folded over, the dagger still clutched in his hands. Words were coming to him now, but he could not hear them.

He did not care to hear them.

One word reverberated in his mind. It rattled in there like an uninvited guest that had long outstayed its welcome. It persisted, even through the congratulations, the calls of acclaim, the shouts that pronounced him the most promising dark knight that had ever lived.

It stayed, though, through all that, refusing to leave, that one word.

The last word that Ameli had ever spoken.

57.

"Please."

The human girl shuddered as she spoke, her voice shaking as she shielded the dwarven children with her body.

Terian blinked. He felt as though he'd just had a spear run into his forehead by a troll at full speed. His jaw dropped slightly open, but no words came. He stared at the girl, her face lined with fear and emotion, the smell of the wood fire in the hearth harkening him back to Sanctuary for some reason.

"Please," she said again, voice nearly a whisper.

"Terian!" Grinnd shouted from across the street. "Get a move on!"

Terian stared into the house, and felt his jaw shake trying to work. "Stay quiet until we're gone." He heard his voice break as he spoke. He cast a last look at the girl huddled over the children in the corner, and he grasped at the knob of the door, and pulled it shut behind him without another word.

The cold, crisp winter air bit at his cheeks, stinging his eyes along the way. He walked to the next house and kicked in the door. He shut it behind him, looking around to see if anyone was visible. He saw no one, and brought his axe across the wooden table in the middle of the room, knocking it asunder and sending the clay dishes upon it shattering to the floor.

"AGHHHHHHHHH!" he shouted, and hit the table again. He blinked then heard a gasp from under the bed. He saw a pair of eyes watching him, and held a lone finger to his lips. "Stay quiet until you're sure we've left." He retreated quietly, closing the door behind him.

He stood in the fierce wind, and saw Grinnd three houses down on the opposite side of the street, the barrel on his back bobbing as he made his way from house to house. A dog's bark cut off in a sudden, pathetic yelp somewhere down the street, and Terian crashed through another door. This one he shut again just as quickly, without so much as acknowledging the half dozen pairs of eyes keeping watch on him.

His axe blade already dripped with blood from the battle with the dwarven men, leaving dots of red on the snow as he crossed the alley to the next house. He saw Bowe standing at the far end of the village in the direction he was heading. With a flash, flame burst from out of the druid's hands and caught the houses at the end of town on fire.

Terian took a ragged breath, watching the flames spread up the homes. He threw himself into the next house and shut the door behind him. He barely saw the faces of the dwarves huddled before him, just as he barely saw a spear race toward him from the left.

Terian lashed out and broke the wooden implement with a swipe of his axe. The dwarf wielding it rushed close in, and Terian smacked him in the forehead with the palm of his gauntlet, knocking the small man back. "Sit down and shut up," he said softly. He turned back to the eyes of the children watching him. "Be silent until you're sure we've all left." He saw the disarmed dwarf look up at him, but his eyes were glazed and he saw no details of the face. "Be quiet as though your life depended upon it—because it does."

"Who are you?" The dwarf asked—the one he'd knocked to the ground.

Terian paused at the door, and felt emotion run over him, bowing his head for him. "Does it matter?"

"You saved our lives," the whispered voice came back.

Terian thumped his hand against the wooden doorframe. "Not yet, I haven't." He spun and looked at the dwarf on the floor. "I've just given you a chance. From here it's up to you." The sound of flames crackling somewhere down the street reached his ears.

"Th-thank you," came the whisper as Terian opened the door.

"Don't thank me until you die old and in bed," Terian whispered. Then he stepped out into the cold night.

58.

The flames roared at the end of the street, burning the houses to the ground. Terian watched them blaze, and turned his head subtly to look at the half-dozen he'd kicked the doors down on himself. They were upwind of the flames, the rollicking blaze which had already engulfed half the town.

"Well done, Bowe," Amenon said as he reached them at a jog. Dahveed was a step behind him, a look of immense distaste on his face.

"This is going to catch attention," Terian said with his jaw clenched. "These flames are visible for miles."

"We have done our duty," Amenon said as he came to a halt next to Bowe.

Grinnd dragged into the loose circle, smelling of blood and gore. His armor dripped red, and his axe blade was covered in the liquid. He did not wear a happy expression. "Let us be done with this mission."

"I thought you liked the slaughter, Grinnd," Terian said, sparing no sting.

The warrior gave him a look like jagged glass. "I have a care for battle, and this was not one. This was duty." He looked away at the flames that burned on both sides of them. Screams tore out of the fiery houses. "This was ..."

"Necessary," Amenon said. "Never forget that." He glanced around the street. "Dahveed and I have traced the footsteps out of town—caught a few people fleeing but surprisingly few. I expect they all huddled together after the men were killed coming after us."

"Yes," Terian said, letting an icy facade settle over his features. "It was mostly women and children in the houses." He felt his teeth chatter, and not from the cold. "They're dealt with, though." *You son of a bitch.*

"Very well." Amenon gave a curt nod, as if everything met his expectations. Terian kept the urge to drive the axe point into his face at bay. "To the mine, then."

Terian followed his father as he broke into a run. They still floated inches off the ground, the Falcon's Essence spell leaving them hanging suspended in the air. *Pointless, now. It's not as though the dwarves would suspect that Aurastra burned itself, even assuming I hadn't left them fifty survivors to tell the tale.* He felt a wave of emotion run over him and clamped his jaw tight. He felt his molars grind together. *If only it could have been more.*

They ran around the edge of the burning village toward the hills backing the houses. The entrance to the mine was visible in the low light cast by the flames, and Amenon led them to it without any hesitation. Terian looked up at the sky, and saw it shrouded with clouds. *No stars.*

"Set the barrel inside—say a hundred feet or so," Amenon said as they came to a halt outside the mine. A sheer face of rock raced upward from the entrance. "Bring this whole mountain down on it."

"But not yet," Terian said, cooler than he felt. "We should confirm that whatever the Sovereign wants buried is within the mine." He felt a vicious smile creep up on his face. *The smile of a man who simply does not care any longer.* "You know, so we're sure we've completed our mission."

Amenon flinched visibly. "The Sovereign assures me—"

"You can face him if we fail, then," Terian said, and started toward the mine. "Me, I'm going to make sure we're not sealing the wrong damned tunnel." He cast a look backwhich was filled with venom. "I didn't just kill gods-know-how-many dwarves so I could have the Sovereign drop the axe on me for stumbling at the finish."

Amenon stumbled over his words. "What—No—what is within is for his eyes only!"

"If I'm not mistaken, it was for dwarven eyes, too," Terian said as he headed into the blackness of the tunnel.

"Now dead!" Amenon called after him.

Terian ignored him and licked his lips as he ran into the dark mine. The cave was chipped out of the mountain, wooden supports placed every ten feet or so to hold it up. The dank, overwhelming smell of the cave was of little comfort to him now. Terian ran on, ignoring every emotion that threatened to overwhelm him. *I won't let these people die without finding out your secret, oh Sovereign. I won't let your servants do their dirty works without witnessing what it is you fear ...*

The tunnel widened, and Terian could see something in the chamber ahead. It was a shape, a shadow, a silhouette of something oddly familiar. He burst into an open room, and stared down at the thing in the center of the room.

It was ovoid but turned lengthwise to the ground. The center was hollow, but glowed with a faint energy that radiated darkness.

He cocked his head, and let out a breath he hadn't even known he was holding as he stepped down to look at the thing. The very ordinary thing. Something he'd seen in every corner of Arkaria.

A portal.

59.

Terian ran his fingers over the stone ring, letting the metal gauntlets poke at the runes inscribed on it. "What ... the hells?"

"Now you've seen it." Amenon's voice echoed through the chamber. Judgment and fury were wrapped up within the words.

"Are you going to kill me for witnessing this very ordinary spectacle?" Terian turned his head around.

"No," his father said, and Terian saw the muscles of his neck bulge under his gorget. "But we need to leave."

"What about if I walk through it?" Terian paused, making a motion as though he were going to do it.

"NO!" His father's cry was sharp and his hand was extended. "Step away ... step away from it."

"So, it's not that it's a portal," Terian said, not taking his eyes off his father. "It's that it leads somewhere he doesn't want us to go." Terian ran his fingers over the runes again. "Where does it go? Did he even tell you?"

"This is all sedition," Amenon said warningly. "Betrayals of the Sovereign—"

"Betrayal requires loyalty," Terian said, feeling his dead gaze fall upon his father, and a smile born of grief and madness split his face. "I have none toward him."

Amenon grew still, his face frozen in an expression somewhere between fear and loathing. "You are my son, and it is expected—"

"I stopped giving a fig about your expectations the day you made me kill my sister to imprison her essence in a soul ruby," Terian said, the hot blood bubbling over, years worth of rage seeping into his words. "I was a fool to come back to Saekaj. I *knew* how it worked. I knew that your city, your nation and your Sovereign coasted along on the blood and pain of good men and women, but I forgot. I can't believe I let myself forget that the darkness in Saekaj and Sovar isn't just some accident of fate, a lack of light because of its location. It's an active scheme, where you and your Sovereign and countless others stand in the light and block it from anyone who grows tired of being kept near-blind."

"You ... you ..." His father pointed a finger at him in fury, shaking like a flag in the wind.

"I ..." Terian said. "Not a word we're free to use in Saekaj. You know what Dahveed said to me, on the day after you had Sareea slit my throat? 'There are no free men in Saekaj and Sovar.'" Terian laughed. "I had forgotten the truth of that in my absence. We are all slaves, bound to be loyal to a Sovereign who does not care a whit if any of or all of us live or die!" Terian laughed, emotion released in the form of grief turned to levity. "We serve him for no purpose but our own survival, and he makes play that it is the most wonderful thing ever brought to us, as though it is our gift and blessing over all other races." Terian shook his head. "I don't want this path anymore. I don't want *your* path anymore."

Amenon shook the finger at Terian again. "You said these things once before. You threw the gifts I have accumulated for you in my face once before. And you came crawling back once you realized that the world was not the shape you thought it was. Be wary of what you say now, because this time, there will be no—"

"Be careful of what I say?" Terian laughed at the absurdity then felt his smile fade as the rage came back. "What I say? Here is what I say:

"*I pray for your death!*" Terian shouted. "I pray that you will die in as treacherous a manner as you have lived, and that in your last seconds of life you recall this moment and the others, and you dwell on what forcing sacrifice on others has brought you! A dying house that will *never* have an heir! A name that will cease to live when you curl up and rot, a legend that will cost you everything! When you die, everything you have worked for will fade and fall into Sovar with the last remnants of your house, and your life will be meaningless!"

"You cannot ... you cannot mean ... you cannot turn your back on—" Amenon's words came out in gasps. "I have given you ... *everything*."

"You've given me nothing," Terian said, striding toward his father and pausing. "You've *taken* everything from me." He spit the last bit as a whisper and a curse. "I will never follow your path. Never. The soul you sacrificed on the day of ascension to knighthood was mine; Ameli's remains on your desk, and it is the closest thing you have to one of your own."

He stormed past his father, down the dark tunnel and out into the cold. He stood there, seething, with the rest of them until Grinnd's barrel exploded and the air was filled with the dust of the mine's collapse. The smell of smoke and char wafted under his nose and the conversations of the others faded into the air behind the ringing left by the explosion.

I pray for your death ...

He looked down at his right shoulder and saw dark soot upon it. He ran a finger across it and looked skyward. Ash was falling slowly, like snowflakes drifting out of the heavens.

"Bowe," Amenon said, drawing Terian to look at his father once more. Amenon did not look back at him. "Take us away."

The wind of the druid spell kicked up around them, stirring the ash in the air to a black cloud around them. Terian stared into it, dark as the Saekaj night, the words came back to him again … and he found he still meant every word of them.

I pray for your death …

60.

"You have failed me." The Sovereign's voice was cold and high and rasped through the throne room of the Grand Palace.

"My Sovereign," Amenon began. "We—"

Terian stood at his side, unspeaking. They had not exchanged a word since the cave, hours earlier. Terian looked down; the soot still covered his armor, and the scorched scent still hung in his nose.

"You have failed!" the Sovereign cut him off.

"We—" Amenon began again.

"*Failed!*" the Sovereign thundered.

"How many times are you going to let Shrawn sabotage our efforts on your behalf before you cut his gods-damned head off?" Terian asked, as calmly as if he had asked a servant for a drink. *Where the hell is this coming from?* Still, he continued to speak. "Five? A hundred?"

"No more, I say." The Sovereign's voice rose, the fury barely concealed beneath the surface. "I grow tired of the House of Lepos and their continued excuses—"

"I grow tired of standing and trying to do your will and getting hacked down at the knees for it," Terian said. The words came unbidden, and no emotion followed them. *I don't care if I die here.*

"If you want us dead, be done with it already and get this farce over with. I can only do so much of your bidding when your 'most loyal' servant keeps trying to thwart my every effort."

Shrawn slipped out from the shadow of the throne once more, tapping his staff on the ground. "You blame me—again—for your own incompetence."

"Indeed, it was my incompetence that led those three traitors to rise against us," Terian said. "Oh, wait, no, that was you, planting them in our ranks to make us look like fools."

"You *are* fools," Shrawn said.

"Yes, we are fools for trying to run an army in spite of your efforts to sabotage said army," Terian said, nodding vigorously. "Just as we were fools to try and carry out our mission without having your agent Xemlinan Eres turn on us, exposing us to the entire dwarven village."

"Lies," Shrawn said coolly.

"Xemlinan ... Eres?" the Sovereign's voice rumbled in the throne room. "The thief that you killed ..."

"Whom you handed over to Lord Amenon," Shrawn said, and Terian could sense his discomfiture. "I have no dealings with him—"

"You mentioned him only last week," the Sovereign said in a low drawl. "An ... information broker, I believe you called him ... someone who provided you with an interesting snippet that led us to execute Baron Metiven."

"An acquaintance only, my Sovereign," Shrawn said, bowing low.

"Lies only, my Sovereign," Terian said without a care. "If you were really loyal, Shrawn, you'd stop trying to sabotage everyone around you to make yourself look better."

"If you were truly competent," Shrawn hissed back, "you wouldn't be constantly tripped up by these betrayals."

"It takes more than competence to dodge arrows shot at your back while you're carrying out a task," Terian said. "It takes a miracle." He shifted his attention to Yartraak, whose visage was still hidden in the shadows. "I don't object to being made a fool of if I'm sabotaged in a task of no significance to you. But when I am made to fail by one of your servants at a task you assigned me to carry out, I have to question their loyalty to you."

"This was your responsibility, Terian of House Lepos," the Sovereign said. "Do you deny your failure?"

"No, we failed," Terian said, shaking his head. *I don't care. Why am I even bothering to argue this with you?* He glanced at his father. *You can all die in the Depths for all I care. So why am I saying any of this?* "Failed horribly. We destroyed the mine and buried the portal, but we were exposed to the dwarves, and surely some of them escaped to tell the tale. Your directive to keep the secret was compromised, without doubt." *Because I made sure it was.*

"The dwarves will blame us if the word gets out," Shrawn said quickly. "They will ... rattle the saber, possibly declare war."

"Because you had your agent expose them," the Sovereign said.

"I ..." Shrawn's mouth went agape. *Bet you haven't found yourself speechless in front of the Sovereign in a long time, Shrawn.*

"Swallow your excuses, Shrawn," the Sovereign said. "Your foolishness has cost us nothing in this instance. War with the dwarves would be a blessing."

"I ... what?" Amenon spoke at last, his tone one of quiet shock.

"We are prepared, are we not?" the Sovereign asked. "Our armies are raised? They are trained? They are ready to strike at whatever target we desire to set them toward?"

Amenon blinked, and Terian stared at him. *The dwarves?* "They were when last I knew their strength, my Sovereign."

"Oh, yes," the Sovereign said. "I had forgotten your fall." There was the sound of strange, steady breathing from the Sovereign's silhouette. "In spite of Shrawn's efforts, I expected more from you, House Lepos. I would have thought you shrewd enough to see Shrawn's intentions and prepared for them."

"It's really hard to prepare yourself for a dagger strike when you have no idea of its origination," Terian said. "Why don't you send Shrawn over here and I'll show you what I mean?"

A gentle laugh came from the Sovereign, followed by a sigh. "You push the bounds, Terian of Lepos."

"I'll push more than that if you'll allow me to drag Shrawn to the edge of a cliff." *And I'd gladly do the same to you, my Sovereign, if I had any hope it could kill you.*

"There must be consequences for this failure," the Sovereign said, ignoring Terian. "Your blindness to the treachery of Shrawn is not a failing I can allow in my inner circle."

"Great," Terian said, shaking his head. "Let's get back to planning the executions, then."

"I have no need to plan executions," the Sovereign said, his voice going higher. "But you will both leave Saekaj today."

"My Sovereign—" Amenon said with a gasp.

"My Sovereign," Yartraak said, mockingly, and he shifted his face into the light. Red, glowing orbs shone when his eyes hit the torchlight, and the three horns gave him a look like some demon. "Why does your son speak all the truth for your House, Amenon? Have you not the balls to speak it for yourself? Living in the soft comfort of Saekaj has made a gelding of you. The darkest knight I ever met rose from the streets of Sovar to become my right hand, and now he stands before me a shade of himself. You have forgotten how to fight. You have forgotten how to claw. Victory has defeated you, and I would send you back to the forging fires to blacken you again or burn you up, I care not which."

Terian blinked as he watched his father's face crumple. *The Sovereign would bind my fate to his. Seal my father to me for all our days. I will be stuck with him in Sovar, and he will drag me down—Unless—*

"I failed," Terian said, staring straight up at the Sovereign.

"Say that again," the Sovereign said, looking down on him.

"I failed," Terian said. "I trusted Xemlinan Eres as a friend, and I was a fool not to see him for what he was—a disloyal traitor to my house. I. Failed."

"And you will accept the punishment for that failure," the Sovereign said. "Time in Sovar will be good for both of you, I think—"

"I'm not going to Sovar," Terian said, looking up at the red eyes. He saw a hint of surprise in them. "I mean no disrespect to you, my Sovereign—but I am going into exile."

There was a steady quiet that settled over the throne room. "You come into my place of rule and tell me how things will be?" The Sovereign's voice was scratchy and tinged with anger.

"Yes," Terian said, staring into the red eyes. "I believe I just did."

"I should execute you right here for your insolence," the Sovereign said in a low rasp. Terian saw Shrawn's eyes light up at that.

"Go right ahead," Terian said with a shrug. "I can't stop you, after all." He looked up at the red eyes again. "That's why I can phrase what I just did as a command—because if you dislike it, you can kill me."

"I ... do not understand," the Sovereign said, and Terian could hear genuine perplexity in the reply.

"You are unquestionably in charge," Terian said. *Where does this bullshit spring from?* "You can kill me—shatter my bones to dust and bloody mess—faster than I can draw my sword. Everyone else around you chatters, they wheedle, they beg, they fight for your favor by kissing your ass and offering you unwanted sacrifices like their daughters to bed. I speak to you and you can either ignore it, listen, or kill me—your choice. Because you have that power. No one else has power in this room, and I never forget it. Which is why I find no need to wheedle, to chatter or beg. You will do as you will do, and I have no need to curry favor. I have failed. Anyone else would tell you that their life is in your hands. I always remember that it is, that you are the God of Darkness, and so I feel no compulsion to remind you. Do as you will, without any of my toadying to cloud the matter."

"Do you think some foolish speech will sway me from killing you, Terian Lepos?" The Sovereign's voice was filled with cold fury.

"I don't think my words will sway you one way or another," Terian said with something nearing indifference. "I was merely suggesting you exile me for my failure. But if you mean to have my death, I'm not going to run." *Because I don't care.*

"Do you think by offering yourself as a sacrifice, you will keep me from sending your father back to Sovar?" There was almost a glee creeping into the Sovereign's words. "Do you think it will spare him the coarsening he needs to survive in my land?"

Terian looked to his father, who turned his head to look back at Terian in return. Amenon's eyes were sunken, the light was out of them, and he looked nearly dead. "Do you not believe that depriving him of his heir and his legacy will not coarsen him enough? Other than your glory, what does he work for?" *He works out of sheer orneriness, out of a desire to hurt others, and the joy of immersing himself in that work. Not that you'd know that.*

A strange, rattling breath came from the throne. "Pain."

Terian stared into the dark, trying to decipher the meaning of the Sovereign's word. "You want to inflict it? Or you want him to feel it? You want to visit it upon all of us?"

"Pain is the fire which burns out weakness," the Sovereign said, his head now shifted back into the shadows. "Your compromise is acceptable to me, Terian of House Lepos, because it will bring your father pain. You will leave immediately from this place, and you will not return until he has suffered enough to pay for his failures and regain his strength. Do not believe for a moment, though, Amenon," he turned his head to Terian's father, "that I am done with you. The Third Army is too high a post for your command. You will join the Sixth Army as a bare Captain, in among the foot soldiers, and march as one of them."

Amenon looked up at him, and Terian saw the barest hint of embers in his eyes. "I will serve you … to the best of my ability, my Sovereign." His voice was hollow.

"Terian, you houseless wanderer," the Sovereign said. "When the day comes that I call you home, you will return to me, yes?"

Don't throw it in his face. "Sure," Terian said, not quite suppressing his sarcasm.

The Sovereign cocked his head, as though trying to ferret out Terian's meaning. "I dismiss you, my loyal servant."

Fooled you, Terian thought. He bowed, deep, deeper than he even normally would have and smiled mockingly into the dark. "Your grace is the stuff of legends."

"It truly is," Dagonath Shrawn said, nodding. He sent Terian a daggered look that told him everything he needed to know about the man. *He won't stop. He will never stop, not until every one of his enemies is dead.*

"He just can't stop kissing your ass, can he?" Terian said, turning to leave. "It's like a syndrome for him; he probably can't even help it."

"Curb your tongue, Terian," the Sovereign said. "Lest it get you into trouble."

"I'm being exiled from my home," Terian said, feeling oddly indifferent about it, "I doubt it'll get me into more trouble than that."

With that, he bowed once more—and left the throne room, oddly lighter than when he had come in.

61.

Kahlee watched him as he packed, filling Terian with the disquieting sense that she was about to explode at him for some reason. As though she would start screaming at him, filling the air with some rage he did not sense from the placid look on her face.

"Where will you go?" she asked when she broke the silence at last.

"Reikonos, I expect," Terian said. "Bowe offered to teleport me there."

"So you'll pick up where you left off?" Her face betrayed no emotion. "Scrabbling for menial work? Walking streets to keep those without homes of their own away from warehouses?"

He blinked and caught a glimpse of himself in a mirror on the wall in front of him as he folded a weathered shirt and stuffed it in his travel sack. "I'll do whatever I have to do to survive on the margins, I expect. Like I did before I came here."

"That hardly seems a task fitting for the greatest dark knight in our land," she said, oddly cool in her pronouncement.

He froze. "Where did you get the idea that I'm the greatest dark knight in our land?"

"Everyone said it on the day of your soul sacrifice," she said, and he met her eyes to find them unblinking as she watched him.

"Do you know how many soul sacrifices I have attended in my years in Saekaj?"

"No," Terian said, feeling his voice go hoarse. "I only ever went to the one, you see. I assumed you were the same."

"The rest of us were not bound by your code," she said. "I have seen countless soul sacrifices." She cocked her head at him. "Do you know what most of them involve? Animals." She wore a look of carefully controlled emotion. "Occasionally some undesirable from Sovar, a complete stranger to the subject of the ceremony."

Terian felt a smoldering in his heart. "Lucky me, to get a sacrifice that truly lived up to its name." He bowed his head, and went back to folding a tunic. "Why are you telling me this?"

"Ameli gave her life for you," Kahlee said.

"Ameli had her life stolen by me," Terian corrected.

"I don't think so," Kahlee said. "She knew. Before it happened. She could have run, but she didn't."

"That is the single dumbest thing I have ever heard said aloud." Terian wheeled on her. "Because it suggests that my brilliant, vivacious sister, who was full of life and wanted to live, somehow failed to act to save herself." He stared her down with burning eyes. "I looked at her in the moments before she died. She was afraid. She may have known just before I stabbed her that she was about to die, but she did not ask for it. She did not walk willingly to the slaughter. She wanted to live and she was deprived of life by me and my stupid refusal to buck every horrible, senseless, ridiculous tenet hammered into my skull by this gods-damned society!" Terian lashed out at the mirror in front of him and shattered it, the glass falling in a rain of shards onto the dresser.

Kahlee let the silence rest for just a moment before she spoke. "You're right, I lied."

"I know you lied," Terian said, staring at his own eye reflected back in one of the shards. "Don't try to make me feel better about the evil things I've done. There is no redemption for the darkness I embraced, and no excuse for my failure to stand up and call it by its name sooner." He looked over his shoulder. "I have stood in the shadows for a very long time, letting myself think that I am a dark knight—a *true* dark knight. 'The greatest dark knight in the land'? I'm a pale shade of dark. I failed to look my father's evil in the face and spit in it once before. Because I ... trusted him."

"Because you wanted to be like him," Kahlee said.

"I was a fool," Terian said. "So, yes, I am going to go back to Reikonos. I am going to do menial things. I will scrape the dung from outhouse seats if need be. I will whack orphans with a stick to ward them away from warehouses where the owner would sooner kill them than allow them to break one of his windows. I will skirt by on the minimums of life and accept it happily as the price I pay for never having to do what my father and my Sovereign would turn me toward ever again." He felt a shudder of discomfort. "I will grant you a divorce if you so desire; so great is my shame that I am without house, and you should not have to suffer—"

"No," Kahlee said, shaking her head. "I don't think so. Married to you, I need never fear I shall have to marry another."

Terian stared at her. "Well. Glad I could serve some useful function to someone."

Her eyes were shaded. "Will you ever return?"

"The Sovereign said he will call me back when my father has suffered enough," Terian said. "But no, I'm not ever coming back. You can live peacefully with the knowledge that no one will ever expect you to marry again, nor deal with the impositions of heirs or anything of that sort." He felt an air of suspicion wash over him. "You're not ... presently carrying an heir, are you?"

"No," she said archly. "I am most definitely not, doubtless much to my father's chagrin."

"Well, that's a relief," Terian said. "No need for more responsibility, you know." He stared down at his pack, only half full, then glanced at the closet. "This is good enough, I suppose."

"I know who you are, you know," she said as he started to draw his pack upon his shoulder.

"Oh, really?" Terian said with a wan smile that turned up the corners of his lips. "Who am I? And please don't say something trite like 'a good man.'"

"I would not say anything so false," Kahlee said, devoid of expression. "You are not summed up into words so easily. But I know this—you are my husband. You are not your father. And you are not who I thought you were when we met again after all your years of absence." She leaned up and kissed him on the cheek, ever so gently. "Good journey, Terian."

"Good journey?" Terian asked, shuffling slowly toward the door. "Why Kahlee … knowing all the places I'm now unwelcome, I don't see how it couldn't be."

62.

There was still almost no light in the Brutal Hole, but he could see nonetheless. It seemed brighter than it had a few months earlier. *Because it's not Saekaj. Everything that's not Saekaj is brighter. Hell, swampy Gren would probably look brighter to me right now.* The loud raised voices of the longshoremen echoed through the establishment, and the smell of the hard whiskey on the table in front of him was not as pleasing as he'd hoped it would have been.

He slugged it back nonetheless and stared at the empty shot glass as Rosalla made her way over. "Another, I take it?" she asked.

"You still don't sound thrilled to see me," he said, staring at the glass. "I've been back for months, and it's been months more since that little incident—"

"That cost me weeks' worth of business."

"I just get the sense you haven't forgiven me," Terian said, letting himself smile.

"I haven't," Rosalla said, without a hint of anything but annoyance. "Another round?"

Terian sighed and slid a few coins her way. "Please." He watched her walk away but without the enthusiasm he might have felt a few months earlier. "I swear, no one's the forgiving sort around here ..."

"Perhaps it is the people you associate with," came a voice from above him.

Terian didn't even bother to look up, but he felt himself smile. "Hello, Alaric."

"Hello, Terian," Alaric said, and slipped into the seat across from his. "Do you mind if I sit down?"

"By all means," Terian said, staring at the paladin in his faded cloak, the cowl turned up to hide his face. "Somehow I doubt you were drinking in here by sheerest chance."

Alaric said with a wry smile. "The Reikonos docks are not known for their abundant hospitality."

"Yet here you are braving them anyway," Terian said. "Not that there's anyone in this room who could be a threat to you."

"Just because I wield the power to harm others doesn't mean I wish to," Alaric said quietly.

"I … had almost forgotten that about you," Terian said, lowering his head to stare at the table, the wood pockmarked from years of abuse. "I had almost forgotten that quality existed at all."

"I assume your sojourn to the homeland did not end as well as you might have hoped?" Alaric asked. Strangely absent was any glee; he sounded genuinely disappointed.

"I found out what happens when power and intention are unfettered by just law," Terian said, not meeting Alaric's eye. "Or maybe I should say I remembered what happens in that instance."

"I see," Alaric said.

"Impressively well for a man with one eye, yes," Terian said as Rosalla sat another glass in front of him. "And one for my friend, Rosalla."

"You have a friend?" Rosalla asked, nearly scoffing. Terian noticed she did not incline her head to look down at Alaric's face.

"Possibly the only one I have left, but yes," Terian said. "A whiskey for my friend."

"Coming right up," she said without enthusiasm, and she sashayed away again as Terian watched her out of the corner of his eye.

"You have other friends," Alaric said.

"No, I don't," Terian said, shaking his head.

"I am certain Niamh would object to your dismissal of her out of hand," Alaric said. "As would Curatio, Vaste, Cyrus Davidon—that bed you gave him was a most curious choice, I might add."

Terian snorted. "I forgot about that. I doubt he's used it like I told him to, though."

"You have friends, Terian," Alaric said quietly. "You need not walk alone down an aimless road."

"I left, Alaric," Terian said. "I left. I did wrong for Sanctuary, and I left in exile." *It's almost becoming a pattern for me.*

"It was your choice, not ours," Alaric said.

"I make a lot of bad choices," Terian said, and the flash of a dagger came to his mind. "More than I can count. And with many of them …" He swallowed deeply. "There is no way to set them right."

"You believe there is no redemption for our mistakes?" Alaric asked.

"I didn't make mistakes," Terian said. "I made bad choices. Calling them mistakes would absolve me of the fact that I knew what I was doing when I made them. They were not accidents. They were choices. Hurtful, cruel, vicious choices that cut me off from people I loved—" His voice choked off. "I don't think I believe in redemption, Alaric. I don't see how I could." Terian kept his face lowered, studying every line of the table, every grain of the wood—

"Terian," Alaric said. "Look up." Terian hesitated then shifted his eyes gradually upward. Alaric sat before him in his seat, helm on the table in front of him, and his cowl back to expose his face.

"Alaric," Terian hissed, looking to the crowds shuffling behind the Ghost of Sanctuary, "this is a dark elven bar! They won't take kindly to—"

"I do not care," Alaric said, staring back at him with his one good eye. "Let me state this in no uncertain terms." He leaned forward. "I am not ashamed to be seen with you, regardless of what might have happened to you in the time since you have left."

"Alaric, I'm not worried about you being ashamed to be seen with me, I'm worried the dark elves in this bar are going to come after you in a drunken fury," Terian said, not bothering to mask his alarm.

"I don't care," Alaric said, still leaning forward. "And do you know why I do not care?"

"Not really," Terian said, still feeling the sense of fear and panic in his stomach. "Alaric, put your helm back on." He shifted to look up. No one had noticed the old paladin yet. *And that is fortunate, but his time is bound to run out, and soon.*

"I do not care because you are here with me," Alaric said and leaned back. "With you and I together, what threat can they pose?"

"Mobs tend to pose a pretty big threat, even to spell casters," Terian said nervously. "All it takes is one nut with a bottle to whack you across the back of the head, and all the spells in the world don't count for much—"

"I have faith in you, Terian," Alaric said, as if Terian had said nothing at all. "I have faith in you—as a man. Faith that you'll do the right thing. Faith that … no matter how bad things get, you'll seek the right path instead of blindly following the wrong one for your whole life. I am proud to be associated with you, if you'll let me—"

"I'll let you anytime," Terian said urgently, waiting to see if the largest fellow at the bar would turn around, "but I'd rather you'd do it with your helm on!"

Alaric let a short chuckle. "Now who's ashamed to be seen with whom?"

How can I more obviously communicate to him that I'm not looking for a barfight? Terian rubbed his temple between his thumb and forefinger, and kept his eyes on Alaric's face. "When we get assaulted by fifty angry longshoremen, I'm going to be asking myself what redemption I'm going to find by caving in some poor, dock working bastard's skull."

"Why, there's no redemption in that," Alaric said as Rosalla set a glass in front of him. He glanced up at her and smiled. "Thank you, Rosalla dear." He slid two coins out of his purse and placed them on the table.

"I didn't know that was you, Alaric," she said, leaning down to scoop them up with a smile. She turned a pointed gaze toward Terian. "Or that you'd associate with such a lowlife vagrant—"

"Take care in how you talk about my friend, please," Alaric said, taking the glass in his hand. He never took his eyes off Terian.

"Because you're the only one he's got?" Rosalla asked, clearly unamused.

"I very much doubt that," Alaric said, "though it may take some convincing."

She gave a slow nod, and her expression softened as she looked Terian over. "Well, Alaric, any friend of yours is a friend of mine, I suppose." She slapped the edge of the table lightly. "Let me know if you need anything else." She turned to walk away and bellowed a shout in dark elven at one of the big men at the bar. It turned the attention of everyone in the place toward them, just briefly, and Terian watched the patrons' eyes fall to Alaric and then slide off, as though he was a matter of little consequence.

"Even here, you're more welcome than me," Terian said with dry amusement. "I guess that's as it should be."

"Redemption does not come overnight," Alaric said, leaning forward toward his glass. "And it does not buy you any friends—at least, not in and of itself. Those require their own sort of cultivation. It is a path that you walk every day. A path that you choose. One that you have walked away from, and one I invite you back to now."

Terian stared at the amber liquid in the glass before him. "How do you know, Alaric?" He glanced up. "Not to sound combative," he kept his voice low, almost mournful, "but how do you know that there's redemption out there for someone like me?"

Alaric stared back at him, that one, cool grey eye. And for just a moment, he blinked, and Terian saw ... pain. "I could not believe otherwise ... and keep walking it myself," Alaric said.

Terian swallowed hard, and nodded, trying to bury the emotion. "What would you have me do?"

Alaric watched him with careful consideration. "I would send you to the Ashen Wastelands."

"I thought you said you forgave me!"

Alaric smiled. "Forgiveness has little to do with it, and I said no such thing. I offered you a chance to walk back down the path of redemption—and that path will lead you to the Ashen Wastelands, where I need you to ask a very important question of some old friends of yours."

"Ahhh," Terian said with a nod. "The brother wurms."

"Indeed," Alaric said, nodding slowly. "There are things hanging in the balance that could destroy us all—questions that need answers." He stared over his glass at Terian. "Are you willing to go wherever the road takes you?"

Terian stared at the amber liquid, sloshed it around one time, and then upended his glass, draining it in a single drink. "Sure. Why not?" He stared at the empty glass, and smiled. "Tell me something, though, Alaric—how did you know that I would be willing—that I'd be willing to come back to you—to help you after our last conversation?"

"Because I know you, Terian." Alaric raised his glass in the faint dim of the bar, and Terian could have sworn he saw a faint hint of a smile on the corner of the paladin's lips. "And I could expect no less from you."

Epilogue

Three Years Later

"Where is he?" Curatio called into the darkness. "Has anyone seen Cyrus?"

Terian could see the end of the bridge, putting the lie to its name. *Oh, but it felt Endless until the scourge hit us. Then, suddenly, the end came all too soon.*

"I'm over here!" Cyrus Davidon's deep voice came out of the darkness to Terian's left, along with the wash of the waves against the sand. "I'm here."

Curatio led them off the edge of the bridge, the healer hurrying toward the origin of the voice that had called through the night. Terian sighed. He could see Cyrus shuffling toward them in the dark, leaning on Windrider with the shape of the Baroness Cattrine next to him.

The favorite son.

Terian drew close to the front of the group, Longwell and Odellan close behind him. He could sense the presence of Martaina close at hand. She had an eye out for him, that elven wench. *Clever, on her part.*

"Ryin," Cyrus said as they approached. Terian glanced over and saw Ryin Ayend, that contemptuous human druid, standing apart from them a little ways. *How long has he been there?*

No matter.

Terian separated himself from the others, drifting toward the jungle to their side. His feet crossed over each other side by side until he stood in the middle between them and Cyrus.

Apart.

"Cyrus," Terian said, his sword in his hand.

Cyrus drew his blade in response and turned slowly toward Terian, dropping the reins of his horse. "Now, Terian?"

Terian felt the twist of emotion near his heart again. "No. Not now. I did what you asked. I fought to the end. Now ... I'm not going back with you. Not to Sanctuary. Not so you can put me on trial like some kind of circus or example. I'm leaving." *And I don't even know to where.*

"Terian," Curatio said with that damnable sternness that the elf could produce on command, "you tried to murder a fellow officer. If you think you can simply walk away from that—"

"No," Cyrus said. The blue glow of Praelior moved in the dark, pointing toward the jungle behind Terian. "He can go."

"I wasn't asking your permission," Terian said.

"I wasn't giving permission. I was releasing you from the charge of attempting to murder me. Go on. Be about your business, then; we have no more between us now to deal with. It's all settled on my end."

Terian felt the grief run over him, and he nodded. "Not on mine. This isn't over between us. Not yet."

A sigh punctuated the darkness. "Fine. But at least do me the courtesy of not coming at me like a sidewinder next time. Try it head-on, like a man. I'll give you the fight you're looking for."

Will you? Terian stared at Cyrus for a moment. *Will you indeed?* Terian felt himself start to move on faltering legs, the sands feeling like they were shifting beneath him. He watched the warrior in black in the dark of the night, his allies—his friends—clustered around him.

His friends. Not mine.

Not anymore.

Terian turned, returning his father's sword to the scabbard. He felt the hilt in his hand as he sheathed it, felt the weight of responsibility—something he could not have predicted he'd feel when confronted with the situation as he had been.

Cyrus Davidon killed my father.

Terian swallowed, the taste of the salt air on his lips and the feel of fresh tears on his cheeks.

But I was the one who put him in Cyrus's path. Who caused him to fall, who arranged his landing in that army, at that time.

I was the one who prayed for his death.

The sand gave way to grass, and Terian fought his way through. The blades of green brushed against his armor near the waist, and he took another step toward the darkness of the jungle beyond.

I think I could have forgiven Vara, if it had been her to do it, Terian thought, his breaths coming choked now. *But Cyrus? The favorite?*

He pictured Alaric as he'd seen him on the bridge. The helm blocked almost all view of his face when he'd appeared—just after that damned bestial scourge king showed up, the one that they called Drettanden—but Terian knew.

He knew. He could read Alaric even with his helm on.

The disappointment was a tangible thing. It had been obvious by the set of his jaw, by the slight squint of his one good eye as he'd looked at Terian while they stood together on the bridge.

"Alaric ..." Terian had said, staring at the Ghost of Sanctuary. "I ... I ... I failed."

"I know," Alaric had said.

"I don't know what to do anymore," Terian had said, staring at the Ghost. Waiting. Waiting for guidance. For forgiveness. For anything.

"I believe in you," Alaric had said.

"Even still?" Terian's voice had sounded brittle in his own ears.

"Always." Alaric had not even blinked, that much had been obvious even through the disappointment. "Remember ... redemption is a path you must walk every day."

Terian felt the choking sense of his throat closing and fought the pain enough to stay on his feet. The smell of the jungle night was rich around him, earthy. The salt air was still present but faded now. Terian felt the stiff lines on his cheeks and eyes where the tears had faded, and he leaned against a tree for support.

"I'm sorry," he said to the empty darkness. "I just ... don't know what to do."

"Perhaps I can help with that," came a voice from out of the dark. Terian whirled and saw a figure moving under the shadow of a tree. A black hood swept down with the motion of hands, and a thin, skeletal face showed itself beneath.

"Malpravus," Terian said, and his sword was back in his hand. He stared at the necromancer, the dry, choking feeling in his throat threatening to overcome him.

"Dear boy," Malpravus said, pulling his fingers together to steeple them as he took another step toward Terian. A smile of confidence, of reassurance—of glee—broke onto his bony face. "Might I offer you ... a path?"

Terian stared at him for a long moment, stared at him, blade shaking in his grasp, not sure how to respond.

And then, slowly, he sheathed his sword.

A(nother few) Word(s) From the Author

So that was Terian's story. Or at least the first part of his story. There's more to come, as you'll see on the next page, because let's face it - I can't just leave him in the apparent clutches of Malpravus and call it a day. Well, okay, maybe I could, but I don't want you all to hate me, so there's another Terian book (with some others as well) after Sanctuary, Volume Five.

If you want to know as soon as I release the next book (because I don't do release dates - there's a good reason, I swear), CLICK HERE to sign up for my mailing list. I promise I won't spam you (I only send an email when I have a new book released) and I'll never sell your info. You can also unsubscribe at any time. You might want to sign up, because in case you haven't noticed, these books keep showing up unexpectedly early. You just never know when the next will get here…

I also wanted to take a moment to thank you for reading this story. As an independent author, getting my name out to build an audience is one of the biggest priorities on any given day. If you enjoyed this story and are looking forward to reading more, let someone know - post it on the site you bought the book from, on your blog (if you have one), on Goodreads.com, place it in a quick Facebook status or Tweet with a link to the page of whatever outlet you purchased it from. Good reviews inspire people to take a chance on a new author – like me. And we new authors can use all the help we can get.

I appreciate your support and thanks for reading!

Robert J. Crane

Cyrus Davidon will return in

Master
The Sanctuary Series
Volume Five

Coming Fall 2014!

AND

Rejoin Terian Lepos
(and others) in Saekaj Sovar in

Fated in Darkness
The Sanctuary Series
Volume 5.5

Coming 2015!

Other Works by Robert J. Crane

The Sanctuary Series
Epic Fantasy

Defender: The Sanctuary Series, Volume One
Avenger: The Sanctuary Series, Volume Two
Champion: The Sanctuary Series, Volume Three
Crusader: The Sanctuary Series, Volume Four
Sanctuary Tales, Volume One - A Short Story Collection
Thy Father's Shadow: The Sanctuary Series, Volume 4.5
Master: The Sanctuary Series, Volume Five* (Coming Fall 2014!)
Fated in Darkness: The Sanctuary Series, Volume 5.5* (Coming 2015!)

The Girl in the Box
Contemporary Urban Fantasy

Alone: The Girl in the Box, Book 1
Untouched: The Girl in the Box, Book 2
Soulless: The Girl in the Box, Book 3
Family: The Girl in the Box, Book 4
Omega: The Girl in the Box, Book 5
Broken: The Girl in the Box, Book 6
Enemies: The Girl in the Box, Book 7
Legacy: The Girl in the Box, Book 8
Destiny: The Girl in the Box, Book 9
Power: The Girl in the Box, Book 10* (Coming Late Summer 2014!)

Limitless: Out of the Box, Book 1* (Coming Late 2014!)
In the Wind: Out of the Box, Book 2* (Coming Late 2014/Early 2015!)

Southern Watch
Contemporary Urban Fantasy

Called: Southern Watch, Book 1
Depths: Southern Watch, Book 2
Corrupted: Southern Watch, Book 3* (Coming Summer 2014!)
Unearthed: Southern Watch, Book 4* (Coming Late 2014!)

*Forthcoming

Acknowledgments, Part 17

I work on so many books that sometimes it's hard for me to remember who all had a part in them. I've mostly got an established crew, but there are just so many people who chip in with an idea or a little help that I always feel like I'm missing someone. Here's my best effort, nonetheless:

Erin Kane, Jessica Kelishes and Jo Evans helped me put the final polish on the manuscript by stomping out those last troublesome errors.

Sarah Barbour handled the editing, large and small, and helped me create a consistent manuscript and story.

Karri Klawiter did the cover, once more turning vague instruction into something really awesome.

George Berger helped me develop a way to feed those poor, abused dark elves in Saekaj Sovar, which was something neither I nor the Sovereign had really considered.

My parents, my kids and my wife provided help and the impetus to get this job done, once again.

And finally, to the most dedicated of fans – this story is for you, because without you, I wouldn't get a chance to delve off course like this. Thank you for indulging my whims and my imagination.

About the Author

Robert J. Crane was born and raised on Florida's Space Coast before moving to the upper midwest in search of cooler climates and more palatable beer. He graduated from the University of Central Florida with a degree in English Creative Writing. He worked for a year as a substitute teacher and worked in the financial services field for seven years while writing in his spare time. He makes his home in the Twin Cities area of Minnesota.

He can be contacted in several ways:
Check out his **website** - http://www.robertjcrane.com
Via **email** at cyrusdavidon@gmail.com
Follow him on **Twitter** – @robertJcrane
Connect on **Facebook** – robertJcrane (Author)

Printed in Great Britain
by Amazon